If You Tame Me

A Novel by

Kathie Giorgio

Black Rose Writing | Texas

ISBN: 978-1-68433-347-9
PUBLISHED BY BLACK ROSE WRITING
www.blackrosewriting.com

Printed in the United States of America
Suggested Retail Price (SRP) $19.95

If You Tame Me is printed in Calluna

To Everyone

Family
Friends
Readers
Students

Thank you for loving me, supporting me, and believing in me... even when I began to write about a woman and her iguana.

If You Tame Me

But if you tame me, then we shall need each other.
To me, you will be unique in all the world.
To you, I will be unique in all the world...
Oh, tame me, please.

–Antoine de Saint-Exupery
The Little Prince

Chapter One

No pussy here. But maybe a little leather...

Audrey never expected a young green iguana to be sitting squarely centered in the picture window of her neat and tasteful living room. But he was there by invitation; Audrey chose him, paid for him, and then drove him home tucked in a comfortable carrier in the passenger seat, and a fully prepared aquarium environment rode in the back. She carried the lizard protectively wrapped in both of her arms into the house. He was a gift, given to herself by herself, on her fifty-fifth birthday. Because she didn't want to be an old lady with a cat.

Old women, she told herself, did not adopt iguanas. She was fifty-five, just today. She adopted an iguana, just today. She was not old. At least, not today.

Audrey sat next to the aquarium now and looked at the green iguana and wondered if the new double five's in her age caused her to lose her mind. She never wanted an iguana. She never dreamed of an iguana. She certainly didn't wake up this morning with plans to adopt an iguana. She didn't know anything about reptiles, other than what the pet store owner, Bob, told her. But squatting on a warming rock, watching Audrey steadily, was definitely an iguana. His gaze was even. He was calm and collected. He didn't seem to think she was crazy at all. She thought his gaze was, actually, affectionate, even though they'd only known each other for a couple hours.

Audrey appreciated this.

Last night, she wasn't fifty-five yet. This morning, she was. And now, fully fifty-five, on the cusp of fifty-five and one day, Audrey appreciated the confidence and calm and care of an iguana she just named after her favorite cookie, Nabisco's fig newton. "Newton," she said, and the lizard blinked. "Newt," she said again and then, "welcome home."

She swore his mouth turned up just a bit in a reptile smile.

She smiled back. "Happy birthday to me," she said. "Happy birthday, Audrey. You're not alone anymore."

•   •   •   •   •

That morning, when she was still iguana-less, Audrey found herself standing in the middle of her living room at the start of her fifty-fifth birthday. Maybe the middle of my life, she thought, as she'd thought on every birthday morning ever since she turned forty years old. Now, she tried to hide from her consciousness that fifty-five could only be the middle of her life if she lived to an unlikely one-hundred and ten. She looked around at her walls, her furniture, her possessions. Her life.

There was a home.

But there was no husband.

There were no children.

And she was fifty-five. Not the big five-oh, but past it, hitting the big double-five. So children were definitely out of the realm of possibility, unless someday, there were step-kids, most likely already too grown to ever call her Mom. Though stepkids required a husband and, well, a husband sort of seemed out of the picture too. Statistically. Even if she was in the middle of her life, the middle of her fifties. That middle still meant there was as much time stretched out in front of her as behind her, right?

Her consciousness pinged, and she acknowledged it, sighed, and moved on.

There was a house, and a house meant something to Audrey's generation, and the generation before, and even the new generation reaching adulthood now. A house was a goal, a dream, and a sign that you were Someone. Audrey couldn't explain it herself, but when she stopped writing checks to landlords and started sending them instead to a mortgage company, it just felt different. When she rented, she pictured the money flying out her apartment window and into her landlord's pocket. She was paying the landlord money for something he or she owned, a two-way win, and she wasn't providing any benefit for herself. Now, with each mortgage payment, she chose a small square foot of her house and said, "There. I own you now."

It was a small house, but its square feet counted. There were three bedrooms. Audrey used one as a study, though she didn't study. She was long past being a student. Calling it a library seemed too nose-in-the-air. It made Audrey expect deep burgundy leather chairs, belted smoking jackets, pipes, and books with leather bindings. Audrey's books were a mix of hardcover and softcover, and her chair was a comfortable and worn recliner in a shade of blue that reminded her of the ocean on some days, and the sky on others. She typically wore yoga pants in here, not a smoking jacket, and she'd never smoked anyway. So she called this room her reading room. She hired a carpenter to build in bookshelves on three walls, and she had a gas fireplace with an antique wooden mantel installed on the fourth. Her recliner with a reading lamp stood in the middle, so it felt like the bookshelves hugged her, and the fireplace warmed her. She happily read in that little room, books that she bought and found places for on her shelves, and books that she borrowed from the city library. She also read in bed before sleep on those nights since menopause moved in and then out, but left residual and infrequent insomnia in its wake.

On the other side of the house was a nice kitchen – Audrey liked to cook. There was one full bath and one powder room. The full bath was in her "master suite", which always made Audrey laugh because how can you be a master if there's no one else to master over? The powder room was in the hallway, between the living room and the guest bedroom. She didn't have a dining room. Where she ate lunch and dinner was always up to mood and timing, sometimes in the kitchen on the nice rectangular wooden table that she found at a rummage sale, sometimes in front of the television in the living room. But breakfast was always a kitchen meal. Audrey really loved the way the sunshine spilled in through the window over her sink. When she saw the house for the first time with her real estate agent, she pictured herself standing there, washing and drying the dishes as she looked out into the back yard, even though the house came with a dishwasher and so this never happened. It was hard to say no to the convenience of a modern appliance. But she compensated, sometimes, by having a second cup of coffee as she stood by the window and gazed. She always imagined a man coming up behind her, wrapping his arms around her waist and resting his chin on her shoulder. But at fifty-five, the only arms that wrapped around her waist were her own.

On this morning, she stood in her living room and looked around at all she collected by her fifty-fifth year. All she earned. But all she noticed was what was missing.

There was no husband. There were no children. There was no chance. Statistically. Realistically. Ping!

So now what?

Audrey sat on the couch and let her hands dangle between her knees.

Was she supposed to feel devastated? Depressed? Utterly and horribly alone?

She didn't.

Was she supposed to feel independent? Empowered? A woman striking out on her own in this cold and cruel patriarchal world? A woman who needed nobody, especially not a man?

She didn't feel that way either.

So what the hell was this then? The only word that came to her mind was loneliness. She wasn't looking forward. She wasn't looking back. She didn't say good morning to anyone until she reached work and she didn't say goodnight to anyone, other than the stuffed cow named Ooshi she kept on her bed.

Was this caused by hormones? Her doctor said she was post-menopausal now because she'd been period-free for over two years. Audrey was sort of disappointed. She'd heard wild tales of the drama of menopause, but hers, like the rest of her life, just seemed to pass on by without much of a fuss. A few sleepless nights here and there seemed anti-climactic. So was this feeling of loneliness a last poke? A lack of hormones? Did she need estrogen?

There really wasn't anyone to ask. Audrey's mother died several years before, so there couldn't be the proverbial mother-daughter walk-talk on the beach. There were no siblings, there were no aunts – she was the only child of two only children. She couldn't imagine her father being much help. But he was dead too, anyway.

She supposed she could talk to her doctor. But how do you call a doctor and say, "Doc, I'm feeling sort of lonely." Can you help? Audrey didn't want a prescription for Prozac. She wanted company. She wanted a partner.

But there was only Audrey. Was that enough? Was she Somebody? She had a house. By her calculations and imaginations, she owned several square feet of it already.

That was when she wondered if her fifty-fifth birthday meant it was time to adopt a cat.

Or if it meant she should sign up for a yoga class. She'd owned yoga pants for years. Or a meditation class. Maybe she should become a Buddhist. Maybe she should join a church, even though she didn't feel particularly religious. Maybe she should sign up for regular massages so that she was guaranteed to have someone touch her body on a regular basis. Even if she had to pay for it.

Audrey tried and couldn't put her finger on exactly when the last time was someone touched her body. Besides Audrey herself.

Maybe, she thought, she should sign up for an online dating site as a final desperate attempt to meet someone. Through the years, Audrey tried it all. The bar scene. The singles clubs. The personal ads. The original dating services, the modern-day (then) matchmaker, where you walked into an actual building, talked with an actual person, took an actual picture, and then became a file among other files that were matched up like a random and odd Noah's ark. In this case, you were supposed to walk on the boat single and then exit down the gangplank arm in arm with your significant other, your soulmate. Audrey talked with the cheery counselor who promised she'd end up happily married, and then Audrey went on an apocalyptic series of dates that were either disasters or just boring. Eventually, that all fell away and the dating service didn't call anymore.

Nowadays, according to night-time television, people went online. Audrey hadn't tried that yet. She wasn't sure she wanted to. She saw the commercials. Christian Mingle. Farmers Only (because city folks just don't get it). Our Time (dating for the "mature"). And the big hitters, eHarmony, and Match.com. Audrey thought it might be fun to date a farmer. Go for a roll in the hayfield. She liked animals. There was that stuffed cow named Ooshi on her bed, which was sort of embarrassing, she thought, given that she was now fifty-five.

The cow was a remnant of a man she dated in her mid-forties, a man who took her to the county fair and won Ooshi for her by bopping fake gophers on the head with a huge mallet. She named the cow Ooshi for the sound the man made as he bopped each one. He and Audrey bopped many times too, and became a regular thing, a couple, Audrey thought, headed in the right direction, but then he turned left when she turned right and bought a house. She didn't know where he went. She was probably one of those people who "just don't get it". She probably wouldn't be allowed on Farmers Only.

Our Time made her feel old. She wasn't old (she hadn't adopted a cat). She'd always hated the word mature, almost as much as she hated the word immature. When she was twelve years old, that was the big insult around her neighborhood. "Oh, you're just so immature!" with the "chure!" final syllable excessively drawn out. The second biggest insult, well, not insult, maybe, but proclamation which always came when someone did something you didn't like, like taking your favorite seat on the bus or grabbing the book you wanted to check out from the library just as your hand was reaching for it, was "It's a free country!" Audrey hated that too. It was just so immaCHUUUURE to think it was a free country.

Anyway, Audrey didn't know if she wanted to date online. She looked around her house again, glanced at her ringless fingers and gave herself a great mental shake. She was a feminist. She'd participated in marches and protests. In college, she wore a shirt that said, "A woman needs a man like a fish needs a bicycle." So she didn't need a man, did she. A man was not required for a woman to be Somebody. Nor was she required to be happy, or to say in a strained Tom Cruise voice, "You complete me." She was complete. She was strong. She was invincible. She was woman. She didn't need a man.

Except, of course, as a solution to being lonely.

Audrey wondered if a fish might need a bicycle by the time it was fifty-five. Didn't things change? Maybe wheels would be an enhancement.

Audrey wanted to be enhanced. There was no husband. There were no children. There was no chance. Statistically. Realistically. Ping!

For today, this fifty-fifth birthday, there was just Audrey. She didn't feel invincible. She felt invisible.

Maybe it was time for a cat. She wouldn't name it Ooshi. No one was making that sound for her anymore. She would name a cat Hope, because that way, she would always have some.

At that time of the morning, at the onset of her fifty-fifth birthday, Audrey didn't yet know that by sunset, she would decide to never adopt a cat named Hope. Instead, her hope would be in an iguana named Newt.

⸱ ⸱ ⸱

At work, there was the usual birthday workday hoopla. Audrey managed the women's clothing sections of a stoic, but nice department store. Not high-end fashion, not high-end cost, but good, solid clothes. Clothes that were in style now, but also racks of clothes that were timeless, that you could wear now, and you could wear ten years from now. You didn't gasp when you studied yourself, wearing the blouses and sweaters, pants and dresses, in the mirror of the dressing room, but you did smile and nod and say, "Yes, that's nice."

Audrey thought the clothes she sold were kind of like herself. Good. Solid. Yes, that's nice.

When Audrey first started at the store, she could still shop in the Junior's section. Eventually, she crossed over to Misses and even Career and also Casual and Sports Apparel. Now, at fifty-five, she mostly shopped in the

Pluses section, but she managed over it all. If you were a female, Audrey knew what you should wear and where you could find it.

Her associates and other managers, the people Audrey called her "work friends", gave her birthday cards with jokes about sagging breasts and disappearing hair (with innuendos as to where that hair was disappearing from) and jokes about hiring a male stripper. They gave her gift certificates for the store they worked in, which they bought with their employee discounts and which meant, with her employee discount, she could buy practically the entire winter line, with change left over for the new spring line. One associate, fairly new, fairly young, gave her a gift certificate to Victoria's Secret. Her card was about a male *stripped*, not a stripper, and this same male being in Audrey's bed. In the silence that fell in the break room, Audrey smiled and said, "Oh, thank you. Yes, that's nice."

There was a birthday cake, of course, white with white frosting. There were a few red and white frosting roses and in red scroll, it read, "Happy 55th Birthday, Audrey!" There were also some illicit bottles of wine, but Audrey was the manager, so she was the only one who would scold over this, and since it was her birthday, she didn't. The other managers, wanting the same treatment on their birthdays, looked the other way.

Because she was the manager, Audrey finished work at four o'clock. When she left the store, she walked down the mall to the Victoria's Secret, where she stood at one of the windows and looked in.

Boobs and butts. Mostly uncovered, but where they were covered was lacy and colorful and provocative. Full to overflowing. Audrey looked down.

There were no children. So her body was still pretty much her body. It hadn't housed anyone else but her for all these fifty-five years. She thought of herself as a good-sized woman, well-rounded, curvaceous, just like the mannequins in the Plus-size department. She wasn't sure what was good about her good-size, actually. She didn't feel fat, but she wasn't skinny, and she surely wasn't athletic. She was pretty much who she'd always been, just thicker here and there. She knew there was some droopage, some slackage. She felt she wore her weight well, back when it was perky and full, and she wore it well now too, when it was a bit larger, a bit broader, but still pleasantly full. She didn't really pay much attention to it. She wasn't sure when the last time was that she looked at herself in the nude. Her bathroom mirror was always steamy when she stepped out of the shower, so she would get dressed and then return to check her reflection. By then, she was covered, combed, scented and tastefully jeweled. She smiled at her reflection, but it wasn't really heartfelt. It was more automatic. The smile of a saleswoman.

A blonde Victoria's Secret employee caught her staring in the window and waved at her. Captured and embarrassed, Audrey went on in.

"How can I help you?" the blonde asked. She was skinny. She would swim in the clothes Audrey wore.

Audrey crossed her arms in front of her crotch, her folded hands suddenly demure. "I was given a gift certificate today," she said. "It's my birthday."

"Oh! Well, that's nice! How much is it for!"

Nice again. Audrey didn't know that Victoria's Secret dealt in nice. She pulled the certificate out of her purse and handed it to the woman.

"This is enough to set you up with at least one bra and panty set! Maybe more, we're having a sale!"

The woman convinced Audrey that she needed to be measured so that the proper fit could be found. Mortified, Audrey followed the woman into a fitting room and disrobed. The blonde introduced herself as Annabel (Annabel? At Victoria's Secret?) and she tsked at what Audrey was wearing underneath. These were from Audrey's own store. Bought with her employee discount, so they cost next to nothing. They covered her up, which was what they were supposed to do. Good. Solid. "We can do better than that!" Annabel said. "Which birthday is this?"

Audrey thought about lying. But then she wondered why. "I'm fifty-five."

Annabel clapped. She actually clapped. "I have just the thing! Several things!"

What followed was a long line of bras whose wires hitched up what droopage there was. Panties that weren't, surprisingly, thongs, but strong, yet soft material that hitched up the slackage in the rear. Audrey didn't know there was slackage in her rear, she never looked. She'd already felt embarrassed and mortified, but now she was just bright red from head to toe. Why was it that when she most wanted to disappear, her body sent out flares to keep her from doing so? How did she not know about the slackage? Why wasn't she familiar with her own butt?

In the fitting room, Audrey avoided the mirror when she was stripped, but she stole fast glances when she was strapped in. She felt overexposed already, with Annabel appraising her, and adding her own eyes to that felt terrifying. But Annabel cheered and clapped some more, so Audrey figured she must look pretty good. When she had the new bras on, her breasts did ride high, and Audrey thought she might even be able to breathe easier. Stand straighter. Her rear felt rounder.

The lingerie (Audrey couldn't call anything in this place underwear) came in animal prints and solids, splashy color patterns, plaids, stripes, polka dots. Audrey lucked out and found some things on clearance, and so she was able to walk out of the store with three sets; two paid for with the gift certificate and one with her own money. One set was zebra, one holy-cow-purple, and one reminded her of the kaleidoscope she played with as a child. She particularly liked that set, and that's why she decided to spend beyond the gift certificate. It was her birthday, after all. Annabel asked if she wanted to wear that one home, but Audrey demurred, and she put on the old things she walked in wearing. The nice ones. It would take a little time to get used to the new. To get used to the double-five, still loud and clear in red frosting on the leftover cake she was toting home. No one seemed to want to eat the age. Tomorrow, she would start with the new.

But she did decide to stop and get some carryout from Applebee's. Again, it was her birthday. She would have steak and their garlic mashed potatoes. She wished she could bring home their sangria, but that wasn't allowed. She was tempted but decided she didn't want to eat there, instead of taking her meal to-go. Not all by herself. Not on her birthday.

So, back into her old things. Her comfortable things. A stop for a dinner, she didn't cook herself, to eat in front of the television, where she and she alone would choose what would be watched. Over the weekend, she would shop at her own store on her off time. Maybe she'd get something different. She could even look in the other departments.

And she would be sure to thank the young associate for the Victoria's Secret gift certificate.

But her drive to Applebee's was interrupted by a whim. Audrey remembered considering a cat named Hope as she stood in her living room that morning, so she stopped at a pet store she passed a thousand times before. But even as she stepped through the door, even as she was inundated with the mixed voices of living breathing animals, from birds to dogs and cats and fish (even the fish seemed to make noise) and rodents and reptiles, the noise of a very small, captured, friendly zoo, Audrey thought loud and clear, I don't want a cat. I don't want a cat. I don't want a cat!

It would just be too much. It would just be too nice. She wanted a pet that would be something like kaleidoscopic lingerie from Victoria's Secret.

Something that lifted up her droopage and decreased her slackage.

As Audrey wandered the store, she deliberately avoided the playpenned area that held the kittens. She knew they were cute, and she didn't want to be seduced by cute. She looked at all the others, and she stood for some time in front of a bright white cockatoo with a huge headdress. He was guaranteed to talk. Audrey thought it might be nice to have another voice around the house. But then, when she heard that "nice" echoing again in her head, she turned away. She wasn't after nice, even if it was an exotic cockatoo sort of nice. She glanced at the guinea pigs, the rabbits, the hamsters. She looked at the puppies, who were just too darn overeager. Overeager was like the bullseye print undies she'd rejected, the push-up bra and panties with red and white targets around her nipples and on her crotch. They tried too hard. And the puppies tried too hard, climbing over each other and lolling their tongues and yipping in strident love-me voices. Audrey turned away and then started to walk right by the reptile wall, a lit glassed-in area of tank after tank, but then felt that wasn't fair. She'd looked everywhere else, so she stood in front of the lizards and snakes and frogs and gaze.

And in the lower right corner, she saw him.

He wasn't nice. He wasn't familiar. He was green.

He was also small, and he had a row of spikes going down his back. His legs bent funny and were longer than a turtle's and had elbows. His eyes were beady, but, she thought, intelligent. He had a tongue, but it wasn't pink, and it didn't loll. Audrey was pretty certain he didn't purr. He didn't yip. And he wouldn't be guaranteed to talk.

The pet shop owner came to her side. "That's a green iguana," he said. "Great creatures. Like miniature dinosaurs. Friendly. Smart."

He didn't say nice. And Audrey was feeling sort of like a dinosaur herself. "How hard are they to care for?"

"They can be tricky," the pet shop owner said, and Audrey appreciated his honesty. "But once you strike a balance, have a good environment for them, they can really thrive. I've known iguanas that grew to be six feet long and weighed well over twenty pounds. In ideal situations, they can live up to twenty years, though I haven't seen that yet. I think the oldest one from my shop was twelve when he died. His owner cried for weeks and then adopted a chameleon." He looked at Audrey. "You seem really interested though. Your face lit up when you saw him. Here I had you pegged for a kitten woman when you walked in, and then I thought the cockatoo might have your heart. But here's where you lit up. Here's where you've stayed the longest." He nodded. "I bet you could handle him."

Audrey smiled at him. Besides honest, this man was also really observant. "It's my fifty-fifth birthday," she confessed. "And I want to buy myself a present. And it can't be a cat."

The owner laughed. "Then let's not get you one. What do you think? Do you like him?"

Audrey looked back at the iguana, who looked back at her. Six feet long, he'd said. Over twenty pounds. Maybe twenty years. This wasn't a pet. This was…a relationship. A commitment.

A partner.

"How old is he now?" she asked. "Where did he come from?"

"I get all of my reptiles from a breeder," the owner said. "This guy just had his first birthday. One year old."

The iguana tilted his head, and Audrey thought suddenly, ridiculously, un-nicely, of WannaDateIguanas.com. She giggled. This was definitely not mature. And while the country wasn't free, it was a free country, and Audrey could buy an iguana if she wanted to. It was her birthday, and she could cry if she wanted to (if she wanted to, if she wanted to). But Audrey thought she wanted to buy an iguana instead and have a relationship with him for the next twenty years. It could potentially last until she reached the big seven-five. Today could be the start of the longest relationship she ever had, except for her parents.

"So it's a boy?" Audrey asked.

"That's what I was told, but let me double-check." The owner picked the iguana up, flipped him over on his back, and somehow checked. Audrey didn't see anything, beyond a white belly that was astonishingly smooth, given the rest of his spiky exterior. "Yes," the owner said. "It's a boy." And then he placed the iguana in Audrey's hands.

He fit there. His skin, while leathery, wasn't cold at all. It was warm. He took his front feet and wrapped his toes around her fingers. It was the closest to an embrace Audrey had all day unless she counted when Annabel reached around her to take her measurements. Audrey didn't. But this was her birthday, a day intended for hugs. And she was a fifty-five-year-old woman who didn't know when the last time was that someone touched her body.

This iguana, in many ways, touched her.

"Yes," she said. "I'll take him."

The iguana looked up at her. Audrey wanted him to smile, in a Disney sort of way, but he didn't. Yet his expression was soft. Audrey found herself gazing back.

The owner, who introduced himself as Bob, began to gather all the necessary things. Audrey held the iguana until the last minute when he was placed in a special carrier for the ride home. There was no one else in the store, and Bob took the time to set everything up for Audrey in a twenty-gallon aquarium. Bob said that a ten-gallon was enough, but Audrey wanted more room for the iguana to move. She chose gravel. The warming rock. The warming lights. The food and water containers. A hammock. A hammock? Iguanas like to lay in them, Bob said. Iguana food, though Bob said there was a lot she could, and should, make on her own. He and Audrey created the perfect reptile environment, and Audrey was delighted. She showed the iguana everything as they put it together and he seemed to approve too. Audrey would make sure he took part in all decisions; they were a partnership, and she wouldn't act like his boss, his master. The aquarium wouldn't even be placed in the master suite because there was no master. There was just the two of them. Iguana and Audrey.

Bob handed Audrey a thick book on iguana care, which included a big section on iguana-friendly recipes. Audrey liked to cook in her nice kitchen. She rarely cooked for anyone else there but herself. Until her parents passed away, holidays were spent in their home. The man, that last man, who gave her Ooshi the cow preferred to eat out. But now, she would cook for two.

Audrey thanked Bob and promised she would be back to replenish her supplies and let him know how the iguana was doing. Bob said the iguana could even come with her, he was welcome for visits. As Audrey loaded the carrier, specially equipped with seatbelt loops, into her passenger seat, she buckled him in, to keep him safe. The aquarium went into the back seat, and she let her hand linger for a second on the glass. Cold. Audrey knew that the perfect environment wasn't cold, it wasn't in the aquarium. It was at home. She was going to give this lizard a home. She was going to be his home. He would keep her company. She wanted company. She wanted a partner.

It was beyond nice. It was, as Bob said, perfect.

$\bullet \quad \bullet \quad \bullet \quad \bullet \quad \bullet$

The perfection continued as Audrey settled her birthday gift in her living room. She had a large picture window, and the aquarium fit in front of it. Natural sunlight would come in and warm the iguana during the day when Audrey was at work. And at night, she could turn on his warming lights. The warming rock was always on. Carefully, Audrey set up the food and water dispensers. She thought about taking the lizard out and carrying him around the house, showing him his entire environment, but he'd already been through a lot of changes on this night. She thought it best to let him acclimate slowly. Bob told her that iguanas didn't do well under stress, so she needed to make this transition as stress-free as possible. This is like all relationships, she told herself. Stress is a deal-breaker. She didn't want the deal to be broken so soon after the iguana's homecoming. She couldn't avoid the stress, but she could offer support and comfort, meeting the iguana's needs and not her own. She really wanted to sweep him up and cuddle him, but now was not the time.

Sitting on her couch, she kept her television off and instead, watched the iguana. She paged through his care book, learning about iguana body language and facial expressions and all of their habits and quirks. She read up on the recipes. And she wondered what to call him. She thought about naming him Bob, after the very nice pet shop owner, but that just didn't seem to fit. This iguana was so much more than a Bob.

It was when she went to the kitchen for a cup of coffee and her favorite snack that she thought of the perfect name.

From the time she was a very little girl, Audrey loved the cookies called Fig Newtons. Other kids went for the obvious, the Oreos, the Chips Ahoy, the Nutter Butters. Not Audrey. For her, it was the ooey gooey rich and chewy inside, golden flakey tender cakey outside. Every day at three o'clock, when she came home from school, that was what she had. Four of them, with a tall glass of milk at first, then a cup of coffee when she got into high school. In later years, when Nabisco attempted to expand the line of Newtons with other flavors, Audrey eschewed them. Only Fig Newtons would do, and she maintained a special spot in her kitchen just for them. The first shelf of the cabinet to the right of the coffeemaker. Coffee mugs were on the left. Reach up, get a mug, pour the coffee, reach up, get four Newtons. As much a part of Audrey's life as her reading room, her job, her solid and steady life.

And at the big double-five and on to the post-menopausal part of her life, it was also important to note that the Fig Newtons kept Audrey regular. They were no longer just a treat. They were a necessary staple.

Because she loved the cookie so much, Audrey dreamed of a husband named Newton when she was a little girl, and she did even now when she still dreamed of a husband at all. He would be her own animated and breathing ooey-gooey inside, tender outside. But of course, he never materialized.

But an iguana did.

Audrey carried her snack and coffee back to the living room and sat down. The iguana seemed quite comfortable; he was moving slowly around his aquarium, checking things out, she supposed, in a lizard-type way. He was a brilliant and healthy green, speckled through with red wine ticking. His belly was a tender white. Audrey never thought of lizards as attractive, but if she looked at him in a lizard sort of way, then this one was. He was gorgeous.

"Newton," Audrey said. "Newt!" she called. He swiveled his head toward her. And then he bobbed.

Audrey beamed. She bobbed her head back, reaching out to the lizard in his own language. Newt approved of his identity. And she more than approved of him.

Setting aside her snack for a moment, Audrey paged through her iguana book until she found a list of acceptable foods. Then she picked up the second ceramic food dish and went into her kitchen again. Bob told her to keep one dish full of Newt's dry pellets and to use the other one for fresh produce. In her fruit drawer in the fridge, she kept some figs. Her love of the Fig Newton translated into a favorite fruit too. Cleaning these and chopping them, and then adding some butternut squash, Audrey made a salad snack for Newt. She sprinkled the food liberally with water because Bob informed her it was one way to make sure that Newt was getting enough to drink. Iguanas, he told her, didn't drink much and when they did, they lapped from their shallow water dish like a dog. They needed to be encouraged to drink more, and water-sprinkling food was one way to do it. Returning to the living room, Audrey gave Newt his snack. Then she pulled over the couch's ottoman, and she sat right next to the aquarium.

The sun was going down on her birthday, and she settled in its glow with Newt. She ate her cookies, he ate his figs and butternut squash, and they chewed companionably together.

Companionably. Together. On her fifty-fifth birthday, Audrey marveled at those words. She woke up without them, but now here she was. With company. A partner. She reached in and stroked Newt's back. Mid-chew, he lifted his head, then pressed it firmly in the palm of her hand. She thrilled.

"Welcome home, Newt," she said. "And happy birthday to me. Happy birthday, Audrey." She rubbed between his eyes. "Happy anniversary as well...to us."

Audrey's favorite t-shirt from college only spoke of men and fish, it said nothing about iguanas. A woman might not need a man, just like a fish didn't need a bicycle, but this woman needed this iguana. And he needed her. She'd found a fresh and creative way to deal with her loneliness. She didn't know this morning that an iguana was missing from her life. She didn't think of that as she looked around her home and thought of the lack of a husband and the lack of children.

But now, that lack drew back a ways. And it didn't take a cat named Hope to do so.

Chapter Two

Meanwhile, back at the ranch (next door)...

All his life, Frank was ducking strike number three. It was his father's favorite crow, "Strike three and yer out!", applied to everything and anything, not just baseball. Frank knew early on with his dad that he always had to get it right within three attempts, no matter what it was he was trying to do. "Three strikes and yer out!" yelled his father when Frank was learning to ride a bike and fell three times. After Frank stopped crying, his mother took over running behind him on the bike, a steadying hand on the seat. His father went inside the house to watch a ball game. Frank noted back then, and he remembered now that he learned how to ride the bike quickly once his mother stepped in. "Three strikes and yer out!" with math problems, spelling lists, being told to put away his laundry, mow the lawn, shovel the snow. If Frank struck out on his chores, he earned a cuff upside the head. Not a hard one; Frank didn't consider his dad abusive. Just...intimidating. Aggressive. A man's man.

They were both gone now. His mother first, his dad, stubbornly, aggressively, last. Frank was sixty-three. His father died last year at eighty-seven. But still, Frank heard his father's voice, his consistent and insistent admonition. It was what kept Frank alone.

He'd had two wives. The next one, if he found one, was his last chance, he figured. "Strike three, and yer out!" He didn't want to be out. He didn't want to be sent to the bench.

This really put the pressure on. He tried to shake it; his father wasn't even around to watch if Frank met, mated and messed up. But that phrase, that possibility of a third strike, just kept circling like a wedding ring. Or a noose. When his father attended Frank's second wife's funeral three years ago, he mercifully hadn't whispered to Frank about strikes as they stood in the receiving line. But Frank knew it was there, unspoken, between them. When his father died, Frank expected to feel like a free agent, able to date, maybe, without his father waiting for the third strike. But he still heard the call. Strike three. Yer out.

It wasn't like Frank even swung at a ball and missed with the first two strikes. Strike One left him. They were married for ten years, from the time Frank was twenty-four to thirty-four. She left him because, at the time, he didn't want a child. She did. She said that he misled her, even though they never talked about children until they both turned thirty. Then they argued for four years, stopped having sex for the last two because he was paranoid that she would trick him, especially after she began to hide her disk of birth control pills, keeping him from obsessively checking it, and then she left. He came home one day and found all of her things gone, except for that missing birth control disk, pink and accusatory, centered in the exact middle of their bed. The last he heard, she got married within a year and had four kids, one right after the other.

Frank figured he was partially to blame for Strike One, at least fifty-fifty. They should have talked about children before they got married.

But Strike Two...his second wife. They were married at forty-five; neither wanted children. So it was awful irony when she developed uterine cancer. She died when they were sixty. Three years ago.

And now he was alone. He felt ready to start dating, but the third strike haunted him. If he blew this one, he would be alone forever. Forever was worse than being alone now. Though it was hard to imagine it being worse than now. Three years and it still felt sometimes like she died yesterday.

Frank moved into this ranch three years after his wife died and a few months after his father's death. He couldn't stand being in the old house anymore, the one he shared with Strike Two. At first, he wrapped those walls around himself like his wife's arms, but as time went on, those arms grew colder, and he felt the house shift into a reminder of her absence rather than a reminder of her. But when he moved to the new house, he found he was more alone than ever, because now he didn't even have the space Strike Two used to stand in. So he adopted six parakeets. He thought it would be hard to feel alone with the racket of six birds in the house.

He was wrong.

But he loved the birds anyway. And so far, there'd been no strikes out. They were all still alive.

But his wife...But his dad...But his mom...

Even Strike One was gone, though he didn't know if she was dead like the others. While she'd been gone for twenty-nine years, just short of three times longer than they'd been together, she now felt more gone than ever. His whole life seemed gone, shrunk down to this house and six parakeets.

Frank liked to stand at his bay window and talk to his birds, even though what he was really doing was looking through the cage bars for any sign of his neighbor. He met Audrey several times in the almost-year since moving in. When winter turned to spring last year, a month into his new house/new life, he began deliberately timing his backyard appearances to fill the birdfeeders when Audrey was outside mowing the back lawn. He'd be outside mowing his front lawn when she came out to get her mail. He'd be getting his mail when she drove in from work.

The onset of winter made it a little harder to bump into her. But he tried. Now that he knew that he could still be lonely with six birds to talk to, Audrey was beginning to feel like a ball that just left the pitcher's mitt.

He liked her.

But three strikes...

Frank didn't want to be out. Not ever.

•   •   •   •   •

So it was a shock coming face to face with Strike One. Frank came around a corner in the grocery store, aisle 7 to aisle 8, Pharmaceuticals to Household Cleansers & Supplies. And there she was, Strike One, looking at the paper towels.

"Oh!" she said when she looked up.

Frank agreed.

"Frank! Well, Frank! How are you! How weird is this!" She fluttered the way he remembered. When they were dating, he referred to her hands as dancing. By the time they separated, he said, those hands were flapping.

"I'm just fine. What brings you here?" He looked around. Surely there were grocery stores where she lived.

"I'm on my way to visit my new granddaughter. My daughter called and said they were out of paper towels, so I stopped." She grabbed a roll and tucked it under her arm like a newspaper. "Well, Frank. It's good to see you."

"It's good to see you too," he lied. Though he really wasn't sure if it was a lie. It was good to see her, in a familiar, but backward sort of way. "Granddaughter?"

"Yes! My oldest had a baby girl. Oh, Frank. From children to grandchildren. It's just such a lovely thing. Did you...I mean, did you ever..."

She looked uncomfortable.

Frank felt suddenly protective of Strike Two, wanting to hide her out of sight behind his back. He didn't want to share her. He didn't want Strike One to know Strike Two died. Actually, he didn't want Strike One to know she outlived Strike Two. Leaving him alone. Again. "I have birds," he offered and pulled out his cell phone. He flipped to the latest photo and showed her. "This is Lucky, Plucky, Ducky, Aristotle, BlueBoy, and Butch. They're parakeets."

"Oh!" she said, and those hands flapped. Much less gracefully than his birds. His birds, when he let them out of their cage, flew around his living room and he liked to lay on his couch and watch them, pretending they were mighty hawks way up high in the sky. He even painted his ceiling blue to further the illusion. Bob, the pet store owner, suggested keeping the birds' wings clipped, but Frank couldn't imagine depriving the birds – and himself – of their flight. In the grocery store aisle, Strike One flapped, like those birds that pretend to have a broken wing to lead you away from their nest. "Well, Frank, it's been so nice seeing you. Congratulations on your...birds." With that, one flapping, limping hand blew him a kiss, and she was gone.

Frank went through the aisles and took an extra long time in the pet section. He bought the birds a couple new toys. He usually got their things from the pet shop, but since he was here and he was just talking about them, he decided to get them a surprise.

When he arrived home, he sat in his driveway for a few minutes and looked at Audrey's house. Her car was in the drive, not in the garage, so she was home and had recently been out, or was planning to go out. He didn't like it when she parked her car in the garage. Then he could only tell if she was home by the lights in her windows or the flicker of her television.

There was something new in her picture window, the window similar to his, but flat. Hers was likely original to the house; his must have been exchanged for a bay window by a later owner. He could see the top of something glass...a terrarium? An aquarium? There was some kind of lamp too. Maybe Audrey had fish now. Or a turtle. He wondered if she'd noticed the birds in his window.

He wondered if she noticed him.

Frank pulled in his garage and then got out, carrying his packages from the grocery store. He walked up and down the sidewalk a few times, trying to figure out what the glass thing was in Audrey's window, and hoping she would appear so he could ask. "Hi, Audrey!" he could say. "You have something new in your window!" And then she would invite him in, and he could see what it was and they would have a cup of coffee and sit at her table, and they would talk, and they'd become friends and...

"And we'll get married and move to a castle and live happily ever after," Frank muttered, suddenly aware of how ridiculous he was, ridiculous and old and stupid, a doddering sixty-three-year-old wallflower schoolboy with a crush, and he stomped off to his own house. He hoped Audrey didn't see him, marching back and forth in front of her picture window like a besotted toy soldier. A wanna-be Prince Charming. A stalker, for Christ's sake.

But he wasn't a stalker. And he also hoped she did see him. And thought about him. And maybe wondered what was in his window.

Frank went inside, greeted his birds who greeted him back and presented them with their surprise. Then standing by the cage, he watched them play, sharing the two new toys. There was much squawking and bickering and flying feathers, except for Aristotle, his quiet bird, who stood on his perch and watched the others from a safe distance. Frank knew he would check out the toys on his own, once the others moved on to something else.

Frank stood at a safe distance too, from Audrey's house and her picture window and whatever was in it. He'd been through a lot of squawking and bickering and flying feathers in his time. Flapping hands too. And dying. Not to mention strike-outs.

He and Aristotle looked at each other. "Thanks for keeping me company, bud," Frank whispered. Aristotle liked soft voices.

The bird bobbed his head.

Frank tucked his hands in his pockets and continued to stand, tilting his body just a bit to the left so he could see the trunk of Audrey's car. But he told himself he was watching his birds. He told himself he wasn't interested at all in what Audrey had in her picture window. But he kept leaning more and more to the left.

Chapter Three

What the f-word?

On the morning Audrey was fifty-five, and one day, she stood in the middle of her living room again, but this time with a case of buyer's remorse. Maybe iguana remorse. She stood at her picture window, looking down on Newt who looked up at her. His eyes twitched down, then up, then down, then up, like a shy boy who didn't think he did anything wrong but was prepared to be guilty.

Audrey checked to make sure his warming rock was warm and that his heat lamp was off as the natural light would do during the daytime. She checked the pellets in his pellet dish that his fresh food dish was definitely removed from the tank, protecting Newt from eating food gone to rot. She'd fed him his breakfast, and he'd eaten it all, but she was still nervous about this. The iguana care book said it was best to give iguanas their food an hour after waking in the morning. Audrey thought they would wake together and then Newt could wait while she showered and dressed, bringing it pretty close to an hour. But it appeared Newt was a late and sound sleeper. When she got up, he was still snoozing peacefully in his hammock. She walked heavily past the aquarium a few times, but to no avail. After Audrey showered and dressed, Newt was awake, but it hadn't been an hour. She considered, but then she fed him anyway, deliberately trying not to look at the time. She wasn't sure if she made the right decision. Was it better that they had breakfast together, having a chance to share in each other's company, or should she have waited until the optimal moment for Newt's digestive system? That would have meant feeding him just as she left, and then his food dish would have been sitting out all day with any food left that he didn't eat. It was nine o'clock now, and Audrey couldn't stick around to see if Newt's stomach revolted. She had to get to the store for her pre-opening chores before the customers were allowed in at ten.

Was this what it was like to care for a child? Or for a partner? Audrey felt so responsible for this little lizard.

She looked at Newt, and he looked at her, and she sighed, and she swore he did too. After she finally went to bed last night, she closed her eyes and pondered Newt and their future together. She saw Newt sitting on the arm of her recliner while they read a book, sitting on her desk while they went on the internet, sitting beside her at meals. But then she began to worry about money. She'd just dropped a cash bundle at the pet shop. A bundle she didn't plan for. Newt was expensive. He was especially expensive for a pet who could die tomorrow if she did one little thing wrong. Like, feed him his breakfast when he hadn't been awake for an hour. Audrey knew about doing little things wrong.

Like so many little girls, Audrey won a goldfish at a county fair when she was six years old. She brought it home, named it Finch (after goldfinch, she told her parents, who thought that was brilliant), fed it for three days and then found it floating belly up. Her parents said she likely overfed it, and then they flushed it the way of all dead fish, down the toilet.

What if she overfed Newt? What if she underfed him? What if she fed him the wrong thing or if the fruit wasn't fresh enough or it wasn't an hour since waking...

He looked up. He looked down. Up. She sighed. So did he.

She remembered the way he pressed his head into her palm the night before. She put her hand into the aquarium, and he did it again. The pressure of his presence, his rough skin against hers, his warmth instead of the expected cold, made her feel better. "You're mine, aren't you, Newt," she said. "I guess we'll learn from each other."

Audrey knew from reading practically every self-help book ever published on relationships that successful relationships were based on compromise and learning about each other. Audrey bought those books in the hopes that someone somewhere finally discovered the absolute right path to finding a partner, but the meet-and-greet chapters were always the shortest. They made Audrey feel as if the way to find your meant-to-be was obvious, too obvious to take time in a book, and that everyone else knew the ropes but her. The rest of the pages were filled with advice on what to do *after the* relationship was underway, and there were always chapters on what to do when trouble fell, which seemed impossible to avoid.

A common theme in the books was that you were always supposed to be open to your partner. You were never to assume that you knew everything, because people...well, partners change. Newt wasn't a person, he wasn't a man, but he was her partner now. And iguanas, she assumed, could change too, over their twenty-year lifespan. Over what would be his twenty-year relationship with her.

She would be open to Newt. She would learn from him. He would learn from her.

"I have to go to work, Newt, but I'll leave the television on for you," she said. "Then you'll have some noise to keep you company. When I get home, I'll make you dinner, and I'll let you out of there for a bit so you can see the rest of the house." She patted him again and triple-checked everything. "You have a good day, okay? You take it easy and get used to being home."

And so she left, with some anxiety. She wondered if she should call in sick, play hooky and stay home. She decided to check into those home security apps that allowed you to see into your house when you weren't there. Then she could see that Newt was okay throughout the day.

She thought even more about the apps and security systems as the morning went on. At work, the worry built. She'd never worried about anyone at home before, and despite the discomfort, it gave her a little thrill. She had someone to worry about. And maybe, at home on his warming rock or in his hammock, Newt worried about her. Maybe he missed her. Maybe he looked forward to her homecoming.

A day ago, Audrey would never have suspected that it was possible to feel this way over a lizard. She thought about the kittens she refused to look at in the playpen. Maybe she would have felt the same way about one of them. But Audrey doubted it...Newt just seemed so special. At lunch, Audrey considered running home, checking on Newt, and then running back. But if there was traffic, it would cut the timing too close. And she wouldn't have any time to eat. She also wouldn't have time to do much more than peek at Newt, and then turn around and return to work. That might upset him more. Audrey didn't want this to be a peekaboo relationship. She wanted Newt to know that when she was home, she was there for him. She wasn't going to just run in and out as if he didn't matter at all. He wasn't an afterthought.

So at her lunch break, Audrey followed her usual routine and went to the food court instead of home. She'd just settled down with her salad from Subway when she heard someone call her name. Looking up, she was surprised, and then pleased, to see Annabel, the young woman from Victoria's Secret, approaching her.

"Hi, Audrey! Happy day after your birthday. Okay if I join you?"

Audrey usually ate by herself. But she nodded at the chair across from her.

Annabel set down her tray and unwrapped her Burger King Whopper Junior. Audrey was glad to see that it was a Junior, at least. If Annabel ate Whoppers and still looked the incredibly skinny way she did, Audrey would have to hate her.

"So are you wearing some of your birthday presents?" Annabel asked in a husky voice.

"I am," Audrey said and blushed. She leaned forward and whispered, "The kaleidoscope set."

Annabel laughed and then tugged at her collar. "God, they always keep the food court so warm." She began to unbutton her bright blue blouse.

Audrey thought it was comfortable. Like Newt, she would have been happy to sit on a heated rock all day; she was always cold. Annabel shucked the blouse, laying it across the chair beside her. Underneath, she was wearing a pink t-shirt with white letters that read, "Not the f-word."

Audrey swallowed and ran the only word she knew of as the f-word through her mind. But that didn't seem to fit. "Not the f-word?" she asked.

Annabel glanced down. "Oh, yeah, isn't it great? I picked it up at a little bookstore near here."

Maybe the f-word referred to a sports team enemy? Or some special social media code? "So what f-word are you...not?"

Annabel opened zesty sauce and dunked an onion ring into it. "Feminist, of course. Not a feminist."

Audrey sat back. "What?"

"Feminist. I'm not one. You know, a man-hater." Annabel licked every finger.

Audrey wondered if it no longer mattered if Annabel ate Whoppers or Whopper Juniors. She wondered if she was going to hate Annabel anyway. "Feminists aren't man-haters," she said.

"Oh, please. It's all that Gloria Steinem dinosaur crap. Men are evil. Men look down on women. Men make more than women. Women deserve to be better than men." Annabel shrugged. "They just want to do to men what they think men have been doing to them. How is that fair? If they want equality, just be equal. Don't try to be better or privileged."

Audrey tried to put this all together. Annabel wasn't a feminist, and she had outrageous views on what feminism was. Audrey's uplifting bra suddenly didn't feel so uplifting. It felt like a corset. She wondered what

Annabel wore under her t-shirt.

It was 2017, and the entire country had just been through the roughest of elections. Feminism, women's rights, whose body was whose, equal pay for equal work, birth control rights, all of it came under a very nasty microscope. A month ago, a new and improbable president had been sworn in, and Audrey did some swearing of her own and refused to watch the event on television. She also refused to call him by name, referring to him instead as only That Man In The White House. The fact that a young woman was sitting in front of her wearing a "not the f-word" t-shirt and the f-word was feminist seemed as wildly ridiculous as That Man In The White House managing to get in there in the first place. It was impossible. It was horrible. It was…

Audrey shook her head and stopped her internal diatribe. She hadn't felt put off by Annabel yesterday. She felt empowered, really. And she enjoyed their time together. Audrey wondered who Annabel voted for. She wondered if she should ask. She knew there were women who voted for That Man In The White House. She just couldn't figure out how they could possibly do so.

Audrey knew she was being ridiculous too. She couldn't say That Man's name. And she promised herself she never would. But her kind of ridiculous felt justified. Not the f-word? Women voting for That Man? How could that possibly be justified?

"Well, enough of that political talk," Annabel said. "Tell me about the rest of your birthday. Did you buy yourself anything else? Or did someone special have something waiting for you when you got home?"

Audrey pushed the negative judgments away. She'd only just met Annabel, after all. Even the anti-f t-shirt didn't mean she voted for That Man In The White House. "No, I'm alone. Not in a relationship right now." She smiled. "So I bought myself someone special for at home." She told Annabel about Newt.

"You bought an iguana for your birthday?" Annabel didn't wait to swallow to comment, and with her mouth hanging open, Audrey found herself no longer craving Burger King's onion rings and zesty sauce.

"He's really cute. All green and white, and just some red flecks that remind me of freckles. Wine-colored freckles."

Annabel resumed chewing and swallowed. "So did you name him Freckles?"

Audrey hadn't considered that; she supposed it was the obvious name.

"No," she said. "His name is Newt."

"Like the lizard? But I thought you said he was an iguana."

Audrey hadn't considered that meaning of the name either. "I guess so, like the lizard. But that's not what I meant. I meant short for Newton."

"Like Sir Isaac Newton?"

Audrey swiped her lettuce through the last of her Thousand Island Light dressing. The science reference helped lift her spirits. Maybe there was more to Annabel than not the f-word. After the Sir Isaac reference, she just couldn't bring herself to say, "Like the cookie." So she said, "Yeah, like that," instead.

Annabel finished up, crumpling her wrappers and pulling her button-down blouse back on. "I've got to get back, but would you like to meet up after work? Go out for a birthday celebration drink? You should have a little fun."

Audrey began to gather her tray together too. "No, but thanks. I really want to get home to Newt, make sure he's okay. He needs his dinner salad."

Annabel paused her hands on her buttons. "You have to get home to your iguana?"

Newt was more than an iguana. Already, Audrey knew that despite the buyer's remorse that morning. But she couldn't say that. She just nodded and told Annabel that maybe she'd see her tomorrow.

On the way back to her store, Audrey glanced at her watch. Another four hours and she could head home. To Newt.

With the exception of her biological clock, before its demise with the onset of menopause, she'd never been so aware of the slow, yet urgent passing of time.

$\bullet$ $\bullet$ $\bullet$ $\bullet$ $\bullet$

As she drove home that night, Audrey thought about what it would have been like to get a drink with Annabel and felt a wave of loneliness pass over her. She couldn't remember the last time she went out for a drink with someone after work. Or went to the movies with someone, or out to dinner. Mostly, she was just by herself. She'd grown used to it, really. But sometimes, it would be nice to share a drink, a dinner, a laugh, with someone else. It was nice today, having lunch, talking, sharing what her birthday had been like, sharing her news about Newt.

Nice. That word just wouldn't leave her alone. On her birthday, she wanted anything but nice. And now the day after, she thought maybe nice would be...nice.

But would it be nice with someone like Annabel? Who wasn't an f-word? And who thought that feminist *was* an f-word, with every meaning that designation put on it? How could putting feminist and fuck on the same level be nice?

But still. A chance to go out. Do something different. Talk. Share.

Though now there was Newt. He was definitely different. Audrey straightened behind her wheel and hit the gas. Oh, yes. There was Newt. Audrey couldn't wait to get home. She would dribble water over his salad and toast him with her glass of wine.

Sharing a drink with a lizard. That wasn't nice. That was spectacular. F-word spectacular. Fucking spectacular.

Within a couple weeks, Newt was only staying in his aquarium while Audrey was at work or out running errands. She'd taught him to hitch a ride on her shoulder, and that seemed to be his favorite place. He pressed his cheek against hers. When they sat in the living room to watch television or in the reading room to read, he either squatted on her lap or on the armrest next to her. They both moved freely throughout the house, sometimes alone, most times together, and when they were together, it was because they both chose to be. Audrey bought another hammock and warming rock for the corner beside her bed, which she laid with patio bricks, and at night, Newt curled up there to sleep beside her. He woke in the morning with her alarm, yawning and stretching in a lizardy way as she stretched and yawned in her bed. He kept her company during her shower, sitting on the bath mat and enjoying the steam and Audrey's voice as she sang to him. He watched her getting dressed, Audrey asking his opinion on different combinations of colors and patterns and accessories, and he shared breakfast time with her in that golden hour after waking. He had his own placemat on the kitchen table, and he stood on it while he ate his fresh food, sprinkled liberally with water, of course. He never tried to jump off the table. He waited patiently until Audrey placed him on the floor or raised him to her shoulder. They were both learning to "bridge"; Audrey would angle her arm downwards, placing her hand at Newt's level, and he would climb up her arm to her shoulder. This took trust on both their parts. Newt trusted her to not jerk or jostle in such a way that he could fall off. She trusted that he wouldn't decide to jump.

Audrey took more patio bricks (Newt liked to lay on hard things; she figured it reminded him of rocks, as if he lived in the wild) and placed them nicely on the living room floor in a corner where two walls met, giving Newt his own iguana-space in the main living area of the house. She knew from her self-help books that in a good relationship, it was important to have spaces that were uniquely your own, where you could still be a couple, but also be your own person. Or iguana. She wanted Newt to have that. He had his own personal spaces now in the living room, the bedroom, and the reading room. She bought a sunlamp for each of his spaces, and more hammocks and warming rocks, and put them on alternating timers, so that Newt had plenty of opportunities and a variety of places to soak in the sun on his warmed rocks or bricks.

She built Newt a special hide box made from plywood, and she painted it a bright green and put his name on the roof. It took up part of his living room space, and when Newt was in there, Audrey knew he wanted to be alone. She respected that. For herself, she really only required privacy in one place, or more accurately, on one place: the toilet. One long-ago relationship involved a man who always left the door open when he was answering nature's call, as he dubbed it, allowing her to hear all of his noises. He even held a conversation with her, calling over his splashes and grunts. Audrey was grossed out and swore to always have a closed-door policy while using the toilet from that point on. Newt respected that. He had his own closed-door bathroom too, which he used responsibly; a litterbox filled with torn-up newspapers that were kept behind an iguana-sized privacy screen in the guestroom. Audrey rarely had guests, so she wasn't worried about what to do if guests had to share their sleeping quarters with Newt's bathroom. She felt that Newt deserved his own private space for bodily functions.

Within a month, Audrey began to trust Newt alone in the house, and the expensive aquarium was stored away in the basement. She just didn't like keeping him trapped in those four glass walls during the day; it felt cruel, like a punishment, like he was a child being sent to his room. Audrey didn't think of Newt as her child; he was her partner, and she wanted to treat him as such, with respect and care and compassion. She'd read in her books that you should never treat a partner in a way that you didn't want to be treated, and Audrey knew she wouldn't want to be relegated to a room, especially one with glass walls that allowed you to see everything you were missing.

Being out of the aquarium, though, meant that he couldn't see out the picture window. Audrey pondered this for a while, but then built a pyramid of stairs from more patio bricks. Newt learned to walk up there to look out and walk down when he was ready for something else to do. Audrey was thrilled. She worried that he spent too much time alone, but his willingness to learn whatever Audrey taught him seemed to show that he didn't feel abandoned or neglected. He even began to sit at the picture window and watch for her car to pull in. When he saw her, he stood on his hind legs and pressed his bare white belly against the glass, and he glowed like a welcome home light on a wide front porch. By the time she opened the door from the garage, he'd scrambled down from the window to meet her, raising himself straight-legged, his limbs moving in his splay-toed iguana way. He moved stiffly and swiftly, but always, always toward her.

He nodded at her often, bobbing his head in the most gregarious way. She pondered buying him a hat. When it grew warm again, she planned on bringing Newt outside. Maybe even taking him for walks. Strolling with her iguana in the budding warmth of spring and sitting with him on the back deck in the heat of summer seemed like wonderful things to do.

"Newt," she said, "I really enjoy being in your company." And Newt seemed to enjoy being with her too.

One evening, as they sat in the reading room, Audrey reading a novel, Newt spread like a lizard tattoo on her knee, the doorbell rang. It was the first time Newt ever heard it, and he quickly rose himself straight-legged. His dorsal spines, the spines along his back, went stiff and upright and his dewlap, the flap of skin beneath his chin, puffed and swayed in a threat. Audrey never saw him look aggressive before and while she knew that iguanas could bite, this tough lizard guy act amused her. He was trying to protect her, but he was still so small.

"It's okay, Newt," she said and smoothed her hand from his head to the tip of his tail. As she did, his dorsal spines sagged and relaxed, and his tail, which was lashing, went still. "Come on, let's go see who it is." She lifted him to her shoulder, and he tucked his head next to her cheek, his tail wrapped around the back of her neck.

When she opened the door, she found Frank, her new next-door neighbor. He'd moved in almost a year ago, she figured. He was friendly, though she didn't see him often, mostly just to wave to and to share some pleasantries with from time to time. She figured him to be close to her age, likely a little older, since he said he was retired.

"Hi, Audrey," he said. "Some of your mail got delivered with mine and – " He stopped, his stare landing just at her left shoulder. "Good lord, Audrey," he said. "What in the hell is that?"

Audrey glanced at Newt, even though she knew who Frank was talking about. Newt's dorsal spines rose again. "This is my iguana, Frank. His name is Newton. I got him a little over a month ago." She decided not to say that Newt was a birthday present. She especially decided not to say that she was the desperate person that gave him to her. She reached up and patted the lizard's head. His spikes sagged, and he pressed against her palm. "He's really friendly. And he's good company."

"Not much of a watchdog though, I'd bet," Frank said, and they both laughed, though Audrey didn't like feeling that it was at Newt's expense. She thought of Newt's straight-legged stance, the quivering dewlap, the stiff dorsal spines. Newt would protect her, if need be. Frank jerked his head toward his house. "I prefer birds myself."

Audrey remembered hearing high-pitched squawks coming from his open windows when the weather was warm. "Canaries? Parakeets?"

Frank nodded. "Parakeets. Six of them."

"Six!" Audrey glanced down at Frank's shirt, his pants, and his shoes, expecting to see him covered with tiny feathers. "Don't they make an awful mess?"

"Just some seed here and there. A few feathers. I have Lucky, Plucky, Ducky, Aristotle, BlueBoy, and Butch." Frank counted them off on his fingers and then started to reach out for Newt as if a lizard would perch on his pointer finger like a bird. Newt's spikes went back up. Frank hesitated and put his hand back in his pocket. "They don't cause any more mess than a lizard, I would think. Does he bite?"

Audrey chucked Newt under his chin. "He's never bitten me. So you said you had some of my mail?"

Frank handed over a few envelopes, then stood there. He looked around Audrey's shoulder in the living room. "Not watching any television tonight?" He smiled and shrugged, adding quickly, "I usually see your light on and the glow from the television screen."

Audrey shook her head. "No, I'm reading."

"Oh, I'm reading the new Stephen King novel myself." Frank shifted his feet. "Have you read it?"

Audrey shook her head again. She didn't read Stephen King, preferring the likes of Elizabeth Berg and Anne Tyler. Sometimes John Irving, when he wasn't too off-the-wall and long-winded.

"Well...you know," Frank said, "I have an idea. It's kinda chilly tonight. Would you like to come over, have some hot chocolate? I have a gas fireplace. We could turn it on. I have some pound cake too, that goes well with hot chocolate." He licked his lips and rubbed his stomach, which freaked Audrey out a little. "Especially on a cold night. It's going to be a long winter, I think."

Audrey considered. She remembered the shot of loneliness she felt after turning down Annabel's offer of a birthday drink after work. It was a month later, and that offer hadn't been repeated, though she and Annabel had lunch together on days when their schedules jived. Annabel was a new number on Audrey's cell phone, which felt good, even though they hadn't met up after hours. Now here Audrey was again, with another chance, this time with a friendly neighbor and pound cake and hot chocolate. She usually had some tea for a snack before bed, but hot chocolate sounded nice. Especially with someone else. And she could trust Newt alone in the house now.

But it was evening. Their time. Newt's and hers.

Newt shifted on her shoulder, and his tail slid along her neck and then down her back. He'd been alone all day. If she had her snack with Frank, Newt would have to have his snack alone when she returned. She supposed she could bring Newt to Frank's, but it was really too cold to walk Newt across her walkway, down the sidewalk to Frank's walkway, up that, then into his house. In a Wisconsin winter, even going to your neighbor's house was a trek, requiring boots and coats and hats and mittens, and you had to be okay with sinking into snow up to your knees. Frank was a case in point, wearing all of these things just to deliver her mail. She also didn't know if Frank and his birds would welcome an iguana in his house. He seemed a little scared of Newt. He asked about biting. And then there was the stress factor for Newt. She was responsible for Newt now. She didn't take that lightly.

"That sounds nice, Frank, but I'm afraid I can't. I have a few things to take care of before bed." There was that nice again. Audrey told herself she needed to become more conscious of using that word. She didn't want nice. She wanted more. Or at least she thought she did. Nice was okay, in moderation. Too much nice, she thought, could be deadly.

"Oh." Frank seemed crestfallen, but then he yanked the corners of his mouth back up into a pleasant smile. "Okay. Maybe some other time." He waved at Newt and said, "Goodbye, little lizard," and stepped off her stoop.

As he crunched the path between their front doors, Audrey thought she heard the sound of his parakeets calling him home.

He did wave at Newt, though, despite asking if Newt bit. And he called him little lizard. Audrey thought that was endearing, in a way.

Nice.

But she wanted more, she reminded herself. Maybe.

She shut the door quickly before Newt caught a chill.

•　　•　　•　　•　　•

Audrey was walking through the mall on the next night, heading toward the parking garage, when Annabel called to her from the entrance to Victoria's Secret. "Hey, Audrey! Any plans this weekend? How's Newt?"

Audrey swiveled and walked over, not wanting to shout out iguana news in front of everyone. "No plans, really. I'll probably watch something on Netflix tonight. Maybe come in here tomorrow. I still haven't spent my birthday gift certificate."

"Netflix?" Annabel laughed. "Really? Girl, it's Friday night! You're single, remember? You should be going out." Annabel leaned against the display window, and Audrey thought how someone would have to wash the smudge off before closing. She wondered if Annabel wore another "Not the f-word" t-shirt under today's blouse. "I sure would be, except I'm the closer tonight. But come 9:05, I am out of here!"

So Annabel would have to wash her own smudge. "Well, I don't have anyone to go out with anyway. Except Newt, of course, and he's not of legal drinking age yet." She laughed.

Annabel didn't.

Audrey started to leave, then hesitated. She leaned against the opposite display window, the entrance to the store a glittery path between them. "You know, I have thought about signing up for one of those online dating sites. Have you ever done those?"

Annabel bobbed her head, reminding Audrey of Newt. "Sure. I haven't done any of the ones where you pay, but I've done some of the free ones. I'm on Fish In The Sea now."

Audrey couldn't help but think that you get what you pay for. And if you paid nothing... "I haven't heard of that one, but I've seen commercials for the ones that cost something. Match dot com, eHarmony, that weird one for farmers..."

Annabel laughed. "Oh, sure, I think there's probably a site for everyone into everything. Have you seen some of those late-night commercials? The ones that are basically for phone sex?"

Audrey had. The barely clad women, breathily inviting men to call, because they just enjoy a good time. Giggle. Coy look. The latest one had a woman biting her knuckle and swaying seductively while the voice-over said, "Your night is in your hands." Then the woman gave a wide-mouth naughty laugh, with plenty of tongue and a wink. Good grief. Audrey usually changed the channel. "I thought maybe…there's that one for people over fifty. I might start there."

Annabel rolled her eyes. "Really? You'd pay to date someone over fifty?"

Audrey frowned. "Well, I am over fifty. So the guy would be with someone over fifty too. I wouldn't pay the guy, of course. I'd have to pay the service –"

"Cripes, Audrey." Annabel straightened as some customers stepped between them into the store. Her head turned to watch them, but Audrey noticed she didn't leave to take up her post. Audrey trained her associates to be surreptitiously near shopping customers, ready to be helpful if requested, ready to be ignored too. And ever vigilant for shoplifters. "You really think anyone meets anyone on those? Just go out. Go to a club. I mean, those 'dating sites' are really all about sleeping together. Why pay for that when you can get it for free? Go out and meet someone face to face. Get some use out of those new undies. Go to *Fish in the Sea* if you want a site. But geez, life is expensive enough without paying to get a date." She glanced at the customers again. They seemed to be zeroing in on a rack of strapless push-up bras. "I'd better go. Text me later."

Audrey watched as Annabel walked back into the store and started to straighten a display within four feet of the shoppers. She remembered Annabel connecting Newt with Sir Isaac Newton, and so she wondered if Annabel was being smart with the dating sites too. If she knew about things Audrey didn't. She was younger, after all. More hip, more with it, or whatever it was called these days.

But she was also not the f-word. Maybe she voted for That Man In The White House.

And Audrey was old enough to say "these days". She was old enough to apply the word nice to just about everything.

And were those dating sites and dating itself really only about sleeping together? Really? That wasn't nice. Was it? Audrey wanted more. She remembered a time when going out, as she and her friends called it, was definitely about sleeping together. But that changed as she got older, especially once she hit her thirties. Now here she was in her fifties. Was she supposed to revert back to casual sex and one night stands? Was she supposed to accept that she was never going to be in a committed relationship, a marriage, and so she should just return to the days of hunting for the next sex partner? Not even a partner. A stopover. A vibrator that breathed and had limbs. And who then walked out the door and Audrey would have to go on to the next club, the next mating, and the next morning with an ultimately empty bed.

Audrey decided she wasn't done with talking with Annabel yet and her thumbs weren't up for a long text-discussion. She walked over to where Annabel was and flipped through a drawer of underwear so Annabel wouldn't get in trouble if a manager was watching. Audrey said, "But what if you want to do more than just sleep with someone? What if you're serious and want something long-term?"

Annabel glanced over and then shrugged. "I guess you hope that you end up liking the guy that you're sleeping with at some point." She smiled. "But hey, you've got Newt, remember? After you've had your fun, you have your guy at home. Even if he's little and green and lives in an aquarium."

Not anymore. Audrey thought of Newt's white belly in the living room window. Of his now familiar weight on her shoulder, his tail embracing her neck.

"Goodnight, Annabel," she said quietly, and she headed out to her car. Newt *was* at home. She *did* have a little green guy waiting for her. She'd go on home and talk to Newt about it. She was a strong and independent woman who didn't need a man to make her life complete. A woman needed a man like a fish needed a bicycle.

But what about *want*? Could a fish want a bicycle? Could a fish have one if it wanted one?

Audrey decided the next time she was in Bob's pet shop, she would see if he stocked little underwater bicycles for his aquariums, like the little treasure chests and deep sea divers. This made her laugh, but even as she did so, she knew she would really look for this when she was there.

Chapter Four

Because, you know, he's haunted.

After Strike One showed up in the grocery store, Frank supposed he shouldn't have been all that surprised when Strike Two made an appearance as well. Even if she was dead. After all, Strike Two spent the first part of their marriage trying to compete with everything Strike One did and didn't do, even though Frank had been divorced for eleven years by the time he and Strike Two were married. "What was your favorite thing that she cooked for you?" Strike Two asked on their honeymoon. "Was she skinnier than me? Did you like her hair long? Do you prefer blondes? And…" she blushed, "what was your favorite, you know, position?"

It took Frank the first five years of their marriage to convince Strike Two that she was unique, that he didn't want another Strike One, that he was happy, so happy, to be with her. Strike Two knew that he and Strike One were married for ten years. Strike Two celebrated hitting their own eleventh-anniversary mark as if she won Olympic Gold. Frank sometimes wondered if their marriage lasted as long and as well as it did because Strike Two was so determined to beat Strike One, to win, to cross whatever that finish line was in her head. Of course, in the end, Strike Two lost, Frank supposed. She died. Strike One was still alive.

Frank felt like he was the one who lost.

So maybe Strike Two's competitive spirit outlived and outreached the grave.

Frank sat on his couch the night after Audrey rejected his offer of hot chocolate and company. He thought of his father, and he figured this might be considered strike one in his pursuit of her. He put his feet up on the footstool and a mug of hot chocolate rested on the shelf of his stomach. His birds, not yet covered for the night, twittered amongst themselves in the bay window. His fireplace was on, and so was his television, and his lamps were off. The flickering lights played over the birds' feathers, and Frank was watching this when he felt the cushion beside him sink down. Turning, he found Strike Two sitting there.

"Holy shit!" he said.

She laughed and said, "I'm happy to see you too, Frank," and kissed him lightly on the cheek. He barely felt it. But he'd thought of her kisses so often in the three years she'd been gone, even this breath of a touch was a feast. "How are you?"

Frank looked in his cup, unsure of what he actually had in there. He glanced around the room; everything was in place, nothing was out of order or a strange color or suddenly animated. So he didn't seem to be hallucinating or stroking out. Except a dead woman was sitting on his couch. "I don't know," he said honestly. "Susan...what are you doing here? Are you here? Am I dreaming? Am I having some sort of..." he sorted through his TV medical shows vocabulary, "...neurological event?" Then he amended, "Or a mental one?"

"I'm here. Really." She rested her hand on that special place on his thigh, the place where it rested so often in their fifteen years together. Frank swore there was a divot in his skin just for her. "I saw that you ran into, well, *her* a few days ago, and then last night, I saw you try to get your neighbor to come over. Frank," she said, and she squeezed his thigh in a grip so soft, it was like a pucker in the denim, "what are you doing?"

"Well, I didn't intend to run into Strike One," Frank said defensively, and then immediately wondered if Susan would understand. He didn't call Strike One by that name until Susan became Strike Two. "I mean, Theresa. I didn't intend to run into Theresa. She was just there."

Susan nodded. "It's okay, Frank," she said. "I know who you mean by Strike One. And I know I'm Strike Two, though you know I certainly didn't want to be. I couldn't help my death. I did everything I could to stay."

His eyes immediately flooded.

She leaned into him.

"And with Audrey...well, it has been three years, Susan. Christ, I miss you every day. And it's not like she'd be a replacement. I just...I just..."

"Need to move on," she supplied. "I agree, hon."

He saw a glitter on her cheeks, and he wondered if ghosts could cry. He also wondered if she was able to tell what he was thinking. Did she know that, while he no longer lived in their old house, he still had all of her things packed in boxes in the basement?

"Yes," she said. "I know. And yes, I can."

In his closet, her bathrobe hung on a hanger next to his shirts. She used to slip into it in the morning before she showered and dressed and she slipped out of it at night, before joining him in bed. On the hard nights since her passing, he held it. On the harder nights, he slept with it. But even on good days, he rested one hand on its sleeve while he pondered which shirt to wear. She always guided him in his clothing choices.

"I know," she said.

He put his hand over hers. It felt like air, but air that had a current to it that kept his hand from sinking through. "I was able to move here," he said. "Away from our home. But I couldn't throw you away. Or donate you. I just couldn't."

She nodded toward the birds, who had gone silent. Frank noticed they were all sitting together on the long perch, facing the couch. He didn't know parakeets could open their eyes so wide. "And those birds? What are they about? Good grief, Frank, six of them!"

"Just someone to talk to," he said. "Someone to take care of."

Susan glanced at the little circle of feathers on the floor around the cage. "You need to vacuum more often if you have those," she said. She always kept their house immaculate. "But with your neighbor, with this Audrey…Frank, stealing her mail?"

Frank fought his blush. He knew it was a federal crime to take someone else's mail, but he needed a reason to ring her doorbell. "I just wanted to talk to her," he said. "It's harder in the winter. We're not out in our yards much. And I thought a cup of hot chocolate would be nice."

She smiled at him. "Oh, Frank. It wasn't a bad idea, even though you could have been arrested. But you don't ask a woman over to your house on a first date."

"It wasn't a date!" he said. "It was just a chance to sit and get to know each other. I can't ask her out without knowing her first."

Susan sighed. "Well, yes, you can. Even to get to know her, you should take her somewhere. Dinner. A movie. Even out for a cup of hot chocolate, but not at your house. That's, well, that's dangerous. In her eyes. In any smart woman's eyes. I know you're not dangerous. But she doesn't. No smart and aware woman goes into a man's house that she barely knows, even if he makes the best hot chocolate in the world." She touched his mug. "And you do. Do you still make it by scratch?"

"I would have, for her. But since it's just me…" He shrugged. "I used a mix tonight."

Susan's face became so sad, he had to look away. "Frank," she said, "please make your very own hot chocolate. Your way. Remember how you used to stir in just a little bit of butterscotch syrup?"

He did. There was butterscotch syrup in his refrigerator right now.

"Make it that way, and then think of me when you drink it. Then I can taste it too. I miss it, Frank," she said. "And I miss you. I didn't want to leave. I love you so much."

"And I love you," he said, and in his voice, he heard every day of the three years she'd been gone. He'd been told grief lasted for about two years, and on the third anniversary of Strike Two's death, he woke up, looked at the ceiling, and said out loud, "Still here." He felt like he was in the same sort of marathon Susan had been in when she was trying to outlast Theresa. But Frank wasn't trying to outlast grief. He wanted to cross the finish line last. He wanted to get lost along the way and never cross the finishing line at all. If he crossed that finish line, he worried, if he won out over grief, he might forget Susan. And that was the last thing he wanted to do.

But he supposed the grief was lessening. He was thinking about Audrey. And it was rare now that he witnessed something and instantly thought that he'd have to remember to tell Susan. Instead, his thoughts now drifted to wishes. Wishes that he could tell her this or that. Wishes that they could share a meal together at their favorite restaurant. Wishes that when he touched the arm of her robe, the sleeve wouldn't be empty.

A night like this one, amazing as it was, Susan's voice in his ear, her hand on his thigh, all the grief came roaring back. But the grief roared before this too, when there was no voice and no hand at all. If this was real, the roar was worth it.

When he turned to Susan, he discovered he was by himself again. The birds resumed their prattling. He wondered, of course, if she'd even been there. But he knew.

She was. As hard as that was to believe, she was.

He got up to look out of his bay window, through the bars of his birdcage. From this spot, he couldn't see to Audrey's house, of course. They were side by side and their houses both faced the street. He really couldn't see Audrey's house at all unless he went outside. Their garages sat next to each other with a swath of green grass running between them. But he knew that her house was dark. There was no patch of living room light setting the snow to glittering. She was either spending another evening with a good book and her iguana in some back room, or she'd gone to bed.

Frank checked his birds' feeder dishes and water bottles. He told them they had about another hour before he'd be covering them for bed. All of them bobbed their heads except for Butch, who always protested bedtime. He opened his wings wide and squawked. "Yes, even you, Butch," Frank said.

He wondered if Audrey covered Newt at night. He wasn't sure if you would do such a thing for an iguana, but why wouldn't you? To Frank, every living breathing species likely enjoyed the warmth of being tucked up into bed. Cared for. Loved. For his part, it was nice to have someone to take care of. He imagined Audrey enjoyed it too.

Then he went to the kitchen to dump out his cold hot chocolate down the drain and make a new batch. Not from a mix, but his own special recipe. With a sweet swirl of butterscotch.

He'd think of Susan while he drank it.

•   •   •   •   •

The next day, Frank's doorbell rang at one o'clock in the afternoon. Frank was startled when he found Strike One on his doorstep. He noticed that while he felt a quick rush of – what? Excitement? Joy? Lust? – at seeing Strike One, it was followed immediately by a wash of loss and then the smack-down of anger. There had been grief at losing Strike One, as there was in losing Strike Two. He'd loved Theresa and then she was gone, just like with Susan.

But oh, the difference in depth with the loss of his second wife. The difference in solidity and continuity. There'd been anger with Susan too, even at Susan for a while, which he knew was illogical and, he was told, normal. But the grief ran throughout. And stayed. The grief over Strike One dissipated. The anger never did.

He decided right then that she would always be Strike One. He would not call her Theresa.

"Can I help you?" he asked, stepping out on his porch and shutting the door to keep the cold air from getting into the birds. "What are you doing here? How did you find me?"

Strike One laughed and flapped. "I'm happy to see you too, Frank," she said, in striking repetition of Susan, but with an extra dose of sarcasm. "There's this new thing now, have you heard? It's called the internet. I googled you." She wrapped her arms around her waist. "I just couldn't stop thinking about you after I saw you at the grocery store. You here, with your birds. Six, you said?"

He nodded toward the bay window. The birdcage was very visible in the winter sunlight.

"Oh, yes, there they are. Well...Frank, could we go inside? It's cold out here."

Frank didn't want to let her in. But it was cold. And she was a woman. He'd been raised to be a gentleman. His father would be handing out strike after strike for Frank's manners and lack of chivalry. In his head, he pictured himself saying no and her saying please three times and his father keeping count. "Strike one! Strike two! Strike three, yer out!" and Frank felt the flare of his own hair as if he'd been cuffed.

He sighed and opened the door, holding it with his arm outstretched so she could go first. She stepped primly inside, carefully stamping and scraping her shoes on his welcome mat before she moved onto the carpet. He was tempted to push her out of the way so he could get the door closed and protect the birds.

"Well, Frank, this is very nice!" she said. She sounded surprised.

He wondered what she expected. "Can you move in further please?" he asked. "I need to get this door closed before the birds catch a chill."

"Oh, the birds!" She walked over to the cage and looked at them. The birds seemed to realize that this was someone Frank wanted to impress, even if he would never admit to that, so they preened and spread their wings and turned in ways that the sun shone most flatteringly on their bright colors. Plucky was green, Lucky was purple, Ducky was yellow, of course, Butch was a mix of green and yellow, Aristotle was white, and BlueBoy was, another of course, blue. Though he would never say it aloud to anyone else, Frank called them his fluttering flying rainbow. He also told them he loved them. Some nights, when he let them out of their cage, they would sit three to one thigh and two to another, with Aristotle sitting on top of the cage. Aristotle wasn't comfortable with being too far away from his perch, but even so, he faced Frank and tilted his head, listening just as intently as the others as Frank talked to them. They always listened, and Frank always thought of their attention as admiring and positive. He was sure they loved him back.

"So what can I do for you?" He wasn't going to ask Strike One to sit down. He wasn't going to ask her if she'd like a drink. He wanted to ask her to leave.

"Well." She turned to face him. "Like I said, I couldn't stop thinking about you. Here alone with your birds. And I...well, I just wanted to see if you're all right." Like the birds, she tilted her head too. But she didn't look nearly as sweet.

"I'm just fine." He nearly said her name, but he stopped himself. He wouldn't do it, no, he wouldn't do it. She was Strike One. Scratch his arm and his anger would flare out like a matchstick.

"Really?" When he nodded, she sighed and folded her hands at her waist. "I know that we didn't separate on the best terms," she said. "And I know it was my fault, Frank, I do. But, well, I'm alone now too, you see. I know what it's like. Though I have the children and now the grandchild." She looked at the cage. "And you have...well, you have your birds."

"You're alone?" The righteousness in Frank reared up for a second. She deserved it. She left him alone. Tit for tat. But then the righteousness calmed again. Alone was never good, he thought. He wouldn't wish it on anybody. "What happened?" he asked gently. And then he went further and motioned to the couch.

She sat on one end and him on the other. Between them was the cushion where Susan sat the night before. "My husband passed away seven months ago. He had a heart attack while mowing the lawn. I found him out there." She stopped, and her eyes welled. "The lawn mower kept going," she said. "It was self-propelled, and the handle jammed. A few days later, a neighbor returned it. It kept going through all the backyards into the next block, bouncing off of trees and bushes, until it ran into the side of a garage and just couldn't go any further. Just like my husband." She pulled a tissue from her purse. "Thank goodness no one was hurt. Well, no one except Dick, I guess."

Dick, Frank thought. Her husband. Her second husband, the one who came after Frank and gave her what she wanted. Children. Dick was an appropriate name. That's what she married him for. But then Frank chided himself for being uncharitable, and he said very sincerely, "I'm sorry for your loss, Theresa." And then he damned himself for using her name. She was still Strike One. If she hadn't left him, if she hadn't suddenly and ridiculously decided they had to have children, something neither ever said they wanted, they'd be together still and neither would be alone right now.

Though she was on his couch, wasn't she. They weren't alone, at least not at this minute.

"Thank you," she said. "So...like I said, I know what it's like being alone. You remarried, didn't you?"

Frank was surprised she knew. But then he knew about her remarriage and the births of her children, so maybe it wasn't a surprise. Mutual friends kept him informed until he met Strike Two and then everyone seemed to scatter. "Yes, I married a woman named Susan. We were together fifteen years, but she died three years ago of uterine cancer."

Theresa looked sad, and her hand pressed a moment against her own abdomen. "And you didn't have any children?"

"No. Neither of us wanted any."

They sat quietly. Frank wasn't sure if he was thinking of the past, present or future. It was all pressing together. Theresa's leaving, Susan's dying, the times of happiness folded in between. The desire to move on now, to find someone he wouldn't lose. Even though he supposed there was never a guarantee.

"Did you adopt the birds with Susan?" Theresa asked.

"No." Frank looked at the cage where the birds twittered about. He noticed they weren't staring at Theresa the way they stared at Susan. "I adopted them almost a year ago. When I moved here, I found the new house wasn't enough. I needed someone to live with, to keep me company." He smiled toward the cage. "They do that."

Theresa took another fast look around and seemed to come to some sort of decision. "How about this, Frank? Would you like to get together now and then? Not for anything serious, really. But just the chance to talk. Especially to talk with someone who has known you for a while, you know?"

Frank was startled at the way Theresa pinpointed his loneliness, just like that. Frank did want to talk to someone who knew him. Even if he hit it off with Audrey, there were all those years he didn't know her and she didn't know him. But talk to Strike One? The woman he didn't even want to let into his house a few minutes ago? "Maybe," he said. "I'll think about it."

She smiled and stood up. "You always did need to think about things." She pulled a small notebook out of her purse and wrote a note, ripping it off and handing it to him. "That's my phone number. Give me a call if you decide it's something you want to do." She walked to the door and opened it herself, Frank still sitting on the couch. "It was nice to see you again, Frank."

The cold breeze from the shutting door worked itself up his ankles to his chest. He looked at the phone number. And then he looked at the door and listened as a car started, pulled out and away. His house settled into a bird chittery quiet of home.

Frank folded the sheet of paper and tucked it into his wallet. He realized he didn't throw it away, but he didn't want to draw attention to that fact, not to his birds, not even to himself. Certainly not to Susan, if she was hovering overhead. He sat and watched the birds, though it wasn't the birds he was seeing at all.

It was Theresa. He wouldn't admit it, not to Theresa, not to Susan, not even to the birds, but yes, it was sort of nice to see Strike One. To talk. Nothing serious. Really.

Chapter Five

When fishes and bicycles become skeletons in your closet...

It was solidly cold out, that kind of bone-drilling Wisconsin cold that announced winter was here to stay, and spring might never come. With the entrenchment of winter, like a standing sheet of black ice and impossible to shatter and push through, came profound nights of deep darkness. Nights left Audrey, from a combination of the recent changes in her life, plus the regret over turning down drinks with Annabel and Frank, with a sudden crushing onslaught of cabin fever, despite having been outside the house and at the mall all day. Still, her only interactions were with customers and an iguana. Audrey needed air, and she needed a voice in her ear. So she decided to take Newt on a visit to Bob's pet store. Bob said Newt was welcome any time and Audrey knew he meant it. When she got home from work, she left the car running in the garage so it would stay warm and when she went inside, she met her happy running iguana in full stride, swept him into a hug, and then tucked him into his car carrier. She talked to him all the way to the store.

"We're going to see Bob, okay, Newt? We'll get you some new food and maybe a few new toys. And I want to talk to him. About you, about how to keep you happy." She glanced at Newt who stared steadily out at her from the mesh on his carrier door. He looked plenty happy and maybe just a bit puzzled over her questioning his happiness. "I just want to make sure that if I'm not around some evenings or weekends, you'll be okay. I mean, I might want to go out sometimes. With people. Maybe. But I don't want you to be sad or lonely."

Now he did look sad, Audrey swore he did. Still, she reminded herself, according to the books on her bookshelves, a solid relationship meant that both partners were able to follow their own interests without necessarily needing the company or the approval of the other. They could spend time apart. In fact, the books admonished, they should.

Though in the examples in those books, the partners were able to talk to each other and explain. Audrey could talk to Newt, but he couldn't speak back, and she was never sure just how much he was taking in. Did that mean she was forever tethered to the house and to a little green iguana?

Who she loved?

Audrey was responsible for Newt. His needs were important, and she had to make sure they were met. But her needs were important too. Compromise, said the books, was everything.

She would try. She would talk to Bob. And Newt would be there to listen and to talk to him too, in whatever way an iguana could, in a way that maybe a pet expert could understand.

There was a parking space in front of the store and Audrey quickly zipped into it. Bob must have seen her pull in and he must have recognized her because he came to open the door so she could run right in before Newt had a chance to catch a chill. Bob greeted them both, then they sat Newt's carrier on the counter, let him out and allowed him to climb up to his perch on Audrey's shoulder.

"Oh, Audrey, he's looking good!" Bob said, patting Newt's head. Newt pressed the flat of his forehead against Bob's palm, just like he did with Audrey.

Audrey remembered the raised spikes and lashing tail that Newt displayed when Frank came over. There was none of that with Bob. Though Frank was a stranger; Newt used to live in the pet store with Bob as his companion for who knows how long before he came home with Audrey.

"So you out shopping today?" Bob asked. "You know, you should have a jacket for him. That would help keep him warmer when you take him out."

"A jacket?" Audrey smiled, picturing Newt in a parka.

Bob showed them a rack of lizard clothes and Audrey was delighted. Together, she and Bob chose a leather bomber jacket for Newt, with his approval. It was lined with soft flannel that wouldn't irritate his skin but would keep him protected from the elements. She picked out a matching leather driver's cap too, and a blue and white checkered button-down shirt and a lizard-sized straw hat for the impossibly far away days of spring. They bought some more food too, and Bob presented Newt with a brightly colored ball that he said Newt would love to roll around. This put Audrey in mind of a kitten, and she didn't like to think of Newt that way. She didn't want to picture him as anyone other than who he was. She didn't want him to think that she was trying to change him into something else, something cute and cuddly, or that she regretted not choosing another type of pet. But Bob promised Newt would enjoy it, and when they stood him on the check-out counter, and Bob put the ball in front of Newt, he obligingly batted at it. So Audrey bought it. She also chose a new hammock, a heated one. Newt loved his warming rocks, and he loved his hammocks and Audrey thought this was the perfect combination of pleasures. She would put it in the bedroom. While she snuggled into her electric blanket, Newt could cuddle into his heated hammock.

As Bob bagged her purchases, Audrey looked at Newt, standing there so squarely on the counter. She noticed how much he'd grown already. "I've been thinking about maybe going out some at night, Bob," she said, and then wished she said it differently. It made her seem like a spinster, and Audrey didn't like to think of herself that way, just like she didn't want to think of Newt as a kitten. "I mean, you know, on dates and such. I've been turning down invitations since I got Newt because I didn't want to leave him alone at night." It wasn't a lie, not really. Annabel had asked her out. Frank asked her next door for a cup of hot chocolate. "Newt always seems so happy when I get home. I hate to think of him sitting in my window, waiting for me and wondering where I am."

Bob smiled and then swung a feather in front of Newt. It dangled from a long red pole and Audrey thought it looked like a cat toy again. Newt stared at it, and Audrey thought he looked baleful. Insulted, maybe. "He'd be okay, Audrey," Bob said. "He's not a baby, you know. He's an iguana. As long as he's warm and fed, he'll be fine."

But Newt was so much more than that. Audrey thought of his welcoming white belly in the window, his straight-legged run to the door. "Maybe I could put my lamps and such on a timer," she said. "Just in case."

Bob nodded. "That would keep him from being in the dark, and it would certainly make you feel better." He took a second to look evenly at her. "I know I like going out after work sometimes. Have a drink, or maybe a little dinner."

Audrey was in the middle of running her hand down Newt's long back, and she paused. She wondered if this was a hint, maybe even an invitation, a little bit of a flirt. She glanced down and couldn't help but notice that Bob's hand didn't sport a wedding ring. He seemed about her age too. But then he went back to ringing up her items, and Audrey reached for the bomber jacket, and it was like someone pressed Play and the moment passed and rolled away, and there was no rewinding. Maybe it never really happened.

She removed the jacket's tags. Bob showed her how to dress Newt, carefully lifting one leg, then the other, The jacket looked like it snapped down the front, but it actually had a hidden velcro strip on the back that allowed Audrey to fold the jacket over Newt's spikes and then carefully seal him in.

He looked amazing. The leather bulked him up, and the dark brown color set off his green face. She thought of his tough guy act with Frank, and she wanted to laugh. This biker jacket was perfect for Newt's wanna-be tough guy image.

But he didn't seem so tough when Audrey thought of leaving him home alone at night. The white belly against her window was vulnerable.

"See, Bob," Audrey said slowly. "I just don't want him to be unhappy. I especially don't want him to be unhappy because of me, because of something I've done or not done. I know I've only had him a short time, and I know he's an iguana, but he already means the world to me."

Bob's face softened, and he pressed his hand against Newt's forehead again. "I get it, Audrey, I really do. I'm in the pet business, remember? But he'll be fine, really. You're taking wonderful care of him. Just look at him! He's thriving!"

Audrey hoped so. It meant a lot, really, to have Bob say that. He was the expert, after all. And so he could tell if she knew what she was doing. She didn't, but he thought she did, and so that counted for something. Audrey tucked Newt into his carrier, said goodnight to Bob, and then they made their way home.

That night, Audrey sat at her desk in the alcove of her bedroom and went on her computer. Newt stood right on the desk's surface, next to her mouse, and from time to time, he put his front foot on hers as she manipulated the cursor. Eventually, he got restless, and she lowered him to the floor, bridging him down her arm. He batted his new ball around for a while before leaving the room. Audrey knew him well enough now to predict that he was heading for a heated rock, where he would wait for their snack time.

It was all right that he left. Audrey wasn't sure she wanted Newt to see what she was about to do.

Fish In The Sea, Annabel said. The first thing Audrey noticed, after landing on the website, was the large flashing banner that shouted, "50,000 New Singles Per Day!" Fifty thousand? At the very top of the screen, it told her that 617,266 people were signed on to FITS right at that very minute.

Audrey instantly felt overwhelmed.

But the site was free. Audrey reasoned that the majority of those 617,266 were probably younger than she was, and there had to be a mix of men and women and even of sexual identities and preferences. It wasn't like she was going to be choosing among hundred-thousands. So she signed up for an account and then worked her way through a number of questions and boxes, creating her profile, trying to be as honest as possible, and then she hit enter. The next step, the site told her, was that they would apply their time-proven algorithm to her answers about herself and her desires for a mate and they would send her a list of possible choices. It was a way to pare down this astonishing group of 617,266. In the meantime, the site explained, she could page through the available men in her vicinity, which FITS already sorted for her, and see if any struck her fancy. Audrey shrugged and clicked on the provided link.

To her shock, page after page after page of men came up. All within the age range she selected: fifty to sixty-five. She didn't care about body types, she didn't care about astrological signs. She didn't care about skin color, eye color, or hair color, or even if there was hair. She did care about education; she wanted someone with at least a bachelor's degree. But wow. Why were there so many single men out there? Not even out there-out there, but right here, in her general area. If this was what came up for Milwaukee and vicinity, what the hell came up for a place like New York City?

Audrey stared at her screen. Her hand was frozen on her mouse.

Did she really want to find a potential partner this way? This felt like online shopping. Pick a size, pick a color, pick a style, choose an amount. Would she want someone finding her this way? It felt...icky. Like a partner was a commodity, sitting on a shelf of commodities, and she just had to pick one up and set him in her cart. Check out!

Ick.

But...if everyone was doing it...

Audrey looked behind her. Newt wasn't anywhere in sight, and it was just under an hour before it was time for their before-bed snack. She glanced at Ooshi on her bed, Ooshi, the stuffed cow given to her by the man from her last what-she-thought-of-as-serious relationship. She wished for summer and a county fair to go to. Should she wait until summer? Try to meet someone at the fair? Maybe she would find a farmer and prove to him that city folk do-so *get it*.

"I get it," Bob said to her at the pet store. It might have been a flirt. Maybe she should ask him out for a drink sometime.

But for now...there were all these pages for her to shop through while Fish In The Sea applied their algorithm. All these men. Men R Us. They were here, and they were free, just sitting on a shelf. She'd gone this far. So she settled in and began clicking through the photos and profiles. She felt like Newt with the feather in his face. Not sure. Not sure at all.

• • •

On Tuesday, Audrey was pleased when Annabel joined her at lunch. Annabel had off the day before, and Audrey actually felt her absence. She was growing used to having someone to talk to at lunch. It felt odd that meeting over bras would lead to a friendship, but Audrey supposed there were stranger ways to meet. Audrey wondered again about Fish In The Sea. Even though she clicked through dozens of profiles, she hadn't done anything with them. Not a flirt. Not a wink. Not anything.

"Hey, Audrey," Annabel said. "How was your weekend?"

"Quiet." It snowed on Saturday, and so Audrey stayed home, not even venturing out to spend her gift certificate, still waiting patiently in her purse. She and Newt watched old movies and napped on the couch. She took a long bath, and Newt kept her company from the fuzzy bath rug. He seemed to like the scent of the bubbles. On Sunday, Audrey heard an odd roaring sound and looked out the picture window to see Frank with his snowblower, clearing her driveway. That was so nice of him. She waved, and he waved back. She noticed when he was finished, he stood at the bottom of her driveway for a bit, as if he was unsure what to do next. She wondered if she should invite him in for coffee, or even a glass of wine, to help him warm up and thank him for the favor. But then he went on to his house. And his birds, she supposed.

"I went to a new club on Saturday night," Annabel said. "It was fun. You should come with me next weekend."

"Make sure you know what kind of fun she means," said another woman, sitting down next to Annabel. Audrey was taken aback. This wasn't a high school cafeteria, after all. You didn't just sit down during other people's conversations without asking to join. "She was surrounded by five guys at one point," this woman explained. "Don't think I was at the meat market with her. She just told me about it already." She extended a hand to Audrey and smiled a tight smile. "Hi. I'm Vicki Beckman." Audrey noticed a name tag on her lapel, indicating she worked at Chico's. "So who did you end up going home with?" Vicki asked Annabel.

"One of them." Annabel shrugged. "I think his name was Jim."

Vicki shook her head. "God, Annabel. That's just so dangerous."

Audrey sat back. "Dangerous? But isn't that what she was there for?" She noticed a sharp look from Annabel while Vicki leaned forward over her pile of noodles and sauce from the Asian restaurant.

"Diseases, Audrey. Diseases! It's not like they've cured AIDS yet, even though no one ever talks about it anymore." She turned back to Annabel. "How do you know who that guy has been with?" she charged. "And what he's done? I mean, he's a *guy.* You know what guys are like."

Audrey agreed about the diseases. Back when she was in college, they didn't have to worry about that as much. There were diseases, but they were more of an inconvenience than a life-threat. That was her era of the one-night stand with someone with no name. But now? She'd need clearance from a doctor before she considered sleeping with anyone. Back in her mid-thirties, Audrey actually had her doctor print a copy of her bloodwork, showing she was clean, so if the opportunity came up, she could reassure the man she was potentially going to sleep with. She reassured a few times after she was reassured in return. But now, the copy rested and waited in one of her desk drawers. It was outdated, and if someone new showed up, she would need to see her doctor and get fresh bloodwork done for it to be considered reliable. Audrey would never consider old results to be a pass to an intimate relationship.

But then there was Vicki's charge of what *guys* were like. Audrey thought of Bob at the pet store, Frank at the bottom of her driveway. "What are they like?" she asked, interrupting a heated discussion that continued without her.

Vicki paused with her mouth hanging open. "What's who like?"

"Guys," Audrey said. "You said, "You know what *guys* are like. What're they like?"

Annabel and Vicki stared for a moment, but then Vicki rolled her eyes and leaped back into the fray with Annabel. Audrey felt dismissed, like someone her age wouldn't need to know what *guys* were like anyway. She thought of the bloodwork form in her desk drawer and how long it had been since she was given a stuffed cow to put on her bed. Audrey calculated. Eight years. Was it eight years since she squealed over a stuffed cow, won by a man slamming a mallet over fake gopher heads? Maybe she would never need to know about anyone's bloodwork anymore. Maybe she just needed to understand her iguana.

Though there was that moment with Bob…And all those men on Fish In The Sea…

"What if you said no and the guy didn't care?" Vicki said. The intensity in her voice made Audrey's shoulders hunch, though it didn't seem to have any effect on Annabel, who kept calmly eating her roast beef sandwich from Arby's. "You know all guys are manipulators, Annabel. And you had five circling you! Wolves on the hunt! The guy you went home with probably just wanted to be the alpha male. The one who conquered. Did he take any pictures of you? That's the big thing, you know. Posting obscene and compromising pictures on Instagram and Snapchat."

"No!" Annabel rolled her eyes too, just like Vicki did a few minutes before. "Really," she said to Audrey. "Don't pay any attention. She believes that all guys are monsters. She's an SJW."

"A what?" Audrey asked, at the same time as Vicki protested, "I am not!"

"Boy, you are out of touch," Annabel said. "SJW. Social Justice Warrior."

Audrey didn't think she was out of touch. She was on Facebook and Twitter. She glanced at Vicki who was turning bright red. "A warrior? For social justice? Isn't that a good thing?"

"No!" they both said together.

Annabel waved at Vicki, pushing away the steam that must have been coming from her enraged pores. "A Social Justice Warrior hates everything. They hate everyone. They're always angry. And they try to change things by shaming, instead of by actually doing something. If an issue does change, then they just go and shame someone else."

Audrey puzzled over this while Vicki tried again. "I am not a Social Justice Warrior! Though yeah, I do think all men are monsters. They are."

Annabel swung her hands toward Vicki as if she were an exhibit. "See? That's what I mean. Let's say that there's a public place that isn't handicapped-accessible. What would you do?" She pointed at Audrey.

Audrey considered. "I'd try to find out who was in charge of that place and then see if I could find a way to build a ramp or something."

"Right! But an SJW wouldn't do that. Instead, they would stand there and shame anyone who can walk."

While Audrey tried to picture this, Vicki said, "I wouldn't do that! I'd try to build a ramp too."

Annabel rolled her eyes again. Audrey wasn't sure what to think.

"Look." Vicki seemed to make a conscious effort to calm down, and her color returned to normal. Her demeanor changed to flat, matter-of-fact. She settled into her lunch. "I don't like men. That's true. They seem fine on the surface, but then they go after women like vultures on roadkill. In the workplace, at home. When you see crimes reported on the news, how often are they done by men? Don't even get me started."

"Don't," Annabel agreed and winked.

Audrey sat back and watched Vicki as she kept her eyes on her plate for several forkfuls. So what was this then? Was Vicki an SJW? And where did that fit on the f-word/not the f-word scale? Was she this caustic about all topics and issues? Or just men? Is this where Annabel's feminist definition – man-haters – came from? Audrey wondered if Vicki voted for Hillary. Or maybe Bernie. Though Bernie was one of those *guys.* "I signed up for Fish In The Sea last night," Audrey said, talking more to Annabel than Vicki.

"You did!" Annabel said at the same time as Vicki, but Vicki used a tone of shock and scorn.

"Why would you do that?" Vicki shivered and sucked in a noodle. "You're just asking for an internet stalker. Remember the Craigslist Killer? And I think there was a Facebook Killer too."

"There have been a few," Annabel said. "And millions who don't kill at all. Imagine that."

She and Vicki fell into another heated discussion over whether it was safer to date men from the internet or men from bars, and then they moved into whether or not it was safe to date men at all. Vicki threw words around like rape, molest, manipulate and beasts. Annabel is syncopated with love, companionship, fun, and sexual satisfaction. She nodded toward Audrey and mentioned the potential for long-term, for a husband, for a family. Vicki suddenly smacked her soda onto her tray and declared, "For God's sake, Annabel, men just aren't necessary! They're not a requirement in a woman's life!"

Audrey blinked. She was reminded again of that fish and bicycle t-shirt she wore back in college. Almost everyone wore it if you were female anyway. For a moment, the food court in the mall disappeared, her practical clothes disappeared, the loud piped-in music disappeared, and Audrey found herself outside in the bright green grass and blue sky and bristling, bustling environment of a college campus. Her hair was down to her waist, and she was braless, her breasts higher and fuller than they were now. She was arm in arm with her best friend, Clara, and they were chattering nonstop as they walked to class, their four breasts bouncing happily and independently on their chests, their backpacks bouncing happily over their hips which swayed in the seductive rhythm of young. They wore matching shirts, though Audrey's was a heather gray and Clara's blue. On it, the fish and the bicycle, the fish's fins waving futilely in mid-air above spinning pedals.

A woman needs a man like a fish needs a bicycle.

Men just aren't necessary, Vicki just said.

Audrey loved that shirt. But she loved men too.

She remembered how she used to have a date every night in college, once classes were done, with a college boy here and a college boy there who she hoped would slip that shirt quickly over her head and remove the last bit of restraint from her breasts. And from Audrey herself.

Out loud in the food court, she said, "A woman needs a man like a fish needs a bicycle."

Annabel and Vicki stopped talking and looked at her. Then Annabel said, "What?"

"A woman needs a man like a fish needs a bicycle," Audrey said again. "It's a shirt I used to wear in college." She shook her head at Vicki's triumphant smile and cut her off before she began spouting with the force of perceived agreement and majority behind her. "But I don't think it means that men aren't necessary. Men have their roles to play too, in this world. I think it means that women can accomplish their goals without the help of men. It doesn't mean we want to wipe them off the face of the earth." She nodded toward Annabel who was now also smiling triumphantly. "It just means we can succeed without them in whatever we choose to do."

"Ohmygod," Vicki said. Her face flushed again. "You just don't get it." She grabbed her tray and left.

Audrey was aghast. "I'm sorry," she said. "I didn't mean to offend your friend."

Annabel shrugged. "Oh, it's okay," she said. "SJW, remember? She gets mad at everything. But I think you're right. We don't need men to succeed, just like men don't need women to succeed. But men sure are fun to be with. This fish would like to ride Saturday's bicycle again." She laughed and stood up. "I'll see you later, Audrey. Think about going out with me this weekend, and let me know who comes up on Fish In The Sea."

After Annabel left, Audrey sat for minutes longer, her chin propped in her hand. She just felt bewildered. *Not the f-word. Men aren't necessary.*

Social Justice Warrior. A woman needs a man like a fish needs a bicycle.

"You just don't get it," Vicki said. Like the dating site for farmers. City folk just don't get it.

Again Audrey remembered the feel of that t-shirt. The linked arm with that friend, the feeling that the future was not only possible, but it was right there, where she could grasp it with both hands. Her own hands. And how wonderful it was to have those hands held sometimes. The knuckles kissed. Even when her hand was held, it was because she wanted it to be, and she could take it back at any time. She could be who she wanted to be. She could be with whomever she wanted, as long as that person wanted to be with her. The different facets of life were whole unto themselves, but they could, if you chose, interlock to form a new whole. One better for some, not better for others.

If you *chose*.

It just seemed like no one was choosing Audrey.

Audrey wondered who young women, women the age of Annabel and Vicki, looked up to these days. Audrey and her friend Clara had Gloria Steinem. There was Hillary Clinton now, of course, but did young women look up to her? Audrey thought of the election that left That Man In The White House and Hillary defeated. She thought of Annabel in her, not the f-word t-shirt, hidden away beneath her blouse. Annabel knew Sir Isaac Newton. But did she really know Gloria Steinem? She referred to Gloria as a dinosaur.

Audrey cleared her place and decided to make a fast stop at the bookstore before returning to work. She wondered what Gloria Steinem wrote recently. Was Steinem even still alive? And why didn't Audrey know this?

. . . . .

It was two o'clock in the morning, and still, Audrey wasn't asleep. She lay flat on her bed and stared at the ceiling. The moon reflecting on the snow threw light into her window, and it was soft-hued and gentle, the way snow was imagined to be. In his corner, Newt slept contentedly in his heated hammock. Audrey had her electric blanket on, and she nuzzled into her warmth as well. On her bedside table, Gloria Steinem's book, *My Life On The Road,* was opened face-down. Audrey was so relieved to find it in the bookstore. Steinem was not only alive but publishing last year, in 2016. But

Audrey wasn't relieved, and she was nothing short of startled to see that the book's description talked about "women of an age", a phrase she was sure Steinem would hate.

But then they were, weren't they. She and Gloria. Women of an age. Though she and Gloria weren't the same age – Audrey was fifty-five, and Gloria was eighty-three. Twenty-eight years apart. Gloria was old enough to be Audrey's mother. And yet it seemed after reaching a certain year – and Audrey was certain that age was fifty – all women were lumped together. If you were over fifty, you were "of an age" if you were gracious. And you were old if you weren't.

As women of an age, Audrey and Gloria were from a time when feminist wasn't an f-word and when women believed they didn't need men any more than fish needed bicycles. Audrey thought of Annabel calling Gloria a dinosaur. She wondered if Annabel thought Audrey was a dinosaur. Was this was how the dinosaurs felt as they were going extinct? Sort of loose-limbed, unhinged, pathless because the path only led one way now? And that way seemed to be over a cliff.

She glanced at Newt. He was likely related to those ancient dinosaurs. They didn't entirely disappear. They just got amazingly smaller. So maybe women of an age weren't going extinct. Maybe they were just shrinking. Certainly, it seemed, their options were.

Audrey felt smaller. She felt very small in this big bed intended for two. That she'd bought with the idea that a man would join her in it someday, and that she had shared with some men, but now, ultimately found herself in here alone. Except for a male iguana on her floor and a stuffed cow, who was somehow male even though he wasn't a bull, named Ooshi on the pillow next to her.

Why was this so important? Why, in the midst of this new battle over women's rights and equality, was she yearning more than ever for a mate? And how did this connect with "not the f-word"? Was she not the f-word simply because she felt incomplete without a man? Did it matter that it was a man? Would she still be not the f-word if she said she felt incomplete without a woman? Was it using a specific gender that made it feminist or non-feminist?

Audrey did feel incomplete. In the middle of the night, with her job far away, in a bed by herself in a house with only her name on the mortgage, she could admit this. She was an independent woman. She felt she was a strong woman. She didn't lean on anybody. She didn't lean on any man. But the absence of a man in her life made her feel incomplete. Maybe even like a failure.

She knew what Gloria Steinem would say about that.

Audrey rolled over in bed and looked through the dark to her desk, where her computer sat, the laptop lid closed, all the pixels, she imagined, asleep. Throughout the evening, Audrey approached her computer and then backed away. She didn't want to check to see the sum total of Fish In The Sea's algorithm. It bothered her that on a day when she remembered proudly wearing the fish on a bicycle t-shirt, she was also going to a website named after fish to see if she'd netted a man. She glanced at Newt again. Maybe she should have gotten an aquarium, one bigger than the one that Newt came in, and filled with a dozen different varieties of fish. That seemed to be the direction her life was heading in, if she opened her laptop and looked to see who, out of the 617,266 people on Fish In The Sea on the night she signed up, responded to her.

What if nobody did?

What if everybody did?

Continuing to ignore her computer, Audrey returned to her back. She hoped her tossing and turning wasn't disturbing Newt. The moon and shadows played on her ceiling, and she folded her hands on her stomach and watched, trying to keep still. She thought about the men she'd known. Some, she was serious about, but somehow, they were never serious about her. When she was younger and had an apartment, she was very similar to Annabel, and there was a steady stream of men in and out of her door. She remembered too shrugging and saying, "I think his name was Jim." There was no danger in being "loose" then; there was only joy and spontaneity and pleasure. She remembered one dazzling weekend soon after college graduation, drunk and heady with independence and her own place and again, the whole world in front of her. She went from one bar to the next, bringing home one boy after the next, somewhere along the way losing count, and laughing, laughing, laughing. Oh, the headache that arrived on Monday morning and a job to go to that paid for the place of her own. The realization that with adulthood came responsibility and still joy, but responsible joy. Careful joy. And then the awful awakening and counting of sins when AIDS reared its ugly head, and she went in for testing to see if the joyful looseness of her youth came with a death sentence before she was old. It didn't. She was fine. And she was grateful. She turned serious. She turned cautious. She presented the print-out of her bloodwork to men who showed the potential of turning into a sexual relationship, but only after a carefully selected number of dates: Five. From a weekend of boy after boy after boy and nary a thought to five dates, a bloodwork printout, and careful consideration.

The love affairs and partnerships began to dwindle then, some in her thirties, more in her forties. Some men stayed around for almost a year, but as that year anniversary approached, something happened, and they wandered away. After buying her own house, the number dwindled to nothing as the man she was dating walked away into the ether. It was as if the men expected a woman who had her own house to expect to stay there alone, to not share, to not expect to link arms with a man in order to create a home. And Audrey didn't, not really; she created her own home as she waited to see if this man would decide to be a partner, would decide to walk through that front door, climb into her bed, and make it his too.

When he left, she grieved, but then she waited to see if another man would cross over the horizon and her threshold, passing the man who was heading toward the sunset. The new man would come toward Audrey as the sun began to rise again.

Audrey stopped at that thought. When did it become *if?* It used to be *when* there would be a partner.

In her fifties, it became an if. In her fifties, it became unlikely. In her fifties, she became a woman of an age. And at fifty-five, she bought an iguana.

This time, when she rolled to her other side and looked at Newt, she saw his eyes were open. He raised his head. Under her heated blanket, she smiled at her lizard on a heated hammock. Not for the first time, she wished he could curl beside her, but she was too afraid he would hurt himself if he fell off the bed. Maybe later, when he was older and larger.

She swore the corners of Newt's mouth turned up in response. But he looked worried.

"It's okay, Newt," she whispered. "Go back to sleep. I will too."

But they stared at each other just a bit more.

Finally, Audrey got up. She padded the floor around her bed with layers of pillows from her closet, the guest room, and the decorative pillows from the living room. Then she picked up Newt and bridged him to the bed, placing him beside her in a nest she hollowed out of the electric blanket. He curled up, but stuck out his front foot and placed it where he could reach; on one of her ribs as she lay on her side and curled herself carefully around him. She sighed. "Goodnight, Newt," she said. "I am so grateful for your company."

As Audrey closed her eyes, she wondered if Gloria Steinem owned a pet. She bet it wasn't a cat. But it probably wasn't an iguana either.

Chapter Six

When The Veil becomes a fine line between being a ghost and being a pest...

Frank stood under the shower, trying to warm up after way too much time spent outside with the snowblower. He'd done his driveway and walkway, and then, in a moment of whimsy, continued down the sidewalk to Audrey's drive and did hers too. There was at least eight inches of new snow, and once it stopped falling, the temperatures decided to fall too. Frank wondered if Audrey would even recognize him, there behind the red snowblower, puffed up as he was beneath a parka, a fur-ringed hood and a hat that turned into a facemask when he unfolded it down to his neck. Whenever he turned up toward her house, Frank looked out the two knit eyeholes and tried to see if she was there in her picture window. Looking through the steam of his own exhaled breath made the scene dreamlike, and so he drifted into a fantasy. Audrey calling gratitudes and waving him inside, tucking him beneath a blanket on her couch, bringing him an Irish coffee, sitting on the footstool and warming his feet with her bare hands...

He began to sweat in his parka when Audrey did turn up in the picture window. She waved at him, and he lifted a heavily gloved hand back and nearly lost control of the snowblower. Smooth.

But when he was done, Audrey hadn't come out. She hadn't waved him in from the window, and she hadn't opened the door and called, "Frank! Come in! I want to thank you for your kindness!" He'd stood at the bottom of her driveway for quite a while, giving her a chance to slip on a sweater or some shoes if she was barefoot in the heat of her house, or even time to check to see if she had the makings for Irish coffee. But she never came. He wheeled the snowblower back into his own garage. Then he pulled off all his layers and now he stood under the beating heat of his own shower.

Alone.

Until he turned around. Then he was face to face with Strike Two. He yelped and quickly covered his manhood with cupped hands.

"Oh for goodness sakes, Frank," Susan said. "Like I haven't seen that before." She smiled. "We used to be quite fond of the shower, remember? Especially on Sunday mornings."

Frank did remember. It was one of the reasons why Sunday was now the loneliest day of his week. "What are you doing here? And why are you dressed in the shower?"

For a ghost, Susan was very well-dressed. Frank figured if he died and became a ghost, he'd want to be dressed comfortably, in loose sweatpants, maybe, a sweatshirt. Maybe torn jeans and a t-shirt. But Susan was in what she used to call a pencil skirt, and a tucked-in pale blue blouse, unbuttoned to show a creamy cami, and heels. It was a look she'd perfected in life; professional, yet sleekly sexy.

Now, she shuddered a bit, and the clothes disappeared. "It doesn't matter, really, Frank," she said. "I can't get wet." Her suddenly naked body glowed with a light that wasn't from moisture. She appeared as she was before she fell sick. This might have even been her body as it was before he met her because he didn't remember ever seeing her so smooth and taut and...perky.

"That's not fair," he said. He wanted to hide his own sixty-three-year-old body, even though Susan was well-acquainted with it, at least until he was sixty. Had he really changed all that much in the last three years? He looked good when he was dressed, he thought. But in the all-together...not so much.

"What? Oh..." Susan said as she followed his gaze up and down her body. "Hold on."

While he watched, she shimmered and became the Susan he remembered on Sunday mornings. And Saturday nights and weekdays and weekends and all the months and years of their marriage. It overwhelmed him with sadness. He turned away and covered his face with his hands, although he doubted she could tell the difference between the shower's waterdrops and his tears.

"Oh, Frank..." and he felt the whisper of her touch on his shoulder. "Look, why don't you finish up and then come out to the kitchen. We'll talk there."

When he turned back, she was gone. He stood under the hot water until it petered to warm and then finally to cold. Then he got out and dressed in the torn jeans and sweatshirt he'd been thinking of as his afterlife's clothes.

By the time he walked into the kitchen, he'd convinced himself she wouldn't really be there.

But she was.

"Make yourself an Irish coffee, Frank," she said. "I know that's what you were thinking of." She watched as he went through the preparations. "I wish I could warm your feet for you. Remember how I always used to do that after you finished with the snow? And I did it whenever you were stressed too." She folded her hands under her chin. "I remember I rubbed your feet the night after your mother's funeral. You stood all day in that receiving line at the wake and then after the funeral and again after the burial. Why do we expect those in grief to stand so much? We got home, and you stretched out on the couch. I put your feet in my lap and rubbed, and you began to cry. It was the only time you cried all day."

Frank remembered too. He also remembered that there was no one to rub his feet the night after Susan's funeral. Or after his father's. He cried on the couch those times too.

That lost intimacy. The sadness welled again, but he pushed it back down. He was composed when he sat beside her at the kitchen table. They'd always sat like this, in their own home. Not at the head and the foot, but beside each other.

"So when you were done with Audrey's driveway, why didn't you just go ring her doorbell?" Susan asked. "You could have said, 'All done!' or 'Whew, what a job!' or something like that. And then she would have invited you in to say thank you, and she would have made you something warm. That was the plan, wasn't it? It was a good plan. Way better than stealing her mail." She laughed.

Frank gazed at his wife. It was amazing how pink her cheeks could be. Who knew death had pink cheeks? "She would have invited me in? But you said she would never come here, to my place."

"Well, no, of course not. That would be going into a strange place with a strange man."

Frank frowned. "But inviting a strange man into her place would be fine?"

"Yes. Look at your sentence. One of the 'stranges' is gone. If she came in here, it would be a strange place with a strange man. Two strangers. If you went in there, it would be a strange man in her own place. One strange. Plus, it was right after you did something nice for her."

Right, Frank thought.

They sat in silence for a while. Frank studied his Irish coffee and Susan waited, her hands folded. "Susan," Frank said finally, "that doesn't make any sense."

She sighed. "I know. It doesn't. But it does. Before, you were a strange man in the dark, bringing over mail you'd filched from her mailbox and inviting her over to your house. That was just creepy. Today, you would have been a neighbor, doing a good deed in broad daylight, and graciously accepting when she offered to thank you."

Frank remembered all the weird and constantly changing rules from both of his marriages. How sometimes it was okay to touch, sometimes not. Sometimes it was okay to tease, sometimes not. Sometimes it was okay to pressure on past "I'm too tired," sometimes not. Apparently, the lack of clarity between men and women continued through all eternity. Forever and ever. Until you thought death parted you, but then the departed came back.

Susan laughed. "Do you think she likes you, Frank?"

"I don't think she knows me enough to know that," Frank said. "We've only just chatted."

"But you like her."

"She seems nice." He considered. "I don't know much about her either, but she's always talked to me. She always smiles. She waves at me when she drives in and out of her driveway or if she's out in her yard or in her window." He wondered if he was hurting Susan's feelings by only coming up with good things about Audrey. He knew how Susan felt about Strike One. True, Susan was the one who brought Audrey up, and he was only responding, but the one thing he knew was that he never knew, with Susan, with Theresa. And probably with Audrey. "She owns an iguana," he said. He figured that could be either positive or negative.

Susan's eyebrows shot up. "An iguana!" She looked toward the living room. "Would it hurt your birds?"

"He. His name is Newt." The Irish coffee was warming all the parts left cold even after his shower. He considered making another one. "I don't know what iguanas eat, so I'm not sure." He looked through the wall at his birds too. He knew them so well, he didn't need to see them to know they were fluttering around the cage, pecking at each other, nibbling on bird seed, and pooping. Aristotle was likely on the back corner perch, where he could sit by himself, watch the others, and look outside. "I couldn't let anything hurt my birds." He turned back to his dead wife. "Susan, it would just be so nice to have someone to talk to, you know?" He thought of his conversation with Strike One, her offer to get together to talk sometimes. *I miss…that.* He almost said "you," but it was more than just missing Susan. It was missing her space. The space she took up. Her effect used to roll away from her in ripples that touched him like radar, even when they weren't in the same room. Sometimes they weren't even under the same roof, and she touched him. She knew just how. It was like the birds. He knew what they were doing even with a wall between them. And Susan…he always felt her, no matter where they each were.

He'd felt her, in steadily decreasing amounts, since her death. But now, here she was.

"I know," she said. "And having someone to talk to isn't quite the same without the warmth of a thigh pressed against yours, I suppose. A hand on your arm. I can still provide conversation, but I can't provide body heat." She patted his hand like a feather. "I'm sorry, Frank. Next time…knock on Audrey's door. Or just ask her out. But Frank, not Strike One, please." Her eyes narrowed. "I know she was here. Remember, there's a reason you called her Strike One."

Apparently, jealousy lasted into eternity too. "There's a reason I called you Strike Two as well," he said softly, but when he turned to her chair, she was gone.

And again, Frank supposed that wasn't fair. But there were times when he still felt so abandoned. Frank looked where she'd sat, noting there wasn't even an indentation on the chair. He sighed and promised himself he'd apologize the next time he saw her. And then he wondered if he was going crazy, expecting to see a ghost again. Believing he'd seen a ghost at all.

Frank got up and looked out the kitchen window. He hoped it was snowing again, so he could clear the driveway another time and knock on Audrey's door. But the sun was out now, and the air was clear. It was so cold, the sun reflected blue on the snow.

Frank thought about going next door and asking Audrey out to a Sunday early-evening movie. But he told himself it was too cold; he'd just warmed up.

Though he wasn't feeling warm at all.

Sundays used to be the best day of the week. Now he hated them the most of all.

Chapter Seven

This chapter is brought to you by the letter F...

When Audrey woke up the next morning, Newt was still curled beside her on the electric blanket. She was so relieved. She hated that her momentary weakness, her not-so-momentary loneliness, might have caused a dangerous situation for her iguana. She swept her legs slowly under the blanket to wake Newt with gentle undulation, watching as his eyes opened. She rubbed him, up his nose, between his eyes and back again. "Good morning, Newt," she said.

He stretched.

Audrey carefully lowered him to the floor. He left the room, his gait stilted and purposeful. Audrey, now used to his morning routine, knew he'd slid behind the screen in the guest bedroom to use his litterbox. She followed her own routine, which Newt knew, and got the coffee going before her trip to the bathroom. Then she cracked open the door to a lizard-sized opening before stepping into the shower. When she got out, Newt would be waiting for her, patiently squatting on the fuzzy rug.

There was such comfort in routine. And even more comfort in a routine shared with someone else. Having someone who knew where she was, even if he was only an iguana, added a dimension of Home to her home.

Only an iguana. Audrey immediately regretted thinking that way. There was nothing "only" about Newt.

When they sat down to breakfast together, Newt on his special placemat just to her left, Audrey thought again of her memories the day before. The fish and the bicycle. Walking to class, body free, mind easy. And her friend. Clara. The friend with the matching shirt, the matching stride, and matching marches and protests, fists raised, voices strong. But a friend who was oh so different from Audrey. Yet she was the friend Audrey once thought she couldn't live without.

"I wonder where Clara is," she said to Newt.

How was it that she didn't know where that friend was, the one she couldn't live without?

When Audrey showed up on the University of Wisconsin – Madison's campus in 1981, Clara was the first person she spoke to. She'd stumbled her way through the towering shelves of books in the University Bookstore, set up by class, professor, lecture and discussion, and was proud that, despite the stumbling, she'd found everything without having to ask for help. Holding her tall stack of books, she got in line, and the woman in front of her turned around, carefully balancing her own books, and smiled. She said hello, and they fell into an easy discussion, comparing schedules and majors. This woman waited for Audrey, and they went out for a cup of coffee afterward.

Clara was the first black person Audrey ever met, ever spoke to, ever saw, really, outside of television and magazines. Audrey was raised in a community that taught its schoolkids about racism but had nary a race represented in its neat houses, outside of white. They'd progressed a bit by the time Audrey graduated – there were two Hispanic boys in her class and one Asian girl.

When Audrey met Clara on the college campus that day, she thought Clara was beautiful. She didn't have the exaggerated speech of Jimmy Walker or the strut of Sherman Hemsley, but she swore like Richard Pryor. Audrey decided she would too. Sometimes. Maybe. She decided she and Clara would be great friends. And to her delight, Clara decided that too.

Newt chewed on a bit of apple, the juice dripping down the sides of his mouth. She wiped him clean with a napkin. Fruit comprised only about fifteen percent of his diet and he loved it. She wished she could give him more, cater to his tastes, but she also had to worry about his health. A balanced relationship, she'd read in her books, teetered between solid support of a healthy lifestyle and the occasional treat. Fruit was a treat for Newt.

"Clara was such a good friend," she said, and she wondered at how good friends could evaporate.

They'd had a fight.

While both wore bicycling fish t-shirts, they had differing views on men. Audrey enjoyed being with a man, as evidenced by her hope after hope that one would come along to lift off that exact same t-shirt. More than one did, and often, more often than Audrey threw that shirt into the washing machine. In the second year of her friendship with Clara, when they were sophomores, Clara came out as a lesbian. As their semesters at school went on, she also became more and more militant. It was a militant time, as many times have been and, Audrey reflected, thinking about all the marches and petitions there'd been since last November's election, will be. Each generation had its own set of causes and effects, uprisings and shut-downs, movers and shakers and shouters and shout-backs. Audrey had been a shout-back in her time, but Clara went further. She pushed, shoved and bared her teeth and, at times, her breasts in very public clashes with authority. Sometimes, Audrey just couldn't agree with her. Clara brought Audrey along on some of the more extreme meetings she attended and protests too. Protests involving sit-ins and take-overs and using handcuffs and chains to connect yourself to trees, fences, and each other. Protests that had tear gas and nudity and police vans and arrests. Clara shaved her head, ridding herself of the burnished black waves Audrey so admired. Clara began to wear camo pants and wife-beater t-shirts. She even cut off the sleeves of the fish bicycle t-shirt.

Audrey went along for a while, though she didn't cut off her hair or her sleeves. But she stopped going along after a meeting where the discussion was on how men's sperm should be harvested so women could become pregnant without actually having to be involved with the male of the human species. This group seemed to think that type of contact was the touch of death. But Audrey sorta liked it. Well, she liked it a lot. Clara moved steadily into the "all men are evil" camp, similar to Vicki now, but years ago, and Audrey just couldn't. She just didn't see why she couldn't be a fully empowered and independent woman who liked to be with a man. Clara argued that men didn't want women to be fully empowered and independent. "You're supposed to be the little woman," Clara said. "They want you to be submissive."

Audrey disagreed. She knew quite a few men who loved it when she wasn't submissive. When she, well, climbed on top and rode her horse home, so to speak. She didn't think they would mind her being on top at other times too. The men admired her in bed. Why wouldn't they admire her in the real world too?

Which, she supposed now, might have been a bit naïve. And maybe it was naïve to still be hopeful now. Except she really wasn't. It wasn't hope that brought her to a pet store and an iguana named after her favorite cookie. Named after a favorite cookie that was supposed to bear the name of her husband.

Audrey and Clara worked hard to remain friends until after graduation, implementing the kitsch "agree to disagree" plan. Clara took a job in a women's shelter in another state and Audrey, unable to find anything with her liberal arts degree, settled into her first retail job, at the same store she was in now, but as an associate in the misses section. One night when she talked to Clara on the phone and told her about her latest string of dates and about having to inventory the new fall lines, Clara suddenly blew up. "You're pushing the women's movement back by a hundred years!" she shouted over the phone. "Fashion! Men! Who cares!"

Audrey did. And she didn't know how it was possible that the friend she couldn't live without wouldn't know that. She didn't understand how a friend she couldn't live without wouldn't support her in what she most enjoyed and in what she felt good doing. Audrey cheered for Clara as she helped organize petitions and drives and marches, guiding women down the path of protest and making a change. Why couldn't Clara cheer for her when she handled the entire summer wardrobe for a well-known television journalist going on a book tour or when she was chosen to dress the mannequins and do the window displays within just her first six months? Clara might organize speakers at the latest women's rights event; Audrey might dress them.

Audrey also didn't understand how it was possible for her to be responsible for pushing the women's movement back into the last century all by herself. Just by doing her job and enjoying men.

But Audrey didn't shout back. She just hung up. They didn't speak again. She wondered what Clara would say if she knew that Audrey was still in the same store, though now she was the one in charge.

She also wondered if Clara was right about a man not wanting to be with a fully empowered and independent woman. If men's sperm was harvested, she could at least have had a child. Though she supposed that's what sperm banks were for. She just never considered that at the time; she wanted the whole nuclear deal. Husband, wife, baby. She also wondered how Clara was faring in this new "I'm not the f-word" environment. Clearly, there were still "all men are evil" believers around, but there seemed to be more Annabels than Vickis. Audrey wondered where the Audreys roamed. Held on for dear life. Wondered where they fit or if they fit at all.

"Remind me," she said to Newt. "I want to look up Clara tonight." She laughed at herself for using her iguana as a memo. She wondered if she should write herself a post-it note and stick it to one of his spikes. She would be sure to see it when she got home. But, she reflected, you don't use a partner that way. You don't use a partner at all. You co-exist, helping each other out.

She helped him out now by bridging him to the floor. After her routine check of his water, heating lamps and rocks, food dish and toys, she waved to him as she headed out the door. He no longer looked forlorn when she left. He seemed to know she'd be back. She loved his faith in her, and she had faith in him. She'd never hang up on him like she did to Clara so long ago. With Newt, she always wanted to leave the lines of communication open. Audrey wondered if they were still called lines of communication in the digital age. She remembered her sleeping computer pixels from the night before. Maybe now it was pixels of communication. She laughed.

At work, she pondered the best way to find Clara. The last Audrey knew Clara was living in Illinois, a little over an hour away. At first, she didn't think that Clara's last name would have changed, but then she reconsidered. Gay marriage was legal now, mostly. It was possible that Clara changed her last name to her spouse's. Audrey doubted it though. That was another discussion in the groups Clara and Audrey used to belong to. It was considered submissive to change your name to your partner's.

Up until her last serious relationship fizzled, the one with the man who gave her Ooshi, the stuffed male cow, Audrey still filled scraps of paper with her first name and her current love's last name. The name-shifting felt like it would be a rite of passage; a literal form of the-two-shall-become-one. Audrey never really thought about her last name much, after she started dating because she figured that one day, she would lose it. Now, it appeared it was going to be who she was all her life. Audrey Franklin. Maybe she wouldn't give it up now if she ever had the chance to. Maybe it was just who she was.

So maybe Clara might still have her last name too since she would likely have never even considered giving it up, marriage or not. Audrey decided to start that night with that great source of people-finding, Facebook.

In the meantime, it was a quiet day. Wednesdays tended to be at the mall. The weekend was busy, and Monday and Tuesday usually held quite a few shoppers who slid in to nab up the week's specials before they disappeared. But Wednesday was for stragglers and for people who didn't like crowds. Audrey took advantage of the quiet to select a few clothes from the clearance section to finally buy with her birthday gift certificate, and she even set aside a few full-priced items. With her employee discount, they wouldn't be full-priced. Then, since the store was calm, she wandered across the aisle to a section the store called the Etc. Department. Audrey called it ragtag. It had things like luggage and backpacks, assorted decor, cookie jars, and knickknacks. It was like whatever didn't fit anywhere else went there.

The man who managed that section, Gilbert, was unpacking new knickknacks and running a cloth over them to rid them of styrofoam bits. "Hey, Audrey," he said. "Slumming?"

That made her laugh. She liked Gilbert, a thirty-something with an unlikely name. He told her once he had a twenty-something brother named Irving. Audrey wondered if he had older parents and if Gilbert and Irving were maybe oops babies and carried the names of past generation remnants. "Just thought I'd look around," she said. "I can see my department from here, and there's a gift certificate begging to be spent in my pocket."

He smiled. "You haven't spent that yet?" Gilbert was one of the managers who happily lifted a glass of wine in her honor that day.

"I keep forgetting." She stopped in front of a luggage display. There was a wild set, four pieces, all done in a bright purple zebra stripe. Audrey ran her finger over the largest one; it came up to her waist. It was smooth, a hard case. Her touch made it rock on its wheels.

Audrey always planned to travel. It was one of those things she really wanted to do but never did because her vision always included sitting next to her significant other on the plane. Sleeping with this man who was as familiar as the place she traveled to was strange, an exotic location, but made comfortable because of the person who wrapped his arms around her and slept with his face pressed into her shoulder. Mostly, though, with the beds in hotels just as empty as her bed at home, she used her vacation days to run down to Chicago or up to Minneapolis, day or weekend trips. She never did more than an extended weekend; she felt lonelier away than she did at home. Away, there was no familiar. A partner would have provided a hand to hold as she traveled through strange places and experienced new things.

She wondered now if it would be possible to travel with an iguana.

Gilbert stopped putzing and stood beside her. He patted the luggage. "It's a cool set, isn't it?"

She nodded. "I suppose so. I've never given much thought to suitcases. They were always just black or blue or gray."

"Not anymore." He pulled the largest one into the middle of the aisle. Squinting one eye, he rocked the suitcase back and forth a few times and then shoved it off into a straight ride into the next section, Men's

Outerwear. "You don't even have to carry them anymore!" he called as he jogged after it. From Men's Outerwear, he shoved the suitcase back to Audrey, and she caught it neatly in her outstretched hands. It reminded her, in a smooth purple way, of Newt running to her when she arrived home and her sweeping him up in her arms. As Gilbert walked back, he said, "But there's a more traditional set over there, if you're looking. It's nice too."

Nice. Audrey didn't want to be nice. She looked at the suitcase in her hands, on sale and basically free with the balance on her gift certificate, and she decided she wanted to be purple and zebra-striped. She wanted to roll easily. And she wanted to travel whether or not she knew the person in the seat next to her. She could always introduce herself, like the woman on top she used to be.

And still was. Or was trying to be.

She was a woman who owned an iguana, after all. Not a cat. And who wore kaleidoscope underwear.

"I'm going to take it," she said.

"Yeah? Well, cool. Let's get the certificate taken care of, and then I'll bring them over to you." Gilbert started the suitcases into swallowing each other, like Russian nesting dolls or a line of bigger to smaller fish, all eating each other for lunch. When Audrey walked out that night, it would look like she was rolling one suitcase, but it would be four. That felt delightfully mysterious like Audrey could have secrets. She liked that.

"Gilbert," she said, "do you date?"

He looked up. "Why? Are you interested?"

Audrey felt the blush. There was probably at least twenty years between them, so she figured he was likely joking. "I'm trying to…get back into it myself," she said. "I haven't dated in a while. Some friends have told me to go to clubs and bars. Some said go online. I signed up on a dating site. Fish In The Sea."

He shrugged. "I'm seeing someone I met on there. So I think anything is possible, I guess. You just have to be open to it." So Gilbert was one of the 617,266 people on FITS the night she signed up. She wondered if the Fish In The Sea algorithm would net them together, even though he was out of her chosen age range. As if he was thinking the same thing, he looked her up and down and then waggled his eyebrows. "There are special sites, you know, for men looking for cougars…or cougars looking for men." He grinned.

"Cougars?" She'd heard the term, but she wasn't sure it applied to herself.

"Older women looking for younger men, or younger men looking for older women, depending on how you look at it." He took her certificate and ran it through the cash register. "You'd make a great cougar."

Audrey wasn't sure whether to be flattered or offended. She wondered what Annabel would think. She wondered what Gloria Steinem would say. She knew Vicki would shriek and run in the other direction.

Actually, she knew what Gloria Steinem would say. That woman was fierce, but she wouldn't be a cougar.

Gilbert leaned on his cash register, slamming the drawer shut with his stomach, which Audrey couldn't help noticing seemed pretty ripped. "When I started looking online, I was just trying to hook up with someone, you know? And I met quite a few women. I've dated this last one a few times now. Maybe it will lead to something, I don't know. But…" His glance slid over Audrey in a different way than it ever had before. Audrey found herself wanting to cross her arms in front of her chest. "…I'm always open to new things. I guess that's why I'm still single. I still like new. You can't have new when you're with someone for a long time. You have to be okay with old then. Routine. Familiar."

Audrey thought of the hand she wanted to hold while traveling to exotic places. That was familiar. Now, she was buying luggage so she could travel alone, or possibly with an iguana. She glanced at Gilbert and wondered if he was being creepy. She thought of Annabel, and the "I think his name was Jim." So did that mean Annabel could maybe start seeing someone more than once? Wake up one morning and realize she slept with someone who she wanted to be with for the rest of her life? To stop being new with?

Audrey was over new. And she was over nice. Familiar didn't seem so bad. Routine, like knowing she was going to pull aside her shower curtain and find Newt on her fuzzy bathroom rug, was comforting.

Audrey wasn't a prude. She'd had her time of men lifting off her t-shirt, of streaks of lust-a-thons, of one-night stands. But she always thought that when she met the man she'd want to spend the rest of her life with, they would be friends first. And it would somehow deepen. Wasn't it supposed to be that way? Or were you supposed to start with this slippery glance up and down? Were you supposed to climb out of bed and then get to know each other? Rather than dating five times, sharing a copy of your bloodwork, and then climbing (safely) into bed?

And why didn't she know this already? She was fifty-five.

Maybe today's women weren't the f-word. Maybe they'd embraced the other f-word. The real f-word. Maybe the f-word was only an activity. An anonymous activity. *I think his name was Jim.*

Audrey was horrified.

Gilbert handed her the receipt and resumed his non-creepy self. They were friends again. Not potential cougar and potential...cub? Prey? "I'll find something to wrap around the handle of this, so it's obvious you bought it, Audrey, and then I'll roll it over to you, okay?"

"Sure." Audrey glanced at the now compact purple zebra-striped luggage set. She could pack, but she had nowhere to go. She had an iguana and no husband. She considered herself a feminist, but she wasn't sure what that was anymore, and if that somehow meant she wasn't supposed to want a husband, which she did. Was she supposed to be on the prowl, like a cougar, or was she supposed to be looking for a fulfilling partnership, or was she supposed to be happy and empowered and self-realized all on her own?

Audrey hadn't known that fifty-five meant confused. Not empowered. Not fully realized. Not in control of her life and self-aware. Not even nice. Hardly familiar.

Confused. She remembered looking into a mirror when she was fifteen years old and feeling like if she stepped through it, like Alice and her looking glass, she wouldn't end up anywhere. She would just disappear.

Maybe at fifty-five, she'd stepped through that looking glass. Maybe she was there, invisible on the other side, with zebra-striped luggage, kaleidoscope underwear, and an iguana named Newt.

Audrey returned to her register. No one was there, but she stood and waited to be needed.

•   •   •   •   •

After work, Newt stood by the legs of a step stool as Audrey climbed up into the recesses of the closet in the guest room. Audrey used this closet primarily for storage, and she knew her college yearbook was in here somewhere.

Audrey only had one yearbook from her four years in college. The yearbooks were horribly expensive, and so she just didn't feel justified in buying them for every year, given that it was for the gigantic University of Wisconsin – Madison and she didn't come anywhere close to knowing the majority of the students. But senior year was different. It was a milestone and graduation was an accomplishment, and so she bought one.

And now she found it again, thirty-four years later. It was on the higher of two shelves in the closet, leaning up against her four high school yearbooks. Audrey grunted appreciatively under its weight. Stepping down, she watched carefully for Newt, who, for his part, watched carefully for her.

Audrey thought about sinking into an Indian-style sit on the floor, as she would have during college or in the first years after. She corrected her thought to the new name in this era of political correctness, criss-cross applesauce, not Indian-style. Someone at work told her that was how it was taught to kids now, and Audrey thought it was ridiculous. How was sitting with your legs folded like a pretzel connected to applesauce? But now, she looked at the floor, contemplated, then discarded the act itself as well as its new name. It had been years since Audrey sat that way, though her mind and body held so many memories of doing so. In dreams, she still folded herself with ease, but that changed when she entered her fifties, and her knees and hips began staging protests of their own. She also knew that if she sat that way, she would have a hell of a time getting back up.

Looking at Newt, she pondered that this would have been one of the benefits if she had ended up with a husband named Newt, instead of an iguana: should she manage to sit Indian-style, there would be a strong human hand to help her up.

But now, it was Audrey who offered a hand and an arm as a bridge to Newt. "Come on, Newt," she said. "Let's go into the reading room." Newt made the ascent to her shoulder. In the reading room, after she settled herself on the recliner, he moved up to the headrest, his tail draping lovingly around her head, the tip tickling her ear.

"Look," she said and opened the book where it was marked with the program from her graduation ceremony. Her face smiled from the center of the page, thirty-four years younger than it was now. "That's me," she said and tapped her finger on the square. Her hair was long then, down to her belt loops on her snug hip-hugging jeans. The back pockets of those jeans gapped, she remembered, stretched out from the number of college boy hands who held onto her butt cheek as they staggered home after a night at the Bucky Badger-themed bars. She wasn't wearing her fish bicycle t-shirt the day the photo was taken; she chose a more serious and classic black sleeveless turtleneck. But underneath, she still wore no bra, her breasts as proud and independent and rebellious as she wanted to be. Her smile was open. For the most part, she remembered being happy.

She flipped a couple pages. Audrey's last name starting with Fra and

Clara's last name, Garrington, starting with Gar, meant they weren't that far from each other in the yearbook. "And here is Clara." Clara's hair was a buzzcut at that point. They made appointments for their photos, provided by the University, for the same day, one right after the other, and they both watched each other pose, making faces to get the other to laugh. Audrey remembered wishing Clara waited to buzz her hair until after the photo so Audrey could brush and tug those amazing waves into place for her friend, taking a few strands from each side of her face, braiding them, then tying them together with a ribbon in the back to form a loose crown. The buzzcut, Audrey remembered, felt like armor to her. A don't-touch-me warning to the world. When she told Clara that, Clara shrugged. "Not don't touch me, exactly," she said. "More like don't fuck with me."

It was the first time Audrey wondered about the future of their friendship. When it did end, with Clara's derisive rant and Audrey's definitive slam of the phone, she mourned the loss, and now, in her recliner, she wondered if the future was still a possibility, if their friendship could be excavated from the past.

Future, like fuck, was an f-word too, wasn't it. And so was *friend*. She wondered if those meanings changed too, like feminist.

"Well," she said to Newt now, "I suppose looking at her picture isn't going to get me any closer to finding her. Did you want to come into the bedroom with me while I work on the computer?" She put down the footrest and offered her shoulder. Rather than climbing on for a ride to the other room, he ran down her arm and then her leg to the floor. She followed him out and then watched as he continued on to the kitchen. It wasn't time for a snack yet, though he sometimes urged her to have it early. She let him go and turned into the bedroom. He would either come back, or he'd find something else to do. As partners, she knew, she didn't have to give in to his demand for a snack. And he didn't have to give in to her desire for company by the glow of the computer.

Sitting at the computer reminded her of Fish In The Sea. She set the yearbook to the side and quietly went to that website, first glancing over each shoulder. She tapped the keys lighter than normal as if she was hiding her destination and intention from the world. She laughed at herself and hit enter hard, sending a crack into her room and throughout the house. Newt appeared in the doorway, looking startled.

"It's okay," she told him. "Didn't mean to hit the keyboard so hard. I'm sorry."

He walked up her leg and then her arm to the desk surface. He stood on her yearbook.

Audrey signed in to the FITS website and waited as her page loaded. And then she blinked.

238 matches and responses.

238?

Broken down, there were 225 matches, but 238 responses. With more responses than matches, some men must have gone rogue, ignored the algorithm and found her on their own.

Audrey wasn't sure she even knew 238 people. And now that many men were considered compatible with her, and they were already reaching out! She didn't see how that could possibly be right. It made her feel sort of…common. She wondered if other women received that many connections. She wondered if she should be feeling popular. Chosen by the masses, the way the cheerleaders were in high school. It didn't matter what little group you belonged to, the drug addicts, the academics, the geeks, the artsy types, the athletes, if a cheerleader went by, you looked. You looked if you were a girl or a boy, straight, bi-sexual, gay (which was all that was identified at that time). You just looked. It felt like it was genetically required, wired into your system.

Audrey wondered if the number 238 should make her feel like a cheerleader. If so, then why did she want to pull on a heavy shapeless sweater instead of turning cartwheels in a teeny skirt that showed her matching underwear ("It's not really underwear!" the cheerleaders would squeal) and a top that lifted easily to show off what was required to be a flat tummy.

Audrey looked down. Her stomach was not flat.

She patted Newt's head for support, then glanced quickly through the list of responses, looking at the computer out of the corner of her eye, as if she wasn't quite sure she wanted to see. And she wasn't sure. Most of these men were indeed algorithm-generated matches, Fish In The Sea going through their resources and matching up her wants and needs with the men's wants and needs and saying yep, this could be the one. 225 times. There were thirteen more responses than matches. Those thirteen extra were not matched with her by the FITS algorithm. So did that make the 225 more likely to be exactly what she was looking for? When she didn't really know what she was looking for? Maybe FITS knew. What did the thirteen non-algorithm men know that FITS didn't? Did they just respond to anyone?

This wasn't match-making. It was math-mating.

And it was overwhelming. It was too much. Audrey hit the X without signing out first, hit it with the same crack that resounded through the house earlier. She just had to get out of that screen. Realizing her breaths were coming fast and too shallow, she forced herself to fold her hands and breathe deeply. Newt, startled again, pressed his forehead against her folded fingers. "It's all right," she said to him. "It's all right," she said to herself. When she calmed, she looked at the yearbook beneath her iguana.

It seemed easier, right then, to look for one old friend than to look at 238 prospective life partners. A life partner that wasn't green and spiked and fit on her shoulder. But that life partner, the green and spiked one, she picked out herself, without using any math at all. She just used her heart.

The steady pressure of Newt's head against her hand made her wonder why she'd ever look further. She stroked his nose and watched as his eyes closed in pleasure.

Her self-help books told her that an inherent *knowing* of each other's needs was a great sign of true partnership. Newt knew her. And she knew him.

Bringing Facebook to life on her screen, she typed in Clara's name in the search box. "Cross your toes," she said to Newt and then hit enter. Firmly, but quietly. Newt didn't startle.

There were seventeen different Clara Garringtons on Facebook. Audrey scrolled down the list, looking at the faces, trying to see from the thumbnails if anyone looked familiar. And then...someone did.

Clara (Garrington) Martin.

It was the wavy hair that caught Audrey's attention. The soft waves that fell down to either side of this particular face, brushing that particular woman's shoulders. The waves ready to be woven into a braid and then a loose crown. Audrey even recognized the shoulders. She knew how they felt beneath her own arm when she slung it around them. She knew the round of the bone and the soft skin when she leaned her head against Clara during late nights of studying when she just needed to close her eyes for a few minutes. Clara always knew, without being asked, to wake Audrey in fifteen minutes. Audrey often returned the favor.

When Audrey clicked on the name, and the profile came up, she saw the brown hair was streaked with a silver gray. No buzzcut. And the clear brown eyes and easy smile contained no anger. Maybe not even rebellion. But it was a face Audrey remembered loving. That she thought she couldn't live without. Clara.

"Look," she breathed, and Newt's head swung toward the computer screen.

But the "About" under Clara's name made Audrey pause and look again. Was this Clara? This Clara had a husband named Bill. And two adult children, making Clara a mother when she was thirty-two and thirty-five. One of those children was a boy. So Clara, who once declared that men should be obliterated from the face of the earth, that men were an evil women couldn't afford, had a husband and a son. In the pictures with them, she was smiling broadly. They were definitely two people that Clara afforded. That she loved. Just as much as she loved her daughter, who leaned her head against her mother's very familiar shoulder.

That face, that smiling face, was definitely Clara.

"What the fuck," Audrey said to Newt. And then she sent a friend request.

Feminist. Future. Friend. And of course, fuck. All f-words.

But nice...nice began with an N.

Audrey didn't want nice. But a friend, she decided, a friend who knew her then. A friend who could know her now and maybe into the future and witness and understand how those three eras braided together, to create who Audrey was then, was now, and would be. A friend who used to wear a shirt with a fish on a bicycle, maybe a friend would be nice. Even if that friend had something that she once said she never wanted: a family. Another f-word. Even if that something that Clara never wanted was something Audrey wanted most of all. And never ever found. Found. An f-word.

It wasn't fair, Audrey thought. Someone who didn't want something got it. And someone who wanted it didn't. But Audrey wanted to contact Clara. She tried to push the unfairness away so that their return to friendship would have the best possible chance. It wouldn't be good to go in with a chip on her shoulder. A shoulder she wondered if Clara would recognize as easily as Audrey recognized hers.

Fair, she thought. Guess what? Another f-word.

She pressed Newt's cheek to hers. Newt. An N-word. Which was nice.

Chapter Eight

Iguana bite your haaa-aa-aand...Iguana bite your hand!

Frank was in his back yard, up to his knees in snow, filling the wild bird feeders, when he saw Audrey's car pull up, but stop just short of her garage. He kept pouring the seeds into the tall feeder, not allowing himself to hesitate, but he adjusted his hips and shoulders enough so that he could be watching her while still appearing to be totally focused on the feeder. He was startled when Audrey popped her trunk and pulled out a suitcase with wild purple zebra stripes.

Was she going on a trip? Who would take care of Newt? He entertained the idea of being asked to watch the lizard, gaining access to Audrey's house while she was away.

Gaining access. Without moving away from the feeder, he imagined whacking himself upside the head. Way to sound like a stalker, Frank, he thought. But he really wasn't. Taking care of Newt while Audrey was away on a trip would allow Frank to get to know her in her absence, discover her likes and dislikes, and then woo her in the most efficient and impactful way possible. It would be like getting a treasure map to a woman, with arrows and directions, instead of having to follow the usual confusing hit or miss relationship development.

Woo. What an archaic word. Did men woo women anymore? Did they want to be wooed? Strike One did. She liked having doors opened for her, chairs held out for her, being helped on and off with her coat. She liked small surprise gifts, popped from his overcoat pockets to her outstretched hands or left for her at her bedside or her place at the kitchen table. Strike Two liked these things too, but there was a limit. Once, just once, Frank made the mistake of planning a romantic dinner for himself and Susan at an exclusive restaurant, which included his choosing ahead of time the perfect wine, the perfect appetizer, and salad, the perfect entrée. They'd been together for five years by then, and Frank knew Susan's dietary likes and dislikes. But she was alternately concise and silent throughout the meal. He noticed she left most of her entrée behind, despite it being prime rib, queen cut, done medium-rare, her favorite. Smothered in mushrooms. When they were waiting for the valet to bring his car around, Susan said, "Frank, I know you wanted to be romantic. But you made me feel like a child. Please, always let me choose my own meals."

So there was a difference, apparently, between working toward knowing a woman as well as he possibly could, from what she liked to eat to how long she liked her coffee microwaved to just how exuberant he could be in the morning, and picking and choosing from all these likes for her. Frank didn't know exactly what that difference was, but from that point on, he was careful with Susan. He always asked her opinion. Though he wondered why the small surprise gifts were okay. He never asked her about those. He just brought her flowers, a candy bar or a scarf. Theresa, he remembered, preferred jewelry, earrings and bracelets and small delicate necklaces.

Frank wondered what would be okay with Audrey. Free rein to look around her house while taking care of Newt could give him a clue. He wasn't stalking, he reassured himself. He was trying to get to know her in the most efficient way possible. He considered it research.

He watched as Audrey rolled the suitcase past the car and into the garage, leaving the engine running. The garages on these older homes were really small and only one car fit, but barely. There were plenty of SUVs that sat out on neighborhood driveways in all weather. Audrey must have wanted to make sure that she could get the suitcase into the house without the car in the way. Frank studied her car and wondered if she was up to date on her oil changes. Maybe he could volunteer to do it for her, once the weather warmed up. Strike Two always said yes to that when he asked. He never asked with Strike One; he just took her car in for maintenance the same week he did his own. Strike Two thanked him; Strike One expected it.

He thought of both the women sitting on his couch recently. One alive, one dead. Both...nice. Both so very different. Theresa, he reminded himself. Susan.

And there was Audrey, who he hoped wouldn't be Strike Three, though she hadn't yet sat on his couch. It was a whole new ball game.

"For God's sake, Frank, quit stalling and go talk to her," Susan said, suddenly appearing next to the pole that held the three feeders. He startled and nearly slipped in the snow. She was wearing a classy winter trench coat with a matching hat and pair of gloves. Typical Susan. Always dressed fashionably and appropriately. He wondered if ghosts could even get cold.

"If you're going to keep popping up like this, we have to come up with a sound or something. Like a knock or a doorbell. You keep startling me," he said.

Susan looked hurt. "I never used to have to knock when I was alive. We never even closed any doors."

This was true. Not having children gave them the benefit of never having to block out eyes that didn't have permission to see. But how do you tell the ghost of your wife that her being dead meant that things were different between you? The same rules didn't apply. Nor did the same intimacy. A relationship between a living husband and wife was complicated. Apparently, though, it only got worse when one of them died, but kept on talking.

"I'm sorry, Susan," he said finally. "But you didn't used to appear out of thin air either."

Her face smoothed and then she nodded toward Audrey's house. Audrey came out of the garage. When she opened her car door, she spotted Frank and waved.

Frank didn't need to be asked twice. "Hi, Audrey!" he called and chugged over through the snow. He was relieved that she waited, standing by her running car. He stepped onto the plowed surface of her driveway, stamping his feet. "How're you?"

"I'm fine, Frank." She smiled at him. "I'm glad to see you. I wanted to thank you for clearing my driveway the other day. That was really nice."

"Oh, you're welcome. I was out here doing mine anyway." He felt a poke on his shoulder and realized, to his horror, that Susan was standing right behind him.

"Ask her out!" she whispered.

He ignored her and went with his own hunch. "So are you going on a trip?"

Audrey looked confused. "A trip?"

"I saw you bringing in a suitcase."

"Oh!" She laughed and turned a little red. Frank wondered at the embarrassment. "I had a gift certificate to use at work, and the suitcases were on sale, and for some reason, I just liked them. They were a total impulse buy."

"She's impulsive!" Susan whispered. "Jump!"

Frank put the bag of birdseed in one arm and waved behind his back with his free hand, trying to shoo Susan away. "Well, they looked really...different. Now you'll have to use them. You know, if you ever need to go somewhere, I'd be happy to watch Newt for you. And your house."

"Newt?" Audrey glanced quickly over her shoulder. It was like she wanted to make sure Newt wasn't listening.

"Well, you know, it's one of the biggest drawbacks of being a pet-owner. You have to find pet-care if you go anywhere." He nodded toward his house. "I haven't been anywhere in a while, because of the birds."

"Oh." Audrey nodded and opened her car door. "Well, thanks for the offer, Frank. It's funny because I was just thinking about that today, about if I could bring Newt with me if I traveled somewhere. I'll keep you in mind if I need someone to watch him. And if you go somewhere, I'd be happy to look in on the birds."

Frank stepped away as she pulled the car into her garage. He waited to see if she was going to come back out, but the door came slowly down. He was titillated at the idea of Audrey coming into his house when he wasn't there; maybe she wanted to get to know him too! He wondered where he could go for a weekend to give her that opportunity. He turned to pick his way home through his footprints in the snow. He noticed there were only his prints; Susan's pristine winter boots left no trail.

"Oh, Frank," she said, trudging beside him. The crunch was there, but he noticed she walked on top of the snow; she didn't sink. "You can be such a dolt."

It was said affectionately, and he smiled at her and wanted to hold her hand. "I just need to do this my way, Susan." Then he had an idea. He hurried to the house, and when he went to hold the door for Susan, he saw she was gone. Shrugging, he went on inside. He told himself to remember to ask her about a simple goodbye when she left; just like the surprise arrivals that startled, the sudden departures left him newly bereft.

He put away the wild birdseed and took off his boots, replacing them with his sneakers. But he kept his jacket on. Looking in the pantry, he saw he was low on the special gourmet birdseed his parakeets so enjoyed. Delighted that there was a practical reason to carry out his new plan, he poked his head in the living room, told the birds he'd be right back, and then went out to his car. It was time to visit Bob's pet shop.

He hummed the whole way there. Susan didn't show up; he wondered if ghosts could ride in cars or if Susan was relegated to only his home.

As soon as he walked in the store, Bob called out a cheery hello, and all of the animals joined in with him. "Hey, Frank! How're you? Need seed for the family?"

Frank really liked Bob. He didn't bat an eye the day Frank came in to buy a parakeet and walked out with six. When Frank admitted he was a new widower, which he wasn't (Susan was two years gone at that point), but his widowhood felt new all over again with the purchase of the new house, Bob suggested that he get at least two birds. "The more, the merrier," he said, and Frank never found a cliché so profound as this. In the end, he bought his rainbow. The six birds were in three separate cages in the store, and they each had a common trait: they hopped to the front to bob their heads and peer out at Frank while the rest just fluttered around. It seemed deliberate, and he couldn't say no to any of them. Bob helped him pick out an appropriately sized cage and all the supplies, and by that evening, his new house was no longer silent and empty. He had a family full of feathers. And Bob referred to them that way every time.

"Just about out," Frank said, and he followed Bob to the bird supplies aisle. Close by were the aquariums with the reptiles. While Bob filled a paper sack with five pounds of the gourmet food, Frank stood in front of the glass wall of green and brown leathery creatures. Chameleons. Geckos. Bearded dragons. Two odd ones with odd names: ackie and tegu. There weren't any iguanas. Frank wondered if Audrey bought Newt from here.

Bob came to stand by Frank's side. "Lizards?" he asked. "Are you thinking about adding to the family, Frank?"

Frank smiled. "Not really. Just kinda interested. My neighbor has one, and I wondered about what it took to care for one. Do you have a book on them?"

"I do." Bob and Frank walked over to a shelf full of books and Frank spied one right away that was just about the iguana. He remembered that Audrey said that Newt was a green iguana. He thought all iguanas were green, and this particular book specified just that. *The Green Iguana; The Ultimate Owner's Manual.* Frank smiled and selected the book. He couldn't help but think that Audrey was the Ultimate Owner. Paging through, he noticed there was an entire chapter on why you *shouldn't* adopt an iguana for a pet, and he was deeply engrossed in that when he heard the pet shop door open.

"Hi, Audrey!" Bob called. "Get in fast, before Newt gets cold!"

Startled, Frank turned. There was Audrey, with a little pet carrier in her hands. Inside, Newt peered out at the store. "Audrey!" Frank said. He immediately wondered how he was going to explain his holding an iguana book. He felt a little like he was caught asking a girl to sign his yearbook in sixth grade.

"Frank!" She smiled and put the carrier on the counter. Bob opened it, and Newt stepped out.

Frank came closer because the iguana looked different. He seemed bulkier. And then Frank laughed as he realized Newt was wearing a jacket. A leather bomber jacket. Frank had to admit, it looked good on the lizard. He looked...tough. "Oh my gosh, Audrey," Frank said. "Look at him! He looks great! Like James Dean!"

Newt butted his head against Bob's outstretched hand as he looked back and forth from Audrey to Frank.

"What are you doing here?" Audrey said and then she laughed. "Well, that was silly." She patted at the bag waiting for Frank on the counter. "You get your birdseed here?"

"I do." He nodded at Bob. "Bob's the best. This is where I got my birds."

"Newt came from here too." Audrey tugged Newt's jacket off, then stretched her arm out, locking the elbow, and placed her flattened palm on the counter. Newt used her like a bridge and walked up to her shoulder. He settled there, wrapping his tail around the back of Audrey's neck. He looked at Frank. Frank waved.

"I take it you two know each other?" Bob asked. He chucked Newt under the chin. "I'm sorry, Newt, I mean the three of you. Frank, are these the neighbors you were talking about?"

"Yep," Frank said. He stood next to Audrey and noticed that Newt's tail lashed a few times. But the spikes on his back remained relaxed. Once the tail stopped, Newt looked friendly. Frank thought about touching him. Bob did. Newt actually craned his neck forward to fit his head against Bob's curved hand. "He really does look great, Audrey, even without the jacket." And he did. He seemed to have a smile on his face. Frank didn't know iguanas could smile. But then, his birds smiled, Frank was sure of it, and so why not a lizard?

"Thanks." She studied Frank for a second. "You were talking about me?"

"I just said I had a neighbor with a lizard." He hid the iguana book behind his back.

Audrey turned to Bob. "Bob, I want to get him something to climb on. He loves to climb. I'd like to have something more natural, like a tree, but not a tree, because I tend to kill plants. Plus Newt might eat it."

Bob laughed. "I have just the thing." He led Audrey toward the cat and dog aisles, and Frank took advantage of their backs being turned to slide the iguana book under his birdseed. Then he trailed after them.

Bob was showing Audrey what looked like a real tree, only without leaves. It had bark and many branches, thick and placed fairly close together, and it rose up to about five feet. It was set into a sturdy wooden platform. "See?" Bob said. "You could put this by your picture window, and Newt could climb up and sit in the branches and look outside. It's intended for cats, a natural scratching post, but it could work for Newt too."

Frank wondered what Bob knew about Audrey's picture window. Had he been inside her house?

Audrey walked around the tree. "I could...I had his aquarium there when I first brought him home. When he got used to the house, and I stored the aquarium, I stacked patio bricks there, like a staircase, so he could climb up and look out the window. He watches for me to come home."

Frank saw Newt sitting in the window on numerous occasions. Frank always waved. Maybe that was why Newt seemed friendlier now. Frank wondered if Audrey ever waved at his birds.

"See if he likes it," Bob said.

Audrey squatted and placed her hand on the floor. Newt walked down her arm and then over to the tree. He stood by it for a second, his strange eyes moving in all directions in their sockets. They were herky-jerky and creeped Frank out a bit, but he had to admit, he could see the wheels turning in the lizard's little brain. Then Newt moved closer to the tree, grabbed it with his front feet, and began to climb. Audrey laughed. "Go, Newt!" she said. She stood close by. Frank bet she was worried Newt would fall. He would worry if it was one of his birds. He wondered if they would like an indoor tree for when he took them out of their cage.

Newt climbed without a slip until he was as high as he could get. He looked out at Audrey. Then he wrapped all four legs around the branch, sprawling with his stomach and head flat. There was definitely a smile. Frank swore he saw Newt's cheekbones rise. Did iguanas have cheeks? He'd have to check in the book.

"He likes it!" Frank said, and Audrey applauded.

"I'll take it," she said. She ran her hand down Newt's length, from his nose to the tip of his tail.

Frank wondered what Newt felt like. "Audrey, do you think he'll let me touch him?"

"Oh, that's right." Bob nodded, and Frank noticed just the smallest twitch to his lips, a know-it-all smirk waiting to happen that he thankfully withheld. Frank withheld a sigh of relief, thinking Bob wouldn't mention Frank's interest in the iguana book, but then Bob said, "Frank was looking at a book right before you got here, Audrey. Frank, it seems like you could learn all you want to about lizards just by going next door."

Frank blushed and wished Bob would shut up. When Audrey looked at him, Frank said, "I just thought…you know what we were talking about, Audrey. If you went on a trip and I look after Newt, I'd want to know what I'm doing."

"A trip!" exclaimed Bob. "Where are you going, Audrey? You know, Newt can always come back here. I could board him in the store."

Audrey shook her head so vehemently, Newt's spikes went up. He stood on the branch and slowly straightened his legs. The smile went away. Despite his size, Newt reminded Frank of a Star Wars AT-AT in this posture, legs impossibly long and straight. An iguana with straight legs definitely looked like something out of a sci-fi movie. "Oh, no," Audrey said, and she quickly held her hand out to Newt. He climbed back to her shoulder. "I'm not going anywhere. I just bought some suitcases, and when Frank and I were talking, I said I wondered what I would do with Newt if I traveled." She reached up and smoothed the top of Newt's head. "It's okay, I'm not going anywhere," she said directly to the lizard, and he seemed to relax. Audrey turned to Bob. "I couldn't bring him back here, Bob. I'd be too afraid he'd think I was returning him."

Bob smiled. "Audrey, he's an iguana."

Her mouth turned down, just a bit, and Frank knew his would too if Bob said his family was just parakeets. "But…he's *mine*. He's so much more than that."

Frank understood. And he appreciated the way Audrey's mind worked. He wouldn't want to bring his birds back here either, even though it was perfectly nice and Bob was nice, and it was where they came from. But it would be like returning orphans to an orphanage.

They walked back to the cash register, Bob carrying the tree. Frank asked, "Do you think my birds would like something like that, Bob? When they're out of their cage? They could pretend they're wild birds, sitting in a tree."

Bob smiled, and Frank noticed Audrey did too. "I bet they would love it, Frank," Bob said. "Interesting, isn't it, that something developed for cats could have so many other uses." He set the tree on the floor. "This is the only one I have right now, but I could order one for you." Frank agreed and then Bob turned to the items on the counter. He held up the book. "Do you still want this, Frank?" he asked.

"Yes, please." He turned to Audrey. "Newt is a neighbor. So I should know about him."

Audrey looked pleased, and so did Newt. Encouraged, Frank reached out to pat the top of Newt's head. He was almost there when Newt suddenly snapped. Frank heard the click as the iguana's teeth came together, fired like bullets in his powerful jaws.

"Whoa!" Bob yelled.

"Newt!" Audrey cried.

But Frank's fingers were intact. He gripped them tightly to make sure, held his hand to his chest.

"I'm so sorry, Frank," Audrey said. She picked up Newt from her shoulder and put him on the counter. "I've never seen him do that!" She was clearly upset, her cheeks flushed, a frown bringing out wrinkles Frank never noticed before. In a bizarre way, he was relieved. Those wrinkles showed that Audrey really was close to his age. Newt seemed upset too, his tail lashing, spikes up, and instead of bobbing his head, it swayed from left to right like a barely contained pendulum. Audrey quickly tugged him into his jacket, then opened the door to his carrier. He stalked right in. Frank thought the lizard would stomp, if he had the weight.

"Iguana bites are nasty things," Bob said. "I'm glad he didn't get you. Those jaws could have taken off your fingertip."

Frank forced himself to lower his hand and then he patted his bag. "Guess I need to read up on what I'm doing wrong with that bad boy," he said and laughed carefully, trying to lighten the mood, to bring the smile back to Audrey's face. "Audrey, do you want help out to your car with the tree?"

"Oh, I'll help her with that, Frank." Bob took Frank's payment, finished the transaction, then reached with his scanner toward the tree's price tag.

Frank fumed. Maybe he didn't like Bob so much. "Oh, all right then. Audrey, let me know if you need help when you get home." Frank left, feeling dejected, leaving behind a silent tail-lashing iguana and Bob and Audrey, deep in conversation. He wondered what they were talking about. Maybe they were lining up whatever they saw as his bad points that could possibly set off an iguana. Frank pictured Newt again, his head pressed against Bob's palm. His imagination expanded the experience, adding in

Newt's half-closed eyes, his lower jaw open and his tongue hanging out like a happy dog's, and a purr rumbling from deep within his scaly belly. Next to this imaginary Newt, Audrey clasped both her hands to the side of her face and she batted long eyelashes over heart-shaped pupils at Bob. "Newt looooooooooves you," she squealed. "And I looooove you too!" Frank mashed his eyelids together to rid himself of the vision so he could see to start his car.

He didn't hum on the way home. He wished Susan would show up.

But she didn't.

Women, he thought. Can't live with'em, can't live without'em.

But he was living without, and he didn't like it. He missed living with.

Even if it meant living with a snapping iguana. But he really wanted Newt to like him. And he wanted Audrey to like him even more.

Chapter Nine

Heading up a creek without a bicycle. But maybe a fish.

For a few days after the pet store incident, Audrey watched Newt carefully. What was it about Frank that made Newt upset? She knew that iguanas could bite, but she never saw that in Newt, never even saw the temptation in an open mouth or a sharp look in his eyes. Did iguanas curl their lips, like snarling dogs did? Did iguanas even have lips?

Audrey studied Newt's mouth. He had lips, she decided. He smiled. How could anyone or anything smile without lips?

She considered sitting down with Newt, trying different movements or actions to see how he reacted. All of her self-help books declared that it was best to not let things fester. Problems should be faced head-on and immediately. But this bad behavior wasn't directed at her; it was toward Frank.

Bad behavior – that sounded like Audrey had to reprimand Newt. Correct him, like an errant child. If Audrey reprimanded Newt, that made her more like his parent. She wasn't his mother. He wasn't her son. They were partners, and partners didn't correct. They suggested, according to her books. They advised. They encouraged. They supported. But it was always up to the individual on what to accept and what not and how, ultimately, to behave. How to choose to behave should be, and would be, Newt's decision.

She thought of Bob saying, "He's an iguana, Audrey."

He was. But he was more.

After sitting with Newt on the couch for several minutes, striking different poses and jolting into sudden moves, all of which Newt looked on with amusement, Audrey decided to leave it for now. It wasn't like she saw Frank all that often anyway. And Newt saw him even less. Maybe Frank reminded Newt of someone in his past. But what kind of past could an iguana have? Bob said Newt was a year old and that he got all of his reptiles from one person. Audrey thought he said "guy". Maybe that was the culprit?

Maybe Frank did something that caused Newt to remember this "guy" and whatever bad action he did? Could iguanas have triggers and flashbacks? Audrey couldn't imagine that Bob would get his reptiles from someone who mistreated them. Bob really cared for the pets in his store.

Though he did keep saying, "Newt is an iguana, Audrey." If anyone would understand that a pet wasn't a pet, but a member of a family, part of a team, and in this case, a partner to Audrey, it should be Bob.

On this day, after dinner, Newt settled himself in his new tree. Audrey was happy with her purchase; it gave Newt a great perch for world-watching, and it somehow made her living room look more…organic. The house was slowly becoming a reflection of who she and Newt were…woman and iguana. Comfy couch, climbing tree. Electric blanket, heated hammock. A recliner and her reading room, warming rocks and patio bricks.

She and Newt fit together.

Audrey patted Newt, then left him in his tree and went to her bedroom. Waiting for her computer to boot up, she glanced at her Gloria Steinem book on her bedside table. "I'm about to check my online dating site, Gloria," she said. "Can you imagine? I certainly never did. I always thought relationships would be natural. I always thought I would be natural. Walking around braless. Hair straight and over my shoulders. Not looking one way or another, not looking for a man, but looking at men. Sleeping with who I wanted, not caring, sex was natural and what I wanted and it would someday lead to love. To a life with someone, I didn't need but wanted. Someone I could live without, but wouldn't want to. I never thought –" She cut herself off, suddenly finding her throat full. She wasn't expecting tears. Especially not while talking to a face on a book cover. "I never thought I would get to be fifty-five and be all alone. It always seemed like life would just happen. As easy as the sway of free breasts in a shirt." She looked down at her chest, at her breasts not so free now, but lifted full in an underwire bra from Victoria's Secret. "And life has just happened, I guess. In a way. Just not all of it. I haven't experienced all the things that I thought everyone experienced. " She touched a finger on the cover, popping Gloria on the nose. "Does a woman need a man to feel complete, Gloria? Do I? Is it in our nature to be part of a couple? Were we wrong to put independence so high on our lists?"

Gloria's face, smiling small on the cover, seemed to take on a stern look.

Audrey sighed. "I know. My life is okay without a man, but it would be better, an enhancement if I had one. Can I have one, like property? Like an iguana? Newt's not property. I don't know how to say this, but look where I am now. Are women supposed to be alone?" She thought of Annabel's friend, Vicki, the man-hater. "Are men supposed to be just sperm-donators? Are women supposed to just lay eggs? Is that all that's necessary about our coming together? So what happens when a woman is an age where semen no longer affects our bodies? Where we don't fire off an egg every month?" Audrey frowned. "I could use some advice, Gloria. And I thought by this age, I'd be past advice. Aren't I supposed to be giving advice now? Aren't I supposed to be growing wise? Becoming a crone?" Audrey always hated that word, picturing a witch of the type that would build houses of candy and entice little children into her oven.

Audrey looked at her screen, going through its light show as it warmed up. She felt infinitely pathetic but saw no reason to not say what she was thinking aloud. No one was there to listen. Even Newt was in his tree. "I don't feel wise. I just feel alone. I feel like I missed something along the way. An important step." She swallowed. And then she said it. The thing that was always hovering in the back part of her brain where doubts hid. Fears hid. And maybe, maybe the truth hid. "Or maybe I just don't want to face that no one has ever wanted me. No one has ever found me valuable enough to be lifelong material."

In the pet store the other night, Audrey noticed again that Bob's finger was ringless. She knew Frank's was too. And she found herself looking at both of these men differently, one who she'd known for a while, but not well, and one who she'd known for a short time, but she felt she knew him better. She wondered if they were possibilities. Bob might have flirted. Frank was really friendly. But neither came forward and asked her out. So maybe the interest was just all imagination, on her part.

Though to be fair, she hadn't asked them out either. She glanced at Gloria. Women could ask men out now. She was sure Annabel did it all the time. Annabel seemed the type that wasn't shy about asking outright for whatever she wanted, when she wanted.

Audrey thought of the way Gilbert looked at her in the store when she bought her zebra luggage. Cougar, he'd said. She thought of the 238 responses on Fish In The Sea. She hadn't checked any of them yet. Possibilities? Though Gilbert's attention made her uncomfortable. And the 238 responses made her nervous.

Neither Bob nor Frank made her nervous.

Audrey sighed. She didn't have to go to the lengths of Annabel's forthrightness, but she had to start being proactive.

Tonight, she decided, she would look at the 238 and just pick one. She would pick from the Sea. She'd go fishing. There was no harm in checking it all out. She wouldn't know until she tried. Platitude upon platitude piled up about a website that was named after a platitude itself and Audrey sat down with her false bravado, and she signed in to Fish In The Sea. She kept her back to Gloria Steinem.

She tried going through all 238 responses one by one. But it quickly became overwhelming. All the cataloging of physical attributes – height, weight, body type, eye, and hair color, if there was hair, and even a report of hair on the body. Hair on the body? Was she supposed to report on that too? She hadn't even noted that in her preferences. And in her profile, she only listed the color and length of the hair on her head. She never thought of…anyplace else.

Finally, she decided to leave it up to Fate. Fate, another f-word. Newt came in and climbed from her leg to her lap, up her chest and down her arm to the desk, where he squatted. Audrey was happy to see him; his presence here would keep her honest. If she vowed something aloud to him, she wasn't the only witness. Newt would remind her of her vow if she began to quibble and back away. Quickly, she explained her goal. "I'm going to hit the scroll wheel, Newt," she said. "It will be like Wheel of Fortune. Wherever it stops, whoever the cursor lands on, that's who I will respond to. No matter what his description says. Ready?"

Newt looked doubtful, but Audrey spun anyway. Her finger pushed the rubber-edged mouse wheel back and forth in an escalating ready-set-go and then she flicked it and the screen blurred in front of her. Then it slowed and stopped.

And there was a man named Mark.

Mark was a good name, she reasoned. Solid. Strong. One syllable. Maybe a bit generic, but there was nothing wrong with generic if it was a good generic. That was the purpose of a generic, wasn't it? He was fifty-six. Six foot two inches. Two-hundred and twenty-five pounds. So he was taller than her, and she weighed less than he did. That was a good combination. He was an accountant. She worked with numbers at the cash register. So maybe there was compatibility. He owned two cats. She wasn't sure about that, with Newt, but this wasn't a marriage arrangement. And it meant he likely understood about pets being family.

Audrey decided straightforward, but innocuous was best. She skipped the flirts, the pokes, all of that stuff that she considered akin to stuffing notes into lockers in middle school. She clicked on "send email". Then she wrote that he came up as a match and she thought there were quite a few compatibility points and would he maybe like to meet for a cup of coffee? She explained that she worked in a department store at a mall and that they could meet in the food court. She figured but didn't say, that this would be a safe public place to meet. And then she sent it into the internet ether.

She wondered what he would say.

"It'll be fine, Newt," she said to the iguana, trying to sound confident. "Don't you let me back out now, if this guy says yes." Newt sighed and lowered himself to his stomach.

After exiting Fish In The Sea, Audrey jumped over to Facebook. Right away, she saw that there was a message waiting. And it was from Clara.

"Oh, look!" she said to Newt, who obligingly rolled his eyes toward the screen.

Clara's message was full of exclamation points.

Audrey!!!!!!!

Oh my god! I can't believe it's you! I can't believe you found me! I'm so glad

I put my maiden name on my page! Wow!

How have you been? What a stupid question! It's been over thirty years! I'm sure that you can see that a lot has happened to me. All good!

I know this is sudden, but I'd like to see you! It would probably be easier to catch up if we just meet! Halfway between you and me is Gurnee, Illinois, where the big mall is. We could meet there.

What do you think?

I'm so happy to see you! I'm so excited!

Clara

In college, Clara was not an exclamation point kind of person. Yes, she did a lot of shouting, yes, she raised her fist in the air, but somehow, exclamation points just didn't fit. At least, not exclamation points like these. These belonged to cheerleaders, the same cheerleaders Audrey just didn't feel like when she found out that 238 men were matched with her on Fish In The Sea. Short-skirted, bare tummy-topped cheerleaders with the bodies to go with the lack of material. Go-Team-Go! types of exclamation points. For Clara? The Clara that used to have a shaved head sneered at cheerleading uniforms as an example of degrading women, and cheerleaders themselves as an example of women who allowed themselves to be degraded. But then, that Clara never wanted to be married, even to a woman, if they could have imagined back then a world where gay marriage was legalized. She never wanted kids. And she certainly didn't want to be married to a man and give birth to a boy.

But here she was. Turning literary cartwheels with exclamation points. Wanting to meet Audrey in a mall. A place she used to call "the throne of American degradation at the bestial hands of consumerism." Whatever that meant. Audrey worked in a mall when Clara came out with that mouthful, and she worked in a mall now. Putting the women's movement back hundreds of years all by herself, according to Clara. And Clara wanted to meet her there! In a big mall, the Gurnee Mills mall, one of the largest in the midwest. Audrey's mall was just a run-of-the-mill mall. Run-of-the-mall, Audrey thought and snickered. Even though it felt like home. Audrey's rolling thoughts paused for a moment at the realization that run-of-the-mill felt like home. It was, of course, nice.

Audrey wondered for a minute if Clara still wore an "A woman needs a man like a fish needs a bicycle" t-shirt. She wondered if Clara went braless. And she wondered where her own fish bicycle shirt was. Did she still have it?

Though it would never ever fit. Audrey remembered the xylophone of her ribcage when she used to run her hands down the shirt to smooth it.

Audrey went back to Clara's Facebook page and looked at her photo again. She needed to doublecheck. Yes, that was definitely her. With hair, with a broad smile, with exclamation points. And with a husband, a son, and a daughter.

Clara. Audrey focused on her smile. That was Clara. There she was.

Audrey emailed back and said she would love to meet. She asked when. She didn't use a single exclamation point. She felt a need to counterbalance and to restore some familiarity to their relationship before their relationship even restarted. And she hit send.

She hugged herself as she allowed a few of her own internal exclamation points. She would love to meet! She wanted to see Clara, a friend she once thought she couldn't live without! In the privacy of her house, with only Newt to see, Audrey gave in to glee and squealed, raising her arms and dancing in her chair. She couldn't wait!

So now she was going to meet Clara in a mega-mall. She was going to meet a man named Mark in her run-of-the-mall.

Audrey stopped squealing. Lowering her arms and making her body very, very still, she looked at Newt. "I wish I knew what I was doing," she said. No exclamation point.

Newt gently placed his foot on her hand.

Audrey smiled. "You always know what to say, Newt," she said. Partnership.

Then Audrey clicked and scrolled herself over to Amazon. Through the miracle of the internet, an internet that sent her 238 strange men to meet, who excavated a friend out of the past and into the present, setting her in the unlikely company of a husband and children and exclamation points, Audrey found a fish bicycle t-shirt in her size. It was vintage. She was vintage. And she ordered it. It would arrive in two days.

She wondered what it would look like if she wore a Victoria's Secret bra beneath it.

•   •   •   •   •

Generic Mark responded almost immediately. Audrey found herself agreeing to a late-afternoon meeting after work when she got off at four o'clock. That morning, standing in her underwear in front of her mirror, after taking forever to choose which Victoria's Secret set Generic Mark would never see on a first date, Audrey wondered if Gloria ever wore holy cow purple underclothes. Would Gloria shop at Victoria's Secret? At eighty-three years old, was Gloria still going braless?

Audrey glanced down. She bet not. Audrey was twenty-eight years younger, and she wouldn't go braless anymore, except around the house when she was sure no one was going to stop by. But would Gloria wear purple? She couldn't imagine Gloria wearing plain white undies, with that common-bra saccharine pink rosebud in the center. Or the...what was it called? The cross your heart bra. Audrey remembered the commercials from her childhood, showing the bra that "lifted and separated", and the spokeswoman whose breasts looked like two melon-esque torpedoes. It struck her now that the Victoria's Secret bras didn't lift and separate, but lifted and pushed together, to create fuller-looking, overflowing cleavage. The commercial image of the best breasts morphed from melon torpedoes to about-to-explode souffles. Taking a deep breath, Audrey reached into her closet and chose a blouse and pants purchased with her birthday gift certificate. Audrey pulled the plum blouse on over her souffles and tried to remember the identity of the lifted and separated woman. Anita Bryant? No, not Anita Bryant, she sold orange juice and hated gays.

Audrey snapped her fingers. "Jane Russell," she said to a clueless Newt who was on the bed, watching. It was Jane Russell, a full-breasted woman who proudly displayed those breasts in, first, black and white commercials, and then colored, and Audrey remembered giggling every time it aired. Giggling, but hoping too that she would someday have something that needed lifting and separating. Did Gloria Steinem like Jane Russell? Audrey thought Jane had something to do with Howard Hughes. Gloria wouldn't like Howard Hughes. Then Audrey's mind bopped back to Anita Bryant. She was pretty sure Gloria wouldn't like Anita Bryant either. Were either of those women still alive? Did they shop at Victoria's Secret?

Audrey finished getting dressed and carried Newt into breakfast. She explained to him that she would be a bit late because she was meeting someone for coffee. He bobbed his head. When it was time for her to go, she lowered him to the floor, and he accompanied her to the back door. By the time she pulled the car out of the garage, he was in the picture window, stretched out on a branch in the sun. He always seemed to raise a lazy front foot to her. Since Newt arrived, Audrey found herself smiling as she drove down the street. She now left to waves goodbye and returned home to a bare white belly plastered in welcome against the window

On her morning break, Audrey sat in the employee's lounge, had a cup of coffee and a cookie and googled Jane Russell and Anita Bryant. She already knew Gloria was eighty-three. Anita Bryant, it turned out, was seventy-seven. And Jane Russell was dead. If she was alive, she'd have been ninety-six, thirteen years older than Gloria. Was thirteen years enough to put Gloria and Jane in different generations? Audrey wasn't sure where the boundaries were. It was odd, though, the different types of women that could come out of the same era. But then, over her coffee, Audrey thought of Vicki and Annabel. And of herself and Clara. Maybe it wasn't so odd. Maybe it was common.

At lunch, Audrey met Annabel and Vicki and filled them in on her Fish In The Sea results (238!), on her Wheel of Fortune method (Annabel laughed; Vicki looked disgusted and said she always hated that show with their perfect-life contestants) and on the final result: Generic Mark. Annabel was thrilled for her and Vicki was appalled.

"You're meeting an online stranger? Here? Ohmygod," she said. "Didn't you listen to me at all the other day? The CraigsList killer? The Facebook killer?"

Audrey and Annabel both sighed loudly enough to be heard and to send their napkins flying to the floor. Vicki was a broken record. She was a broken record who would have absolutely no clue what a record was, and she was a broken record who wasn't really broken at all because she was too young to be and had her entire life before her like a yellow brick road glittered with gold and good intentions and good luck and unicorns and rainbows...

At times, Audrey was amazed at how jaded she could be.

"Has there been a Fish In The Sea killer?" she asked, and Annabel laughed.

"No," Vicki said evenly, drawing out the O's. "But I bet there will be. I hope you're not the victim." Her eyebrows came together in such a stern and foreboding warning that Audrey actually shrunk, her shoulders drawing in and neck retracting like a turtle, lowering her chin almost to her chest. "And I hope you don't take the rest of us with you. I know you're supposed to meet with these...these...online meat market hook-ups in a public place with lots of people. But this just feels like you're taking your choice to put yourself at risk and throwing it all over us too, like a net. What if he shows up with a gun?" She huffed and walked away.

Even though Audrey was glad to see her go – she didn't much like Vicki – she wondered if Vicki was right. Audrey was meeting a strange man. She did meet him via the internet, and the news was always full of internet-driven crimes. But all first meetings involved strangers, right? The choice of a public place was for her safety.

She never really considered that she could be bringing danger to the public as she used the public to protect herself from danger.

Her mind flitted briefly to the mall shootings in the news. She'd meant to sign the last gun control petition she received. Did she? Or had she let it slip? Not that her one signature would have made any difference. Not that the petition or any petition would make any difference. She shook her head. She remembered when having her one voice joining many others felt like power, like bringing about change. When did it start feeling futile?

Probably when her voice, along with the popular majority of others in this country, failed to keep That Man In The White House out of the White House, because of the antiquated electoral college, which failed to give the majority, the raised voices, what they chose. One more voice just didn't seem to make a difference anymore. Involuntarily, Audrey's eyes filled, and she tried to hide the sudden tears from Annabel.

Annabel patted her hand. "Don't worry about it," she said. "Vicki just spends her life paranoid. Social Justice Warrior, remember? Can you imagine being that way? But I'm happy for you. You're doing it the right way. Meeting him here, where people know you, and it's a public place. Nothing is going to happen. Not to you, not to any of us."

Audrey heard the echo of her own thoughts.

"You look very nice, by the way," Annabel said. "Is that new?"

Audrey nodded. The plum blouse was a good color for her, and the V was fairly deep, allowing her to show off her newly enhanced assets, thanks to Annabel and the holy cow purple Victoria's Secret bra. The black pants were of this new trend – still yoga pants, but styled for work – and they were comfortable and hugged her snugly. It was nice being snugged without being tight. When Audrey asked Newt that morning what he thought, he tilted his head and then bobbed. That was approval, Audrey decided.

Now, Audrey shook everyone and their breasts and their votes out of her head. "I think I'm nervous," she told Annabel.

"Of course you are," Annabel said. "Who wouldn't be? But the thing to remember is this isn't a life commitment. You don't owe him anything. He doesn't owe you anything. Fish In The Sea matched you, and you're just getting together to see if the computer figured right."

That didn't sound so bad. It was just coffee. With a man. A strange man. A man that Audrey already knew had very little body hair if that mattered to her, and she wasn't sure if it did, and she wasn't sure if she should even know that about him yet. How was it that she knew about his lack of body hair before she knew about his upbringing, what his childhood was like, what his middle name was? All she knew was that he was a fifty-six year old, six-foot-two, two-hundred and fifty-five-pound accountant with two cats and very little body hair. And they were having coffee. In a public place. This was just coffee. That's all. That's all it was.

Audrey was nervous. She said goodbye to Annabel and walked back to work.

When four o'clock came, Audrey made sure everything was set for the evening associates, then she grabbed her jacket and her purse. As she walked down the mall corridor, she saw Annabel standing in the doorway of Victoria's Secret. Vicki was just inside the window of Chico's, holding very still behind two mannequins like she was trying to camouflage her nosiness. "Good luck!" Annabel called. "I'm here for another hour, so come back before you go home and tell me how it went. I'll wait! Unless you leave with him, of course. Then text me." She winked.

It felt good, knowing someone was watching out for her. Audrey tried to straighten her posture as she strode into the food court and headed for the Starbucks. She saw a man sitting by himself at one of the little bistro tables right outside the coffee shop. She loved those little tables. They made her feel like she wasn't a part of the food court at all, even though if she walked just a few steps further, she'd be smack dab in the middle of crying toddlers, harried mothers, privileged shoppers who didn't need to wait until the weekend to shop, and cryptic businesspeople, trying to get something done fast while they had a few minutes. Starbucks had tall plants in pots scattered around and, with the mall's skylights, it was almost like being outside. This man sat in a ring of sunshine, next to a potted palm. He was watching her, and as she got closer, he raised his hand halfway.

That must be him. Generic Mark.

Audrey went to him before ordering. "Hi," she said. "Are you Mark?"

"Audrey?" He extended his hand, and she took it. His grip was firm. Audrey noticed there was no hair on his knuckles. She wondered if she ever noticed that about a man before. "Nice to meet you," he said. He gestured at his cup. "I went ahead and ordered. I didn't know what you would want."

"Oh, that's okay. I'll go get mine." Audrey walked into Starbucks, feeling better. She was an independent woman. Buying her own coffee on a sort-of date. Gloria would approve.

Though he could have waited until she got there to order. Even if he didn't offer to pay, that would have been nice. It was sort of rude to go ahead without her, wasn't it?

But she didn't want nice, she reminded herself.

She returned to the table with her own latte, and she sat. She and Generic Mark looked at each other for a few seconds. Then Audrey offered a weak, "So you didn't have any trouble finding the mall?"

"Oh, no," he said. "I've been here lots of times. Which store do you work for?"

That seemed safe enough information to offer, so Audrey told him.

"Oh," he said. "My ex-wife used to shop there."

Ex-wife? Audrey didn't remember reading about a previous marriage on Generic Mark's Fish In The Sea bio. He only said he was single. There was a checkbox for divorced, Audrey was sure of it. But then if you were divorced, you were also single, she supposed, so it wasn't really lying.

"It's a really great store," Audrey said. "I've worked there for a long time.

I started right after college." They nodded at each other, and he didn't offer anything else to the conversation. Audrey noticed he didn't share his workplace, now that she divulged where she worked. She wondered if she was supposed to ask. Eventually, she decided it would be a good idea to let Generic Mark know that she had reinforcements nearby. "I have friends that work in the mall too. At my store, of course, but also at Victoria's Secret and Chico's."

"Oh," he said. And he nodded again. He took a sip of his coffee.

Audrey wondered what he was drinking. She thought maybe she could get a handle on his personality by his choice of Starbucks drink. Was he a macchiato man? A white mocha latte? Did he just drink plain black coffee, no sugar, no creamer? She hoped he wasn't a chai tea drinker, but she couldn't have said why. She just thought chai tea at a coffee shop was weird. She wondered what he would think of her if he knew she drank a cinnamon dolce latte, extra hot in the winter time, iced in the summer, and she always asked the barista to cut the amount of syrup in half. But she decided not to say another word. It was his turn. Let him come up with something. All of her self-help books said that the responsibility of getting to know each other was a teeter-totter. Or tit for tat. She titted and teetered. It was time for his tat and totter.

Finally, he said, "My second wife shopped at Chico's. My third was too fat; she shopped at Lane Bryant. She didn't shop at Victoria's Secret either, they didn't carry her size, but my other two wives did." His face did a twitch that might have been a muffled leer, and Audrey noticed his gaze dropped to her chest.

Second wife. Third. Too fat? Audrey oversaw all the female clothing departments for women, but on the floor, she worked primarily in the Women's Department, which was code for plus size. Was she too fat? She'd been known to shop at Lane Bryant. She crossed her arms. "How...how many times have you been married?"

"Three. Well, no, four. But that one only lasted a month. I don't really count it."

Where in the line-up was that one? And were there others that lasted less than a month that he didn't count? Audrey swallowed. "Which one shopped at my store?"

"The first." Nod, nod. "She might even have checked out with you. That's kind of weird, isn't it? Almost like serendipity."

Audrey decided to nod too, though she was pretty sure that was not the definition of serendipity.

"So..." His voice dropped. "I do need to come clean about something." He leaned forward.

Audrey thought he already had. "What is it?"

"Well...I said on that form that I have very little body hair. Actually...I shave it off. If I let it grow, I'd be a bear. So I don't know if that counts."

Just like not knowing if a marriage that lasted less than a month counted. Audrey had no idea what to say to that.

"I just always heard that women prefer smooth bodies. So I shaved everywhere." He waggled his eyebrows. "*Everywhere*. I thought I'd make the effort, you know?"

Audrey nodded quickly, and when she thought of *everywhere*, her stomach turned. "I see," she said, and she looked around. "You know, I think I'd better go."

Generic Hairless Mark looked startled. "What? But we just got started."

"No...no, I think I'd better go. I need...I forgot..." Audrey scrambled and tried to find solid ground. She thought of Gloria on her bedside table, face up, somehow watching her telepathically from her book cover and shaking her head. What would Gloria do?

Gloria would get the hell out of there. Audrey was pretty sure Jane Russell and Anita Bryant would too. So would Lane Bryant, the secretive Victoria and whoever the hell Chico was. "I'm sorry, I just don't like you," Audrey blurted and then cursed herself for apologizing; why did she feel the need? And then she apologized again. "You're creepy. I'm sorry." She saw his face flush red and she shot out of her seat and moved away as quickly as her new professionally-styled yoga pants would allow. She liked their flexibility even more now.

Audrey flew to Victoria's Secret, looking over her shoulder several times to make sure she wasn't being followed by the first ever Fish In The Sea killer. She wasn't. There was no sign of fake-hairless, married, not-married, who's counting? Generic Mark. Her first date in a long, long time.

Disaster.

Annabel was helping a customer, so Audrey waited, shifting from foot to foot, slurping her cooled extra-hot latte to try to calm down. She didn't even pretend to be looking at the merchandise, not even to cover Annabel's butt with her manager. Across the hall, Audrey could see Vicki peering out at her, eyes wide with alarm. She waved frantically, but Audrey shook her head, holding up one finger, trying to indicate, Just a minute, let me talk to

Annabel first, I don't want to talk to you right now, you might have been right, oh, ick. Ick, ick, ick! Audrey's one finger just wasn't enough. All of her fingers joined in, and she began to flap.

As soon as the customer walked away, Annabel ran to Audrey. "Why are you here already? What happened?"

Audrey just opened her mouth to speak when there was a flurry behind her and then Vicki was there. "Fast!" she said. "Talk fast! I've got to get back to the store!"

Audrey grabbed both of their arms. "He's been married four times. Except he doesn't count one. He didn't have that on his form. And he told me he shaves his body hair and then tells women that he's smooth-bodied. And that his third wife was too fat for Victoria's Secret and then he looked right at my chest."

The ew's echoed. There were even several that weren't from Audrey or Annabel or Vicki but from the overhearing customers. Audrey couldn't blame them; she was just too unnerved to speak softly. Her voice, like her flapping hand, wouldn't calm down.

"I told you!" Vicki hissed. "I told you! It's not safe! There's all sorts of creeps out there!"

Audrey was ready to agree. She even called Generic Hairless Mark creepy. In this case, it looked like Vicki was right.

Annabel shrugged. "Calm down, Audrey. There's losers out there, for sure. You just found one. Don't give up! You got over 200 responses. That means there are more options. There will be some nice ones, really."

But Audrey didn't want nice. She didn't, did she? Maybe she did. Generic Hairless Mark was not nice. Maybe nice would be safe. Maybe nice would be comfortable. Maybe nice would be nice. Audrey was on overload. "I can't even think about that now," she said. "I'm going to head home."

Vicki zipped ahead of her back to Chico's. As Audrey approached the doorway, Annabel called out. "Audrey! Meet me for a drink tonight? We can talk more about this."

Audrey shook her head. "No. I think I just want to go home to my iguana." Eyebrows shot up on the overhearing customers' faces. But Audrey didn't care. She just needed Newt.

Newt, she realized, was nice.

•　•　•　•　•

That night, Audrey sat in her reading room, the overhead turned off, the three-way reading lamp on low, the gas fireplace glowing and warm. There was an iguana in her lap, not a book. Her recliner's footrest was up and, between her raised toes, she watched the fireplace, and she stroked Newt, from his nose to the tip of his tail. He was actually big enough now to create some weight in her lap, and tonight, she relished it. A good relationship, she'd always read, was grounding during times of stress. Newt was grounding her. His eyes were half-shut under her ministrations.

She hadn't been on her computer. She didn't even turn it on. She wondered if Fish In The Sea offered reviews of dates, of people. She'd heard some dating sites allowed that. Would Generic Hairless Mark give her any stars? Were there any stars to give? She hoped not. Maybe she would get off that site altogether. She also needed to check to see if Clara answered. But she couldn't take an exclamation point right now.

Sitting there that night in the firelight, Audrey only knew what she didn't know. She didn't know what she wanted. She didn't know what she needed.

Except mute. She needed to put her life on mute tonight. She needed soft. And she needed her iguana, who wasn't soft at all, but who made her feel soft.

Audrey thought about all of it. Turning fifty-five. Being alone. The f-word, what it meant, what it didn't, who was to say. Audrey thought she was a feminist. Annabel, a not-the-f-word. Vicki, rabid. Possibly an SJW. There was Gloria, a dinosaur. And That Man in the White House. There were petitions left unsigned in her email box. There were years gone by since she was braless. And she was all alone, uncoupled. Annabel and Vicki too. Maybe even Gloria. Maybe Jane and Anita. Well, to be fair, Jane was dead. And Audrey had Newt. She rubbed his head.

Not the f-word. At a time when That Man was in the White House. When That Man made it to the White House despite admitting that he'd sexually assaulted women. That he didn't respect women. And when he'd pledged himself to tearing down laws and institutions that were devoted to women, to making women's lives better, to making women's lives their own.

What did it mean to have your own life? Audrey wondered if having her own life meant that it was hers alone. All alone.

She wondered again if Gloria was married. Audrey remembered reading from a quotations website that Gloria once said that marriage ruined relationships. But Audrey's relationships were ruined before they ever got to marriage. And now she didn't even have a relationship to ruin.

Except with Newt.

Not the f-word. Maybe Audrey really wasn't either. Maybe she was a fake. Another f-word. Sitting here, craving a man. Going on a site like Fish In The Sea and meeting someone like Generic Hairless Mark. Audrey bet he voted for That Man. She wondered, idly, if Melania liked smooth-bodied men and if That Man In The White House shaved. *Everywhere.* Then she shuddered and pushed those thoughts away.

"It's not like I did a lot to prevent That Man from being there," she said to Newt, who widened his eyes to look at her. "It's not like I've gotten involved." She thought of the unsigned petitions that filled her inbox before, during and after the election, how many of them she glanced at, thought to sign later, and then didn't. She remembered the protests and marches she went on with Clara when they were still in college. The Women's Studies classes she took. Reading *Our Bodies, Ourselves* and feeling enlightened, feeling with it, feeling empowered.

When she was younger, she volunteered at a women's shelter. She licked envelopes and answered phones and had to hold herself back from tracking down the men that caused the bruises she heard about, the ones so visible on the skin, the ones not so visible, but deeper. Tracking down those men and doing...something. She was never exactly sure what. But something. Something was better than nothing. Though answering phones and licking envelopes counted. Even if Generic Hairless Mark wouldn't count it at all, because he was married to a woman, he didn't count as a wife.

Audrey also used to volunteer during elections. At twenty-two years old, she campaigned rigorously for Walter Mondale and Geraldine Ferraro, cheering until she was hoarse for the woman who dared run for vice-president. She liked Mondale, but she voted for him because of Ferraro, which, she supposed now, might have been a bit narrow-minded of her. But years later, she cried when the Johns, Kerry, and Edwards, lost. And then she felt guilty for crying because of news reports that Edwards cheated on his wife while she had breast cancer. Was it wrong for her to like a candidate who did something like that? Was she supposed to change her like to hate because of it? She voted for him. She didn't regret it. Was being with another woman who said yes while your wife went through cancer and didn't know worse than assaulting women who said no? Was there even a comparison?

And now women voted for That Man In The White House. They attended his rallies wearing t-shirts that shouted, "Hey, Donnie, grab this!", with arrows pointing toward their crotches.

She thought of Annabel and her theory that feminists were men-haters, like Vicki, who protested being a man-hater and denied being an SJW. But Audrey knew she'd grown since the Mondale and Ferraro election. After all, she didn't vote for John McCain and Sarah Palin just because Palin was a woman.

And ultimately, Geraldine Ferraro was one hell of a woman. Palin, not so much.

But That Man.

Everything was getting all mixed up together. What did her being a feminist have to do with her being alone? What did her wanting to be with a man have to do with being a feminist? How could the three of them, Audrey, Annabel, Vicki, all exist at the same time, the same riotous period of history? And the other two were so young; Audrey had the experience. She should be teaching them, not looking at them and wondering about herself and her place in this world.

She wondered what age you have to be in order for things to start making sense. She wondered if she would ever reach it.

"I haven't even done anything since the election," she said to Newt. Though if she was being honest, she didn't do anything before either. She didn't volunteer during that election. She just watched and read the news. She got angry over and over again. She posted on Facebook, and she felt like that was enough, like she was doing something, she was raising her voice, though who knew who heard it. Who cared. She told herself the world would be able to figure this out. The world had common sense. The right outcome was so obvious. The election and everything about it, the debates, the commercials, the news articles, were so ludicrous. So she didn't volunteer. There was no need, she thought. It would all be okay.

And then her voice didn't matter. And now That Man was in the White House.

She didn't vote for him. But ultimately, she didn't do anything to stop him either. Not before. Not after.

"There was this march," she said to Newt. "All over the world, women marched. And they put on these pink knit hats that looked like cat ears. Because of That Man's comments about 'grabbing pussies'." She flinched at the word as her fingers put air quotes around it. She preferred the real word – vagina. Her generation was encouraged to eschew the slang terms and derogatory phrases for the human anatomy and go straight to the real thing.

"I didn't go on the march, not here nor in Washington DC. It was January, and it was cold. And honestly…" She looked around the room as if someone else might hear, though she knew it was only the two of them. Gloria, at least Gloria's face on her book cover, was down the hall in the bedroom. "…I thought it was kind of useless. What was it going to do, putting on kitty cat hats and yelling in the cold?" She sighed and thought about her fish bicycle t-shirt. When she wore that shirt and marched years ago, her fist held high, her breasts and hips swinging freely, she felt better. Like she was doing something. Something was better than nothing.

Though she didn't know anymore if what she did then had any effect either. Look where they ended up now as if history had no influence at all. But maybe she would feel better when her new old fish bicycle t-shirt arrived tomorrow. When she pulled it over her head. And tugged it down over her Victoria's Secreted breasts.

That Man In The White House. Voted there, at least in part, by women. Not stopped by women like Audrey.

"Maybe I should have marched," she said to Newt.

He blinked.

But even if she had, That Man would still be right where he was now. Half of her bed would still be empty. She was pretty sure his bed was never empty.

Feminist. Not the f-word. Man-hater. Audrey's head spun. Newt pressed his face into her palm, and he didn't release until she let out a breath and loosened her shoulders. He sighed too, an iguana sigh that heaved his ribs and rustled his spikes.

Audrey thought about turning on her computer and checking to see if Clara answered. She thought about retrieving Gloria's book, settling back, and reading. But she didn't. She needed mute tonight. She needed soft. She sat in her recliner, watched the flames in her fireplace, and stroked her iguana.

Chapter Ten

Ya can't live with 'em, ya can't live without 'em,
even when they're dead.

In the middle of a sunny afternoon, Frank sat on his couch with the iguana book open on his lap. The birdcage door was lifted, and five of the birds were out and about. Aristotle, the homebody, was out, but not really about, at his spot on top of the cage, just over his regular perch. He faced the bay window, and Frank could see his tiny head turning this way and that. Frank wondered at how different the world must look when it wasn't striped with metal bars.

There was a bird now on each of Frank's shoulders and another on his right knee. A third parakeet sat companionably on the cushion next to him, and Butch, the most active, the alpha-hawk, was on top of the curtain rod, chirping a constant conversation to whoever would listen. Frank thought of the tree he ordered that was like Newt's. It should arrive soon. For a long moment, Frank closed his eyes, pictured his bay window with a tree in front of it, on which sat six colorful birds...and one iguana.

Though in all likelihood, he wouldn't put the tree in front of his bay window. That was where the cage sat since the day Frank brought the birds home. He thought he might put the tree in front of the window in the dining nook, giving them a whole new view. It wasn't a picture window, but it was tall as well as low; it dropped to just about six inches above the floorboard.

He returned to the iguana book. The section on possible bad behaviors and specifically on biting let him know he dodged a bullet when Newt's teeth missed him the other day in Bob's pet store. The book told of iguanas who clamped on to a variety of human body parts and wouldn't let go, of powerful jaws that needed a vet's intervention to unlock, of lost fingertips and infections. Frank pointed one of his narrowly missed fingers and Blueboy took it as an invitation to perch, fluttering from Frank's right knee to his knuckle. The rough twig-like toes and tiny claws didn't hurt at all. Not like that iguana's teeth would have.

Frank raised Blueboy up and addressed him directly. "How am I going to get close to Audrey if her iguana doesn't like me? I know I wouldn't be happy if you guys didn't like her." Blueboy tilted his head. "Newt doesn't seem to mind Bob. It's me he doesn't like. I don't know what I did to upset him."

He lowered Blueboy, and the bird hopped back onto his knee. Frank studied his book more. None of the human behaviors that the book described as threatening to an iguana were typically in Frank's repertoire. They certainly weren't present at the pet store, in front of Audrey. Frank was particularly mindful of his manners around Audrey. And thus, around Newt too.

Maybe the iguana just didn't like him. Maybe the iguana liked Bob better. Maybe the iguana knew that Frank just wasn't the right man for Audrey. Maybe Audrey liked Bob better.

Frank slammed the book closed, and the birds jumped. Even on top of the world on the curtain rod, Butch flapped. "Sorry, guys," Frank said. He dropped the book on his coffee table, and the birds reacted again.

"Geez, Frank, what's got your gander?" Susan was suddenly there, on the cushion not occupied by Ducky. "Oh, for heaven's sake, these birds! You let them loose? In the house?" Susan hugged herself, pulling her tangerine cardigan, which nicely matched the print blouse beneath, closed over her chest.

"Well, I can hardly let them loose outside, Susan." Frank remembered that Susan had a thing about birds. About small animals in general. The big ones, she didn't mind. The little ones, she said, could run up your pants leg and get into all sorts of places you didn't want them to be. Birds, while they wouldn't go up your pants leg, could get in your hair or fly down the collar of your shirt. And they could bite your ear. Frank once teased her by setting off a wind-up mouse in the kitchen where Susan was reading a book and drinking coffee. That hadn't ended well.

"They just come out for some exercise sometimes," he said now, "or when I clean their cage. Watch. They're really well-trained." Frank moved carefully to the cage, not dislodging the two birds on his shoulders, though BlueBoy flew from Frank's knee as it unbent. He landed on top of Frank's head, and Susan let out a little screech, seeing one of her small-pet-fears come to life on her living husband. Standing by the cage, Frank let out a low whistle, just three notes then paused, then repeated. One by one, the birds flew from wherever they were, perched for a second on his pointing finger, and then hopped back into the cage. Aristotle was first in, and he greeted each of his siblings, as Frank liked to think of them, with a happy tweet. Butch, practicing his alpha-hawkness, was the last, flying down from the curtain rod, exchanging a few words with Frank, who saluted, and then he flew in too. As Frank shut the door, the birds all began to tuck their heads, ready for a nap after their burst of freedom. Frank sat down next to Susan again, who'd been sitting with her hands over her mouth in horror ever since BlueBoy landed on his head.

Now she lowered her hands. "That was pretty impressive," she admitted. "I never knew you were so good with pets. Or that you liked birds."

He shrugged. "I didn't know that either, until...until you were gone. I thought when I sold our house and moved into this one, I'd be okay, that you wouldn't be so...missing. Absent. In our old house, I always noticed your empty chair in the kitchen, your empty recliner in the living room, the empty side of the vanity in the bathroom." He looked away. "And your empty half of the bed. But even here, you were still obviously gone. Even though this wasn't our house and you never lived here." He looked over at her. "I think you felt even more missing because you'd never been here. It was a place I saw, I chose, I moved into, that you would never see, and that you had no say in." He attempted to pat her on the knee but didn't feel much of anything. It was like patting almost threadbare material, with no limb inside. "I guess you've been here now." He felt the corners of his mouth turn down, and he fought it. "I missed you before when you never lived here. And I miss you now, when you're right beside me, even though I'm not quite sure you're real."

Her mouth turned down too. "I'm sorry, Frank. Do you want me to stop coming? I thought about appearing to you earlier, even before you moved here, but I was afraid it would upset you too much. But then, when I saw Theresa at your door..." She looked at her lap. "Well, if she gets to see you, I should get to see you too. She chose to leave. I didn't. It's just not fair."

Frank couldn't help but smile, even as he felt the full weight of that unfairness. "It's okay. I'm glad you're here." He picked up the iguana book and held it out to her. "I got this at the pet shop. Audrey showed up there too, with her iguana. I went to pet him, just a really friendly gesture and Audrey said I could, and then Newt nearly bit me."

She took the book and Frank was pleased to see it didn't just fall through her hands. He just didn't understand the physics of all this. "Why did he try to bite you?" she said.

"I don't know. That's what I'm trying to find out. What am I going to do if her iguana doesn't like me?" Frank sank back in the cushions. "He lets the pet store owner, Bob, pet him."

Susan paged idly through the book. "Do you really think you need to worry about that? Surely she doesn't just let him roam through her house; he'd be in a cage or something. I think we have to worry more about if *she* likes you, Frank. Newt is just a lizard." She set the book back down.

Frank thought about his conversation with Blueboy just a few minutes before. He didn't want to upset Susan by telling her she was wrong, but she was. Newt wasn't just an iguana. Frank would never be able to leave his birds locked up all the time if Audrey didn't like them out and about. He glanced at Susan. Until she died, he was never even allowed to have birds or any small pet. And he didn't mind. He didn't really understand the pet connection then either. But now, he wouldn't want to be without the birds. It was more than a pet connection. They were family.

Susan leaned forward. She put her hand, a featherweight, on his arm. "Don't forget I know what you're thinking."

Frank was horrified.

"It's okay," Susan said. "I know things have changed since I've been...gone. That had to happen. You had to find your way. I know, Frank, I know deep in my heart that if there was a choice to either have me back or keep your birds, I know who you'd pick."

Frank closed his eyes and hoped he'd never have to face a choice like that.

"You won't." Susan sat back. "I am really dead, Frank. I can't come back." She crossed her arms. "So about Audrey. Maybe she's ambivalent right now, and the lizard is reflecting that."

Frank considered. Pets were supposed to pick up on the emotions of their owners. "That's possible, I suppose."

"I really wish you would just get to it and ask her out."

But it seemed like there should be more to it than that. Frank felt all at sea when it came to women and what women wanted these days. It was different than with Strike One and Strike Two. The rules had changed, or at least, he thought they did, from what he read and saw in books and on television shows and in movie theatres. And it had been so long since he was unfamiliar with the woman he was with. With Susan, it got to the point that he could predict almost exactly what her reaction would be to just about anything. Even her reaction to the wind-up mouse wasn't off the mark. He just didn't know that a broken mug and a coffee stain on the wall would be part of it. "I just –"

"I know. You want to do it your way. That's not working so well, though, is it?" Susan said.

He frowned. Since Susan's death, he'd forgotten that she could be a little bit bossy, a little bit blunt. He had to admit, he hoped only to himself, that he didn't miss that part. For years, he watched along with the rest of the world as teary bereaved women turned to friends on television shows and said, "If only I could hear him snore now!" That wasn't true. You grieved the good things, and you just forgot about the snoring. He bet Susan didn't miss his snoring, something she complained bitterly about throughout their marriage. At one point, he slept with a necktie slung under his chin and tied in a bow on his scalp, in an attempt to keep his mouth shut during sleep.

"I do miss your snoring, Frank," she said.

He damned her telepathy. Again. So maybe women were different from men. Again.

"Sometimes, when you sleep, I stop by your room just to listen."

Frank thought that was a little creepy and he didn't think fast enough to block his thought, and Susan suddenly snapped into a straight-ahead position on the couch. Her angry pose. "I'm sorry, Susan," he said.

She folded her hands.

"Susan...why are you trying so hard for me to get together with Audrey? You don't like thinking about me being with Theresa."

Her hands went from folded into fists. "Honestly, Frank! Really?" And then she crossed her arms, and Frank really dreaded that. It was another rung up the anger ladder. "You don't like Theresa, remember? Why would I want you to end up back with her? I came after Theresa, and I don't want you moving backward. Backward, Frank! Theresa hurt you!" She looked at him and her eyes filled with tears. He wondered if ghost tears were salty. "Audrey hasn't hurt you. She seems really nice."

Frank tried to make light. "Well, her iguana nearly hurt me. Theresa doesn't have an iguana. She just has a grandchild. I suppose that could nearly bite me too."

Susan's mouth went into a straight line, the line of no return, he used to call it, and she disappeared. That was familiar too, and something he'd forgotten, or at least not had in the grief-filled forefront of his mind. She would end arguments by just leaving the room, and when she returned, she pretended nothing happened. He used to shout after her, but she always claimed she didn't hear him. He would just have to wait until she climbed back down the ladder of anger and returned it to the closet.

Women. Maybe he should just stick with his birds.

Frank sat back again and put his hand on the cushion where his dead wife just sat. He wrapped her familiarity around him like her matching cardigan. Maybe he did miss the bad things. That ladder? He didn't like it. But he would climb it beside her every single day and night if that's what it took to bring her back. He would buy a ladder for every room in the house.

•   •   •

With the arrival of February came the first winter thaw and Frank welcomed it, even though he knew from experience it wouldn't last. There were a series of thaws that occurred during every Wisconsin winter, and they always brought the optimists out of hibernation. Suddenly, there were people on the street, wearing shorts and t-shirts, slogging through the melting snow to catch summer Frisbees and softballs. Only to have the snow return, and then return again. Still, it was hard not to feel your spirits lift toward a sun that promised summer, even when you knew that temperatures below zero were still in the forecast.

Frank went out one afternoon in his middle jacket, as he called it, lighter than the winter one, heavier than the summer windbreaker, and worked on clearing the bottom of his driveway and the edges of his sidewalk. It was good to see the blacktop shining against the melting snow and blades of grass sticking out, even if that grass was yellow. Some people looked for tree buds as a sign of spring; Frank looked for the return of his entire driveway.

He decided to clear the bottom of Audrey's drive too. He looked up at her picture window. Newt was there, in his tree. From the sidewalk, it looked like the iguana was asleep, but Frank was suspicious. He moved a bit to the right and the left and sure enough, Newt's head swung with him. Frank was being watched. He raised his hand and waved. He knew Newt wouldn't wave back, but he still felt crushed at the lack of reaction. He knew from the book that a head bob was friendly, a "Hello!", an "I like you!", but Newt's head remained steady. At least it wasn't doing that threatening left to right sway Frank saw in the pet shop. He couldn't see Newt's eyes from this distance, but he imagined them beady and cold.

"Why couldn't she just get a cat?" Frank mumbled, trying one more wave, but there was no change in Newt.

He was halfway through Audrey's melting slush when a car pulled up in front of his house. Theresa's face, Strike One, was behind the windshield and he shook his head, gently, so he could still react, but she wouldn't see. He wondered if not only Newt was watching, but Strike Two too. Susan. She wouldn't be happy to see Theresa. He wasn't either, not really, but Susan would be unhappy in a different way. He glanced around but didn't see her. Which didn't mean a damn thing, when it came to a ghost.

He seemed to be spending an awful lot of time with his wives, even though he was divorced from one and the other was dead.

"Frank!" Theresa called, getting out of her car. "What are you doing? A man your age shouldn't be shoveling."

A man his age? Frank rankled, but then quickly reminded himself that she was a widow, given that role by a man who keeled over while mowing the lawn. He straightened and waited for Theresa to join him on the sidewalk. "It's not really shoveling, Theresa. It's all melt. It's more like sweeping."

She looked at the slush with an expression of disgust. "I hate when it gets like this. I'd rather just have snow."

Frank remembered that about Theresa. She didn't like messes. It was one of her quirks, really, given that personally, she was disorganized and scattered. If she said she'd meet him at one, he knew to wait until one-twenty. He also knew that she'd thrown on an outfit that she selected at the last minute, unlike the carefully coordinated Susan. But her house and her car were always impeccable. Her car had scented plastic garbage bags that hung from the doorknobs in the front and back seats and were replaced weekly, whether they needed it or not. She vacuumed her trunk every time she changed the garbage bags. A mechanic once said that Theresa's trunk was cleaner than his mother's bedroom. "I know. At least I can clear it away now. And when the temperatures drop again tonight, it won't freeze back into ice."

She looked back at his house. "This isn't even your driveway."

"No. I'm just being neighborly."

There was a movement in the picture window, and they both noticed it. Newt moved forward on a branch, planting his front feet in a straight-legged stance on the windowsill. It was like he wanted to get closer to them. There was still no evidence of a head bob.

"Good lord," Theresa said. "What is that?"

"My neighbor's iguana. His name is Newt." Frank waved again. Then he shoved the last of the slush into the gutter. "Would you like to come in, Theresa?" He felt Susan's frown, whether it was there or not, and wondered again if she was watching.

"Yes, please, that would be very nice." Theresa always had the best manners.

Frank led her inside and deposited her at the kitchen table. As he hung up his jacket, he called, "Would you like a cup of coffee?" He'd started a fresh pot before he went out to shovel, knowing he'd want to come into a hot cup and a treat as a reward for a job well done. There were doughnuts from his trip to the grocery store that morning. His sludging through the slush had a double intention: gain Audrey's notice and justify a high-sugar treat in the afternoon.

"That would be nice," Theresa said again.

If he'd been alone, Frank would have taken his mug and the white box of doughnuts to the couch and had his snack while watching late afternoon television. He'd grown fond of Judge Judy. Judge Judy, he thought, made no bones about where she stood. He wondered if Judge Judy's husband was ever as confused as Frank was about the women in his life. But there would be no Judge Judy today; Strike One was impossibly here. Again. He placed the two mugs on the table and set out the sugar bowl and poured creamer from the carton in the fridge into a little matching pitcher. Then he arranged the doughnuts on a platter. He brought them over with two plates.

"Oh, my," Theresa said. "This is wonderful, Frank. I remember how you've always had a sweet tooth."

He remembered she did too. It was amazing, really, what he remembered after so many years. He knew before she did it, that she would pick a doughnut, tear it in half and put one half on her plate. Depending on her mood and what the scale said that morning – he remembered she always weighed herself after her morning shower and going to the bathroom, but before putting on her clothes, though she did comb her hair first to get rid of any extra-weighty water droplets – she might allow herself the other half later. But she would never have a whole doughnut at once on her plate.

He realized with a start that when he chose his assortment in the bakery department that morning, he chose one that was Theresa's favorite: caramel Pershing. He looked quickly and breathed a sigh of relief when he saw that Susan's favorite, a cheese danish, was there too. This was hard work, balancing the needs of one wife he was divorced from and one who left him a widower. He was used to not having to worry about either of them anymore, and now here they were, back in his life and in his doughnut selection. He wondered idly what Audrey's favorite doughnut was. He made a bet with himself, thinking it was a white-frosted long john. She seemed the type. He sighed and reached for his own favorite, a maple-frosted. He took the whole thing. He smiled and decided he never did anything halfway.

"So how've you been, Frank?" Theresa asked, daintily licking her fingers.

"I've been fine. Are you here today for a reason?"

She sat back and looked affronted. "I just thought I'd stop by. Do I have to have a reason?"

Frank wanted to say yes. Yes, there should be a reason to suddenly start visiting her ex-husband who didn't become an ex-husband by any choice of his own because she chose to leave him behind all those years ago, after ten years of marriage, and she hadn't seen him since. He considered all the years gone by. The eleven-year gap after Strike One divorced him and before he married Strike Two. His whole time with Susan, fifteen years, and then the three years since her death. That added up to a twenty-nine-year gap in their relationship. "No," Frank said evenly. "You don't need a reason. It just seems sort of odd that you're suddenly popping up again."

"Well." She eyed the remaining half of her doughnut and Frank pushed the plate a little closer to her. Her weight must have been good that morning. She looked great. Frank's chair moved suddenly sideways as if it had been kicked, and Frank wondered if he imagined it. "You know how we left it last time...I gave you my phone number and told you to call if you wanted to get together sometimes to talk. You haven't called me, and I thought I'd stop by to see if maybe you'd lost my number."

Frank couldn't help it. He smiled. Theresa just couldn't stand negative outcomes. She was definitely a woman with a positive spin. "I didn't lose it, Theresa," he said. "I just haven't had the time to call." He didn't add that he didn't have any intention of calling. Frank just wasn't a cruel man. Theresa was a positive woman. Until she decided that she just had to have a child, they did so well together.

She took the other half of her doughnut and set it neatly on her plate. Frank refilled her coffee cup. He refilled his and took a second doughnut and then sat back and looked at his first wife, his first love, and remembered Sunday mornings. He and Theresa lived in an apartment with a balcony that overlooked a river. When it was warm, they would sit out there on Sunday mornings, eating their favorite doughnuts, reading the paper, lifting their faces to the sun. Often, they laughed. Often, they held hands. And often, they returned to bed, and this went on for years of Sundays until the times between them turned cold. The bed turned cold with it.

He remembered. And he knew he wasn't a cruel man. The woman before him lost her husband just a few months ago, in the heat of a summer day, a time of family barbecues and pushing grandchildren on swings and going to county fairs. Nights of sleeping with the windows open. Mornings of fresh breezes on bare skin. He let himself wonder, just for a second, if seven months ago, Theresa woke up in her bare skin next to her husband. He and Theresa used to sleep in the nude. He and Susan were the same way, even bare-skinned at sixty years old, even as sick as she was. Especially as sick as she was. But he didn't know what changes might have come between sixty and sixty-three if Susan had lived.

Frank looked at Theresa and sighed. He'd lost his wife. Twice. She lost her husband. Twice. The loss happened between the two of them, even though they used to share those Sunday mornings. They even treasured them. Frank treasured the memory now.

Loss was hard, Frank thought, no matter how the losing was done.

He pulled out his cell phone. "Tell me your number again, Theresa."

She gave it to him, and he made as if he was adding her to his contacts. But then her phone rang. "Oh! Excuse me," she said. "I normally wouldn't be rude and answer it, but with a grandchild now…"

He waved his acceptance and then turned a bit so she couldn't see him lifting his phone to his ear.

When she said hello, he said, "Hello, Theresa, it's Frank. I've been thinking. I think it would be nice for us to get together sometimes to talk."

She stared across the table at him and then she began to laugh. He remembered her laugh. He remembered how he used to smile, just thinking of her laughter. Of her face, when it lit up. He remembered scheming, planning, coming up with ways to bring that laughter to the surface. There wasn't much laughter at the end of their relationship. But there was plenty at the beginning and even in the middle.

It was amazing how much he could remember about someone who made him so very angry. It was amazing how she could still make him laugh.

His chair bumped again. He was very sure he didn't imagine it. Susan, he thought, since she said she could read his thoughts, I have good memories of you both. Let me have them.

His chair didn't move. But somehow, it felt accusatory.

When he hung up his phone and reached over to pat Theresa's hand, he was struck by the warmth. He remembered that too, of course, but it had just been so long. He thought of touching Susan the last time, the ephemeral feel of her knee, the featherweight of her hand.

Theresa was warm. And solid.

His hair flew up from behind, and he was pretty sure he was just cuffed upside the head by a ghost. A ghost he used to be married to. A ghost who tended toward jealousy.

But still. He kept his hand on Theresa's and leaned in to talk.

Strike one. Strike two. He wasn't out yet.

Chapter Eleven

The obligatory viewing of obligatory sex.

"So tell me," Audrey said, sitting across from Annabel in the food court. "Last month, did you go on any of the women's marches? The ones against…That Man in the White House?" Audrey couldn't imagine that Annabel wouldn't know who she was talking about. She hoped she didn't have to break her vow and say his name.

Annabel shrugged. "Yeah, I did it. Vicki asked me to come, and we went to the one in Madison. It was fun. Cold, but fun."

Audrey leaned forward. "How did you feel about it? I mean, when it was all over, did it make a difference, do you think?"

Annabel laughed. "Of course not. I went because it seemed like a big party. And hey, I don't like Trump either. He's an asshole. So I went because I figured it would be a fun way to express that, to work off some steam. But cause any changes? No. What changes could it cause? Was Trump going to slap a hand to his forehead and shout, 'Oh my god, you're right! Women are equals!' Was he going to whip out his phone and call Hillary or Obama and say, 'Hey, I'm in over my dumb blond head here. Can one of you take over?' I don't think so."

This was something Audrey hadn't considered; protesting as a way of letting off steam and of simply expressing what she felt. When she went on marches with Clara in college, it was always focused on bringing about change. But on the day of the Women's March, all of the women's marches, she watched the faces of the women on the news, women from all around the country and the world, women with signs and shouts, but faces that ultimately smiled. Maybe it did help, at least toward recovery from what was a sickening, and then disheartening unbelievable election. Maybe it would have helped Audrey. But still, wasn't change the ultimate goal? Wasn't there a hum of hope going through all the crowds that day? "So you don't think it had any impact?" she asked Annabel.

"I didn't say that." Today, Annabel was eating Subway, and she happily unwrapped a long 12-inch loaded sandwich. Audrey noticed she even added bacon. "It had an impact on the women that were there. They felt better. They felt engaged, involved. It felt good to be doing something. To be noisy. But it didn't do anything overall. Of course not. He's still in the White House, isn't he." Annabel shook her head. "I don't think many of us had the real expectation that the march would do anything, other than express our beliefs and our anger. If there were some who truly expected change to come out of marching around with signs, which were really, really good signs, by the way, well, then we had dreamers amongst us." Annabel took a big bite of her sandwich and then said, around chewing, "I think it's a good thing that we still have dreamers. But you know, ultimately, we have to live with reality. Those of us in the streets can't really do anything. We're not the ones who can kick Trump out."

That was true. Audrey sat back in her chair. A government by the people, for the people, of the people. Except the people had nothing to do with it anymore. Even when they were in the popular majority.

She glanced around; no Vicki in sight. She'd grown used to Vicki swooping in whenever she and Annabel were together. "How did Vicki think it went?"

"Oh, she loved it. But you know, she's one of those dreamers. I think she was actually disappointed when he didn't cower in fear and instantly resign. It was like she thought that a huge group of women, more than huge, from all around the world, would somehow intimidate Trump. Scare him, beat him down. But it didn't, and that made her sad." Annabel shook her head and took a bite. "I think Vicki would likely support any possible way to get Trump out of the White House. Any way, even violence, as long as it ended up with that result. Vicki is a bit of a feminazi."

Audrey sat back, horrified. "A what?"

"Feminazi." Annabel looked around quickly too, dropping her voice to a low whisper.

"Where did that word come from? Why would you use it?" Audrey thought she might actually begin to feel sick. She wanted to feel sick. Why would anyone take the horror that was the Nazi regime and attach it to feminism? How could being a feminist be anywhere close to being someone who wanted to murder an entire race?

Annabel looked puzzled. "Audrey, come on, you've heard Vicki. She says she doesn't hate all men, but it sure doesn't seem that way. Look at how she reacted to your Fish In The Sea date the other day. She probably thinks all men should be euthanized. Just like Hitler thought that of the Jews."

Audrey nearly protested, but then stopped. She thought of Vicki saying that the male gender just wasn't necessary. And Annabel just now saying that Vicki would support any possible way to get rid of the president, even violence when the president was That particular Man in the White House. But did that mean that Vicki wanted to kill all men? Audrey just couldn't equate Vicki with Hitler.

"Anyway." Annabel brushed her hands, wiping away the drippings and crumbs and the salt from her chips and the topic. "How about a movie tonight? That new Fifty Shades movie isn't doing so well, so the Majestic is combining it with the first one to make a double feature."

"Fifty Shades of Gray?" Audrey hadn't seen the first movie a couple years ago when it came out originally. She didn't read the books. She refused, after reading the book jacket. The book was placed bizarrely in the romance section when it was clearly pornography. Even erotica didn't fit what was contained inside the covers of what the publisher said was romantic. Audrey refused to support anything that exploited women, even if the author was a woman. Audrey remembered putting the book down and having to restrain herself from shaking her finger at a display that included a photograph of the author. She wanted to yell, "Shame! Shame on you!" But she didn't. She just didn't buy the book or go see the movie.

Just like her vote in last November's election, she wondered if her opinion and action counted. If it had any impact at all, against the millions who bought the books and who lined up on Valentine's Day 2015 to see the first movie's grand opening.

Now, Audrey wondered if Annabel might be willing to see a different movie. A night out with a friend would be fun, and it was exactly what she needed. No more dwelling or ruminating. No sitting in front of the computer. "A movie sounds good, but I'm not sure about that one. Is there anything else?"

"Oh, sure, but I really want to see this. I mean, it's a double feature, two movies for the price of one. How often does that happen?"

Audrey couldn't even remember if she'd ever sat through two movies in one night. It was practical, like a BOGO sale or a final clearance. But taking a night off from reading Gloria Steinem in order to see a Fifty Shades double feature seemed…hypocritical.

Still, it was a night out, and she'd been trying to shake up her stay-at-home routine. Maybe, in the dark of the movie theater, she could lose her restraint and shake her finger at the screen. "Okay," she said. "I'll go home after work and feed Newt and then meet you there."

"Maybe we should invite Vicki," Annabel said, and Audrey surprised herself by joining in her laughter.

At dinner that night, Audrey explained to Newt that he was going to be on his own for a few hours. While he ate his vegetable plate, she munched on a salad too, but hers was topped with cheese, ham, and turkey, reminiscent of Annabel's earlier sandwich, and a generous helping of Thousand Island dressing. She even threw in bacon bits. But she wanted to save room for popcorn and soda. "I know we usually spend evenings together, Newt," she said. "But tonight, I'm going to the movies. With a friend. I hope that's okay. I'll turn the lights on, and I'll leave the television on, so you have some sound and something to do." Newt seemed to actually pay attention when he and Audrey watched television movies and shows. "I'd take you with me, but I don't think they allow iguanas in movie theaters." She smiled at this and Newt shook his dewlap. She hoped it was with humor and not protest.

After she turned on the lights and the television and took a moment to carefully flip Gloria's book, so she was face down and not watching where Audrey was going, she headed to her garage. Newt followed her. He looked surprised. She bent down to the floor and let him climb on her arm. Then she stroked him the way he liked, from the top of his head to his tail. She walked him back to his tree. "I won't be late, I promise, Newt," she said and put him on his favorite branch. Then she walked briskly out, trying to ignore the scrabble of iguana claws behind her. By the time she pulled out of her garage, Newt was back in the picture window. His hind legs were on a branch, and he stretched straight up against the glass, baring his white belly against it, just like he did when he welcomed her home. But this time, his white belly seemed plaintive.

Audrey felt awful.

But she didn't cancel. As she drove to the theater, she told herself that Newt would be all right. She wouldn't be gone that long. She reminded herself again that partners needed to let each other have some time on their own every now and then. This was good for the both of them.

Though it didn't seem fair that she was off with a friend while Newt stayed home alone. If only he had a friend…

She thought about dog parks and doggie daycare and puppy playgroups.

She wondered if there was a playgroup for iguanas.

But Newt wasn't a puppy. He wasn't a child. He was her partner. But he was a partner that was dependent on her. He couldn't leave the house without her. Audrey hadn't thought about that when she brought Newt home. What if she found a babysitter for Newt? Her mind tripped over to Frank. He'd offered to watch Newt if she ever traveled anywhere with her zebra stripe luggage. If Frank and Newt ever became friends, maybe Newt could spend some time over there, when Audrey was out.

She shook her head. She could hear Bob saying, "He's an iguana, Audrey." And he was.

But he wasn't. This was something Frank really seemed to understand, and Audrey appreciated that. She wondered if Newt ever would. She could still hear the click of Newt's teeth as his amazing jaws came together.

But for tonight, Newt was home alone with the television for company. And Audrey was going to see a movie that she never wanted to see and its sequel, just to get out of the house for a little while.

Audrey met Annabel outside of the theater and to her surprise, Vicki was there too. Audrey couldn't help herself. "Really?" she said directly to Vicki.

Vicki shrugged. "You're here too," she said. "I figured I might as well see what all the fuss is about."

Audrey thought that was a good way to look at it. Annabel winked at her.

They loaded up on popcorn and Sno-caps and licorice and soda, though Vicki had a bottled water. She added a salted pretzel with cheese dip to their pile. They went in and sat, Audrey in the middle of the other two, in a theater that wasn't very crowded. The lack of an audience surprised Audrey. She remembered the news articles that went out two years ago when the first Fifty Shades was released. There were stories of having to buy tickets far in advance, lines reaching around blocks. And there were stories of boycotts and protests. Audrey herself donated to *50 Bucks, Not 50 Shades*, a movement that encouraged you to donate fifty dollars to your local domestic shelter instead of spending it on dinner and that movie.

That Movie. That Man In The White House. Women flocked to That Movie and women voted for That Man. They attended rallies, wearing those t-shirts with down-pointed arrows and invitations for Trump to grab them where the arrows pointed. Audrey wondered if the same women who attended That Movie also attended Those Rallies and also voted for That Man.

But now, here she was. She didn't donate fifty dollars this year. She tried to shake the guilt.

The three of them chattered amiably as they waited for the movie to start. They passed the popcorn bucket, and the candy and Vicki split her pretzel three ways. When the theater darkened, Audrey cast one more thought toward Newt and his bare white belly gleaming against her window, and then she settled back, straw in her mouth.

That didn't last long.

"Ohmygod," Vicki said, the salt on her fingers glittering in the movie's light as she pressed her palm to her mouth.

"Oh my god," Audrey said, doing the same.

"Ooooo," Annabel said and leaned forward.

"I can't watch this," Vicki said. She began to shift and gather, shoving napkins to the floor, picking up her purse. "This is...this is a crime."

"I can't either," Audrey said. She reached for her coat.

"Shhhh," someone in the audience hissed. "Be quiet!" It was a masculine voice, Audrey noticed.

Annabel shrugged. "You won't get your money back. And I want to see the rest."

"I don't care." Audrey stood, Vicki behind her, and they abandoned Annabel there, by herself, surrounded with movie food and movie sounds and whatever that was on the screen in front of them. As Audrey pushed her way through the doors and stepped into the lobby, she found herself wondering if Annabel might go home with that masculine voice that night.

She hoped not.

Audrey didn't hesitate, but continued through the lobby to the outside, Vicki right behind her. It startled Audrey when she realized Vicki was hanging on to the back of her jacket, like a child following her mother through the crowd. Once they were in the fresh night air, Vicki let go, and they stood side by side.

Audrey hugged herself. "I want to wash my hands." She actually wanted to take a shower, and not a cold one. A hot one. Hot as she could stand it. "But I didn't want to stay in there any longer than I had to."

Vicki was taking deep breaths. She swayed a bit, and Audrey put out an arm to steady her. To her surprise, Vicki leaned into her and closed her eyes.

They stood for a moment, the cold air that Audrey suddenly hoped held a hint of spring washing over them. Audrey wanted warmth. She needed it.

"Do you want to go get coffee?" Vicki asked finally. "There's a Starbucks down the street. We could just leave our cars for now and walk there."

"Sure," Audrey said.

And so she ended up sitting across from Vicki The Feminazi at a Starbucks on a night when she thought she was going to see a movie she never wanted to see with Annabel The Not-The-F-Word instead of sitting at home with Newt, her partner who happened to be an iguana. It was a different Starbucks than the one in the mall where Audrey last sat across from Generic Hairless Mark, and Audrey couldn't help but feel relieved to be here instead with Vicki, even though Annabel called her a feminazi and even though Audrey herself wasn't too crazy about her. But tonight, Vicki looked smaller. She hadn't taken off her coat, and she huddled into it, her hands wrapped around her for-here mug.

Audrey loved that Starbucks had for-here mugs, that she could get her favorite drink extra hot in ceramic. The ceramic instead of the heavy cardboard just seemed to tell her to breathe, sit back and relax.

But Vicki didn't look so relaxed. Audrey thought she looked genuinely unhappy. Audrey expected Vicki to look angry. Enraged. Ready to run off on another march, pull on a pink hat with pussycat ears, throw her fists in the air and yell. Audrey expected a lecture on the evils of men. Although Audrey had to remind herself, 50 Shades was written by a woman. Which just made it that much more confounding. And women voted for Trump, wearing Grab My Pussy t-shirts. Which made it even more confounding. Audrey wondered for a moment who was worse. The men who treated women this way, or the women who felt that this treatment was all right. That it was what they deserved. That they were supposed to like it, want it, flock to bookstores and movie theaters to enjoy it, vote for a president that grabbed them just like his next cheeseburger, but not with nearly the same amount of respect.

But Vicki didn't spout any speech or lecture. She looked sad.

Finally, Audrey said, "How could anyone watch that? How could anyone read that?" She looked up at the ceiling as if the answers were there. "For that matter, how could anyone write that? How could a woman write that?"

Vicki straightened a bit. "Annabel called it a romance. The commercials called it that too." She opened her hands, empty, questioning, wanting to grasp something that just wasn't there. "So did the publishers."

Audrey remembered finding the book in the romance section of the bookstore, and she thought of what she just saw on the screen. She thought of what she'd experienced with a variety of men over the years, some who stayed a while and some who didn't. But none of them were like what was on that screen tonight. *She* wasn't like what was on that screen tonight. What was on that screen was what you were supposed to walk away from. Run away from. Whether you were a feminist or not.

Vicki seemed to melt a little bit more. She took another sip and then said, "Some people called it erotica too. That wasn't erotica. And others compared it to Erica Jong and *Fear of Flying*." Vicki's knuckles turned white. "I read that. A long time ago, but I read that. And it wasn't what was on the screen tonight. That was abuse. That was rape. Right there. In front of everybody."

Audrey nodded. She'd never been raped or abused. But she didn't think she needed to experience it to identify it.

"Do you know," Vicki said slowly, "there were some mother/daughter book groups that read 50 Shades? Discussed it? Can you imagine? What mother would want to teach her daughter that that was the type of relationship to look for?"

Audrey wondered if Annabel read That Book in a book group. Did they sit around and drink wine and talk about it? Did they "ooooo" the way Annabel did in the theater?

How could any woman read That Book and not throw it across the room? Audrey didn't condone book-burning, but she wondered, if she had the chance and if there was an open flame if she could do it with That Book. With the others that came afterward.

She thought she might. She felt the anger.

That Book. That Movie. That Man In The White House.

Annabel called Vicki a feminazi. But feeling anger like this didn't make you a Nazi, Audrey decided. How could you feel anything but anger? Annabel also called Vicki an SJW; a Social Justice Warrior. Vicki wasn't either. She was angry. And with good reason.

Annabel stayed to watch the movie. What did that make her?

It was confounding.

Vicki shrugged out of her coat. She looked a little bit better. "Audrey," she said. "That happened to me. Once."

Audrey thought of book groups, of mothers and daughters, and she was confused. "What do you mean?"

"Rape." Vicki's lips closed over the word. They pressed themselves white. Then she said, "I was seventeen. On a date. My boyfriend took me out to a park shelter late at night so we could, you know, be alone."

Audrey tried to breathe.

"His friends met us there."

That was all she said. Several tears rolled down her cheeks.

Suddenly, what Audrey knew of Vicki made sense. Suddenly, Audrey understood.

She thought she just might type that word, feminazi, on her computer, print it out, and then burn it. Maybe burn it too, along with a few books. Maybe.

Leaning forward, Audrey wrapped her hands over Vicki's. She squeezed. And then she held on.

• • • • •

Late that night, Audrey found herself again in her reading room, not reading, the light off, the fireplace on, her iguana in her lap. Newt was dug in tight, all four of his feet and their attending claws clinging to her thighs. Audrey kept one hand on him, and the other rested on the cover of Gloria's book. Gloria's face peeked out between Audrey's pointer and middle fingers. Audrey wasn't reading, but she needed Gloria to talk to.

"Can you imagine," Audrey said softly to Gloria, "a world that uses the word feminazi?" Then she remembered that Gloria Steinem was alive and well, not just residing on the cover of her latest book. "Well, of course, you don't have to imagine it, you're living it." She shook her head. "Are you as stunned and horrified as I am? I imagine you've been called one."

Under her palm, she felt Newt's breath even out. He was frantic when she walked in the door. She'd carried him with her as she moved throughout the house, changing into her pajamas, making him a snack and herself some hot chocolate and a piece of toast with boysenberry jelly. She checked her email with Newt on her shoulder, his face pressed to hers. Throughout, she kept saying, "I'm sorry, Newt. I'm sorry." But she also explained that he would have to get used to her being out every now and then. She did so with a soft voice. She did so with a comforting hand. Newt was her partner. His feelings mattered. She needed to help him understand and believe that he was always safe, whether she was in the house or not. This was her home, and it was his as well. He was dependent on her, and she would keep him safe, and she would keep him happy.

She was dependent on him as well, in a way that went beyond being able to walk out a door.

125

Clara emailed. They were going to meet at the big mall in Gurnee on Saturday. Clara suggested making a weekend of it, staying in a hotel, but after seeing how Newt reacted that night, Audrey wasn't sure an overnight stay was a good idea. He'd have to be alone for such a long time. If she brought him along, he'd be left behind in the hotel room, a strange place, while she and Clara were at the mall, and she'd be worried about the maid going in and Newt slipping out the door. Audrey just didn't trust the Do Not Disturb signs. And who knew what perils there were for an iguana in a hotel room? She'd have to bring his old aquarium, and he'd feel trapped within the glass walls that used to be spacious but were getting smaller every day. She didn't think either of them was ready for that kind of stress, or for that kind of separation if she kept him at home. So she and Clara would only meet for the day.

But now, Audrey sat in the quiet, the fire glowing, her iguana mostly stiffly asleep in her lap, the scent of chocolate surrounding them. Gloria at her fingertips.

Audrey thought of Vicki.

And she thought of Annabel too, of Annabel's quickly putting not one, but two labels on Vicki without questioning what it was that made Vicki say the things she said. Feel the things she felt. Audrey thought of how quickly she fell into judgment too.

Feminazi. SJW. There was a reason for such intense anger. Was it justified to feel it against all men? Of course not. But was it justified to feel it?

Yes. Of course, it was.

Audrey looked in the fire. She thought about marches, and she thought about burning things. Bras. Books. Words. Maybe even effigies.

She wondered if any of it would make her feel better.

．　　．　　．　　．　　．

On Saturday morning, Audrey left the house with minimal fuss from Newt. Newt really didn't know weekdays from weekends. Most days, he knew Audrey left the house early, and some days, she stayed at home. To an iguana, there weren't days of the week or months or even years. There was when he was awake and when he was asleep. There was when Audrey was home and when she wasn't. So when she followed her weekday routine this morning, he went about his business as usual too. He'd recovered from her being out late with Annabel and Vicki.

Audrey still felt guilty about leaving Newt behind, whether he was aware of it or not, so she took Frank up on his offer and had him over the night before to teach him how to make Newt his dinner. Maybe, Audrey thought, maybe Newt would grow to like Frank if Frank offered him food. Audrey knew the old adage that the way to a man's heart was through his stomach and she thought that was ridiculous...but Newt did like to eat. The iguana followed them around balefully as Audrey showed Frank where everything was. Frank, to his credit, talked to the iguana constantly, in a warm and friendly tone, and Audrey was impressed with his effort. When the dinner was prepared, she had Frank set it on Newt's placemat and then she showed him how to bridge Newt up to reach it. Instead of setting Newt in his place, she put him back on the floor and then Frank held out his arm, just like Audrey did. Newt looked stunned. Frank looked cautious.

"C'mon, Newt," he said, despite that caution. "I won't hurt you, buddy. I think you'll like what I made for you."

Newt hesitated, looking several times between Audrey, who stood with her arms folded, to Frank, whose arm was extended to the floor. Finally, he huffed, blowing his dewlap out and setting it swinging, and then he walked stiffly up Frank's arm. Frank lifted him like an elevator and bridged him to the placemat. Then he sat across from Newt and watched while he ate, and Audrey ate her dinner too. She offered some to Frank, it was a simple dinner of a grilled cheese sandwich and tomato soup, but he'd already eaten. Instead, he talked, with the both of them, regularly interrupting his conversation with Audrey to direct some comments to Newt.

Audrey liked how he called Newt buddy. So she left today, feeling fairly comfortable with Newt staying behind. Frank promised he would text updates. She also knew he was well aware of the perils of an open door to the outside, particularly in wintertime. She knew he would open it quickly, then shut it long before Newt would have the opportunity to slip out.

And with all of this, she knew she would still worry. But not to the point of canceling her day with Clara.

As she drove, she glanced down every now and then at her t-shirt. Her fish bicycle shirt showed up in the mail without a hitch, and Audrey loved it. She told herself she didn't mind that it was a larger size than her old one. It was comfortable. It was purple, a color she hated in college, but loved now. And it reminded her of Clara. She wondered what Clara would be wearing and then she chided herself. What did it matter?

She thought of Clara's photo on Facebook, how she looked so nicely put together, and Audrey wondered if she should have worn a new outfit from her store. The yoga pants. A nice shirt.

But when she was with Clara, in their past, she wore mostly jeans and t-shirts. And that's what she wore now. She felt like she had one foot in the past and one foot in the present. Or one sleeve each, actually.

Audrey sighed and drove over the Wisconsin/Illinois border.

The Gurnee Mills mall was always packed on a Saturday. The largest mall in the midwest before the birth of the Mall of America in Minnesota, Gurnee was still a travel destination. Audrey enjoyed it, relishing the different stores and the wide variety of people wandering from wing to wing. It was an outlet mall as well, and so she knew she'd find things there that she couldn't find anywhere else, and sometimes for a cheaper price. There was a twang of nerves today, though, knowing Clara would be there, stepping out of her past and into her present. They were meeting at the east food court.

When Audrey got there, she looked around. She didn't see Clara, but she wasn't sure she would recognize her right away if she did. So she sat down at a table near the edge of the court where she could look out on the aisle at all the passing people.

It only took moments. She saw the shirt before she saw the face. A bright red shirt, with a white fish pedaling a bicycle. And then, above it, the wide smile of her old friend.

They both stopped dead and stared. And then, like the college girls they used to be, they squealed and ran toward each other. Audrey was newly fifty-five, and Clara was right there with her, but Audrey didn't care, and Clara didn't seem to either. Audrey fell into Clara's embrace, and they hugged with their arms around their expanded bodies. Clara felt just like she used to, though softer. Audrey remembered being able to rest her elbows on the rack of Clara's ribs. Now, it was a roll of woman flesh that Audrey's elbows rested upon and Clara was squeezable. And there was something else too, something pliant and full, but still oh so familiar.

"Clara!" Audrey cried. "You're not wearing a bra!"

Clara laughed. "Some things don't change. I'm still me, Audrey."

"I can't believe you have the shirt!"

"It's not the same one. I bought one off of Amazon when I knew I was meeting you."

"So did I!"

Laughing, they wrapped their arms around each other's waists and walked into the food court. They decided to eat an early lunch, have a chance to talk, and then wander the mall.

"So..." Audrey said after they returned to their table and unwrapped their burgers. She was pleased to see that Clara ate meat. That was also a change. Clara used to be a staunch vegan. Audrey remembered her quoting the late great Euell Gibbons from his television commercials: "Ever eat a pine tree? Many parts are edible." Audrey used to retort, "Many parts of a cow are edible too." Now she said, "You know I have to ask you what happened. I was just astonished to find out you were married with kids. In college, you were, you know, a lesbian. A pretty damn committed lesbian too."

Clara laughed. "Yes, I remember. I was there. And I suppose it was a shock for you. It was a shock for me too." She chewed for a moment. "Something in me shifted when I hit thirty. I wanted a family. I wanted children. I know I could have done all that with a lesbian partner, but that's just not who walked into my life at the right time. Bill did. And before I knew it, I was walking right alongside him, up the stairs of the county courthouse. Shortly after, I began pushing a stroller."

This was confusing to Audrey, but she tried to work her way toward understanding. "Can that happen? I mean, can you just switch off your sexual identity like that?"

Clara shook her head. "I don't think I did. I identified as a lesbian when we were in college. But I was always attracted to both sexes. I've had relationships all along with both men and women. If I'd found the right woman, I might have settled down with her and had children. But that's not what happened. I found the right man. And I'm so happy with him. And with the kids."

Audrey wondered if maybe she would have had better luck if she'd become open to both sexes. But like Clara said, that just never fell into Audrey's path. "I haven't," she said. "Found the right person, I mean. The right man. Every now and then, I think I have. But then they wander off. The last one wandered off years ago. I'm thinking...I'm thinking I might be spending my life alone." To her embarrassment, tears welled up, and she grabbed for a napkin to wipe her eyes.

"Oh, Audrey." Clara reached out, grabbed her hand. "I'm sorry. It's not over yet though, you know."

It wasn't. Audrey knew that. But at times, it felt like it was. The part about having children through the set pattern of conception and childbirth and child-raising was certainly over. The dream of family life, of a family portrait showcasing a husband, a wife, and at least two children disappeared with her last period. There was still time left to be part of a couple. But Audrey didn't know if that would constitute a family.

"Sometimes I wonder if I'm even supposed to want to be with a man," Audrey said. "Or feel bad because I'm not."

"Why?" Then Clara's eyes dropped to Audrey's shirt. "Oh...you mean because of this? Because a woman needs a man like a fish needs a bicycle?"

Audrey nodded.

"Yeah, I know. I felt that way too when I met Bill. When I wanted children. When I had them. Hell, for a while, I even stayed home and was a full-time mom. I felt like a full-out defector to the cause."

Audrey leaned forward. "The cause? Feminism?"

"You bet. Here I was, this leftover from college, still full of memories of pumping my fist in the air and yelling about equal rights for women, and down with The Man. The Man was the enemy, and suddenly, I was married to one, staying at home, taking my kids to playgroup, cleaning my own house. And, God forbid, liking it." Clara shrugged. "Do you remember me telling you that you were setting the women's movement back a hundred years by working in a department store, selling clothes? Well, I felt like I was setting it back to prehistoric times. I felt like a hypocritical dinosaur." Clara grabbed Audrey's hand again. "But I was a happy dinosaur, and I was still contributing, and I just had to learn to see things differently. Audrey, I am so sorry. I am so, so sorry. What a godawful, ridiculous thing for me to say to you back then."

Audrey was shocked.

"At the time, I don't know, I guess I thought we all had to be in the trenches. Fighting The Man. I thought there had to be violence. Shouting. Massive change. Revolution. I am woman, hear me roar. It was like there had to be one or the other, men or women, that only one gender could win, only one gender could be on top, and I wanted women to be on top. To hell with equality! I wanted women to be in charge of the world. Hell, I wanted to be in charge of the world. And while I was fighting The Man, there you were, having fun with men, sleeping with men, and working in a department store, selling clothes."

Audrey remembered the hurt of that time. The complete dismissal from her best friend. She'd marched beside her and felt like she was still marching, even as she went out on dates and went to work every day. "It was a hard time."

"And I just made it harder." Clara sat back. "Things changed after I met Bill. Well, they changed before, really. I didn't see where all the noise we were making was actually accomplishing anything. I began to get involved in the elections, the quieter types of protests, writing senators and congresspeople, going door to door, talking to people about the issues, getting petitions signed, that sort of thing. I do volunteer work for NOW, and Planned Parenthood and I volunteer for every election. I even drove people to the polls during our last election, people who couldn't get out any other way. That seems to have more impact. Despite who we have in the White House." She rolled her eyes.

Audrey nodded. "I've done that too, though not so much, recently." She thought of Annabel and Vicki. "Do things seem weird to you now?"

When Clara shrugged, her breasts bobbled, and Audrey couldn't help but admire them. Clara was fifty-five like she was, and she wasn't afraid to show herself. Audrey glanced down. She was wearing one of the new Victoria's Secret bras, the zebra stripe, which, she suddenly realized, would coordinate with her luggage, if she ever went on a trip. She wondered if Clara ever set foot in a store like Victoria's Secret.

"A lot of things seem weird," Clara said, "especially since this election. We've gone backward, thanks to our new president. Thanks to those who voted for him. Thanks to those who didn't vote at all, or who voted for a third party, knowing that was a sure way to shoo Trump in. Can you imagine voting for a reality TV star? For someone who admitted to assaulting women? For *him*? For God's sake, for *him*? For who he's been forever, before the reality TV show, before that videotape was made?" For a moment, Audrey thought Clara was going to throw her burger down in disgust. "He's revolting."

And so they began to talk, burgers forgotten, fries forgotten. Audrey felt the clock, and the calendar fly backward as they leaned together, finished each other's sentences, laughed at the same time, and thoroughly understood each other. Audrey even told Clara about Newt, and after Clara finished laughing, Audrey showed her photographs.

"He feels like a partner to me, Clara," Audrey said. "Which I know is strange. But I feel stuck. Like I've always wanted to be married, I've always wanted to have kids, but I've also always been a feminist, and maybe somehow that's where things went wrong. Maybe who I am, my personal recipe just doesn't mix well. And maybe I haven't done enough to be a feminist, because look where we are now. I didn't vote for That Man In The White House, but I didn't do anything to stop him either because I never imagined, not in a million years, that he would actually win. And I haven't done anything to officially protest him either. I didn't march in the Women's March. I didn't wear a pussycat hat. And I'm really missing having a man in my life, and I'm wondering if I'm ever going to have someone permanent, a partner, like Newt is to me, and I don't even know if I should be wanting that. If that makes me not a feminist. If I'm a fraud." Audrey looked down at her t-shirt. "Maybe I shouldn't even be wearing this."

"I'm wearing it, and I'm married," Clara said. "And a former stay-at-home mom. Well, not former. I still stay at home, even though my kids are grown. Not to mention I lived my life as a lesbian for a long time. What does that make me?"

There was all that. But all Audrey saw when she looked at Clara was her friend. Whether she slept with women or with men, Clara was Clara. The love Audrey always had for her, the connection, came roaring back as if there weren't any years in between.

"I think..." Clara said slowly, and she stopped to consider her words. Audrey thought of the words that fell out of both Annabel's and Vicki's mouths, at an amazing clip where Audrey sometimes felt she couldn't keep up. She liked Clara's pace. It matched her own. "I think maybe feminism doesn't have anything to do with our personal relationships with men. I think it only has to do with women's rights, with how women are treated." She looked at Audrey. "Why would being a feminist mean the exclusion of men in our lives? It's like when I used to want to be in charge of the world, and I wanted women to be in charge of the world, and to hell with men. But being equal to men doesn't mean wiping them off the face of the planet. How can you be equal to something that doesn't exist? You have to live side by side to be equal." She nodded, as carefully as she was measuring her words. "My life is better, because of Bill. But I still want quality healthcare for women. I still want control over my body. I still want women to earn equal wages. Why should my validity be changed just because I'm married to a man? He and I treat each other as equal partners. That's what it's supposed to be all about, isn't it?"

Audrey sat back and stared at Clara. To have it stated so flat-out, to have it out loud, made it seem so simple. She remembered wondering if Gloria was ever married if Jane Russell or Anita Bryant were ever married.

She decided she would look that night.

"Clara," she said now. "Clara, I love you. I'm so glad I found you again."

They stood up and, across the table, embraced each other, their fish and their bicycles blending.

Then Clara said something that Audrey would never have believed possible from the braless free-wheeling rebellious, angry college woman who was her best friend. "Let's go shopping," she said.

Audrey was thrilled.

Chapter Twelve

When you give an iguana a cookie...

Frank had to admit, he was nervous when he turned the key to Audrey's front door at six o'clock that evening. Newt's dinner was to be at six-fifteen, and Frank put off his own meal until after what he dubbed The Ceremonial Feeding of the Iguana. He wanted to do everything right. He wanted to make Audrey happy. And he wanted to find out just how to do that. If Newt cooperated, Frank might have access to a wealth of inside information that probably even Bob hadn't seen.

Had Bob been to the house? Frank didn't think so. He figured that Bob would likely have been the one asked to take care of Newt, if that was the case. But she asked Frank! Despite the near-bite!

"Too bad, Bob," he said out loud.

Newt behaved himself the other day when Audrey was still there. The memory of those snapping jaws in the pet shop still haunted Frank, but he told himself he and the lizard were friends now. He'd fed Newt. Frank made friends with his birds through food. So maybe that was the way to an iguana's heart too.

Frank quickly went inside, making sure the door was securely closed behind him to prevent iguana escape before he turned to look for Newt. And Newt was right there, standing in the archway between the living room and the kitchen. Frank wondered if it was possible for the lizard to grow from the previous night to now; he sure looked bigger. Then Newt straightened every part of his body – his legs, his spikes on his neck, back, and tail – and the bobbly wobbly thing under his chin grew round. Audrey said that was his dewlap. Frank flinched. He knew this was a defensive pose. Maybe Newt wasn't going to like him if Audrey wasn't around.

"Hey, buddy," he said, his voice a tenor croon. "Are you ready for dinner?" He bent and placed his hand on the floor, offering his arm as a bridge. Frank knew from Audrey that this was an invitation to Newt, and one of his favorites.

Newt hesitated, then lowered himself bow-legged again. He walked over and moved up Frank's arm, stopping on his shoulder. Frank wondered if his ear was safe. Then he shoved the thought out of his head. He knew that all the programs on Animal Planet said that an animal could sense fear. He wasn't going to let Newt sense that. He was going to get him to sense friendship. Camaraderie.

"Oh, there you go," he said. "Let's go make you some dinner. I bet you're hungry."

In the kitchen, Frank found everything just where Audrey said she would leave it. Newt remained steadily on his shoulder as Frank made up a salad of crunchy vegetables and some pellets of iguana food, Bob's gourmet blend, making sure to sprinkle everything liberally with water. Audrey told Frank that it was important to make sure that Newt kept himself hydrated, and so his meals were always served wet. Audrey shuddered when she said that the most common cause of death for homebound iguanas was dehydration.

Newt wasn't going to go dry on Frank's watch.

He bridged Newt to his special placemat on the kitchen table. Then he sat down beside him and watched Newt eat. He used the same chair as yesterday, thinking it would be best if he didn't take Audrey's spot. That might confuse Newt, and Frank didn't want a confused iguana. He noted that Newt, despite his dinosaurish appearance, was a dainty eater, each piece chewed separately and carefully. Frank told him about his day as the iguana ate. He told him about his birds, including names and descriptions. He snapped a photo of Newt in mid-chew, and he texted it to Audrey. Audrey replied back with a thumb's up and a heart. Frank smiled and showed her response to Newt, who seemed to study it for a moment before resuming his meal. Frank said, "I really like your mom, Newt."

Newt stared at him, his eyes steady.

"Mom? Is that right? Do you call Audrey Mom?" Frank called himself his birds' dad. "Anyway, I like her a lot, Newt."

Frank hoped again that the way to an iguana's heart was through his stomach because he already knew that the way to Audrey's heart was through her iguana.

When Newt was done, Frank lowered him to the floor, then he thoroughly cleaned out the dish. After carefully folding the dishtowel and hanging it in its spot, Frank turned and found that Newt was still in the kitchen. "I bet you'd like some company, wouldn't you, Newt."

"You can't use him for justification," Frank heard. Susan was suddenly seated at the kitchen table. She eyed the iguana. "My gosh, he's ugly."

Frank bent quickly and offered his arm to Newt. Newt ran up and settled back on Frank's shoulder. "You forgot to knock again," Frank said to Susan. "And he's not ugly. This is how an iguana is supposed to look." He wondered if Newt could see Susan. Newt's head was turned to the table, but his eyes weren't steady. He seemed to be looking everywhere. "Can you see her, Newt?" His birds seemed to notice when Susan was around.

Susan shrugged and stood. "I doubt it. Audrey didn't see me the other day. I think I can only be seen by people I know."

Frank noticed she didn't respond to his prod about knocking first. He patted Newt's back. "Are there animals in Heaven, Susan?"

"Not in my portion of it."

Frank supposed that made sense. If you weren't an animal lover, spending eternity in Heaven with them wouldn't seem so heavenly. He hoped his portion of Heaven would have animals. Birds, especially. He wondered if animal-lovers could cross over to the non-lover side to visit with friends and family who didn't care for pets. "I'll stay for a little bit, Newt," he said.

"Oh, come on, let's get on with it. You know what you're here for. I don't condone it, but I'll help you." Susan headed down the hallway, followed quickly by Frank and Newt. Frank glanced in at a room lined with bookshelves before he turned into the bedroom.

"Her bedroom?" he asked. He looked around, uncomfortable. He'd been planning on just poking around her kitchen, her living room. Maybe the room with the books. He figured the books on the shelves would tell him a lot about the woman who bought them.

Susan shook her head. "No, Frank," she said. "Whatever you want to know about a woman, you can find out in her bedroom, and possibly in her bathroom too." She pulled open a dresser drawer and held up a bra, scattered and sprinkled with colors. "Nice bra. Victoria's Secret. She shops well."

Frank thought the bra was nice too. Theresa was a utilitarian underwear woman. Everything was white so that it always matched. Susan liked colors, but solids, and nothing too outlandish. Black. Navy blue. A nice teal, maybe, a gentle lilac. She also liked to match.

But these color swirls...Frank liked them. He wondered if, like his two wives, Audrey's above matched her below. She'd be covered with swirls and sprinkles. Like a cupcake.

Susan rummaged around a little more but didn't bring out anything else. Both she and Frank glanced around the room and noticed the book on the bedside table at the same time. They made a beeline to it.

"*My Life On The Road,*" Frank said.

"Gloria Steinem," Susan said. She looked at Frank. "Are you sure Audrey likes men?"

Frank was startled. He hadn't really considered anything else. He thought of Audrey's job in the department store, selling women's clothes. He thought of the way she dressed and the purple zebra-striped luggage. He thought of the color-confetti bra. "I'm pretty sure…" he said.

"Has she ever been married?"

"I don't think so. She's never mentioned a husband. She's always said she's on her own."

Susan rolled her eyes and sat on the bed. "Oh, no, Frank," she said. "Have you gone and picked yourself a lesbian?"

Frank patted Newt. "She has Newt. Would a lesbian own an iguana?" He stopped. *Would* a lesbian own an iguana? He thought of how Audrey said she didn't want to own a cat. He tried again. "If Audrey is lesbian, wouldn't Newt at least be female?" That sounded ludicrous as soon as he said it, so he expected Susan's laugh. But it didn't come.

"I don't know," she said slowly. "Most of the lesbians I ever knew were strictly female about everything. Artwork with women. Books about women. Dogs and cats that were girls."

Frank looked around. The artwork on Audrey's walls didn't show women. There were landscapes, and one, a really interesting one, was a painting split over the four panes of an antique window. Frank wondered if Audrey did it herself or if she bought it somewhere, maybe at an art show or a flea market. He hoped she liked flea markets; he loved puttering around those on a summer weekend. He'd only discovered flea markets since Susan's death; she only appreciated the modern. And Strike One was too nit-picky about germs to go to a place that had things previously owned by others. But he liked scrounging and imagining the life an object had before he held it in his hands.

Now he turned back to Susan and saw a stuffed cow propped against the pillows on Audrey's bed. "Look," he said. "She has a stuffed animal on her bed. A cow. Would a lesbian have a stuffed cow on her bed?"

They studied the cow. Then Frank sat on the bed. "This is ridiculous," he said. "This is awful. What are we thinking? We're not thinking. We're being stupid. Of course, lesbians can own iguanas. They can have stuffed cows. And straight women can read Gloria Steinem." He patted the cow on the head, then patted Newt too.

Susan looked at him and then she laughed. "You're right. It's really easy to slip into that mindset, isn't it? Too easy." She picked up Gloria Steinem, flipped her over, seemed to read the back of the book. "It actually looks interesting," she said, and Frank took that as a surrender, a giving up of the idea that Audrey was gay. Susan put the book back down.

Frank started to leave, intending to stick with his original idea of reading the titles of the books on her bookshelves when he saw Audrey's laptop on her desk. Her laptop – the modern person's receptacle of all things personal and private. It was like finding his sister's diary when he was only twelve years old, and his sister was fifteen. And he quickly found that the laptop would be even easier to break into than the flimsy lock and key that his sister claimed was foolproof. When Frank lifted the laptop lid, the screen came to life. Audrey hadn't signed off.

He sat down in the chair and Newt walked down toward his elbow. Frank bridged him to the desk's surface. When Frank started directing the mouse, Newt put his clawed front foot on the back of Frank's hand.

Was Newt trying to stop him? Encourage him? Just have a comfy connection?

Susan came to stand behind him. "Maybe there is a better way than a bedroom or a bathroom," she said. "I didn't like these things when I was living. I always felt like someone was watching me from the other side of the screen."

Given today's technological advances, Frank figured that particular paranoia likely wasn't too far from the truth. He felt uncertain. This was far worse than looking in Audrey's underwear drawer. He fought the temptation to look in her email or any of her files, and he tried to find a happy medium. Something that would allow him to get to know Audrey, but would still not have the taint of invading where he wasn't supposed to be. Slowly, he moved the cursor to the drop-down menu that would tell him what sites Audrey visited recently.

Google.

Amazon.

Facebook.

Fish In The Sea.

"What's that?" he asked Newt as much as Susan. He hadn't thought of Audrey as an outdoor person, someone who would go fishing or camping. He clicked on it.

A dating site exploded on the screen, bright and busy enough to make him blink. Complete with neon colors and smiling faces and hearts, along with bubble-blowing fish making googly eyes at each other.

"Oh," Susan said. "Is that what I think it is?"

Frank nodded.

"Well, there's your answer, then, Frank. See what type of person she's looking for. And Frank, this could be a good thing! It means she's looking for someone!"

But why, Frank thought, look for someone when I'm right next door? Clearing out your driveway? And now feeding your iguana.

Though he supposed it might mean that she wasn't looking at Bob either. That could be a good thing too. It was hard to compete against a guy who owned a shop full of adorable animals.

He found the spot for signing in to an account. Luckily, Audrey was the type that said "yes" when the computer asked if it should remember sign-in names and passwords. Frank bet most everyone over fifty loved that little perk. He did. When he was in her account, he clicked on "My Preferences".

Susan placed her featherweight hands on either of his shoulders and leaned forward, her face like a breath next to his. Newt kept his foot firmly on Frank's hand. Frank scrolled through the questions, looking at each box that Audrey clicked.

Frank fit in Audrey's age preference. He was the right height, he was the right build, he had an educated background. He liked animals. Audrey didn't seem to care about eye color or hair color or even if there was hair. She didn't seem to care if the man was single, divorced or widowed, which was good since Frank supposed he was all three.

Frank sat back. This was good news. But…he clicked on Matches. Audrey had already put her profile out there. She already had responses.

238 men.

Apparently, Audrey was popular.

Frank stared at the impossible number. He was never popular. He wasn't good at sports. In high school and college, he went out with the studying girls, the good-grade girls. And pitiful few of those. He wondered if Audrey was a cheerleader.

She had a stuffed cow on her bed. That was a cheerleader sort of thing, he figured. More so than a lesbian thing. He remembered giggling girls walking through county fairs and state fairs, clutching outrageous stuffed animals. Their arms were always linked with the athletic guys who won them by swishing basketballs into hoops, knocking down pyramids of bottles with a baseball, shooting a water pistol into a target. Frank never won a stuffed animal in his life, not for himself, and certainly not for a girl.

238 men.

"Susan," Frank said. "How will I ever stand out among all of these guys?"

Susan wrapped her arms around Frank, pressing her breezy cheek to his. She felt just short of warm. He closed his eyes and remembered the way she would hug him like this at his desk. At the kitchen table. Kneeling behind him on the bed. "Frank," she said, "those 238 men are in there." She pointed at the screen. "You're here. Right next door. And you've made friends with her iguana."

Newt turned to look at him then. His face molded into that impossible iguana smile.

Frank felt warmth from this creature that he considered cold-blooded. From his wife, who was dead. No-blooded.

He thought he felt Susan's lips against his temple, a favorite spot of hers. "I'm going now, Frank. I'll talk to you later." And she disappeared.

She remembered, he thought. She remembered to give me a goodbye.

Then her voice drifted back. "Ask Audrey out."

After returning the computer to its original condition, Frank carried Newt back to the living room. He turned lights on, made sure the heating rocks were working, set the television to Animal Planet, then checked his watch. An hour and a half had gone by. Audrey asked him, if he had time, to return to the house around eight o'clock if she wasn't home yet, to give Newt a snack. She said she would leave him a strawberry, just for this purpose. Iguanas, she said, could only have fruit now and then, so she saved them for special treats. The strawberry tonight was because she wasn't going to be home at the usual time. Frank glanced at his watch again. It was already almost eight o'clock, so he might as well stay and have a snack with Newt now. He bridged Newt to the couch, his favorite place for watching television in the evenings, Audrey told him and went into the kitchen in search of the strawberry.

Audrey said that iguanas ate better when things were chopped, so Frank took a knife and chopped the berry into little chunks. Then he scrounged and found a couple cookies for himself. There was still coffee in the coffeepot, so he poured himself some of that too, heating it in the microwave. When he returned to the couch, Newt was still there, apparently mesmerized by a show about a woman who whispered to dogs.

Frank was drawn in too, and he sat on the couch for a time with Newt. He ate a cookie, and the iguana ate his strawberry. Frank split the final cookie with Newt, three-quarters to a quarter. Then he patted the lizard on the head and told him he'd see him later. He carried him to his tree and settled him on a branch. "Audrey will be home soon, Newt," he said. "Don't worry." He told himself he'd watch for Audrey's car, and if it was more than an hour later, he would come back to check on Newt.

But it wasn't the iguana Frank was checking on. He knew that. By Newt's smile, Frank figured he knew it too.

•   •   •   •   •

But Audrey's car arrived home within the hour. Her headlights passed from left to right through Frank's picture window, highlighting each of his birds and setting them fluttering. He couldn't see Audrey pull into her garage, but he stood anyway and studied the red glow of her taillights on the driveway until they disappeared. Then he sat down again and continued watching television. He sighed as he did so. Even though it was late and almost their bedtime, he let the birds out of their cage. Aristotle went to his usual place on top of the cage, and the other five sat with him on the couch, Butch on one side, the remaining four on the other. The birds were quiet, seeming to sense his melancholy and need for silence, and his need for company, despite the silence. Butch moved onto his knee. Frank patted each bobbing head, saving Aristotle's pat just before he whistled them all back into the cage. After he covered them for the night, he stood and looked out his window. He could see a portion of Audrey's front yard, and there didn't appear to be any lights reflected on the snow. She must be asleep. He sighed again, patted the cage, and went on to bed.

He spent a longer time than usual, staring at the ceiling. He wondered what it would be like to have Strike Two beside him. Would she provide any warmth to the sheets at all?

At least there'd be a presence. A presence that loved him as much as he loved her. There'd be a Someone.

The next day, it was just after noon when his doorbell rang. Lately, it was Strike One dropping in for surprise visits, so that was who Frank expected when he opened the door. But Audrey stood there without her coat on, even though the temperatures were still in the twenties.

"Audrey!" he said. "How're you? Come on in!"

She shook her head. "No, I have to get back to Newt, Frank. But I have to ask you...was he acting weird at all last night?"

"Weird? No. Why?" He stepped out beside her and shut the door. "Sorry. I can't leave the door open, the cold breeze will make the birds sick."

The iguana owner seemed to understand. "Of course. But Newt is just acting kind of funny. Lethargic. He didn't eat much breakfast this morning. He's been visiting his bathroom a lot."

A red flag raised for Frank. Had he done something to make the iguana ill? He hadn't hurt him in any way, he didn't drop Newt or step on him. "He seemed fine last night. Ate his dinner and everything. I stayed and talked with him for a while, kept him company. He seemed happy. I gave him the strawberry before I left, your special treat since you weren't there." Audrey glanced toward her house, and Frank saw the worried frown between her eyebrows. "Let's go see him," he said impulsively. He knew that if one of his birds were sick, he'd want company and a second opinion.

There was still snow; the thaw ended as unhappily expected and dropped another half a foot of white. They walked down his sidewalk and then up Audrey's driveway. Frank could see Newt sitting in his tree in the picture window. His belly was flat on the branch, his four legs dangling below it. His spikes seemed to be drooping, and Frank verified that when he stepped into Audrey's house.

"Hey, buddy," he said, and Newt rolled his eyes to look at him. The iguana did not look happy. The smile from last night definitely wasn't there now.

Audrey and Frank stood by the tree. Frank patted Newt's head and thought how he was no longer scared to do so. "Did you put water on his food?" Audrey asked.

Frank nodded. "I did. I even drenched the strawberry before I gave it to him." Then he remembered the cookie. "I did give him a bite of a cookie. I didn't put water on that. It was just a piece."

Audrey swung toward him. Her movement was fast enough that Newt's spikes came up. "A cookie? Frank, iguanas, aren't supposed to have stuff like that!"

"They aren't?" Frank immediately felt guilty. He hadn't even stopped to think about giving the iguana a cookie. It was like Newt was a puppy – he offered him a bite of table food.

Audrey was stroking Newt head to tail. "Does your stomach hurt, Newt?" she asked. The iguana half-closed his eyes. "Let's check this out," she said to Frank.

Frank followed Audrey down the hall into her reading room. He was relieved her voice didn't sound accusatory, and she didn't seem ready to chuck him out forever into the snow. He tried to quickly take in the titles of the books that he didn't get a chance to discover last night, the books he intended to explore before he got pulled in by the allure of Audrey's bedroom and her computer. There were some nice novels here, titles he recognized – *Catcher In The Rye, To Kill A Mockingbird* – and more modern novels too. There were a couple shelves scattered with what appeared to be self-help books, and they seemed to center on relationships. He only saw one he was familiar with – *Men Are From Mars, Women Are From Venus.* Susan read that one and Frank agreed with the title. The books weren't standing, but laying at various angles. A couple were open and spread face down. Frank wondered if Audrey read all of any of them.

Audrey went straight to a certain shelf and pulled out a book that was resting on its side...the same book that Frank had. Green iguana care. He bet she bought it from Bob. Quickly, she looked through it. "It says that nothing in the cookie is poisonous, but that it can cause stomachaches in iguanas. It suggests a warm bath." She shut the book firmly. "Looks like it's time for Newt's first bath."

Frank was relieved to see Audrey smile. "I'm so sorry, Audrey. I didn't know."

She patted his arm as she went by. "It's okay. He's going to be fine. You're right, you didn't know. I should have told you what not to feed him, instead of just what to feed him. Newt!" she called. "Want a bath?" They went to the kitchen and Audrey ran the faucet, holding her finger under the stream to gauge the temperature. She had a big farm-style sink that Frank admired the night before; she must have replaced the standard aluminum double-sink most houses of this era came with. Like the one in his own kitchen. She placed a rubber mat on the sink's floor. "Want to help?" she asked him.

"Sure!" Frank was delighted. While Audrey prepared the sink, he went back to the tree in the living room. After Frank placed his hand on the branch, Newt was very willing to climb up his arm and settle in his spot on Frank's shoulder. To Frank's surprise, Newt's tail came up and draped around his neck. It was like an embrace.

Frank wondered how many people in this world found their hearts melting for an iguana. Especially for one that you might have hurt by giving him a cookie.

"Audrey!" he said as he came back into the kitchen. "Is Newt hugging me?"

Audrey glanced over and then beamed. "He is! I've never seen him do that with anyone but me!" Then she laughed. "Though it's not like I've seen him with a lot of people. Just Bob, and I've never seen him do that with Bob. That's great, Frank. He seems to like you now. Of course, you gave him contraband." She shook her finger at him, and then placed a towel at the ready on the counter next to the sink. "All right, Newt, we're all set." She flattened her hand against the front of Frank's shoulder.

Her palm was warm. Frank knew the touch wasn't for him. But it thrilled him anyway.

The iguana stepped from Frank to Audrey's arm and then up to her shoulder. She guided him down to the counter, then picked him up, wrapping both of her hands securely around his...armpits? Frank wondered if the area behind and beneath Newt's shoulders would be called armpits. Did iguanas have arms? Maybe these would be called *legpits*. "Okay," she said. "I've never given him a bath before. You stand by, Frank, in case he wiggles out of my grasp."

Frank stood close, wishing he had a catcher's mitt or a butterfly net. "I'm going to use the towel, just in case," he said. "I'll put it back when you're ready." He took the towel and then held it between his hands like a hammock.

"Good thought." Audrey slowly lowered Newt into the warm water.

Newt sighed, relaxed...and pooped.

"Oh, great," Audrey said. "Put the towel back, Frank." After he did, she put Newt on the towel, wrapped him up, and handed him over like a newly swaddled lizardy baby. She quickly cleaned the sink, then washed her hands briskly in warm, soapy water. "I was reading in that iguana book that the one thing you have to be careful of as a human with an iguana is washing your hands if you come in contact with their feces. It contains salmonella."

Frank didn't know this. Newt looked mortified.

When the sink was ready again, they returned Newt to the water. This time Frank was the one to lower him in. Newt sighed again, closed his eyes, and relaxed.

"Maybe that was just what he needed," Frank said. "To...evacuate."

Audrey smiled, Frank figured at his choice of words, but he wasn't sure what word to use around a woman. Especially around this woman. He would have said poop around Theresa, who was delicate about these things. Defecate around Susan, who liked scientific terminology. He'd say shit around his guy friends. But Audrey? He just didn't know. She said feces, and he thought evacuate seemed to go with that. He wanted to be polite, to make sure he didn't offend. "That's possible, I suppose," she said. "Can you watch him a minute while I go get the book?"

"Sure." Frank pondered this when Audrey left the room. Not only did she let him take care of Newt while she was gone, but now she was leaving him with Newt in a potentially dangerous situation…in the sink. It seemed she trusted him. Even though he was the one who gave the iguana a cookie and caused Newt's distress.

There was a whisper in his right ear. "You're doing great, Frank! Ask her out!"

He glanced quickly over his shoulder, but Susan was nowhere to be seen. He knew she was a ghost, but invisibility was creepy. "Go away!" he whispered back. "I'll talk to you later!" He wondered, if things went well with Audrey and if one day, they were, well, intimate, if Susan would –

"Ew!" she whispered. Frank heard a whisk, and he assumed that was his cue that she was gone.

Newt was staring at him.

"It's okay, buddy," he said and stroked the iguana between his googly eyes.

And then he had to stop. He was standing at a farm sink filled with an iguana. An iguana he talked to as if the iguana was a person. He was giving this iguana a bath in a woman's house. He just talked to his dead wife and sent her away, and any minute now, his phone could bing with an incoming text from his first wife, who he swore he never wanted to see again. For a moment, Frank had to look out the window, getting his bearings, trying to ground himself. His life was becoming weird. But the world outside looked normal and when he looked down at the iguana looking back up at him, an iguana who seemed to smile, Frank decided that maybe he was just heading into a new kind of normal. It didn't feel like a bad thing.

Audrey came back, the iguana book opens in her hands. "So I'm not supposed to use any soap on him. Just water. And look, it says that water is a cue for an iguana to poop! How weird is that!" She set the book on the table. "So maybe that was his issue. I didn't find anything in his litter pan, even though he was there a lot this morning. Maybe the cookie made him stuck, and the water helped relax and get him unstuck."

Audrey and Frank stood side by side and watched the lizard, who almost seemed to be going to sleep. His breathing was nice and even, Frank noticed. He knew that increased respiration was a sign of distress in his parakeets. If it was in an iguana too, there was no distress here.

"Well," Audrey said a few minutes later, "we should probably get him out. We don't want him to get chilled."

Frank stood back, and Audrey took over, placing Newt on the towel and gently patting him dry. Newt's eyes opened wide and settled brightly on Frank. Frank thought he looked much better than at the start of this visit. "Good job, buddy," he said. "You'll never talk me into giving you a cookie again."

Audrey laughed and put Newt on the floor. "Go get a drink, Newt," she said, and the lizard obligingly trotted off. "Frank," she said, turning back to him, "speaking of a cookie, would you like a cup of coffee? And a cookie? Thank you so much for helping me with this."

"Oh," he said and blushed. "It was the least I could do. I mean, I'm the one who caused the trouble. And I'd love a cup of coffee and a cookie."

Frank sat down at the kitchen table and watched Audrey putter, putting the snack together. He thought of the other afternoon with Theresa, with the coffee and doughnuts, the neat way he put the mugs and sugar and creamer on the table, the doughnuts on a matching platter, because he knew that was what she would like. It wasn't what he liked. Audrey heated the coffee in the microwave; she didn't make a fresh pot. The mugs didn't match. She tossed the cookies in their package on the table. And she placed a paper towel in front of him and one in front of her chair. She hummed quietly as she worked.

She was casual. Frank liked that. And he liked the sound of her voice. Neither Theresa nor Susan were hummers. He wondered if Audrey sang. Frank liked to sing, and he did so often, in the shower, in the car, with his birds, and whenever he was working at a chore.

Frank was sorry he gave Newt the cookie. He really was. He would never do anything to hurt the iguana or any living little creature. But he was so happy a misplaced cookie brought him to this moment, in this kitchen, with Audrey. Newt was fine. And so was he.

"What are you smiling at, Frank?" Audrey asked.

Newt came back into the kitchen, and Frank saw his chin was dripping.

He'd actually gone to get a drink when Audrey told him to. Frank put his hand to the floor and Newt walked up to his shoulder. His green tail came to rest again around the base of Frank's neck. "This," Frank said, one finger stroking Newt's nose. "I'm just so glad he's okay."

And he was happy as well to get a chance to know Audrey, in a way that didn't involve breaking into her computer or peeking into her underwear drawer. Though, in his deepest thoughts, in the shadows thrown by the back of his mind, he supposed that drawer was in his sights. Maybe he would have looked in it, after reading Audrey's book titles, if Susan hadn't gotten there first. Maybe he would have looked in her bathroom, in her medicine cabinet, that tell-all of the human condition. Maybe.

He wondered again if Audrey matched in sparkles and specks, above and below.

He hoped so.

Chapter Thirteen

Ken Kesey, who's to say that lizards don't pray to the sun?

Audrey closed the door behind Frank later that afternoon, the both of them full of a couple cups of coffee and most of the package of fig newtons. She leaned against the door and looked at Newt, asleep in his heated hammock, swaying gently above his patio pavers in the iguana corner of the living room. Newt looked fully relaxed, and Audrey tried to relax too. She tried not to think about how it could have easily turned into a disaster.

What if Frank had given Newt a whole cookie? Or something else the iguana couldn't stomach?

It wouldn't have been Frank's fault. She thought of the careful way he held Newt, rubbing the crease between Newt's eyes, how he called the iguana buddy, how Newt tucked his tail around the back of Frank's neck.

The fault was hers. She was responsible for Newt. She was responsible to him for his lifetime.

"It's okay," she said aloud into the quiet room. "He's fine."

But it was what almost happened that scared her. It was the *could have*. The *might have*.

"But it didn't," she said. She tried to hear herself. With one more look at the napping Newt, she went to her bedroom. Before Audrey became worried about Newt and his tummy, she'd noticed something else amiss in her house. But Newt's distress was distressing for Audrey, and so she set all other concerns aside until after it was clear he was going to be okay. Now, she sat down on the bed, by the other thing that wasn't quite right when she came home last night.

Gloria. Gloria was face-down on her bedside table. Audrey was sure she left the book face-up. She liked having Gloria's face to speak to. The first thing she did when she returned after the Fifty Shades fiasco was come into the bedroom to look at Gloria and say, "What *was* that?" But now, Gloria was face-down.

Audrey wondered if Frank poked around her house. He stayed longer than just the time required to feed Newt, Audrey knew that. Frank told her so. He kept Newt company. He gave him the special strawberry treat and a bite of contraband cookie. But did he and Newt take a tour of the house?

Audrey glanced around, then walked through the guest bedroom, her reading room, the bathroom. She knew nothing was out of place in the living room, and kitchen and everything seemed okay in these rooms too.

It was possible, she figured, that she simply put the book down incorrectly when she went to sleep the night before meeting Clara. She was excited and distracted by the trip to the mall the next day, getting to see someone, a special someone, after a 34-year absence, and having to leave Newt behind. Trusting his care to a neighbor she barely knew, but who seemed really nice. Turning a book upside down was inconsequential, a momentary lapse, and something she could have done without thinking about it.

But she always said goodnight to Gloria after reading for a bit. She was pretty sure she remembered saying goodnight to Gloria on that night too.

Audrey stood at the head of the hallway, her living room opening in front of her, her kitchen to the left, everything else behind her. It all seemed fine. And what was the harm, really, if Frank wandered through? Would she have done the same if she was watching his parakeets?

Audrey smiled. Of course, she would have. It was what you did. Snooping in such situations was almost a requirement. It was human nature.

Settling on her couch, Audrey decided to join Newt in a Sunday afternoon nap. Despite the iguana's momentary illness, it was a good weekend. She'd reconnected with Clara, and it turned out well. Despite the husband and kids, Clara was still Clara and, to Audrey's surprise, she was still Audrey. Together, their fit remained solid, in a postmenopausal older adult way. Audrey pictured them each riding a bicycle, a fish in a basket hanging from the handlebars. She watched as their waists thickened, their hairstyles changed, they pedaled slower, and the bikes became those three-wheelers, those large tricycles for adults. She laughed out loud. She so enjoyed her visit with Clara yesterday. It was different than when she had lunch with Annabel and Vicki, when she went with them to the movies when she spoke with each on their own. She and Clara shared history, and while Audrey was often astonished by Annabel and Vicki, she was comforted by Clara. While they'd lived different and separate lives for three and a half decades now, their experiences were still similar, their thoughts and feelings running parallel.

It was, she realized, a relief to find that she wasn't an oddity.

This afternoon, she enjoyed Frank's company. Newt enjoyed Frank too. It was nice to have someone to talk to, within the familiar walls of her kitchen.

Audrey glanced once more at Newt, sprawled in his hammock. He slept as soundly as he did every Sunday afternoon. She was willing to bet that Frank too, despite the coffee, was stretched out on his sofa, the television on, his birds in their cage with their heads tucked under their wings, and Frank would be sleeping. Clara too, down in Illinois. Maybe she was on the recliner, her husband on the couch, while the kids were out doing what adult kids did. Napping was what you did on a Sunday afternoon after you reached a certain age. She bet even Gloria was Sunday-napping. Audrey, enjoying the company, joined them all.

· · · · ·

Near the end of February, the snow disappeared again, and the temperatures soared into the fifties. The second winter thaw in Wisconsin was a tricky thing. Even life-long Wisconsin residents fell prey to the early April Fool of a second barrage of a decoy spring in the middle of winter. The first was a fake, everyone reasoned, the second must be sincere. Even though there was bound to be more snow. There was bound to be more cold. But everyone, whether life-long Wisconsinite or recent transplant, heralded the second serious thaw as spring. Maybe.

These peekaboo days always enthralled Audrey. It was easy to understand why spring was the season of rebirth as the air warmed and windows were opened in her house and in her car and as winter-barren streets suddenly became populated with walkers and the muddy yards with kids kicking and throwing balls. Wearing lighter jackets, or exposing only long sleeves, or on particularly bold days, venturing out in short sleeves, all seemed to Audrey to signal a stepping away from the dark and the cold. She supposed if spring was a rebirth, then the second thaw was a premature birth. Or possibly false labor. Yes, she decided, false labor. A dry run for warmer weather before you settled back into the inevitability of the rest of winter.

When you worked in a department store, particularly in the women's section, the seasons passed in sleeve lengths and the thickness of material, hanging from racks on the department floor. Newt's world was in Audrey's house and in Bob's pet store, and Audrey wanted Newt to experience the season change too, in a way that a domestic iguana would understand.

So after dinner on one of these flukey warm nights, with temps flirting with sixty-three degrees, she pulled on a light jacket and then tugged Newt into his bomber jacket. He was always patient now when she dressed him, lifting first one front foot, then the other. The jacket had a hook midway down the back, and Audrey affixed a slender leash to it, though she felt guilty as she did so. Tethering someone wasn't a sign of a good relationship. She thought back to the Fifty Shades double-feature she abandoned, and she shuddered. That movie's budget for leather and chains must have exceeded what they paid the actors. But in this case, the leash was for Newt's own well-being. He was growing longer and heavier and becoming faster and faster. If he startled in the new outside, charged off her shoulder and began to run, she could lose him in a heartbeat.

So really, she considered, the leash was also for her well-being. She couldn't stand to lose Newt.

She knew Newt had to be surprised when she offered her hand and arm for him to climb up. Usually, his jacket meant going into his carrier, and then the carrier into the warmed-up car. His jacket meant a trip to the pet store, to get a treat from Bob and probably a new toy from Audrey. But not today. Today was pre-born spring, at least for the moment. "It'll be okay," she said to the iguana as he climbed stiffly up onto her shoulder. The jacket kept his movements from being their usual iguana-fluid. "You're going to really like this, Newt. You'll get some fresh air, and the sun is out, and you'll see trees and grass and flowers." She patted his head. "Well, maybe not flowers. If it's still warm enough when we get back from our walk, I'll let you down into the grass in the front yard. You'll feel grass for the first time!" Audrey wondered what it was like to not know what grass was.

When they stepped outside, and the door closed behind them, Audrey felt Newt hunch down on her shoulder. His face swung in, and he plastered his cheek to hers, and she felt the movements of his eyeball as he tried to take everything in. For him, the world he viewed through the window suddenly went from framed to everywhere. There was air that wasn't from a furnace, there was direct sunlight. She imagined it must be like seeing a painting come suddenly to life. She crossed his leash over her body and held it with her right hand, while her left curved up and rested gently on his back. When partners had challenging moments, she knew, you were supposed to offer comfort and support. Under her hand, she felt Newt relax, and he moved away from her face so he could turn his own head and look around.

Audrey strolled down the sidewalk, trying to move smoothly so as not to startle Newt. As she passed Frank's house, she glanced at his bay window. She could see the birdcage and the blur of the parakeets fluttering around inside. Six of them, she remembered, though she couldn't recall the names. Aristotle, for sure. Butch. But not the rest. She was sure they were happy for the pretend spring too, and she wondered if Frank ever took the cage outside. She supposed you couldn't leash a parakeet, let alone six of them.

Audrey talked quietly to Newt as they continued around the block. She pointed out the grass, which was still winter yellow as it stretched toward the sun after being squashed by snow for months. She told Newt that the grass would soon be as green as he was and he looked appropriately surprised. The sun was just starting its descent and hadn't begun spreading colors, but it sparkled yellow and white in the blue sky. "I know it sounds weird, Newt," she said, "but I think the blue sky looks different in each of the seasons. This blue...this blue is like a robin's egg. Isn't it pretty?"

Newt didn't seem to think it was weird at all. He bobbed his head. His breathing was steady under her hand, so she knew he wasn't scared. He seemed to be enjoying himself.

They were on the third leg of the four-street block when a couple kids came running up. Audrey felt bumps appear under Newt's jacket. She knew his spikes were trying to come up.

"Wow, lady," one of the kids said. "Is that a lizard on your shoulder? Is it real?"

"He's scary," the girl said, stepping behind the boy, and Audrey assumed they were brother and sister.

"He's an iguana," Audrey said, and she stopped walking and angled her shoulder forward so they could see Newt better. "A green iguana. He's a little over a year old."

"Can I pet him?" The boy reached a hand up, and Newt shrunk back. His tail came up and circled Audrey's neck.

She pressed her hand down more firmly and took a tighter grip on the leash. She thought of the way Newt nearly bit Frank. The sound of those teeth as they clashed together. "Probably not," she said. "Sometimes iguanas get scared of strangers, and they bite. Maybe after you get to know him better."

The boy quickly pulled his hand back.

There was a slam of a door, and a woman came walking quickly across the golden lawn, her sneakers squelching with every step. She put a hand on each of the kids' shoulders when she joined them. "What's going on?" she asked.

"This lady has an iguana!" the boy said.

Audrey smiled. "Hi, I'm Audrey. I live just around the corner. It was nice out tonight, so I thought I'd bring my iguana out for a stroll." She was struck with how odd that sounded. But that was what she was doing. It was no different, really, than if Newt was a dog. Though she knew that Newt was much more than a dog. "He's never been outside before."

The leash felt so wrong.

"Does he bite?" the woman asked. She must have been putting pressure on the kids' shoulders; they each took a step back.

Audrey started to shrug but stopped when she felt her shoulder rise under Newt. "He never has," she answered truthfully. Newt attempted to bite, but he didn't succeed. And it was only Frank. Audrey didn't want to create fear and concern where there didn't need to be any.

"Well, you have to be careful around kids," the woman said. "Kids don't know any better. Iguanas are wild creatures," she said directly to the boy. "They shouldn't be kept as pets."

"That's not true!" Audrey's voice went up, and Newt rose straight-legged, pushing strongly against Audrey's fingers. "Newt wasn't born in the wild. He was born at a breeder's. He's domestic. He's never even been on grass, let alone out in the wild."

The woman rolled her eyes. "That's no better, really," she said. "He should have been born in an iguana climate, in an iguana-friendly place. He's not intended to be a pet. It's like someone trying to keep a tiger or a raccoon or something. A wild animal." She patted her kids' backs. "Go on inside, guys. It's about time for baths."

The kids protested but ran off, and Audrey started to move away. She didn't really know how to respond to this woman. She would have to talk to Bob about how to deal with Newt and the public, or maybe she would just keep Newt in her own yard. The back yard, maybe. No one would bother her or Newt there.

But the woman had one more thing to say. "Don't those things carry AIDS?"

Audrey flushed hot. "No, they don't. That's ridiculous." She started to say that iguanas carried salmonella, but then she thought better of that. It wasn't something the neighborhood needed to know.

Newt turned a bit on her shoulder, and Audrey looked to see what caught his attention. Frank joined them. "Hi, Audrey," he said. "Hey, buddy," he said to Newt. He looked at the woman. "Iguanas don't carry AIDS. And all Audrey is doing is walking around the block, giving her pet some fresh air and sunshine during this great break in our long winter. It was your kids that ran up to her. She didn't approach them."

"Even so," the woman said, "please don't talk to my children when you have that thing out with you." She stalked away.

The bumps under Newt's jacket went down, and Audrey felt her own hackles release. "Whew," she said. "I wasn't expecting that. Though I suppose, to be fair, she wasn't expecting to see her kids talking to an iguana. Thanks, Frank."

"Well, of course." Frank patted Newt's head, and Newt leaned into his palm. "I saw you walk by earlier and stepped out so I could say hello when you got back. When you seemed to be taking a while, I started walking the opposite way around the block to see if you were all right. I figured it was Newt's first time outside." He tilted his head toward the house. "You're fine, but I think Ms. Whackadoodle doesn't know much about reptiles. AIDS?"

Audrey laughed and began walking. Frank fell into step. "Do you ever take your birds out, Frank?"

"On really warm days, when there's not much wind, I put their cage on the picnic table in the back yard. They seem to love that. I can't let them loose, though, because they're still able to fly. I felt like it was cruel to clip their wings." He put his hands in his pockets and looked a bit wistful. "I think they'd come back if I called them, but I just couldn't take the risk."

Audrey thought of how she felt when she put the leash on Newt's jacket. "I understand," she said, and she did. "I thought when I got back, I'd let Newt onto the grass. Let him see how it feels."

Frank smiled at the iguana. "I bet you'll like that, buddy." He looked back at Audrey. "You don't treat your grass with anything, do you?"

"Nope. Just the lawn mower." She turned onto the walkway up to her door, and Frank followed. "I read in the iguana book about letting your iguana outside. It said it was okay as long as there were no chemicals. There shouldn't be. I've never used anything, and I've lived here for years."

"Can I watch?"

Audrey sat on her front step and nodded, and Frank lowered himself beside her. "Want to step in the grass, Newt?" she asked and lowered her hand into the lawn.

The grass was a bit stiff from the winter. The soft, lush carpet-feel of green grass would have to wait until it was really spring, and then summer. Newt walked down her arm. As he set his first foot in the grass, he stopped and raised his foot right back up. Balancing on his three remaining legs, he turned into an iguana statue. His upraised toes were spread.

"Can you see his face, Frank?" Audrey asked. "What does his expression say?"

Frank laughed. "He looks a little shocked." Frank moved to a squat a few feet away. "Come on, buddy," he said. "Give it a shot." He put his hand out on the grass and Audrey realized he was offering Newt a chance to escape as he explored. How nice, she thought. And in this case, nice was a good thing. Nice was exactly what she was looking for when it came to how she wanted others to treat her iguana.

"It's all right, Newt," she said softly. "I'd never do anything to hurt you."

Newt glanced over his shoulder at her, and the movement nearly caused him to topple. He had to put his foot down quickly. Then he moved his other feet, one slowly after the other, into the grass.

Audrey supposed she was feeling more maternal right now than partner-like. She was proud of Newt for doing something new, for attempting something that made him a little bit nervous. "Good job!" she said, just as Frank echoed with his own, "You're doing it, buddy!"

They watched as the iguana moved between them. Then he stopped and lowered his face into the grass. When he came up, golden blades were sticking out of his mouth, and he was chewing.

Audrey didn't want a repeat of the stomachache, even though she read that grass was okay for iguanas to eat, so she prepared herself to swoop him up after he swallowed this one mouthful. But instead of lowering his face to the grass again, Newt walked over to Frank's hand and up onto his shoulder. Audrey had to let the leash out to its full length to accommodate the distance. She and Frank stood up together, making sure the leash didn't yank Newt back to the ground.

Audrey stepped closer and put her hand against Frank's shoulder. "Come on, Newt," she said. The sun was still out, but she shivered just a little. "Time to go in. It's not summer yet." Iguana-bodies adapted to their environment by becoming whatever temperature surrounded them, and she didn't want Newt to go cold.

"Audrey?" Frank said. Newt was stepping onto Audrey's arm, his front feet on her, his back feet still on Frank's shoulder. "Would you like to go to a movie on Friday night? Maybe dinner too?"

Newt stopped in his half and half stance. He looked right at Audrey. Audrey knew that she saw him smile before, but this looked more like a smirk. She raised her eyebrows at him.

And then she looked at Frank. What could she say, really? He stood there, with half of her iguana on his shoulder. He called Newt buddy, even though Newt once tried to bite him. He knew iguanas didn't carry AIDS, and he knew that their feces carried salmonella and he didn't care. He petted Newt in the groove between his eyes.

She was about to accept a date. With the boy next door. The outdoor temperature suddenly didn't feel so cold as she felt her face flame with the heat of hazy summer nights.

"Sure," she said, her voice so high, Newt flinched. She dropped it an octave. "That would be nice. Just text me what time you'd like to go. I want to get Newt in now before it gets too cold. Just like you, with your front door and your birds." Newt came all the way over to her shoulder, and he wrapped his tail around her neck. She smiled at Frank, and she bet her teeth looked blindingly white in the stop sign red of her face. She supposed the white was a good thing; on commercials, wide-grinning women always ended up with a man. She and Frank agreed on a time to meet and then she said goodnight and went inside her house.

As she undressed Newt, she said, "Frank? I'm going out with Frank?" And she wondered what Gloria would think about dating the boy next door. Or in this case, the old man next door. Though he wasn't that old. Just like she wasn't old. She wasn't young, like Annabel and Vicki. She wasn't young like she used to be with Clara.

But she wasn't old.

She was going on a date. She thought it was a date. Was it a date? She thought of how Frank asked, how he said a movie, and then said dinner. Dinner and a movie had to be a date. Weren't they always a date when presented together like that? It was a classic first date.

At fifty-five, and after a very long and dry spell, Audrey had a date. She hadn't had a date since the man who gave her Ooshi the cow. Ooshi, in stuffed animal years, was old.

She wondered if Frank voted for That Man In The White House.

Frank was good company, that day Newt had a stomachache. He'd been willing to watch Newt, even though Newt nearly bit him. He might have snooped around her house, but if he did, he put most everything back in its place. Frank and Newt had a good time together. Frank and Audrey had a good time together too, sharing coffee and fig newtons after bathing an iguana.

Audrey set Newt on the floor, and he scuttled over to the picture window and up into his tree. He looked outside, and Audrey wondered if he was recounting to himself what it was like to be out there. What the world felt like when it wasn't beyond a plate of glass.

Audrey was going out there too. On Friday. With Frank.

Audrey remembered again that Gloria had said that marriage was a sure way to ruin a great relationship. She also remembered her decision to dig through Google to find out if Gloria ever got married. In all the excitement of meeting Clara and then Newt seeming sick and then regular life, Audrey forgot. She wanted to check on Jane Russell and Anita Bryant too, even though they really didn't have anything to do with anything. They were just somehow all a part of this. Audrey headed down to her bedroom to do some research.

As she sat down in front of her computer, she chided herself. Marriage. Why was she researching marriage? This was a date, that's all. A first date. A classic first date with the boy next door. Dinner and a movie.

At least, she thought it was.

•

Before Audrey got to the facts and figures of Gloria's marriage status, she fell into BrainyQuote.com and pages of little boxes filled with Gloria's most memorable words. Audrey scrolled through them and found several more disparaging marriage, besides the one that said that marriage ruined relationships. Apparently, Gloria really did have a dim view of the covenant. "The surest way to be alone is to get married," Gloria said, and Audrey read.

She looked away from her computer and around. She was sitting in her bedroom, where she slept alone, unless Ooshi the cow counted until she adopted an iguana and then she shared it with him. Her bedroom was in a house that she owned by herself. When she left in the morning for work, the house was empty, except for an iguana. When she came home, the house was empty, except for an iguana. An iguana that she loved, but still, the house was empty of human companionship. When she went in for her first colonoscopy five years ago, when she turned fifty, she had to take a cab to and from the hospital because there was no one to drive her, no one intimate enough that she was willing to have sit with her as she woke and passed the dreaded colonoscopy gas.

She went through that alone, with only a nurse to check on her. In the curtained cubicle next door, she heard who she assumed to be a husband and wife, and the husband was waking from his colonoscopy. When the inevitable occurred, they both laughed and made fart jokes and Audrey, in her half-awake phase, experiencing her own stomach rumbles all by herself, marveled at the amazing connection. There was no embarrassment. Just good humor and understanding. "Just wait until it's your turn," the husband said. "I'm going to record it and play it on Facebook." The wife shrieked.

Audrey, in her own cubicle, waited by her windy self and didn't laugh at all. When the nurse said she could go, she escorted her to the waiting taxi. Audrey sat in the back seat by herself. At home, she took care of herself. And then she went back to work. She spoke about her colonoscopy, clean and clear, to no one. And she felt lucky but bereft.

Now, Audrey looked at Gloria's words on her computer screen. The surest way to be alone was to get married? Wasn't she alone as she paid her mortgage, collected her bills, farted uncontrollably in the recovery room?

She wasn't alone anymore; she knew that. She had Newt. But Newt's name wasn't on anything. And he would never be able to accompany her to anything other than the pet store and pet-related events.

So where did that put her? Gloria had a dim view of marriage. She thought that marriage ruined relationships, that if you married, you would find yourself alone. Yet alone was where Audrey was finding herself now. Even though she wasn't married and never had been. And this wasn't where she wanted to be. Being alone was never in her life plan.

If you married, you were ultimately alone. If you stayed single, you were alone. So being alone was inevitable?

Audrey fetched Gloria's book from the bedside table and then returned to the computer. She placed Gloria where she could see her and ask her questions as she scrolled through more quotes.

God may be in the details, but the goddess is in the questions. Once we begin to ask them, there's no turning back.

Audrey smiled. "Guess I must be a goddess then, Gloria," she said. She scrolled. "See, there's this man." Then she stopped and backtracked. "Well, there were these men," she said, "238 of them and..." And she backtracked further. "There's me, Gloria," she said. "See, there's just me."

And then she brought the cursor to a screeching stop.

A woman needs a man like a fish needs a bicycle.

Audrey looked from the screen to Gloria's face to the screen to the face. "*You* said that?" she said, her voice rising. "You? You said my favorite t-shirt? How did I not know that?"

She felt a tug on her pants leg and looked down to see Newt. She carefully and slowly moved her chair back, and he climbed up her pants leg to her lap, up her shirt, down her arm, and onto the desk. He looked at the screen too and put one foot on Audrey's hand.

Audrey picked up the book and set it upright so that Newt could see Gloria's face too and join in the conversation. "Gloria said the quote on my fish bicycle shirt," she said. "Can you believe that?" Then she leaned over her keyboard. "Okay, Gloria. Here's the big question. Were you ever married? Did you pedal that bicycle?"

After typing her question into Google, Audrey found, among other things, an article from People Magazine. "Feminist Ms. Steinem A Mrs.!" crowed the headline. Audrey read the article aloud to Newt and discovered that Gloria was married when she was sixty-six years old on September 3, 2000. "Listen to this," Audrey said to Newt. "Gloria said, 'I'm happy, surprised and one day will write about it, but for now, I hope this proves what feminists have always said: That feminism is about the ability to choose what's right at each time of our lives.'" Audrey sat back in her chair and looked directly at Gloria, barely smiling on her book cover. "The ability to choose what's right at each time of our lives. And you got married. After saying everything you did. You married someone that you didn't need any more than a fish needs a bicycle. Wow."

Digging further, Audrey found that the marriage was short-lived, but only because Gloria's husband died. Three years in, he was gone. And since then, Gloria was alone.

Audrey wondered why. Because of heartbreak? Or because she'd found marriage wasn't worth it? Did she find herself more alone when she was married than when she was single? Was she more alone in marriage than when she was widowed, a state that must have felt like a whole new level of aloneness, a deep-under-the-sea aloneness? Even Gloria Steinem couldn't fight death.

Audrey paged a bit through Gloria's book, moving into the parts she hadn't read yet. At least with this kind of cursory glance, she could find no mention of David Bale, Gloria's husband.

The surest way to be alone is to be married. Gloria ended up alone. So was she alone before marriage, during and after? Or did Gloria's own words, her own beliefs, change over the years she was married? Did she find comfort in such close company?

"You're not helping me here, Gloria," Audrey said. She turned toward the wall to her left, where she had an old window frame hung, There was a painting on the glass as if she was looking through it to the outside, and she could see a green hill, dotted with flowers, leading up to a blue sky and a forested horizon. If she looked harder, Audrey knew, if she had x-ray vision, she would look through the wall to the guest room, and through that one to the living room and through the outside wall of her home. The house with only her name on the deed.

To Frank's house. Which he bought on his own too. And where he was in the company of parakeets.

Audrey was here, in the company of an iguana.

Friday was two days away. And so was the date with the boy next door.

Newt patted her hand.

$\bullet \quad \bullet \quad \bullet \quad \bullet \quad \bullet$

In the morning, Audrey ate her breakfast with Newt while checking her email on her phone. Each morning, as she did so, she marveled. She remembered the era of waiting for the mailman to come, of waiting for her landline to ring, in order to have any contact with her world. Then the computer arrived and the internet, and at first, she really only used it at work, inter-department and corporate communications. But then the internet opened the world for everyone, and now, instead of spending her breakfast reading a book or watching the news on television, Audrey scrolled on her phone and learned what was going on that way.

For the most part, she thought this was a good thing. She looked at Newt. Maybe, if she'd gotten married, if she had a family, this wouldn't be seen as good. She should be spending this time in early-morning chats with her kids, checking on their schedules, their social lives, their psyches, she should be kissing her husband good morning and goodbye and sharing a meaningful glance, reflective of the night before or possibly an invitation for the night to come. Or both.

But there wasn't a husband, and there weren't children; there was just her iguana. And he didn't talk much, though she talked to him. Returning to her phone, she said, "Look, Newt, an email from Clara."

He munched and looked interested.

Opening the email, Audrey read about a resistance call to action that Clara said they should follow. Clara was very involved in the resistance movement against That Man In The White House. Ever since Audrey told her that she didn't do anything, really, to stop That Man except vote against him, Clara was determined to get her involved. "You'll feel better," she insisted. "You'll feel like you're at least doing something."

Audrey wondered if feeling like you were doing something was enough, if you didn't really feel like that "something" was going to change anything.

Clara wrote now, "This is a national effort, maybe even international, I'm not sure. We're supposed to write postcards. They should say exactly what we think about Trump. You can decorate your postcard however you like. And then we're all going to mail them on the same day so that they arrive there at approximately the same time and we'll inundate him. Millions of postcards, Audrey, can you imagine? I think we should do it. This weekend? We can Skype and do it together."

At first, Audrey rolled her eyes. Postcards? What was this really going to accomplish? That Man In The White House didn't have to read them. In fact, he likely wouldn't. Plus, he fed off of attention, both negative and positive, so he'd likely enjoy being inundated. He'd want to know the numbers without even looking at one of the postcards, or even one of the words on the postcards. He might even consider comparing the number of postcards he received with the number of postcards President Obama received during his tenure.

Audrey barked a sardonic laugh that startled Newt. Then she closed the email and focused on her Banana Nut Cheerios.

But she thought of what both Clara and Annabel said about the Women's March. How it made them feel better, and that maybe that march, that protest, was more about making the protesters feel involved, feel like they'd done something, even if it didn't really change anything at all. Which, in the end, it really didn't. At least, not in the White House.

But it did bring a huge world community together. It allowed that community to raise its voice. And…Audrey hadn't raised her own voice in a very long time.

Audrey opened the email again. As she read it through, her eyes focused on the name, Trump, the word that she could not say. Would not say. She supposed that her calling that man That Man In The White House was her own personal protest, and in the end, what did it accomplish? Nothing. But it made her feel better.

So maybe she'd try this postcard thing. Maybe. With Clara. She didn't actually have to mail it.

Breakfast over, she lowered Newt to the floor, cleaned the dishes, checked that he had everything he needed, kissed him on the top of his scaly head, and she left for work. As she pulled out of her garage, she waved at Newt, already stationed in his spot in the picture window. She marveled at how she could depend on him to be where she expected him to be.

She glanced over at Frank's house, and she saw the parakeets fluttering in his bay window. Frank wasn't standing there with them, but that didn't mean he couldn't be. Someday. Waving at her as she pulled out of her driveway. Waiting for her when she came home.

She shook her head. She was putting the cart before the horse. She was leaning out over her skis. She was being silly.

But she smiled anyway.

Thursdays were relatively busy days at work, preparing for the weekend crowd. Racks needed to be re-organized, new inventory hung and displayed. The spring line was out in full force and the clearance racks, filled with winter, were jumbled and crunched. As Audrey worked, she noticed movement and noise across the aisle. Gilbert was reorganizing too. He waved at her.

"How's it going?" he called.

Audrey moved to a rack that was next to the aisle so she wouldn't have to shout. "It's going well," she said. "How're you?"

He shrugged. "Same ol', same ol'. Get a chance to use your new suitcases yet?"

She shook her head. "No. But it's nice to know they're there. If an opportunity comes up, I only have to pull them out." She wondered idly if there was a matching carrying case for pets. An iguana-sized one. Newt would look amazing in purple zebra stripes. She didn't know if her current carrier was TSA-approved. She told herself to check at the pet store the next time she saw Bob.

"How's the online dating going?" Gilbert asked.

It was her turn to shrug. "Not so great. I met one guy, and he was just weird. But I am going on a date tomorrow night with my neighbor."

Gilbert lifted down a handsome set of deep burgundy suitcases and replaced them with a new set, whimsical, sky blue, covered with yellow and white daisies. Even luggage had seasons. "A neighbor, huh?" he said. "Is he new? Just move in?"

"Not real new. He's been next door about a year." She'd been in her house for almost eight years, Audrey realized. She'd had the house that long. The Ooshi-man left a year later. She was forty-seven when she suddenly found herself alone with a stuffed cow.

Now, she was halfway through her fifties.

Suddenly, Audrey felt really, really old. Suddenly, she wondered if it wouldn't be better to just stay alone with her iguana.

"Have you gone out with him before?" Gilbert asked.

Audrey frowned, disoriented, thought Gilbert was asking about Newt. Then she realized he meant Frank. "No," she said slowly. "He didn't really seem like someone to go out with." She tugged a blouse free from the others, shook it out, then filed it neatly back. Another rack wasn't quite so full, so she selected some items to move over there. "It doesn't seem like the usual way of meeting someone, does it? Right next door?"

Gilbert laughed. "Good grief, Audrey," he said. "The boy or girl next door? Ever hear of that concept?"

She had. She'd used it just the night before. But...Frank? "I guess I never thought of him that way," she said. "He was just the guy who moved in a while back. The guy who owns a lot of parakeets and who likes to feed the wild birds outside. He has like six bird feeders."

"Parakeets. Birds." Gilbert shook his head. "Well, at least it's not cats."

Audrey thought of Newt and her birthday and her own anti-feline decision.

"So you're going out with him now, why? Is it because you know he's available now? Or because you really like him?"

Audrey was getting flustered. "I don't know, Gilbert. Am I supposed to? I mean, I never considered his availability before. I knew he lived alone, so I guess at some level, I knew he was available. But...he was just my neighbor. I do like him, though. He's really nice to my iguana. And to me. He used his snowblower to clear my driveway. He walked with me yesterday when I took Newt outdoors for the first time. He helped me with this really crabby lady who thought Newt might hurt her kids."

Gilbert crossed the aisle and pushed her gently on the shoulder. "Relationships have been made with less than that," he said. "I'm sorry, I shouldn't be asking you all these questions. Don't overthink it. He seems like a nice guy. He likes your iguana. Not all guys like iguanas, Audrey." He shuddered. "And let's talk about this. You have an iguana?"

Audrey laughed. "Yes, Gilbert. I have an iguana. His name is Newt. I bought him for myself on my birthday. I didn't want a cat." She remembered the slinky look Gilbert gave her the day she bought the suitcases when he was talking about cougars and the panic she felt at it. But even if she'd been flattered, attracted, pulled into the slink, his shuddering at Newt would have brought everything to a halt. Newt was now part of her package.

And Frank liked iguanas. Or at least, he liked *her* iguana. She wondered if she would like his parakeets. Six of them. There was only one of Newt. But the birds were a part of Frank's package.

And, though she would never ever admit it out loud, not to Annabel, definitely not to Vicki, maybe not to Clara, though maybe she would, she let her thoughts drift for just a few seconds to Frank's package. *That* package. The one that didn't involve birds at all. Unless she used slang, and she didn't, and she felt her cheeks begin to flush.

"Well," Gilbert said now. "If you have an iguana and your next door neighbor is nice to him, I'd say that's a match made in heaven. As long as you like parakeets." He patted her shoulder again and then turned back to his daisy-filled suitcases.

"Thanks, Gilbert," she said, and she turned away and got back to work. Then she stopped and watched him lifting the suitcases to their varied-height pedestals, turning them this way and that, apparently checking to see how pleasing the display was. She thought of the postcards from Clara's email. She thought of the marches. Men were in the marches too, even though the march was called the Women's March. She waited until her face cooled and then she called, "Hey, Gilbert?"

He looked up.

"Would you consider yourself a feminist?"

He leaned against a display table and considered. Audrey decided she really liked Gilbert; he always seemed to take her seriously. Even momentarily considering her a dating possibility was serious, she supposed.

"Yes," he said finally. "I guess I would. I support women's rights. I think they should be paid equally for equal work. They should be in control of their bodies. I think a woman can do anything a man can do. Except maybe get another woman pregnant. Well, she can, you know, with a turkey baster. But I mean biologically. Or anatomically." He nodded. "Can a man be a feminist?"

"I think so. I don't remember there being a requirement to be female." She slid some more clothes down the rack. "You don't think a feminist is a man-hater?"

Gilbert looked startled. "No. I think, if you wanted a two-word definition of feminist, I would say that a feminist is a woman-supporter. It's not about hate at all. And I don't think a feminist is identified by his or her gender. Just by the support and beliefs."

Audrey couldn't help herself. She beamed and ran across the aisle and threw her arms around his neck. "Thank you, Gilbert!"

Now it was his turn to flush. "Anytime, Audrey." He turned toward the suitcase display. "Do they look okay? Do they make you want to go on summer vacation?"

Audrey laughed. "They do. If I didn't have my purple zebra stripes, I'd buy these right now." She stopped for a second and considered the suitcases more thoughtfully. "You know…if you have any green material that could go under them, it would feel more organic. Like grass. Then you have grass and the sky and flowers. That would really be spring."

Gilbert snapped his fingers. "You're right! I'll go see what we have in the back."

Audrey took one more look at the daisies and then crossed back to her department and her own work.

At lunch, Audrey sat in the food court with Annabel and Vicki. They were across from her, and she wondered why that always was. She never sat beside either of them. They were next to each other, but they were also always at each other's throats, with Audrey acting as the buffer.

She thought of her conversation with Gilbert, his reaction to the phrase "man-hater". "I want to ask you both something," she said.

They stopped whatever today's squabble was and looked at her. "Oh, no," Annabel said. "I'm going to stop having lunch with you, Audrey. Lunch used to be fun. Now it's always so serious. You make me think."

"There's a first," Vicki said. "Don't sprain your brain."

Audrey laughed. "I've been thinking a lot about feminism and what it means to be a feminist today," she said. As she could have predicted, Annabel rolled her eyes, and Vicki sat up straighter. "Annabel, I know you said you're 'not the f-word.' But what does that mean exactly? Where do you fit in with some of the things on the feminist agenda? Do you believe women have the right to control their own bodies? Do you think that women should not be seen as sexual objects? Do you agree that women are discriminated against?"

Annabel held up her hands in surrender. "Geez, hold up there, Gloria," and Audrey startled in surprise, almost looking around to see if she'd accidentally brought Gloria along. "Of course and of course and of course." Annabel smiled. "Though there are lots of times I want men to see me as a sexual object." Vicki snorted, and Audrey thought of their Fifty Shades film festival. "But I don't believe that all men are evil. I don't believe that all men are out to hurt women, and I don't believe that the only way for us to be equal is for us to be greater. That makes no sense to me." She shrugged. "I think feminists go too far."

"I don't think all men are evil!" Vicki cried out, and given what Audrey knew now of Vicki's past, Audrey was happy to hear that. "Well...most of them are, maybe. I admit that I think of them as pigs. They can't see a woman in a skirt without wondering what's under it and how they can get to it. They're like dogs that way, always trying to get their noses in your crotch. For that matter, no matter what a woman wears, the men are seeing her stripped. We can be dressed from our eyeballs to our ankles, and we're still naked." She shoved her glasses up her nose. "And I think that a woman who wants to be seen as a sexual object doesn't have any self-respect."

"I have self-respect! I'm bursting at the seams with self-respect! Why would being aware of and acting on my sexuality mean I don't have self-respect?" and Annabel swung toward Vicki.

Quickly, Audrey stepped in. "Annabel, you said you think That Man In The White House is an asshole, right?"

Annabel glared at Vicki but then turned back to Audrey. "Trump? Well, yeah. Of course."

"So you didn't vote for him?"

Annabel suddenly seemed very interested in her burger.

Even though she was in the middle of her lunch, Audrey felt her stomach drop. Like she hadn't had a meal in ages and never wanted another one. "Annabel? You didn't vote for him, did you?"

Annabel took an inordinate amount of time to chew. Then, studying her fries, she said, "Well...actually, I didn't vote."

"What?" Audrey heard Vicki's voice echo with hers.

Annabel dropped her burger. "Look, I didn't like either of them. Trump's an asshole, but Hillary wasn't much better. She's bossy and privileged. She didn't leave Bill when she found out about Monica Lewinsky." She glanced at Vicki. "Talk about a lack of self-respect. Ultimately, I just didn't like her. So I didn't vote." Annabel shrugged. "I just couldn't reconcile myself to voting for someone I didn't want to be president to block the person I wanted most to not be president."

Audrey fell back in her chair. She knew, of course, that not even half of the country voted in that election. But she never thought she met a non-voter before. Especially a woman. Her mind boggled at the idea that a woman could vote for That Man In The White House. But her mind exploded over the idea of not voting at all.

"Ohmygod," Vicki said. "How could you do that? It's your responsibility!"

Again, Audrey heard the echo. She turned to Vicki. "You voted then?"

Vicki nodded vigorously. "Sure. I voted for Bernie Sanders."

"But he wasn't even running anymore! He dropped out! He even backed Hillary and asked his followers to vote for her," Annabel said. "That was a wasted vote that Bernie didn't even want!"

It was Vicki's turn to shrug and study her food court tray. "I know. But I didn't like either of them either. Bernie was really the only one with any integrity and any solid plans I could back."

Audrey wanted to be gentle at the same time that she wanted to scream. "Even though his plans didn't matter anymore? Except for his plan to get Hillary into the White House? Why didn't you listen to him then? He told everyone that to vote for him was to usher That Man into the White House."

Vicki folded her arms. "It was the only thing that felt right," she said. "I just couldn't vote for Hillary."

"Even though she's a woman?" Annabel said.

This surprised Audrey too. Despite her backpedaling a little bit here, Vicki had pretty much declared herself as a man-hater. Audrey would never have predicted that she would vote for a man, any man when a woman president was possible.

Vicki frowned. "Gender couldn't be the deciding factor in this," she said. "There are lots of women I'd never vote for."

Audrey could definitely think of a few. Both she and Annabel nodded.

Then Annabel seemed to gather herself. She straightened and looked flat-out at Audrey. "It was a difficult election," she said. "No matter who you are, no matter what you believe or who you ended up voting for, or if you didn't vote at all, no matter if your vote won or not, it was just a horrible, difficult election."

Audrey nodded. "I'm pretty sure that's something we can all agree on," she said.

They each studied their food for a few minutes.

Audrey considered all of them, all of these women that were suddenly in her life, old and new. Clara, who voted for Hillary and who took part in protests, even though she knew from experience and history that nothing was going to come out of it. She no longer pumped her fist in the air and shouted for change, but she joined with others and hugged herself and them in an attempt to help herself get through all of it. Annabel, who decided to hell with it and just went on with her life. Vicki, who voted for a man who had no hope of winning because she just couldn't get herself to vote for the one person who had the chance to block That Man In The White House. And Audrey herself, who didn't do much during this election because she never believed for a moment that That Man could possibly win. And now, she felt helpless.

Gloria, at home, stood with her hands on her hips on the cover of her book and glared at all of them.

How could they create a force on the playing field when none of them were on the same field to begin with?

Audrey thought of Clara's morning email and Gilbert's woman-supporter definition, and she looked up and leaned forward. "There's something I think we should do," she said. She pulled out her phone and brought up Clara's postcard article and showed it to Annabel and Vicki.

"Why?" Annabel said. "It won't make any difference. He probably won't even read them." Which was, of course, just what Audrey said.

Vicki took Audrey's phone and read it over for herself.

"I think it might make us feel better," Audrey said. "You know, to express it. That's just what you said about why you participated in the Women's March, Annabel. Remember?" Silently, Audrey wondered about this. Annabel didn't vote, but she went on the march. Maybe not voting taught her something? Though at the same time, Annabel didn't vote because she didn't think her vote would do any good. She also said that she didn't think the march did any good either, at least on a political scale. Why would Annabel make a practice of doing things that she felt wouldn't do any good? She called the march a party; was that all she was interested in?

Vicki voted for Bernie, even though she knew it wouldn't make a difference. But Annabel said that Vicki was crushed that the march didn't bring about any change.

Confounding. Audrey was back to the scattered playing field. Everyone was doing, thinking, believing something different.

She shook her head. "I think making the postcards might make us feel more connected." She looked at the two of them. "Sometimes I feel like we're all the same gender, but we don't speak the same language."

Vicki handed Audrey's phone back. "I'd give it a try."

"Do you guys work this weekend?"

"I work Friday night, but I'm off Saturday," Annabel said. "I was planning on going out that night."

Vicki rolled her eyes. "You always plan on going out. I'm off Friday and Saturday, but I work Sunday."

"Well, I'm going out tomorrow night," Audrey said and witnessed all four of their eyebrows raising. "We could do this on Saturday afternoon, and then Annabel could still go out Saturday night. I'll stop at the post office for postcards and then an art store for some supplies, like markers and gluesticks."

"Maybe glitter!" Vicki said, and Audrey smiled. Vicki didn't seem like a glitter kind of person, but Audrey would get some.

"What's going on with you tomorrow night?" Annabel said.

Audrey filled them in on Frank.

Both women sat back and considered. "An old guy who owns parakeets?" Annabel said. "An old guy who lives next door?"

"He's not that old," Audrey said. Yes, Frank was retired, but that didn't mean old. Did it? She hadn't really considered his age.

"At least he's not some stranger," Vicki said. "Not some whackazoid from the internet or stalker in a bar."

And they were off. Audrey let them go and started wondering what she should wear to dinner and a movie. With the boy next door. Who might be old. Who owned parakeets. But who liked her iguana. Maybe, like Gilbert said, it was a match made in heaven.

If you believed in that sort of thing. If you believed your vote could make a difference, even when your candidate lost to someone whose claim to fame was lechery, family money, and reality show stardom. If you believed that marching down a street, carrying clever signs and wearing pink pussycat hats, could create change. If you believed in postcards in the era of the internet, of Facebook and Instagram. Of Twitter.

Audrey finished her lunch as she listened to her squabbling friends. She would email Clara when she got home.

Chapter Fourteen

Dating in your sixties is like riding a bicycle... when you're a fish.

After ushering Audrey and Newt to their front door after Newt's first walk in the outside air, Frank walked himself to his own house, determined to keep his shoulders back, his stride steady. He whispered, "Left foot, right foot, left foot, right foot," to keep himself going, to move like a normal man. And not a man who just asked a woman on a date for the first time in years.

And she said yes.

Frank closed the front door behind him and leaned against it. He looked at his birds. "What have I done?" he asked them. "This is so great! But...what have I done?" His face felt like a rubber mask as it alternately nearly split in two with his grin and then crumpled in on itself in a bewildered frown. "I don't know what I'm doing."

The birds lined up on the perch closest to him, tilted their heads and shrugged their wings. Butch let out a chirp sharp enough to draw blood. Frank winced. "Get over myself," he said and nodded. "Thanks. You're right. But...what have I done?"

"Knock, knock," Susan called and then appeared on his couch. He appreciated the warning. "For God's sake, Frank, what is your problem? You asked her out! She said yes! This is what you wanted."

"I know." He sat down beside her. "But now what? What do I do? Does she realize it's a date? Maybe she said yes because she thinks it's just a nice time between friends. Between a woman and her iguana-sitter."

Susan huffed. "Frank, what do you think a date is? That's how it starts. Don't you remember?" She rested her hand on that special spot on his thigh. "You met me at the bookstore. I was grabbing a book from one shelf below where you were, and our elbows banged. Remember?"

Frank did. He smiled. He wasn't even looking for a book in that section. He was looking at magazines when he saw Susan, and he was struck by her, by her neatness, her coordination, just how perfectly lovely she was. So he followed her and pretended to reach for a book when she did. To this day, he had no idea what section of the bookstore they were in.

Susan laughed. "Don't you think I know that? You're just not the best at stalking. It was the memoir section. I'd been feeling so down, and I wanted a book on someone who had it worse than I did and survived. So do you remember what happened after our elbows took a beating?"

Frank put his hand over her ethereal one. "You asked me if I wanted a cup of coffee. I said yes."

"And we had the best time. We talked. We had fun. We gave each other our phone numbers and the next day, you called and asked me on an official date. But I consider the bookstore coffee shop our real first date. We became friends."

"You're right, of course." Frank knew because she told him so, that Susan was always right. But she really was, this time. That was how their relationship started, as simply as a random sighting, then a clumsily orchestrated meeting in a bookstore. He and Audrey already had a series of random sightings and meetings, moving through his babysitting her iguana, helping out when Newt was sick, and walking with them outside on a pseudo-spring day. It was time for the next step. Random, clumsily orchestrated, then planned. At least there weren't bruised elbows with Audrey, though there was a plugged-up iguana. "But what if I screw up? What if I say the wrong thing? All I know about her, really, is that she has an iguana, she reads Gloria Steinem, she works in a department store, she has a stuffed cow on her bed, and she has underwear with colorful speckles. And I'm not even supposed to know most of that yet, other than about Newt and the department store."

Susan sighed and took her hand back. "Oh, Frank. You're the only person I know who gets what he wants and then worries about it." She gave him a half-smile, and Frank knew it was affectionate, if exasperated. "I'm going to head out now. I'll come back when you're trying to figure out where to go and what to wear. I can help with that." And she was gone.

Again, she was right. Susan wasn't much good at the emotional support stuff. With practical, organizational details, she was the best. Frank had no doubt that when he left on Friday for his date, he would be dressed and groomed perfectly. Susan would help him pick out the restaurant and get together a list of possible movies with their showtimes. She was very forward-moving, forward-thinking. She wasn't great at the sitting and holding hands and commiserating part.

But Strike One, now...

Frank looked quickly around, fully expecting Susan to come whipping back into view, hand upraised for a smack upside his head. But she didn't. He pulled out his cell phone and found Theresa's number and texted her. "Theresa, if it's not too late, would you like to meet for coffee? I need to talk to someone." He named a Starbucks located right between his house and the town where Theresa lived now.

It only took a minute before his phone pinged with an answer. "Glad to! Meet you there in twenty minutes." She included a smiley face.

Frank switched out his light jacket for a heavier one – the bogus spring temperatures were already dropping, and they were due for a return to the deep freeze – and he waved at his birds who bobbed in return. Aristotle turned toward the bay window to watch him go while the others put their heads together, likely to chatter about this new development which could affect their lives.

Could affect their lives. As if he'd found his birds a mother. He laughed at himself. He was leaping ahead way too fast, acting like a ten-point buck in a rut instead of a thoughtful turtle. Which made him wonder how turtles ever did the act of procreation. Which made him wonder if he would ever perform such an act again, and if he did, would he find that, in the three years since Susan died, the five years since he'd had sex, he'd become as slow as a turtle. Or worse, as fast as...well, what? The only thing he could come up with was a fifteen-year-old virgin, which he'd been once and he never wanted to be again, especially at sixty-three. Especially with a younger woman. Especially...

And then he smacked himself upside his own head, stopping his runaway thoughts, doing for himself what he knew Susan would want to do.

"For heaven's sake, Frank," he said in his best Susan imitation. "It's a date, nothing more."

And then he felt a second, softer smack. He thanked the gods or the universe or whoever was in charge of ghostiness that Susan's afterlife punch didn't carry near the power of her living one.

As he drove down the street, he remembered Susan's description of their first meeting and the way she said that she considered their talking over cups of coffee in the bookstore a date. And now here he was, years later, heading down the street to another coffee shop, another woman. And then he slammed his car to a stop, and there wasn't even a stop sign. Luckily, no one was behind him.

Because now, there was a third woman to consider.

Would Theresa think of this cup of coffee as a date? Or would she see it his way – a cup of coffee with a friend? But they were divorced. She had to know it was just a cup of coffee.

"What have I done?" he said out loud. Then he moved forward, like Susan.

He arrived at Starbucks first, which he expected, given his years of living with Theresa's perpetual twenty-minutes-lateness. He selected a nice table directly in front of the fireplace. It was roaring, as if somehow, Starbucks knew that the weather was shifting back to winter and customers would need the warmth. Frank relished the sun that was out earlier, but the cold that sank over him in his walk from the car to the café went deep into his bones, which ached with an I-told-you-so feeling. He sat and waited, planning on ordering Theresa's coffee with his.

When Theresa flew in, he appreciated her scatteredness, which was nice after Susan's supreme coordination. True to form, Theresa looked like she'd just thrown herself together. Frank knew that after she received his text, she probably ran a comb through her hair, decided what she was wearing was good enough (it was – a white sweater over a pair of jeans), pulled on a pair of sneakers because she rarely wore shoes in the house. Skechers, he saw, still her favorite brand, though these were slip-ons, no longer the ones that laced up. He attributed that to age – he wore slip-ons now too. So much easier than bending to tie the laces. She saw him right away and trotted over, a smile on her face. He smiled too and thought how, just a short time ago, he would have ducked behind posts and baristas and then dodged out the door, just to avoid her. He never thought he would get to a point where he'd be inviting interaction with his first wife. The only wife whose title bore an "ex".

"Frank! How nice that you asked me for coffee! And you got the table by the fireplace!"

Frank worried for a moment that the roaring fire might seem romantic, so he quickly doused those flames in practicality. "It feels cold tonight, after the warm day we had. I thought this would keep us comfortable. What would you like to drink?"

She unzipped her coat and then stood, waiting, until he slid the coat off her arms, settled it on the shoulders of her chair, and then pulled her chair out for her. Theresa was a stickler for etiquette; he remembered her pleasure at his serving the doughnuts on a platter, the creamer in a pitcher and the sugar in a bowl. "Oh, gosh, are you buying? Thank you! I'll have a grande toffee nut latte in a for-here mug, please." She leaned forward and whispered, "If you order the grande in a for-here mug, they put it in a ceramic mug that actually holds a venti. You get more."

"Thanks for the tip." Frank went to the counter and ordered two of Theresa's drink, though he made his extra-hot and added whipped cream. When he sat down across from Theresa, he wasn't quite sure where to begin.

Theresa took care of that. "So," she said, "your text said you needed to talk to someone. I'm surprised but glad you chose me. What's going on?"

Frank moved from not knowing where to begin to not knowing where to go next. How did he tell his first wife that he asked someone on a date and he didn't think he knew what he was doing? Especially when he had a second wife too? One would think that with two wives, he would have a battle plan, a reference from the past, that led him to the point of being a man with two wives. But he didn't. He couldn't have explained his two-wife status to himself, let alone to anyone else.

"Well..." Frank decided to go with Susan's practical, move-forward approach. Get it out there. "I asked a woman on a date. But I feel like I'm not sure what's supposed to happen next. Or what to do at all, really. How to behave. What to say." He thought of Susan. "Even what to wear. What do you wear on a first date these days? It's just dinner and a movie, nothing fancy."

Frank couldn't have defined what expressions went across Theresa's face just then. It was like watching a disco ball flicker. Eventually, she took a breath and became a smooth, blank canvas. He couldn't read her face when it was flashing, and he couldn't read it now when it said absolutely nothing. "Oh," she said. "I didn't know you were interested in anyone."

"She's my neighbor," Frank said. "I've known her for a while, and I like her, but it took me a long time to work up the courage to ask her out. I asked her once to come over for some hot chocolate, but she said no. Today, she said yes. To the dinner and a movie." That giddy rubber face feeling went over him again, and it was impossible to hide his grin.

"You asked her to your house?"

Frank recognized this expression. It was hurt. When Susan learned about the hot chocolate fiasco, she was mortified. But Theresa's voice wasn't sharp; it shrunk. The corners of her mouth turned down. He remembered how he nearly didn't ask Theresa into his house the first time she came over.

And how she essentially manipulated and finagled her way to his kitchen table and into his cell phone, without any real invitation from him. But this meeting, right here, was his own orchestration. He called her.

"Is this the neighbor with the iguana?"

Frank wasn't sure what Newt had to do with anything, but he nodded. Theresa sat silently for a moment, and he decided she was waiting for some more information. "She's a little younger than we are, I guess. She said she just had her fifty-fifth birthday. She asked me to watch her iguana one night, and I did, and so I thought she was getting friendlier and so I –"

Theresa shoved her chair back. The legs squawked on the floor, putting Butch's chirp to shame. Theresa's cheeks were flushed, and Frank didn't think it was from the fire. "Frank, I thought that maybe you and I could start seeing each other. Why do you think I kept coming over? We have a history, you know."

Frank was dumbfounded. "What? But, Theresa, we tried already, didn't we? We failed. I mean, yes, we have a history, but it's not a great history, is it? I never once thought –"

From behind his right ear, he heard an intense whisper. "Frank! Shut up! Just shut up!" Susan was at Starbucks. He was trapped between his two wives, one standing invisibly behind him, one standing very visibly with flushed cheeks and hunched shoulders in front of him.

Susan was always right. Frank listened. He stopped.

Theresa's face now read stricken. "It wasn't all bad, Frank," she whispered. "It wasn't all bad." She grabbed her jacket and flew from the coffee shop.

Theresa wasn't the only one left stricken. Frank stared at the empty chair, at the empty space on the other side of the table.

Slowly, almost cautiously, the air colored in and then Susan was sitting there. She wrapped her hands around Theresa's abandoned mug. "I wish I could drink this," she said. "And I wish it could make my hands warm." She looked at the fireplace. "I can't even feel the fire, can you imagine that?" she said quietly. "It's not like I'm cold. I'm comfortable. One thing about being dead like this – I'm always comfortable. My body's thermostat never changes." She looked back at Frank. "It's nice, I suppose, to never be hot or cold. But I miss feeling the way a fire sweeps you with heat. I miss feeling it chase away the cold." She raised the mug, sniffed the toffee nut.

Frank didn't know what else to say, so he said, "What would happen if you took a sip?"

She shrugged. "I don't know. To anyone else in this shop, the mug is still on the table. Only you can see it's in my hands. Can I taste something no one else can see?"

"I can see something no one else can see," he said.

Susan considered this, then brought the mug to her lips and sipped. Her eyebrows arched. "I think I can taste it," she said, her voice barely above a whisper, which Frank knew meant she was excited. Susan was the only woman he ever knew who got quieter with heightened emotions. She took another sip. "I don't know if I can really taste it or if it's my imagination, but there's something. It's delicious!" She seemed delighted.

Frank wondered how she could be dead for three years and only discover this now.

"I've only begun to be seen recently, Frank, and only by you. I haven't really done earth things yet. I haven't wanted to, not without you. You're not the only one who's been grieving, you know." She took another sip and her smile, while pleased, was restrained.

Frank took up his own drink. "So what the hell just happened?" he asked. "I mean, with Theresa."

"You might want to just think your conversation to me, Frank," Susan said. "To anyone else here, you'll look like someone talking out loud to yourself."

Frank glanced around. The coffee shop wasn't very busy and, so far, no one seemed to be watching. He imagined trying to talk to Susan without saying a word. What would he do with his hands? His face? He glanced at his phone. "I think I'll just pretend I'm on my phone. People will think I'm talking on that."

Susan waited until his phone was pressed to his ear. "So here's what happened, Frank. It seems like Theresa was hoping that maybe you and she could be an item again." She curled her lip in distaste.

"But why would she think that? I mean, we're divorced, for god's sake. We left each other by choice. It's not like you and me, where neither of us wanted our relationship to end. God, Susan, I just don't understand women." Frank rested his forehead in his palm. "What am I going to do about Audrey? Do I even want to pursue this? Is she going to be this difficult too?"

Susan laughed. "Probably. But all people are difficult, Frank. It's not just women. Men aren't easy either. Look at you." She pulled his hand away from his face so that he had to look up. "Trying all sorts of schemes instead of just asking Audrey out. Living with parakeets, and not just one, but six! I was married to you for fifteen years, and I never would have predicted that you wanted birds. It's always about figuring someone out. Not just once. But every day. Frank..." Now Susan curled her fingers around his on the coffee mug. He felt wrapped in ribbons of warmth. "Theresa just lost her husband, right? Last summer?"

Frank nodded. "Seven months ago, I think."

"Don't you remember what that first year was like? After me? I don't want to feel sorry for her, but Theresa is lonely, Frank. She's still in shock." Susan squeezed his hand, and to Frank, it was like the barely-there pressure of a leather glove. "What would you have done if you saw her during that first year after me?"

"Run," Frank said automatically.

Susan shook her head. "No, you wouldn't. Not during that first year. I don't like her either, you know. The whole reason I started showing up was because she did and I wanted to protect you from her." Her touch lightened from glove to knit mitten. "Well, maybe not protect. That's more my deal, I guess. I wanted to keep you from her. I couldn't stand to think of you with her. But Frank, remember that first year? Remember it. And then imagine that someone familiar comes in. Someone who knew you as well as I did. Someone who lived with you like I did. Someone who was married to you, who shared things with you...like I did."

Susan's eyes welled with tears which slid down her cheeks. Like a mirror's reflection, his did too.

He thought of that first year when Susan's absence was like a hole he stepped into constantly, and each time he did, it became deeper. He knew he was in danger of being swallowed and he felt like he was looking at the world like Kilroy, only his eyes showing over the fence of grief.

If Theresa showed up then? If she said, "Hi, Frank," and he knew just how her voice would sound? If she laid her hand on his arm and he would feel the weight of it before she even touched him. If he hugged her and he knew exactly how their bodies would fit together, how he would have to stand to get her as close as possible. Just like he knew with Susan. Just like he missed with Susan.

"I would have reached for her," he whispered out loud.

"And that's what she did. She reached out for you. Meeting you in that grocery store must have felt like kismet, like fate. Like a miracle. Then you started talking about a new woman. Taking her out, when Theresa was so hoping you were taking her out. For a cup of coffee. Which you paid for. And you even ordered the same thing she did. And you sat in front of a fire. Never sit in front of a fire with a woman you're not serious about, Frank."

Like the winter in his bones after an almost-spring day, Frank now felt Theresa's stricken, her red cheeks, the squawk of her chair legs, through his entire body. "Oh, no," he said. "Susan, why didn't you stop me? You must have known I was coming here."

Susan took another sip and then she began to fade. Just before she disappeared entirely, she said, "Because sometimes, Frank, even in death, when it comes to you and when it comes to Theresa, I'm still a heartless, mean bitch. But then I saw her face, Frank. I'm so sorry."

And then Frank was alone. Deserted by a first wife who was hurt. Deserted by a second wife who felt to blame. And with a date with a new woman on his horizon in just two days.

"What have I done?" he whispered.

He drank both lattes, figuring he wouldn't be able to sleep anyway.

• • •

The next day, at Susan's suggestion, Frank texted Theresa. "I'm sorry if you misunderstood my intentions," he typed. Susan wanted him to stop there. It was succinct, she said, and it was enough. But Frank knew Theresa, and he wanted to say more. "I didn't mean to hurt you," he added. Susan pressed her dead lips together and disappeared.

Theresa hadn't responded. He thought how quickly she answered the night before and he sighed. He didn't want to cause any more pain for Theresa. He knew what this type of loss felt like. But he didn't want to date her either. He'd been there; he'd done that. He didn't want to do it again. But a friendship...maybe. They'd already been flirting with that idea, hadn't they? Though maybe Theresa took the word "flirt" a little too seriously. But the thought of a friendship with Theresa, which used to seem impossible, now filled him with something warm and familiar. He remembered what he always heard about grandchildren; you could love them, enjoy them, and then send them home. He wondered if that was the same for ex-wives.

Sitting on his couch, he thought about this as he watched his birds. The new tree was finally here, after being back-ordered, and he'd set it in front of the dining nook window, just as he planned. Then he let the birds out. Five of them were in the tree, squawking up an involved and excited conversation, with Butch in the uppermost branch, holding forth the loudest. Aristotle, Frank noticed, didn't join the others, but sat in his usual spot on top of the birdcage. He wasn't looking out the bay window, though, the way he normally did. He pivoted, his clawed feet grasping and turning as gracefully as any ballerina, and then he watched the others enjoy their new exotic environment. Frank wondered how long it would take before Aristotle felt comfortable joining them. Maybe he never would. It was hard for some to try new things and Aristotle was definitely one of these.

Frank thought he might be too. Three years since Susan's death. And only now was he asking someone else out.

Tomorrow. The date was tomorrow.

Overcome suddenly with fatigue, Frank allowed his head to drop back, and his hands folded easily over his belly. His eyes closed. Just for a few minutes, he thought.

He woke up an hour later. The birds were still on the branches, no longer talking, but all facing the dining nook window, taking in the new view. Frank quickly scrambled to his feet and crossed to the birdcage. He whistled his three-note song, and the birds returned, one by one, Butch last, as usual.

But Butch didn't go in the cage. Instead, he settled on the opened door and spread his wings wide. That's when Frank realized. One, two, three, four, five. Where was Aristotle?

He wasn't on the top of the cage. He wasn't in the cage. He was a bird who never went anywhere else unless he was carried there.

Trying to keep calm, Frank whistled the song again. The four birds already in the cage looked at him, puzzled. Butch flapped and squawked, and his tone blared frantically. Frank began to search, pushing aside his own mounting frantic, and called out, "Aristotle! Where are you, birdie?"

Not on the floor under the cage. Not on the windowsill. Frank looked up, though he doubted that Aristotle would ever be as daring as Butch and land on the curtain rods. No Aristotle. Then Frank dropped to his knees. He put his hands over his eyes for a moment, trying to block an imagined vision of his shy bird, flat on the floor, little bird body not moving, not breathing. Frank wouldn't allow that. He wouldn't.

Lowering his head to the carpeted floor, he looked under the couch, the recliner, the television stand and then over to the dining nook.

Under the table, tucked behind a leg, was a white and very puffed-up bird. Frank thought he looked like the robins outside when they came back for spring and found a blizzard.

"Hey," Frank whispered and crawled over, the first time he'd crawled in what was probably years. He felt every day of those years in his knees, and his hips weren't too happy either. "Hey," he said again when he arrived at Aristotle's side. He thought for one mad moment about sitting Indian-style, but then he realized he'd never get up again, certainly not while holding a bird. So he knelt, parking his butt on his heels. "Bud, what are you doing here?"

Carefully, Frank circled his hands around Aristotle, until the bird's head popped out of the circle made by his thumbs and index fingers. When he felt Aristotle's clawed toes step onto and cling to his palms, he raised the bird off the floor and drew him to his chest. His thumbs could feel the pounding of the little heart. "It's okay," he whispered. "It's all right. I've got you." He cradled Aristotle, then braced his elbow against the tabletop to help himself to his feet.

Moving slowly, both for his cramped joints and for Aristotle, Frank returned to the cage, murmuring the whole way. "Did you decide to join the others? And then you got scared?" He looked back at the tree. To get there, Aristotle would have to fly from the top of the cage, across the width of the living room, over the table, and then set down on a branch. That was farther than Aristotle had ever flown. The only time he ever sat anywhere else was when Frank brought him over to the couch and perched him on his knee for some special one on one time.

"How brave," Frank whispered. "How brave you were. It's okay that you didn't make it. Next time, I promise, I'll carry you over there if it seems like you want to go."

Aristotle's heart rate slowed, and Frank raised him up, planting a kiss on his feathery head. "I'm so sorry I fell asleep," he said. "I should never leave any of you unwatched." Then he put his cupped hands into the cage and set Aristotle back on his usual perch. Aristotle was no longer puffy. But he immediately tucked his head under his wing. Frank discovered it was possible for parakeets to sigh.

Butch, when Frank withdrew his hands, went into the cage. He settled on the perch next to Aristotle and moved in close, feather to feather with his cage-mate. BlueBoy came up to Aristotle's other side. Lucky, Plucky and Ducky chose perches that were as close by as they could get, and they formed a protective triangle. One by one, their heads tucked under their wings. Frank quietly closed the door.

When he sat back down on the couch, Frank gave in and let the tears come. How fast, how easy it was to lose someone. He gave Newt a cookie. He fell asleep when his birds were loose. He nearly lost Aristotle.

Here one minute, gone the next. He thought of Susan and wept. Even though she'd been ill before she died, even though her death was expected, it still wasn't. In their bedroom, in their bed, Frank had held her hand and watched as she breathed...and then she stopped. Just like that. One minute. The next.

Through his tears, Frank looked again at the birdcage. His family was asleep. No worse, he hoped, for wear. They're all right, he told himself. It's okay. This time. It's okay this time. No one was lost.

When his hands stopped shaking, he drew out his cell phone. Finding Theresa's name, he texted, "Theresa, I am so sorry. I hope we can be friends. You are my friend. You always have been." He scrolled through the emojis until he found one he thought looked beseeching and he sent it.

When five minutes passed, and she didn't answer, Frank wept some more.

Here one minute, gone the next.

•   •   •   •   •

And then it was Friday, the day of the date, the real date with Audrey. He stood in front of his bedroom mirror, considering the clothes Susan picked out for him. She'd shown up in the early afternoon, telling him when to have a snack (so he wouldn't be starved at the restaurant and embarrass himself with a growling stomach), to include coffee (to make sure he stayed awake and alert – he was sixty-three, after all), and when to take a shower so his nervousness wouldn't have a chance to "foul him all over again", making the shower useless. While he was carefully scrubbing himself, Susan sorted through the clothes in his closet and dresser. She was familiar with most; Frank didn't like to go shopping much. The only things he'd replaced since she'd been gone was underwear and socks. She was bemoaning this fact when he stepped back into the bedroom, wrapped in a towel.

"These clothes are pretty tired, Frank," she said. "For heaven's sake, I'm dead, and I'm more with it than you are."

"I haven't really felt a need to look all that nice," Frank said, sitting on the bed. "You were gone. There was no one else I wanted to impress."

Susan turned and looked at him then. Her smile was gentle, and she hugged a sweater, still on its hanger. "I always loved the way you looked," she said. "I liked buying you blue. Blue shirts, blue sweaters. They brought out your eyes."

And so they went with blue. Susan even picked out his underwear and socks. She tried to match his t-shirt color with his boxer briefs. "Just in case you get lucky," she said. "You want to be coordinated."

Frank knew that Susan loved coordination. Theresa was coordinated too since her white underthings couldn't help but match, but coordination wasn't her goal. She liked being able to scramble through any drawer and not have to worry about finding sets. As for Audrey, he still didn't know if what was up top matched what was down below. "I don't believe Audrey is the type to let me get lucky on the first date," he said.

Susan shrugged. "She reads Steinem. Feminism includes freedom of sexual expression too, you know."

Now Frank had something else to worry about. "Should I change my sheets?"

Susan shook her head. "No. The first time will be at her house. She'll be more comfortable that way."

"What about my comfort?" Frank thought about Newt and wondered if Audrey would let them shut the door. Then he shook his head and reached for his boxer briefs, a navy blue and white stripe that Susan matched with a navy blue t-shirt. Why was he even thinking about Audrey's bedroom?

"Because you're a man," Susan said. She held a crew neck sweater, also navy blue, to the window, using the light to check for pulls and pills.

"But I don't –"

"Yes, you do."

Susan was always right.

She handed him the sweater and his tan slacks. For under the sweater, she chose a blue and tan checked shirt. It was missing a button, but Susan said that didn't matter. "Only the collar and cuffs are going to show," she said, "and they're fine."

Frank figured that if the time came that he took the sweater off, he would just turn his back to Audrey.

"See?" Susan said. "What're you thinking about, Frank?"

Frank gave up and just focused on getting dressed. The shirt's missing button made it difficult, and it took him three times to push the buttons through the correct holes.

When he was finally dressed, all the way down to his dark brown leather shoes, Frank had to admit he looked pretty good. He knew that Susan always chose blue for him, but he never knew why. Now he did, and he could see it. His eyes looked bright above the dark blue sweater. Susan hummed in approval and gave him a gentle hug. "You're perfect," she said. "Now you did make reservations, right?"

He had. Susan helped him pick out a small, privately-owned Italian restaurant. She said Italian was always a great bet for a first date. There was plenty of selection to choose from, and if Audrey was a light eater, Italians loved salads and soups. Susan also helped him pick out a movie, though Frank would give Audrey several choices. But the one he hoped for was a light romantic comedy. "You'll laugh," Susan said. "You have a great laugh, Frank."

He did? But then he didn't know he had great eyes either. Maybe his laugh and his eyes were part of the reason why he found two wives. Maybe they formed the battle plan he wondered about. His path.

In Audrey's case, Frank knew that liking Newt was a big plus too. Even bigger was Newt liking him.

As Frank pulled on his overcoat, his phone pinged. He immediately wondered if it was Audrey, canceling their date, but he was surprised when it was a text, finally, from Theresa. She said, "Good luck, Frank. Let me know how it goes." He showed Susan, who shrugged. He texted a thank-you back, along with, "I'm so glad to hear from you." He was.

Susan kissed his cheek. "I won't be going on the date, Frank," she said. She looked at the floor. "As much as I want you to be happy, and as much as I support you in this, I just don't think I can watch. It's difficult."

Frank hugged her, as well as a man in a winter overcoat can hug a dead wife who is a ghost. "I'll look for you when I get home," he said. Just like I used to when you were alive, he thought. For a moment, he wanted to pull off the overcoat and just stay home with her. He didn't want to look for her anymore. He'd found her.

The corners of her mouth tugged down, and Frank damned himself for not controlling his thoughts. "It's all right," she said. She sat on the couch. "But tell me about it before you tell Theresa."

He smiled and stepped out of the door. There, on the stoop, he considered. He was driving, but Audrey lived next door. Should he drive his car from his driveway to hers and then pick her up? Or should he walk to her door, then escort her here to his car?

Already, he was worried.

Finally, he pulled his car from the garage to the bottom of his driveway.

Then, leaving it running, he went to fetch Audrey. He waved at Newt, who was in the window. Newt bobbed his head.

When Audrey answered the door, she smiled at him. He stepped inside, shutting the door quickly, to protect Newt. "You look great!" he said to Audrey, and she did. She was wearing a blue sweater too, though hers was a lighter shade, a baby blue, with tiny white buttons that reminded him of pearls. He crossed over to Newt and chucked the lizard on his wattled chin. He congratulated himself on not being afraid to do so anymore, and Newt seemed to like it. "How are you, buddy? You'll be okay while I take your mom out to dinner?"

Newt pressed his head against Frank's palm.

Audrey laughed. "I'm not Newt's mom, Frank," she said. "I guess I think of him as more of a partner."

Frank took her coat from her hand and helped her into it. "I understand that," he said. "I call my birds my family. I take care of them, and they take care of me too."

Audrey beamed at him, and he felt like he got an answer right on a game show. "That's exactly it. I'd like to meet your birds sometime, Frank."

Frank wondered if this was a way of hinting he'd get lucky on the first date. Susan said the getting lucky, when and if it occurred, would happen at Audrey's house, but she wouldn't meet the birds here. Then he shoved that out of his mind. After they both waved at Newt, Frank took Audrey's hand and led her out the door. They waved again at Newt, as he stood up on his hind legs on his tree and pressed his white speckled belly against the window. They walked to Frank's car, Frank marveling at the feel of Audrey's mitten in his. Her skin was warm, even through the knit. Her grasp was strong, but her hand was smaller than his, and it just felt good, wrapping his fingers around hers. When he glanced at her, she had a small smile on her face. It wasn't of amusement, and she wasn't beaming like she did when he answered the question correctly. It was just happy. She looked happy.

He opened her car door for her and shut it firmly. If he was younger, he would have jumped in the air and clicked his heels together as he rounded the back bumper. But he wasn't younger. Still, the thought was there. The feeling was there. The desire to slip on the ice and break a hip on a first date...not so much.

He glanced at his bay window and saw Susan standing on the other side of his birdcage. She raised her hand and Frank thought of Newt baring his belly. He nodded, not wanting Audrey to possibly notice his wave, though he supposed he could have said he was waving at the birds. Susan didn't look happy, though Frank remembered a time when that small smile that was on Audrey's face graced Susan's. And Theresa's too. And even his own.

He was awash for a moment in a deep ache. For his two wives, one lost by divorce, the other by death. And for himself too.

But then he got into the car. As he told Audrey where they were going to eat and she exclaimed in pleasure, and then he brought up the list of movies, he hoped fervently that she wouldn't turn out to be Strike Three. He just didn't think he could bear to be called out.

Chapter Fifteen

If a feminist falls in the forest, should you offer to help her up?

In the restroom after the movie, Audrey slowly ran her fingers through her hair. She wasn't the type of woman to carry a comb in her purse, and now she wished she was. Her hair looked fine, but combing your hair in the restroom before you leave with a man was what you did. You freshened up. Checked your make-up, but Audrey didn't wear any. Spritzed on perfume, but Audrey only wore after-shower spray. Combed your hair, but Audrey only had her fingers. Smoothed your clothes, and Audrey could do that, so she ran her hands over her sweater, making sure the little pearl buttons were all lined up and neat. For an extra measure, since no one was sharing the mirrors with her, she put both hands below her breasts and lifted a few times, like she was plumping up pillows. She was wearing her Holy Cow Purple Victoria's Secret bra, and she shouldn't need any plumping. She plumped anyway. It made up for all the things she couldn't do.

She wondered what came next. First, there was dinner. Then a movie. Now a breather away from Frank while she freshened herself up for...something. She didn't know what. During the movie, Frank pressed his thigh against hers a few times. She didn't know if it was intentional and so she didn't press back. Then he rested his hand over hers, like a blanket for her fingers. That was intentional, and in that moment, Audrey felt like her fingers were precious things. She hadn't felt like any part of her was precious for a long time.

Dinner was wonderful. She had a great time with Frank. They talked over pasta, he sharing bird stories, she sharing Newt stories. He had more to tell because he had more birds and he'd had them longer. He told her a little about his previous wives; the plural took her aback, but when he explained his last wife died, somehow that made it better. It wasn't like he had two failed marriages, two rejections. One marriage failed. One wife died. That was a different thing. He didn't speak of either wife with derision; she felt that was a particularly important detail.

She told him some about herself too, though she mostly focused on the present. She sensed him wanting to ask why she was still single. He did ask her if she was divorced, a subtle way, she thought, to find out if she'd ever been married. She smiled and said no and then she raved about the fettuccini.

If he'd gotten the question out, she wouldn't have had an answer. She had no idea why she was still single. It wasn't out of choice. But here she was.

He held the car door for her and the restaurant door too. He helped her on and off with her coat. He slid her chair out and waited until she was seated and comfortable to seat himself. To her surprise, she liked this. Was she supposed to like this? She remembered women at her meetings in college laughing over what they termed "macho" gestures. "What?" Clara said once. "I don't have the strength to open my own door? Sweet little fragile me?"

Audrey wasn't fragile. But when the doors were opened and her coat held, and her chair pulled out, it felt nice. But she thought she didn't want nice. This felt better than nice, she amended. She felt cared for. Even respected.

Respected? How could having a man do these things for her that she could obviously do for herself make her feel respected? Was Frank going to wipe her nose next? Cut her meat up for her? Pat her on the head and tell her she was a good girl?

But of course, he wouldn't. It didn't feel like that. This was courtesy. This was manners. What used to be called being a gentleman. But Audrey was no lady. At least, she didn't think she was. She was a woman. W – Oooooooooh – M – A – N. "Let me tell you again," she said to her reflection. But then she found she had nothing to say.

She supposed she stalled enough. She'd done her version of what women were supposed to do in the bathroom while on a date. She had no idea what came next. She thought about texting Annabel or Vicki, but she knew if she did, she'd get two different answers. Annabel would likely say she should grab Frank by the collar and haul him home to bed. Vicki would suggest sneaking out the back door. Which answer would she most prefer to hear right now? Audrey supposed she felt a little bit like she wanted to do both.

Now Clara would be different. Clara knew her, and she would laugh at her hesitation. "Just get on with it, Audrey," she would say. "See what comes next without knowing what comes next."

This didn't use to be so difficult. It wasn't like she never dated. But she supposed she never dated successfully, at least if success was to be measured by the end result of marriage, by a permanent relationship. She was successful if the point of dating was to end up with a man in your bed. She was very successful. But he always went home, and at that point, her bed was empty again. Audrey didn't want dating to be like basketball, where the ball going through the net was a big thing, but only lasted for a moment before the net was empty again and ready for the next ball. She tried to think of a sport where the ball didn't just keep on going once it reached its goal. The only thing she came up with was golf. In golf, when your ball ended up in the little cup, you pulled it out and carried it with you to the next green, where you attempted to get it in a different cup, further down the line. Audrey liked that. She wanted someone who would be trying to get her in the next cup, whatever it was.

But it never seemed to happen. Somewhere along the way, she must be making a mistake. With so many guys revolving in and out of her life like it was the outside door to the department store, how could she be the one not in the wrong?

And now they didn't even revolve. Not for a long time.

She looked in the mirror again and wondered if the mistake lay there, in the way she didn't have a comb in her purse, she didn't have make-up on. Maybe she just made too many mistakes. Maybe she was a hopeless case and right now, Frank was looking at his watch and wishing she would come out so he could dump her at her door and return to his six birds and get on with his life.

He wore a watch. Imagine! He actually looked at it instead of his cell phone for the time. She found that charming. And she didn't want to be dumped at her door.

Audrey looked around the room to see if she missed something. If there was just one more thing she should do to make this work. Wash her hands again? Make sure her fingers were dry? Push her hair just a bit more to the left, instead of standing straight up in the spiked look she loved? She willed an answer to come flying out of her mouth and print itself on the mirror.

She'd looked so long for some answers. She thought of the self-help books on the shelves in her reading room and all the books that came in and out like the men through the revolving door. All those books and no one in her bed but an iguana. That wasn't supposed to happen. There were no chapters about that. Though she was glad Newt was there; she loved Newt.

But everything felt so different now. In this day and age. She felt so old, saying that. This day and age as opposed to her day and age. But whether she was old or not, it was different now. It felt like either the clock turned back into an archaic past or moved forward into a horrific future. What were women supposed to want? What was going to be taken away now that That Man In The White House was there? If she didn't yank her chair back from Frank and plunk her own damn ass down on it, putting the chair where and how she wanted, was she no longer a feminist? To be equal to men, did there have to be no give and take, just a standing side by side with no touching at all? No exchange? Could only one gender be the boss? Is that what pulling out a chair or holding a door meant?

Everything changed with this last election. Audrey wondered if Bill held out Hillary's coat for her. She wondered if Hillary held out Bill's. Or did they each pull on their own coats, their backs to each other, no familiar touches as the coats were settled on shoulders, no happy pecks on the cheeks.

Audrey decided she was thinking too much. She was on a date. With a man who owned six parakeets. He was on a date with a woman who owned an iguana, and he seemed to be enjoying this date as much as she was. At least, before she looked at herself in the bathroom mirror. She gave her hair a final finger-comb and left. She hoped Frank wasn't looking at his watch.

He wasn't. He was looking at her. Frank leaned against the wall, her coat draped over his arm. When she came up, he smiled and held the coat open for her. She slid into it. "So," he said, his hands resting on her shoulders as she buttoned up, his voice behind her ear, "would you like to go out for some coffee? Or a drink? What type of nightcap would you prefer?"

Nightcap. She liked that word. And so maybe this was the next step, this was how the evening ended. "I think I'd prefer coffee," she said.

As he drove them to a Starbucks, they chatted about the movie. It was an easy conversation; the movie wasn't controversial and didn't require any heavy thinking. Audrey was relieved. Serious thought was just impossible. She was too busy trying to figure out how to position her body language to say what she wanted to say when she had no idea what she wanted to say. In the café, Audrey was delighted to see a table was available in front of the fireplace. Frank looked at it a little oddly, and Audrey wondered if he was feeling too warm in his sweater. But she loved sitting by a fireplace, and so she chose that table. He had a shirt on under his sweater; he could always take it off. She wondered if she wanted him to, and then she batted that thought away. He pulled out her seat, and she sat down. "How about if I pay for this?" she said. "You've paid for everything else." Then she wondered why she sat down if she was going to order. Did she only sit down because he pulled out her chair? She stood back up.

Frank seemed ready to protest, but then he sat down. Audrey wondered if she should have pulled out his chair. "Sure," he said, "that would be fine. Thank you. I'd like a grande toffee nut latte, please, extra hot, with whip, in a for-here mug."

She smiled. "Oh, you know the for-here mug trick too. Be right back." She went to the counter.

When she returned with their drinks, Frank was looking into the fire, one of his hands resting gently over the other. She thought he looked melancholy and she wondered why. They sipped for a while, and Audrey worried they'd run out of things to say. It wasn't uncomfortable though; the silence was just fine. She enjoyed the heat from the fire and from the mug as she wrapped her fingers around it.

"Audrey?"

The voice wasn't familiar, and at first, Audrey was surprised that there could be another Audrey in this particular Starbucks on a Friday night. But then the owner of the voice stepped to the table, and Audrey's heart sank. It was Generic Hairless Mark, the creepy man from Fish In The Sea, the man who confessed he shaved his body hair. The man with a million wives, at least one of whom he wasn't sure counted.

"Mark!" she said. And she wondered why, when you try so hard to clear your voice of disgust, it comes back three times more disgusted than you tried to hide. "How are you?" she tried to amend.

"Oh, just great." He looked at Frank. "So is this why you ran out on me the other day? You'd already met somebody else?"

Frank seemed startled, and Audrey couldn't blame him. Quickly, she said, "Mark is someone I met on a dating site. Fish In The Sea. It...didn't work out."

Generic Hairless Mark snorted. "Like you gave it a chance. You were with me for, what, fifteen minutes?"

If even that. Audrey didn't know where to look, so she looked in her mug.

"We met at the Starbucks in the mall," Generic Hairless Mark said. "No fireplace." He nodded toward the flames. "Smooth move, man. Gotta remember that."

The silence turned awkward. Audrey wondered who should be responsible for making Generic Hairless Mark go away. Frank, who held out her coat for her and opened doors? Mark himself, realizing he was an annoying third wheel? Or Audrey, who was supposed to speak up for herself, demanding her rights and her wants, from equal pay, to good sex, to telling a man to get out of her way so she could talk with another man who interested her.

Frank was a gentleman, but Audrey was no lady. "Mark," she said, "if you don't mind, we're on a date here. Can you leave, please?"

A look passed over Mark's face then that almost made Audrey regret being forthright. It was there just for a second. Maybe, Audrey thought, maybe we're all just lonely.

But then his face grew hard. He yanked his coat together as if it wasn't already zippered shut and then he stomped away.

"Well." Frank leaned forward, his hands settled around his mug. He smiled. "Looks like we have something to talk about now. What the hell is Fish In The Sea? What kind of bait were you using?"

Audrey startled, then she laughed. "Oh my god, Frank, I'm so sorry."

"Don't be." His hands moved, covering hers, and her fingers were encapsulated in warmth. Warmth from her own mug. Warmth from his, still resonating from his skin. The fire to their side, flickering light, and shadows over Frank's face and over hers too, she imagined. She'd always heard that everyone looked attractive in firelight.

She felt attractive. She marveled at that.

"The only bait I used," she said, moving her body forward so that their faces were close together, "was me."

She didn't remember dates being this difficult. But she also didn't remember them being this warm. She began to tell Frank the story.

• • • • •

That night, Audrey sat up in bed and Gloria opened her book on her lap to the next chapter. Newt was beside her. The house was dark. Only her bedside lamp was on. It was warm and cozy. Not for the first time, she considered having another fireplace installed, this one in her bedroom. Imagine falling asleep to the gentle crackle of flames, shadows dancing like dreams on the wall.

She pictured Frank in the house next door, tucked into his own bed. The birds wouldn't be with him; their cage was out in the living room. But she imagined him calling out a goodnight to each of them, just the way they used to on that old television show about the family living bravely through the Depression. *The Waltons*. She could hear Frank, his voice deeper now with oncoming sleep, calling out his bedroom door and down the hall, "Goodnight, Lucky. Goodnight, Ducky. Goodnight, Plucky. Goodnight, Aristotle. Goodnight, Blueboy. Goodnight, Butch." And the birds, she imagined, would chirp right back. "Goodnight, Frank."

"Goodnight, Newt," she said to her iguana, and he blinked at her.

It was a good night.

After the coffee shop, Frank drove them home. He parked in his garage, then told Audrey he would walk her to her door. Once there, he reached for her key, but she demurred and unlocked the door herself. This was something she decided to do, even among all of the other nice things of the evening, her coat held, her chair slid, his standing until she sat. *She* decided, she noted. She held her own key and opened her own door. That was what made it all right. It was her decision.

Frank waved at Newt in the picture window while she unlocked the door. Then she turned to Frank. "This was so much fun," she said.

"Even when your ex-date showed up?" He laughed, and Audrey thought he had a nice laugh.

"Well, maybe not then." She patted his arm. "We'll do this again?" She held her breath.

"Yes!" he said, and the way he said it made Audrey sure it was as good as a promise. Then he leaned toward her. "Do you mind?" he asked.

Audrey knew what he was asking for. And it was her decision. "Not at all," she said.

And they kissed.

When Frank pulled away, Audrey wondered why she let all that time go by, ignoring the nice man with the parakeets next door. "Goodnight, Frank," she said.

He kissed her one more time and then walked away. He waved as he unlocked his own door and then they both went inside. Audrey knew both doors closed quickly, in protection of the iguana and the birds. Their families.

In these houses now, she imagined, he said goodnight to his birds. And she said goodnight to her iguana and to her friend, Gloria, who was a photograph on a book.

Before Newt, Audrey used to sleep with Ooshi the stuffed cow. But now, at bedtime, Ooshi the cow rested on her desk chair. She was afraid the cow might fall over on the little lizard, who wasn't so little anymore and suffocate him. Now, she wondered if she might soon be moving Ooshi into a closet or dropping him off at Goodwill. She hoped that maybe it was time to remove all reminders of previous relationships from her home. Maybe especially so from her bedroom. But maybe it was too soon to be hoping for that.

She looked over at the stuffed cow, sitting like a human on her desk chair. It didn't seem fair, really, that she hoped to send him away. They spent so much time together. While the man who was the cow-giver was gone, the cow stayed and lasted. He sat next to her when she read in bed. He allowed himself to be squashed against her stomach on nights with the flu. He waited for her to come home.

No, she wouldn't get rid of Ooshi. He was more than a reminder, and he would always have a place. So she turned her hope onto Frank instead. She hoped Frank wouldn't mind sharing a bed that was used during the day by a stuffed cow given to her by a former lover. A stuffed cow she now loved more than the man who won it for her.

Audrey closed her book and put Gloria face up on the bedside table. She remembered another Gloria Steinem quote, one that she used to have pinned to her bulletin board in college. "I'm not just a dreamer," Steinem said. "I'm a hopeaholic." Audrey decided she was too.

After she turned out the light and settled onto her pillow, Audrey couldn't help but wonder what it would feel like to have Frank in bed there with her. Just the two of them.

Well, not quite just the two of them. There would be an iguana.

"Oh, dear," Audrey said into the darkness.

Chapter Sixteen

When a ghost waits up for you, there is no sneaking in.

Frank was still thinking about Audrey when he stepped into his house that night and so when he turned on the light and found Susan sitting on the couch, he yelped. "Susan! My god, you scared the hell out of me! Why are you sitting in the dark?"

Susan looked hurt. "Waiting for you, like I said I would. Light or dark doesn't matter much to me anymore, Frank." She started to fade. "I'll check on you tomorrow, I guess."

"No! I'm sorry!" He quickly took off his overcoat and hung it in the front closet. Susan filled in again, and he sat down beside her. Glancing at the birds, he saw they were all lined up on one perch, looking at him. Aristotle was in the middle, as he often was now, ever since the day he was lost. It was like his siblings wanted to make sure they always knew where he was. "Hi, guys," he said, realizing he hadn't greeted them the way he always did. Satisfied, they resumed their motion and chatter.

He tried hard to block his thoughts from Susan, not wanting to make her upset. But he'd been looking forward to sitting in the dark himself, with just the fireplace on, reliving the date, going over the date, the date, the wonderful date, following himself and Audrey through every step. He didn't know if he wanted to rehash it with someone else yet. It felt like a secret that he shared with just one other person. A special person. Audrey knew the secret. She was the secret. And she was the secret-sharer too.

"Oh, Frank," Susan said, and her voice broke in a way that Frank never heard before, not even when she lived. She began to fade again. He had to find a way to block his thoughts from her. There also had to be a way that he could tell her about this, the success of what she herself helped to set up, without forever hurting her feelings.

"I'm sorry, Susan," he said, and she came back. He hid a smile; her desire to hear was stronger than her hurt. "Do you want me to make some of my hot chocolate, now that we know you can taste it?"

She brightened. "That would be so nice!"

They moved to the kitchen and Susan took a seat while Frank gathered his ingredients. He glanced out the window, looking toward Audrey's house. Her garage blocked his view, but he could see the edge of a square of light shining on her back yard's snow. She was in her kitchen, maybe looking out the window where she and he stood, bathing Newt on that special day. Maybe she was making a snack for herself and for Newt. Maybe she was going over the date too, talking to Newt about it. He supposed talking to an iguana about a date wasn't any weirder than talking to the ghost that used to be his wife.

"Frank!" that ghost said sharply.

He hadn't realized he'd come to a stop by the window. Quickly, he got back to work, and soon, he had their hot chocolate, laced with butterscotch, thick with real milk, ready to go. He sat down with Susan, and they raised their mugs. Toasting each other was a ritual.

It was such an odd thing, a form of déjà vu, but with newness sparkling the edges. Just a short time ago, he was with Audrey. Learning about her, talking to her. Everything was new. And now, he sat in a kitchen with Susan, as they did countless times over the years, drinking his special hot chocolate. This wasn't their kitchen, it was his kitchen, but here Susan was, and Audrey was across the yard, just past her garage. He felt familiar and disoriented all at once. Excited by the new. Comforted by, not the old, but the familiar. The remembered. The held dear.

"So tell me how it went," Susan said.

Frank did. He tried to remember every detail. Susan laughed when he got to the part about the guy from the dating site. "See?" she said. "I told you that you didn't have anything to worry about with that Fish In The Sea thing. And that was really good timing. Audrey could compare the both of you, the crazy guy from the computer and the nice guy from next door, right there. In front of her face!"

Frank remembered Audrey's face. She was so embarrassed. At first, it seemed like she was turning to him for help, but before he could do anything, she took care of Mark herself. He admired the way she firmly marched the guy out of the door and out of their date.

Theresa used to look to him for help, and she would just keep looking until he did so. Susan usually just took care of things herself but looked to him later to see if he thought she'd done the right thing. Audrey just acted.

"I really like her, Susan," he said. He put his hands around his mug, remembered Audrey's hands under his.

"I can tell." Susan took a sip, closed her eyes, savored. But Frank could see that her mug was still completely full. She hadn't really had a sip at all. He just couldn't figure out the logistics of all this. She drank, she swallowed, she savored...but where did her sip go?

The look on her face told him she tasted it. That she loved it as she always did. He was happy to be able to do this for her. He wondered at a heaven that didn't have a favorite drink, that didn't have hot chocolate or butterscotch.

"It does," Susan said and set her mug down. "It has that and more, Frank, everything that anybody could want. But...not made by you. And you're not there." Her voice was soft. It was the soft of their late-night talks, their heads on their pillows, the house quiet. Talks at night in bed required a low volume; Frank didn't know why that was, there was no one else in their house to disturb, never any children and not even the birds at that point, but he enjoyed it. It brought them closer, literally. They were practically nose to nose in bed when they spoke. Now, he leaned across the table, and she leaned forward too.

"I think that I might be able to move on now," she said.

He was startled. "What does that mean?"

She put her feather hands over his. "I've been thinking about it while you were gone. I think it's time that I stopped visiting. Stopped meddling. I'll still be able to see you, and I will, from time to time. But I can only bear to watch so much, Frank. I just wanted to make sure you were happy. I felt you wanting to be. And I felt that it was me holding you back."

"You weren't holding me back." He considered all the time he spent watching Audrey, but not saying or doing anything. "It was me. I just didn't know how to move forward."

She nodded. "You needed a nudge. And I needed one too, and that was to see you happy. Well, see you to a certain point. There are some things..." She looked away. "There are some things I don't want to see, Frank."

Frank ached. He wanted to hold his wife, comfort her. But she was a ghost. She'd been gone for three years already. He wanted to hold Audrey too. He just wanted to be himself again, and being himself now was being with someone else. Someone else besides his birds, though he loved his birds.

"I want you to love more than your birds, Frank." She glanced toward the entryway to the living room, and Frank saw the expression of distaste cross her face. He never would have experienced his birds if it wasn't for her passing. But then he would have had her.

Give and take, he thought. Pluses and minuses.

She turned back to him. "I'm going to go, Frank," she said in the pillow voice again. "I love you so very much."

"And I love you," he said. "I wish…"

She waited.

"I wish you were here. For real."

"Me too." She stood and crossed over to him. Pressing cool paper lips to his cheek, she left him with a kiss that used to be warm. That used to be a part of saying good morning, goodnight, I'll see you later. That used to be a part of just because.

He missed the warmth. He missed the surprise of the just because, the clocklike regularity of the good morning and goodnight. He missed her.

And then she was gone.

Frank sat on for a few minutes, looking at the still full mug across from him. He wondered, for a bit, about his own sanity. His own imagination. His own voracious missing of his wife. Eventually, he took both mugs and rinsed them out before putting them and the pot in the dishwasher. He stood, looking inside at the racks. A few dishes. A few mugs and glasses. Some silverware. The pot. It took days now before he had enough to run a load. He wondered if he should just do the dishes every night by hand, or if he should switch to paper plates, styrofoam and plastic cups, plastic silverware.

Then he turned out the lights in the kitchen and went to do what he meant to do when he got home. He turned on his fireplace, switched off the lamps in the living room, and sat in the company of his birds and in the flickering mix of heat and shadow to think about his date. His date. His wonderful date.

He tried not to think about losing Susan. Again.

Chapter Seventeen

You can send an ass a postcard,
but you can't make him think.

Audrey moved around her kitchen table, getting everything all set up for an afternoon of creating postcards she was sure would never be read by That Man In The White House. She was frustrated at the lack of a real point to this activity but excited to have these three women in her home. She couldn't remember the last time she had any type of party or get-together. Frank had been in her house but giving a belly-achy iguana a bath didn't really count as a party on her social calendar. At least, she didn't think so. A pool party, maybe. She did have fun that day, once she knew that Newt was going to be all right. And she had fun last night too. With Frank. On a date. That truly was a social event. And his goodnight kiss was the most social of all.

If it wasn't for the postcard party, Audrey knew she'd be laying on the couch, staring at the ceiling and thinking about Frank. And that kiss. And possibilities which maybe weren't possible at all. It was probably best that she had this distraction.

For the party, she decided she would sit at the head of the kitchen table, and her computer was set at the foot; she would Skype Clara in from there. Vicki would be on the right and Annabel to the left. Newspapers layered the tabletop. There were little bright blue plastic cups of water at everyone's spot and neat piles of paintbrushes, colored pencils, tubes of acrylic paint, Sharpie markers, glue sticks, and glitter sticks. There was construction paper, tissue paper, and stickers of stars and hearts and emojis. There were stacks of postcards, so they could make as many as they wanted, or start over if there was a mistake. When Audrey went to the post office, she was delighted to find that there were two different sizes. There were the 4 x 6 standard postcards, but also just a bit larger 5 x 7 ones. Audrey knew she'd be working on the 5 x 7's. The bigger space made her feel like she had less chance of messing it up, more room to work. Plus, she thought she might have a lot to say.

Newt was on the floor, following her every move, and Audrey had to keep stepping around him. She knew he wanted to see what was happening on the table, but she couldn't let him get into this stuff. She was terrified he would eat glitter or get paint and glue on his sensitive skin. "Okay, Newt," she said finally and offered him her arm. He strode up to her shoulder, but when she stood, she didn't provide him with a bridge to the tabletop. He shifted, expecting to be lowered, but then rose straight-legged and stiff. Audrey assumed it was because the table looked different than it ever had before. "See?" she said. "I'm not putting out food. It's not dinner time. These are art supplies. I have friends coming over this afternoon. We're going to be making art on postcards for That Man In The White House, and we're going to tell him just what we think of him. And Clara is going to Skype in." Audrey ran her hand down Newt's back, hoping to soften her next words. "You can watch, Newt, but you can't join in. I can't even let you touch it, this stuff is unhealthy for you. Okay? When they get here, I'll fix you a nice tea, and you can eat it in the living room." She felt badly for leaving him out. She reminded herself again that the books on her shelves said that it was good for partners to do things separately from each other. But that felt like a going-out thing. Going out with friends while your partner stayed home or went somewhere else. Here, they were both in the house and Newt was going to be excluded, right in their own kitchen. That didn't seem right. Newt was an equal member of her household, even if he didn't contribute to the mortgage payment. This was his home, and he should be allowed to participate if he wanted to. Audrey decided that after everyone was settled and Newt was done with his snack, she would let him ride on her shoulder if he showed any interest in observing. She would just have to make sure he didn't try to climb down.

Satisfied, she continued her preparations, filling her sink with ice cubes and nestling in bottles of wine and beer and setting wineglasses and tumblers off to the side. She made a pot of coffee and had the teapot filled and ready to go if someone should prefer tea. Vicki seemed like a tea person. Audrey had no doubt that Annabel would head straight for the beer. Audrey put out snacks too, nuts and pretzels, cupcakes that she made herself, and a loaf of fresh-baked banana bread. Newt rode along on her shoulder, cocking his head and looking at everything. She was grateful for his patience. It was something she appreciated about Newt; he never had to be told something twice. And he always seemed to try to understand and honor her point of view.

When the doorbell rang, Newt startled, and Audrey winced as his claws dug into her shoulder. As he grew larger, he also grew stronger. Audrey walked to the door, patting Newt on the back the whole way, and she tried to remind herself to ask Bob about this – was there a way to train Newt so that he wouldn't dig in, even when he was scared? Was she supposed to be trimming his claws? They didn't seem to be getting longer, he was just stronger and more capable of causing pain. She didn't want a time to come when she could no longer carry Newt on her shoulder because he could hurt her. This mode of iguana-transportation was something they both enjoyed.

Four eyes widened when Audrey opened the door, and she and Newt looked out on Vicki and Annabel. "It's okay," Audrey said quickly. "This is Newt, remember?"

"I sorta forgot about the iguana thing," Annabel said. She edged sideways around Audrey. "Yikes, Audrey. He looks kind of scary. Like a dinosaur."

Audrey was affronted, though Newt seemed to take it in stride. He bobbed his head, then tilted it in a way that Audrey knew was a greeting. "He's not a thing, Annabel," Audrey said. "Nor is he scary or a dinosaur. He's just an iguana."

Vicki edged around the other side. "But you let him run loose? Don't you have a cage or something for him?"

Audrey felt Newt press tightly against her cheek and neck. He bowed his legs, hunching low on her shoulder. He seemed to be picking up on the women's anxiety, and so he was making himself smaller, meeker, less scary. Audrey was amazed at how empathetic Newt was; this was a far cry from the iguana who tried to bite Frank. "He's fine, you guys. He has the full run of my house; it's his home. He wouldn't hurt anyone." She patted Newt's head, and he bobbed agreeably. Audrey told them to toss their jackets on the couch and then she led them into the kitchen.

"Wow," Vicki said as she sat down. "It looks like you thought of everything." She smiled a little and nodded toward Newt. "Everything down to the reptile."

Audrey laughed. "There's wine and beer in the sink, and there's food on the counter. Help yourselves. My friend Clara will be Skyping in just a few. I'm going to get Newt a snack and get him settled in the living room." As she prepared some veggies, Newt paddled his front feet against her shoulder, his version of happy dancing. "Try to be aware of when you move your chairs," she cautioned the women. "If he's on the floor, you don't want to run your chair over him." She wondered if she should lock Newt in the bedroom, but that seemed even meaner than not letting him participate in the party. "Newt," she said quietly. "You need to be careful, okay? These women aren't used to you like I am. After your snack, you can ride on my shoulder, if you want."

Newt was more interested in the vegetables. Audrey hoped he would stay that way.

She brought him to the tree in the living room and bridged him onto his favorite branch. She'd hung a small basket from an upper limb, and she put the veggies into it. This allowed Newt his favorite view in his favorite spot while munching. Audrey likened it to eating at a sidewalk café, sitting at a table and eating lovely things while watching the world pass by. For Newt, the world passed by out the picture window and lovely things were fresh-washed vegetables. She popped him a kiss on the top of his head and returned to the kitchen. Next up was getting Clara there.

Vicki and Annabel were sorting through the supplies. "I like these bigger postcards," Annabel said. "What were we supposed to be doing again?"

Vicki rolled her eyes while Audrey tapped on the computer keyboard. "Let's wait until I get Clara here. Then we can talk about it as we all get started."

"And who is Clara?" Annabel asked.

"My best friend from college. She lives in Illinois. She was the one who emailed me about this postcard thing, and Skyping her in is a way for us to do it together."

The computer went through its usual beeps and boops as it prepared Skype, and then Clara's face popped up like a miracle on the screen. "Hey, Audrey!"

"Hi!" Audrey said. She introduced them all. Clara must have her computer set opposite her on the table too because Audrey could see all of her art supplies spread across a newspapered expanse. Clara bought many of the same things, scattered loosely from one side of the table to the other. Audrey was much more organized, setting up what she thought of as "centers".

Clara laughed. "Your table looks like it belongs in one of those wine bars where you paint. So neat, Audrey!"

Audrey had never been to a painting bar, though she wanted to see what it was like. "We should go to one of those sometime," she said.

"Oh, god," Annabel said. "That's so middle-aged housewife, Audrey."

"I am not a housewife!" Audrey said and then wondered if she should have since Clara was a stay-at-home mom for so many years. But Clara didn't seem to mind.

"We're way beyond middle-aged unless we live to well over a hundred," Clara said. "So respect your elders, young lady."

"Yes, ma'am," Annabel said and saluted.

"I'm going to come stay with you for a weekend, Audrey, and we'll hit up one of those painting bars and bring these two young'uns with us and show them what's what with the crones." She stopped to cackle, and Audrey joined in. "Where's Newt? I wanted to meet him." Clara leaned to the left and right as if that would somehow give her a better view from her kitchen in Illinois.

"He's in the living room right now, eating a snack. I'll bring him in here after we get going. So do you want to explain to Vicki and Annabel just what this is all about? And can I get anybody anything while she's explaining?"

Annabel requested beer, which wasn't a surprise, and Vicki wanted wine, which was, and they both asked for some of the banana bread. Clara called from the screen that she was having coffee and a brownie. While Audrey pulled it all together, she listened to Clara's explanation. She remembered so well Clara's voice from when they were in college. She had a way of speaking that demanded attention, but not in a show-off way. She was firm and straightforward.

"I'm not sure who came up with the postcard idea," Clara said. "It somehow stems from the Women's March back in January. The thought is to inundate Trump with postcards from people, women especially, telling him exactly what we think about him. You can decorate the cards however you want. And you can talk about whatever you want too. It can be a general statement, or you can go after a certain issue. Healthcare. The economy. The climate. Women's rights. We're supposed to all mail them on the same day, so they start arriving at the same time. Instead of a sporadic trickle, he should be smacked outright with a deluge, like after a dam has broken."

"Or like that old Christmas movie, *Miracle On 34th Street*," Audrey added. She remembered that scene, where the mailmen brought in bag after bag of letters to Santa Claus, piling them on the judge's desk. She pictured That Man In The White House being buried at his desk in the Oval Office under a mountain of colorful, expressive postcards.

Vicki looked doubtful. "Do you think he'll really look at them?"

Clara fell quiet. Audrey set the drinks carefully by the women's elbows and then said into the silence, "I doubt it. But that doesn't mean we shouldn't say what we want to say. There's a difference, I think, between being silent and not being heard. He might not hear us, but we should still say what we mean. Someone somewhere will listen, even if it's just us to each other." She paused. "If we choose to be silent, then we're choosing to not be heard. We can't control if he listens, but we can control if we speak." Audrey couldn't have been more surprised at her own words. She'd been thinking this was a pretty futile exercise too, but the more she tried to figure out what she wanted to say, the more she wanted to say it.

"That was nicely put, Audrey," Clara said. "We can't control if we're heard, but we can control if we speak. It's always about having a choice, isn't it."

Maybe it was time for Audrey's voice to be outside her own head. The problem was that, unlike her neat table, Audrey's mind was a jumble of protests and horrified exclamations. It was like her inner voice kept bursting in little one-word incomplete, sometimes repeated thoughts. *How! What! Why! You? Racist! Sexist! Sick, sick, sick! Abuser, abuser, abuser! Pussy! Really?* The only truly coherent thought she had was *How the hell did That Man end up in the White House? How? How?* That was still just so incomprehensible, it was hard to focus herself on any one single clear sentence.

She took a postcard and set it in front of her. "Well, why don't we just get started? Grab a postcard, whichever size you want, and then think for a moment about what you would say to That Man In The White House if he was standing right in front of you. And if he couldn't answer back, couldn't shout over your words. Pretend he's gagged and bound, so he can't speak, and he can't walk away. He can only listen. What would you say?"

Clara laughed. "Still can't say his name, can you?"

Audrey shook her head. "No. And I don't think I ever will."

"That's silly, Audrey," Annabel said. "Trump. Trump, Trump, Trump. See?"

"That's not his name," Vicki said quietly. "Not in my house. I call him Asshat."

Audrey sat back in surprise and then laughed out loud. Annabel smirked but didn't argue. For a change.

They all grabbed the 5 x 7 postcards. Clara had them too. Audrey got herself a cup of coffee and turned on some music. She could hear Clara humming along with the song.

They talked idly for a while as they sketched and thought. Two of them, Annabel and Vicki, put their first postcards to the side and grabbed a second. Audrey stared at the blankness of hers, folding her hands neatly, not reaching for anything yet. The jumble of words in her mind, when faced with the blank field of a simple postcard, seemed to throb a disco neon. But which words were the most important? What did she need to say?

Then Annabel said, "So you two were friends in college, back in the day of the dinosaur? And I don't mean Newt."

Audrey laughed while Clara huffed. "Well, not quite dinosaur days. It was the seventies."

Vicki said, "And you marched in a lot of protests?"

Audrey nodded while Clara said, "You bet. We did a lot of marching, a lot of shouting, a lot of pumping our fists in the air. We did sit-ins. We tried a hunger strike once, but that only lasted until a little past lunchtime." She laughed, but Audrey remembered how disappointed she felt in herself that day when she gave in to her stomach over justice. She didn't remember what it was they were protesting, but by two o'clock, the only thing that felt important was a cheeseburger. "It was an exciting time. Everything felt possible. Everything had potential for change. We felt like we were instruments of it." Clara leaned over her postcard, vigorously drawing with an orange Sharpie. "That's why it's so hard now." She glanced out of the screen at Audrey.

"What's so hard?" Annabel sat back. So far, it looked like she was drawing a crowd. Audrey could see round shapes that could be faces and heads. "That you can't keep up anymore? You go on strolls instead of marches?"

Audrey threw a Sharpie at Annabel while Clara laughed. "No, it's not that. Though we probably couldn't stride the way we used to. It's just that we truly believed by doing all that we did, we really changed the world. We thought we accomplished something," Clara said. "But look where we are. Again. Look what we're fighting. Again. Apparently, we were totally wrong. Is it even possible to accomplish equality for women? Healthcare for women? Allowing women to actually control their own bodies?"

How the hell did That Man end up in the White House? "I never would have believed it," Audrey said softly. "Never. I still don't, most days."

Vicki was being quiet, and Audrey glanced over at her. She was painting on her postcard, using a delicate brush and a red paint and Audrey was surprised to see the image of a curvy woman. Vicki herself tended to wear bulky sweaters that came down to mid-thigh over leggings. If she had a body like what was appearing on her postcard, she kept it carefully hidden away.

Audrey heard a scuffle and looked down to see Newt on the floor by her chair. "Hey, bud," she said. "You can come up on my shoulder, but you can't go on the table, okay?" He climbed up her offered arm and settled, his cheek against hers, his tail draped in a hug around her neck.

"Hi, Newt!" Clara called out. "Nice to meet you! My gosh, Audrey," she said, dropping her voice as if Newt couldn't possibly hear, "he is an ugly thing, isn't he?"

Audrey flinched. She never thought of Newt as ugly.

Vicki looked over. "Actually, for an iguana, I think he's pretty handsome. He doesn't make a very good cat or dog or a person, but he's a great lizard."

While the others laughed, Audrey beamed at Vicki. What a nice thing to say. And what a really important thing to say. Newt didn't have to be a handsome man or any kind of man. He was a lizard. An iguana. Expectations should be reasonable. So should judgments.

Grabbing the green and tan Sharpies, Audrey leaned over her postcard. Newt leaned with her, his taut tail against her neck keeping him steadily on her shoulder. Falling silent, Audrey sketched to the backdrop of her friends' chatter and laughter and the music from the radio. A cartoon Newt showed up on the postcard, his iguana body draped on its side on an ornate burgundy velvet couch. Audrey made sure to feature his bright white lightbulb belly, his wine-colored ticking matching the velvet. She thought about putting Newt in a fish bicycle t-shirt, but that would have covered his glorious tummy.

"Does that look like you, Newt?" she whispered. He bobbed his head.

Using a glitter stick, Audrey dabbed gold glitter over cartoon Newt's green body, making him sparkle. Then she took the black Sharpie and began to write above the couch.

"Iguana. Youguana. Weguana. Together."

And then she laughed out loud.

"What?" Clara called from the screen while Annabel and Vicki looked up from their own work.

Audrey showed them her postcard.

"An iguana?" said a voice Audrey didn't recognize. She looked over the postcard to see a young woman sitting at Clara's table. She had a postcard in front of her, and she was sketching something in colored pencil. "Why an iguana?"

"This is my daughter, Sylvie," Clara said. "She joined us while you were off in iguana-land."

Audrey patted Newt's head. "I own an iguana," she said, though she hated using the word "own". She changed it to, "I chose him." Newt bobbed his head. "Newt's decision too. He chose me."

"Hello, Newt," Sylvie said and waved. Audrey instantly liked her.

She set the iguana postcard aside. "That's not what I want to say to That Man In The White House," she said. "It's just what came out. Newt is so important to me, and I guess I had to find a way to say it. Maybe now I can get down to business."

And so she hunkered. Her friends' voices fell away again as she took a green Sharpie and followed her hand's wishes around a curve. She recognized a question mark. Grabbing Sharpie after Sharpie, she filled her postcard with question marks, big, little, zig-zagged, sideways, upside down, like the jumble in her head. She reached inside her brain and drew what ran about, in circles, endless, never coming up with any answers. Then, she took a black Sharpie and carefully wrote across the top of the postcard, "I have so many questions." And then across the bottom, "And you are not the answer to any of them. You are the cause."

She nearly added, "Mr. President" after the "you", but she couldn't. She couldn't give him that title. Just like she couldn't say his name. Watering down the blue acrylic paint, she washed it over the whole postcard, then blew on it to help it dry.

Newt bumped his cheek gently against hers, and Audrey sat back. The other four women were looking at her. "Wow, Audrey," Clara said. "You were lost in your own zone there for a bit. I can only see tons of colors from here. What did you draw?"

Audrey held her postcard toward the screen.

"Question marks," Clara said. "And the need for answers. I get it."

Annabel and Vicki nodded. Sylvie sat back, and Audrey saw there was a message on her t-shirt. It said, "Not the F-word? Well, then F-U!" Audrey glanced quickly at Annabel.

Who saw the message too. She crossed her arms over her chest. "Hey," she said. "I'm not the f-word." Audrey heard the challenge in her voice. "I'm not a feminist," she said.

Clara's daughter stood up and peered closely into the screen, like someone observing an animal in the zoo. "Really?" she said. "Then why are you doing a postcard?"

Annabel laughed, though she didn't sound amused. "I don't think you have to be a feminist to dislike Donald Trump," she said. She looked at Audrey. "Trump, Trump, Trump. Just because he's an asshat," she nodded at Vicki, "doesn't mean I want to hate all men. And I don't want to be an SJW."

"Feminists don't hate all men," Clara and Sylvie said together.

"And they don't have to be social justice warriors either," Vicki said. "I'm not an SJW. I'm not a man-hater."

Audrey thought about how worried she was over feeling so desperate to have a man in her life. That not having a partner brought a feeling of emptiness to her. But did feeling incomplete without a man mean she wasn't a feminist? "I like men," she said, "and I think I'm a feminist, though I have wondered about the definition lately." Both Vicki and Annabel groaned. Audrey ignored them. "I just went on a first date with a man last night. I like him very much." And she was horrified to hear her tongue roll and linger over the L in like, and her voice drop into a seductive octave, and then she giggled. How utterly *unfeministy* of her. She slapped a hand over her mouth. But then she took her hand away. Why couldn't a feminist giggle? Did Gloria ever giggle?

"I'm married to a man," Clara said. "I created this young woman next to me with him, and her brother too." She hugged Sylvie. "And I'm a feminist." She winked at Audrey.

"I don't like men, but I don't hate all men, and I'm a feminist," Vicki said quietly. She looked at her postcard, then arched her hands over it so no one could see. "It's about choice, Annabel," she said. "Just like Clara said. The ability and the freedom to make choices. You choose to be with men. I choose not to be. But that doesn't mean we're not both feminists." She leaned forward. "How would you feel if one of the men in the clubs you go to made you do something you didn't want to do?"

Annabel shook her head. "That would never happen. I'm careful."

Audrey didn't think she ever saw such a level gaze as she did coming from Vicki then. "I was careful too, Annabel. But then my choice was taken from me. I had no choice at all." She held that gaze, strong, Audrey thought until Annabel's face seemed to darken in recognition of what Vicki was admitting to. She looked away. Vicki didn't. "Now, I make the choice to stay away. That might change someday. But not now. And I have the right to choose that isolation, and the right to change my mind. Just like you have the right to go home with any man you want. And to say no to those you don't want." She lifted her hands away from the postcard.

Audrey saw that the curvy woman had grown. The postcard, held vertically, was the woman's entire nude body from her neck to her upper thighs. She was all curve, and her energy emanated from her in waves of red and purple, following those curves to the edges of the postcard. "Can I see?" Audrey asked.

"It's still wet, be careful," Vicki said. Then she slid the postcard over.

In the middle of the woman's belly was what looked like a poem. Audrey read:

This body, my own.
Treasure trove to be opened by whom I choose.

The O in "to" in the second line was the woman's navel. Audrey read the poem aloud to the others. Then they all sat for a moment. Vicki's head was bowed. "That's lovely," Audrey said finally. "Vicki, is this yours? I didn't know you wrote poetry."

"I do," Vicki said. "I wrote that in my head as I was making the little picture. It's a haiku."

"Bless you," said Annabel. It took a moment before they all laughed.

Vicki pulled the postcard back. "I kinda like what I made. I wish I didn't have to mail it."

"You don't have to," Clara said. "But you could make a copy of it and keep that. Audrey, does your printer do color copies?"

Audrey nodded. She looked at Annabel, who was amazingly quiet, especially for Annabel. "So see?" Audrey said. "You don't have to be a man-hater to be a feminist. You can hate men if you like. You can love men if you like. That's not what it's about. It's about women. And it's about having a choice. It's about women being given the same choices as men. It's about being equal, about being treated fairly."

"All right then," Annabel said. She nodded. "Then I guess I'm a feminist." She turned her postcard around and held it up.

Annabel used Sharpies and colored pencils. There were bodies everywhere, dancing, moving, hair flying and arms up. Music notes dashed over the crowd's heads, and there was a sparkly disco ball hanging over them all, glowing with silver glitter. On the lower left-hand corner, one woman stepped away from the crowd and faced out of the postcard to the viewer. Her hair scattered like a blown dandelion and her hands were flung open and wide above her head. Her smile was dynamic. Across the bottom,

Annabel wrote, "I should be able to do just what I want and still know that I am safe."

"Yes," Vicki said. "Yes, Annabel, that's it exactly. You should be able to be safe in your own choices."

Annabel turned toward the computer screen. "So you guys used to burn your bras. Can I burn my not the f-word t-shirt?"

"Absolutely!" Sylvie and Clara held their hands up to the screen, and Annabel pretended to high-five them. Then she reached for Audrey and Vicki. Newt jumped a little at the slap, but Audrey quickly reassured him it was all right.

"I'd high five you too, Newt, but I'm not exactly sure how," Annabel said.

Audrey laughed. "So let's see your postcards," she said, turning back to the computer screen.

Clara used both the paints and the Sharpies. An inked rainbow arched and extended across the entire postcard. At the bottom, there was a long row of stick figures and more behind them, narrowed so that it looked like the crowd went on for miles, past a distant horizon. Over the picture, Clara created the same wash as Audrey with her own watered-down blue acrylic paint. This made the rainbow and the people look muted, almost hidden behind a fog. In the arch of the rainbow, Clara wrote, "Rainbows are meant to be free." Audrey thought again about the Clara she knew in college and the Clara she was getting to know now. She called herself a lesbian then and called herself bisexual now, but living a heterosexual lifestyle. She wondered how many people knew that about Clara, as she stayed home and raised her children. She wondered if her children knew. And she wondered if it mattered. If it was anyone's business but Clara's.

Sylvie's card was vertical. On it was a raised fist, the universal symbol for solidarity. But this fist had remarkably groomed fingernails. They were a luscious shade of deep pink, and silver stars sparkled from the thumbs. Bangle bracelets were tumbling down her wrist, and a tattoo of a rose tucked just under the palm. Over the fingers, Clara's daughter carefully printed in shiny block letters, "Woman Power."

"Those are excellent!" Audrey said. As the others left their cards to dry and helped themselves to more snacks, Audrey went into her bedroom, Newt riding along on her shoulder, and turned on her printer. She figured everyone would want to make a copy of what they made before they dropped their postcards into the mailbox.

Audrey turned to Gloria, resting on her bedside table. Gloria gave her the now familiar controlled smile from the cover. Audrey wondered about that smile many times. It wasn't open and gleeful, and it wasn't forced. But it was careful. Audrey didn't think of Gloria Steinem as being a particularly cautious person, but maybe, when so many people listened to what she had to say, she did have to be careful.

Audrey picked the book up and sat by her computer. Newt climbed off her shoulder and stood beside her, one of his legs resting on the cover of the book. Waking the screen, Audrey googled, again, Gloria Steinem quotes. Something was nagging at her memory. Something about husbands.

Scrolling down, Audrey found what she was looking for. Gloria Steinem said, "We are becoming the men we wanted to marry." She followed a link from that to an article written about Steinem and published in 2016 in the Daily Mail. There, Steinem mentioned this quote and said, "When I said women have become the men we once wanted to marry, I didn't mean it deeply. I just meant occupationally, because I think in the past, women who wanted to be writers or lawyers themselves married a man who was a writer or a lawyer."

Audrey thought about that. Here she was, owning her own home, involved in her own career, owning her own car, providing her own health insurance, her own life insurance. Things that traditionally, she would have done with a man. Things that traditionally, a man would have provided for her, as the part of the couple who had the better job, the better pay, and the better benefits.

But she did these for herself. She did them on her own. She did just what a husband used to be expected to do for a wife, just what her father did for her mother.

And yet, even though she'd proved herself self-sufficient, she still wanted a man. A mate. A partner.

In this article, Steinem also said, "Feminism has not been a failure. We have achieved a great deal, but we still have a long distance to go. Perhaps one of our greatest achievements is to know that we are not crazy."

Audrey looked at Newt and smiled. She was living with an iguana, calling him her partner, and she wasn't crazy, at least according to Gloria Steinem. Well, that was a relief. "Thanks, Gloria," she said, and then returned to her friends in the kitchen. After cutting herself a large slice of banana bread, slathering it with butter, and pouring a hot and fresh cup of coffee, she also sliced a few pieces of banana for Newt. It was nice, sharing snacks with friends in her own kitchen.

When everyone prepared to leave, Audrey felt good. She found she wasn't thinking about the likelihood of That Man In The White House reading her postcard anymore. She made it, she created it, she spoke in it; that was what was important. And it was going somewhere – she would mail it. It would travel to the White House. Whatever happened then was up to fate. But she raised her voice.

The iguana postcard, she decided, she would frame and put on the side table by her recliner in the reading room.

Audrey gave Vicki and Annabel their copies and hugged them both as Clara reminded them to mail their postcards on Wednesday. Then they all said goodbye to Clara and Sylvie, and Audrey shut down her Skype account. Vicki and Annabel put on their jackets. Annabel was wished a good night at the clubs. Vicki was planning on a quiet evening at home, watching Netflix and eating popcorn. She smiled at Audrey and said she might stop at a pet shop and think about getting her own version of Newt.

"I think, though, that in this case, I might not mind being a cliché. A kitten would be cute," she said.

Audrey was surprised again, just as she was with the wine. She never would have pegged Vicki as a wine and kitten woman. It was a nice surprise and a reminder to Audrey that not everyone was as they first seemed. She thought of Frank and how he was no longer just the nice man who lived next door who fed the birds. To Vicki, Audrey recommended Bob's shop and told her about Frank's six birds, and she made herself proud by reciting each of their names. She knew this was important to Frank. She would meet these birds, and she would call them by their names.

When the women asked about Audrey's plans for the evening, Audrey thought of how she just saw Frank out her kitchen window when she was collecting the dirty dishes into the dishwasher. He was in his back yard, filling his bird feeders. She'd waved, and he waved back. "I'm thinking about asking someone over," she said, and suddenly waggled her eyebrows. She realized this invitation didn't have anything to do with the names of Frank's birds.

"Go, Audrey!" Annabel said and pumped her fist in the air. Audrey noticed her nicely polished and decorated fingernails and thought of Sylvie's postcard. Woman Power.

Audrey thought she might have power.

Vicki said, "Just be careful."

Her voice sounded like Gloria Steinem's cautious smile. Audrey gave

Vicki an extra hug. Audrey did have power. She would be careful. She always had a choice.

After bridging Newt to his tree, Audrey followed Vicki and Annabel out to their cars. She waved at them as they drove down the street, going in opposite directions, as they always did, Audrey thought. She stood there, at the bottom of her driveway and looked at her picture window, where Newt watched her. His legs dangled over the branch, and Audrey knew he was about to take a nap. She glanced over at Frank's bay window, his birds jittery, blurry blips behind the glass, and she thought about what she'd been wanting to do for a really long time. Something that at first seemed like it had nothing to do with birds' names which were important to Frank. Just like Newt was important to her. She remembered his buying the iguana book because he said he wanted to know more about Newt. More, she realized, about what was important to her. Suddenly, that something, which seemed like it had nothing to do with what was important to Frank and what was important to her, had everything to do with it. Maybe that importance was what made all the difference.

Maybe Frank had been wanting to do this for a long time too.

She moved down her sidewalk to the gap in their properties where she could see between her garage and Frank's into his back yard. He was just finishing up with his bird feeders. "Hi, Frank!" she called.

He looked over and lit up. "Is your postcard party done?"

She nodded. "Just now. Would you like to come over?"

"Sure," he said. Audrey didn't think his smile could get any broader. "I'll be right there."

Audrey went into the house, leaving the door unlocked so Frank could come right in. She checked to make sure that Newt's heated hammock was on in the iguana corner of the living room. Newt tended to sleep deeper and longer when he was surrounded by warmth. She picked him up and nestled him into the hammock's fold. He looked at her, his eyes droopy from the afternoon's activities. Audrey's, however, were not drooping. Her whole body felt alert. "Newt," she said softly, in case Frank was coming in. "I might close a door for a while. Don't be mad. I'll explain later."

Newt bobbed his head and burrowed into his hammock. They'd been together long enough now that Audrey knew he'd be out in minutes and likely sleep for the next few hours.

Perfect.

When Frank walked in, he looked around and his gaze settled on Newt.

"Hi, little buddy," he said softly. "You look sleepy."

Audrey thought his voice, deliberately hushed and gentle for her worn-out iguana, was the biggest turn-on ever.

She crossed the room in three steps and wrapped her arms behind Frank's neck. He looked surprised, but when she urged his face down to hers, he didn't resist. His hands slid around her waist. Their kiss was the exact something Audrey had been waiting for and led her to want what she'd been wanting for a very long time even more intensely.

It was her choice. And she was going to say yes before he even asked. She was going to do the asking. She had the power. But he had a choice too.

"Frank," she said, "do you mind my being forthright?"

"Not at all," he said and laughed.

"Then let's go to my bedroom."

As Audrey took Frank's hand and led him down the hall, she waved at a sleeping Newt and then thought about how her question mark postcard might go totally unnoticed by That Man In The White House. But Frank was a man who would notice her postcard. Frank would listen. She decided that later, after, she would show him what she drew.

Maybe he would even want to make one.

But first...

Audrey giggled. And she wasn't horrified at all. It was, she decided, perfectly feministy to giggle when you were making a choice to do something you'd been wanting to do for a very long time, with someone who made the choice too. With someone who made all the difference.

• • • •

Audrey's eyes were slow to open the next morning. She wasn't sure she wanted to lift her lids, because she knew from her first moment of wakefulness that her life changed overnight and she wanted to relish in the dark behind her eyes and the warmth that wrapped around her waist and pressed against her from her shoulders to her heels.

Frank.

His breath created a warm patch too, a circle on the back of her head. Beneath the electric blanket, turned on high, her fifty-five-year-old body was naked, as usual. But it wasn't alone, which wasn't usual at all. Not like it was usual in her twenties and thirties, and even somewhat in her forties, until the man who gave her Ooshi went away. And yet, she didn't feel the post-first night urge to pull the covers up to her chin. Or to slide out carefully from under Frank's arm and slither off the edge of the bed, then run to the bathroom and pull on some clothes from the hamper. She knew, from the rosiness of the insides of her eyelids, that it was daylight and sunny in her room and if she wanted to hide, there was no nearby darkness to duck into.

But she didn't want to hide. Audrey hugged the surprise of that. And she hugged the exuberance of wanting to fling the blanket off, open her arms and her legs to Frank, and shout, "I'm here! You're here! Let's do that again!"

Again, Audrey giggled.

Against her tummy, there was a stir, and Audrey agreed to open one eye and peek at the day. Well, actually, at her iguana. Newt was curled in his electric blanket nest. He lifted his head, shook his dewlap, and blinked. She remembered lifting Newt to the bed the night before, when Frank left for just a few minutes, fifteen, she counted, to run back to his house, turn off the lights and say goodnight to the birds. "I just don't want them to worry," he said, "but I just don't want to leave either." The warmth Audrey felt then had nothing to do with an electric blanket.

When Frank returned in those fifteen minutes later, Audrey whispered, "Do you mind if Newt is on the bed?"

"I wouldn't have it any other way," he answered.

Now she smiled at Newt, and she was pretty sure he smiled back. Then Frank stirred too. He kissed the back of her neck, raising goosebumps despite the heated blanket. And then he moved his hand from her waist and tucked it under the blanket, cupping her breast. "Good morning, Audrey," he said. And then he said it again, putting her name first. "Audrey, good morning."

Audrey felt the pressure that let her know he wanted to fling back the covers too. "Good morning, Frank," she said, "and just a minute." Scooping Newt up, she placed him in his heated hammock. She'd turned it on the night before, in case he wanted to sleep there, in case there were nerves or sulks because Audrey wasn't alone in the bed. There weren't; he was fine. "Stay here, Newt," she said now, and she realized she was bent over, bare ass up, naked everywhere else, depositing her iguana into his hammock, right in front of her new lover.

And she didn't care. Instead, she patted Newt's head while allowing her hips to wiggle. Just a little. Just enough.

Returning to the bed, she flung back the covers and there Frank was, stark naked too. She slid into his arms and said, "Well, good morning, good morning, good morning."

Breakfast time.

Chapter Eighteen

When a woman needs a fish, and a man has a bicycle...

On Monday morning, Frank stood by his bay window and watched over the birds' featherheads as Audrey pulled out of her driveway and set off to work. She raised her hand, and he knew she was waving at Newt. She didn't wave his way, but that was all right. He'd come back from her place late last night, and she wouldn't know that he was up right now, watching for her out his window. But he was. And he watched. And then he glanced at the digital clock on his television to see how many hours it would be until she got home again. He wondered if it would be too much if he went to the mall and met her for lunch.

Because he wanted to. Oh, he wanted to.

"I'm smitten," he said to his birds. They stood with their backs to him, likely because he was over at Audrey's house for most of the weekend. With a lizard. Butch fluffed his feathers. Even Aristotle seemed miffed.

Frank knew he would have to start figuring out a way to balance his family with his new love. With Audrey. With Newt.

But right now, all he wanted to do was go over to her house, go into her bedroom, fall into her bed, breathe in where they'd been, and been, and been, and wait for her to come home.

"I guess I have a few things to do," he said to the birds. "Smooth some feathers, so to speak. We'll start with you."

After going to the kitchen to gather some supplies, he returned to the living room and opened the door of the cage, allowing the birds to come out. They fluttered around the room, settling on the tree, the couch, the recliner, the fireplace mantel, and Butch went to his favorite place on top of the curtain rod. Aristotle just moved to his safe spot on the roof of the cage and watched as Frank began to clean. He talked to the birds as he did so, but he mostly looked at Aristotle, who was often the best listener. He tilted his head, blinked, and, at times, even appeared to smile.

"I really like her, guys. I mean, really. I might even use the word love pretty soon. I'm just...smitten, there's that word again. Over the moon. Enraptured. For heaven's sake, I'm sixty-three years old, and I'm enraptured!"

He glanced at the couch, expecting Susan to show up, disappointed when she didn't. He understood why. But he really wanted to celebrate. Part of being a committed couple was always having someone to celebrate with, but he and Audrey weren't committed yet, and he wanted to celebrate her. The fact of her. The solidity. The possibilities and potential.

"I think we're a good fit for each other. I really do. And she's right next door so we can take it slowly, but I don't know if I want to take it slowly. I'm tempted to go to the mall, today, right now, go to a jewelry store, get an engagement ring, give it to her at lunch, get married by dinner. Honeymoon tonight." He laughed, but he wasn't so sure he meant it as a joke. "I know that's ridiculous." But was it?

Calm, steady, shy Aristotle bobbed his head one time. Frank looked around the room and saw the other birds regarding him, quietly. Butch let out one squawk.

"All right. I get your message. Slow down. Breathe. There's time." Frank sighed and laid down fresh paper on the floor of the cage. He liked using the comics. He didn't know for sure if birds saw in color – he told himself to ask Bob the next time he saw him – but he liked giving them color. It was something for them to enjoy when they were in the cage.

Just like they would enjoy Audrey. And Newt. Could birds and a lizard be friends? They'd be like step-siblings. He smiled.

"I think you'd enjoy having a woman around," Frank said to all the birds. "She would be something different for you, for sure. She'd talk in a softer voice. But I bet she'd like you. She says she wants to meet you." He hoped Audrey wasn't like Susan in that regard, scared around small animals. She wasn't scared of Newt. You would think that someone who loved a lizard wouldn't have a problem with birds. "And you'd have two people paying attention to you then." Frank filled the feeders with their special gourmet bird seed. "And a lizard too." As soon as Frank stepped away from the cage, Aristotle zipped back inside. He found his favorite perch and began to preen. Ever since he got lost on the way to the tree, Aristotle enjoyed being out of the cage even less. He tolerated the top, but as soon as he could, he went back inside. Frank even tried carrying Aristotle over to the tree, but Aristotle wouldn't leave his extended finger. Not one to push, Frank honored

Aristotle's fears and trepidations and returned him to the cage. If Aristotle felt safe there, then that was where he should be. Frank wondered if Aristotle would feel safe with an iguana looking in at him. Newt could look a little...intimidating.

For just a moment, Frank allowed himself to remember the sound of Newt's jaws when he snapped at Frank's finger. The image of his finger transformed into a bird's slender neck. Would Newt look at his birds as a meal? He tried to remember what the book said; he didn't think that iguanas were carnivores. He never saw Audrey give Newt meat, but he wasn't sure what was in the pellets from Bob's store.

Standing by the open door of the cage, Frank whistled his three notes, and the birds started to file in. As always, Butch refused to move, always choosing to be the first one out, the last one back. After the others passed through the door, he flew down, sat on Frank's shoulder for a few minutes, preening his hair, and then he went inside.

Frank smiled. He knew the bird would obey within a reasonable amount of time. Frank didn't mind a little show of independence. He honored that, just as he honored Aristotle's shyness. The birds were a flock, but they were also individuals. Locking the birdcage door, he watched the six of them as they hustled around, making the cage their own again.

Then he stood and looked at the empty couch for a few seconds before he went for his coat. He decided to visit the place he thought he'd be able to leave behind, once Susan began to show up in his life again.

Even before Susan's sudden and surprising reappearance, Frank didn't visit the cemetery often. He went on the special days, of course – their anniversary, her birthday, Christmas, Valentine's Day, and, the one time he could handle it, the date of her death. He'd made it there for the third anniversary of that date, missing the first and second of that awful time. But now that Susan was gone again, Frank felt compelled to visit her resting spot. He knew from her visits that she could hear him at any time, but he needed something to look at as he spoke to her. So he chose to look at her headstone. At least it held her name.

He stopped at the florist first, even though he knew flowers wouldn't last long in this weather that was still cold and threatened snow. Susan wouldn't have cared. He chose her favorite, pink roses with a random daisy stuck in, creating what Susan always called "a mostly lovely lack of symmetry', and headed off for the cemetery. As he drove, he thought how Susan was a mostly lovely lack of symmetry too, and he smiled.

He was the only one at the cemetery. Except, of course, for the ones underground. "Hi, Susan," he said. He dug away at the remaining snow, pushed up tight against the headstone, and found the attached vase for the flowers. More snow was expected tonight into tomorrow, and he hoped the flowers would at least have a few hours before freezing. "I wish I'd thought to have these at the house while you were still visiting. Then you could have smelled them. Maybe you can now too." He tucked the flowers in. He kept the tissue paper around them, in the hopes it would provide a little protection.

"I just wanted to talk to you. To tell you that, well…Audrey and I seem to be hitting it off. I spent Saturday night there. All night. I nearly stayed Sunday too, but we decided she needed her rest because she had to go to work today." He felt the leer that was pulling at his face, and he tried to control it. There was so much more to what was happening between him and Audrey, but if he even mentioned the sex, even glanced at a thought of it, his face did this thing that he didn't want it to do, but it did anyway. "I think I needed the rest more than she did," he said finally. "Holy cow."

Frank didn't know if he was being insensitive by discussing his and Audrey's sexual athletics with his dead wife, but he remembered how Susan decided to step away from their visits once the first date seemed to go well. He moved sideways from the topic and talked just about Audrey instead. "I think this could work out, Susan. I really like her. And she seems to really like me. Imagine that!"

He thought of how Susan talked with him, encouraged him, coached him, how she was visual one minute and then a voice in his ear the next. How she picked out his clothes for him on the night of the date. How she told him he looked handsome.

"I just wanted to say thank you, Susan," he said. "And this is such an odd mix. I can't tell you how much I miss you. And I can't tell you how happy I am that it seems like Audrey and I might just have a future." He looked at the roses and the one asymmetrical daisy. "You must have really loved me, to do this for me. You must love me still." He fought his own tears on a day that he really felt happy. "I still love you too. I always will. If you hadn't died, well, I would be the happiest man on earth." He put both hands on Susan's stone and squeezed as if he held her shoulders. "But now I know that I still have the chance to be just that. Thank you, Susan. Please…feel free to visit. If it's still possible." He patted the stone, checked the flowers once more, glanced at the sky to calculate the snow's arrival, and then he said goodbye.

He touched his fingers to his lips, then touched the first S in Susan's name.

In the car, he pulled out his phone. He scrolled until he found Theresa's number. "Theresa," he texted, "I really want to talk to you. Would you meet me for coffee at that Starbucks? If you will, I'll head there right now and reserve the table by the fireplace. If someone is already sitting there, I'll kick them out."

Her answer came almost immediately. "Be there in fifteen minutes."

He knew that in Theresa's world, fifteen minutes meant thirty-five.

. . .

Luckily, the Starbucks was fairly empty this mid-morning, and the table in front of the fireplace was vacant. Frank preferred to be a nice-mannered man, and his promise to kick someone out would have been difficult for him to fulfill. Instead, he made sure that the table and chairs were clean and positioned just so that the heat would blanket him and Theresa both. He ordered their drinks, getting them each a grande toffee nut latte. He asked that the drinks be made in ten minutes so they would be fresh and still hot when she walked in the door. Then he sat down and looked at the empty chair across from him. A chair that was recently occupied by first Theresa, then Susan, then Audrey. When Theresa was there before, she stormed out. Susan faded away. And Audrey kissed him.

Audrey kissed him. He propped his chin on his fist and let himself go all moony.

Theresa arrived just before the barista called out their order. She looked at Frank in surprise as he jumped up to get it. "Well, this is really nice," she said when he returned. "Such service, Frank!"

He laughed and set the mug in front of her. "Maybe I should get a job here." He sat back down. "I'm so glad you came," he said, "and on such short notice. So I thought I'd get your favorite drink ready to show my appreciation."

She smiled, and her smile was soft and warm and familiar. Frank remembered it from years ago, when they weren't much more than kids, though, at that time, he didn't think they were kids at all. In her face now, with years behind them, her smile was the same. "You were always nice that way, Frank," she said. "I could never say that I felt unappreciated."

They sat for a minute, both of them adjusting their mugs and taking their first sips. Then Theresa folded her hands. "So what did you want to talk to me about?"

"Well...I texted you that the date went well, right?" Frank remembered Theresa's reaction the last time he brought up Audrey, and he didn't know if this was the best way to lead the new conversation. Not for the first time, he wished he knew how to finesse. Especially around women.

Theresa's lips turned down. "Yes, you did."

"It's actually going better than well. Audrey and I spent most of the weekend together." Frank hesitated. Theresa was stirring her drink with a wooden stick, and she suddenly began to stir even faster. "And I...well, I wanted to talk to you about it."

Theresa dropped the stick and pushed her chair back. "Why, Frank? To rub my face in it? To let me know that you found someone and I haven't?" She became scattered, standing, trying to pull her coat off the back of her chair, but her purse was there too, and a sleeve and strap became entangled.

Frank got up quickly and grabbed the chair before it fell over. "No, Theresa, that's not it at all! Please, sit back down."

Theresa's shoulders drooped. She looked around the café and then sat. She didn't say anything, but picked up her drink and took a sip without raising her eyes from the table.

Frank sighed and returned to his seat. "Look," he said. "I know you hoped that maybe we could...reconnect. But we are reconnecting. Just not in the way that we used to be. We tried that before, and it didn't work, remember?"

"Well, sure." Theresa shrugged. "But we didn't have problems in our marriage until we talked about kids. And now kids don't matter anymore."

That was true. But... "I know that. But there's a grandchild, and even though we didn't have kids and the kids you did have with Dick are adults, it creates a divide between us. A divide of experience, and of what we each think is important. I don't think I want to return to our old relationship, Theresa," he said quietly. "We're different people now. The experiences you had with Dick, the experiences I had with Susan...we can't blend them together back into the experiences we had with each other. But we do have history, just like you said. And what I really want...what I really think I need is..." He couldn't get the word out. He suddenly felt like he was a card in a Hallmark store.

Theresa still wouldn't look at him. "What, Frank?"

"A friend." There. He said it. He sat back in his chair. "Someone who knows me well. Who knew me then. Who still wants to know me now. Who

I can sit with and talk to about things that we remember, and talk about things that are happening now and might happen in the future. You know? I mean, I'm really excited about Audrey. But even if things move ahead with her, she and I won't ever have what you and I have. Our history. Our past."

Now Theresa looked up. "But you said our history wasn't great."

Frank leaned forward. "I know I did. And I regret that. I really do. I was just thinking of our divorce and what came right before and during." He took her hand. "But you're right. We had some wonderful times. And because we have our history, we also have plenty to talk about. And we can also talk about things that happened while we didn't know each other. But we both know what it's like to be married. To each other, to someone else. You could tell me about Dick. I could tell you about Susan. You could tell me about what it was like to be a mother. I could tell you about...what it's like to own birds." And hopefully, an iguana, he thought.

Theresa laughed. Then she said slowly, "Sometimes, over the years, I would want to tell you something. I'd see a place where we visited or think about something we did, and I so wanted to say, "Frank, remember?" and I couldn't. Dick didn't like hearing about you."

Frank thought of Strike One and Strike Two. "Susan didn't like to hear about you either." He couldn't say for sure, but it felt like his chair shifted a bit, like the leg had just been kicked. He smiled. "There's a lot we could talk about, Theresa. Without the pressure of being a couple. You know, I really think we can be completely honest with each other. We've known both the bad and the good."

She sat back and seemed to consider. "And you'd want to talk about this Audrey, I'm sure."

He nodded. "I would. You know, I can't talk to Audrey about Audrey. Well, I can, but you know. It's good to have someone to run things by. And maybe, if you get out there too, you'd have someone to tell me about."

Theresa looked at him. Steadily. Straight on. That unwavering gaze he remembered so well. Sometimes, he'd felt like he was being drilled. Other times, examined, and still other times, thoroughly adored. Now, meeting her unblinking gaze, he felt measured. And then, when the corners of her eyes crinkled, accepted. Met head-on. Understood. "Friends," she said.

"Yes." He took her other hand, and their fingers and palms made a little warm pile in the center of the table, in between their two white coffee mugs.

"Okay," she said. "We'll give it a try. I could use a friend too, Frank. You're further ahead in this widowhood thing than I am." Her eyes filled. "I need someone who knows me too. It's like once people send you a card and a casserole, they think you're going to be all right. They can all just move ahead. But I'm not moving anywhere. When the casseroles and sympathy cards and the funeral were all done, it wasn't like life returned to normal, like it did for everyone else. Dick never came home." She shook her head. "I don't know when I'm going to be all right."

He squeezed her fingers. "But you will be. It just takes a long time."

The fireplace threw warmth and light and shadows over them. Frank felt it as a moment to relish. In just the last little bit of time, he reconnected with his dead wife, felt her presence, felt her love, and knew it was still there, even though she was gone again. He reconnected with his first wife and felt again the friendship that started their relationship in the first place. And he moved toward Audrey. She moved toward him. He never thought he could love another woman, and he never considered loving a woman with an iguana. But it turned out that life was full of surprises, just like they claimed in those Hallmark cards.

He sat back to enjoy a conversation.

•   •   •

When Frank left Starbucks, he planned to head for the mall. And for Audrey. But when he was driving past Bob's pet store, he decided to pull in. He thought a surprise for the birds would go a long way toward assuaging the guilt he felt for abandoning them. And maybe, maybe he'd get something for Newt too, even though he saw a lot more of Newt than he did his birds these past couple days. But he also distracted Newt's – what did Audrey call herself? – partner from paying attention to her little lizard. Her attention was on Frank this weekend. A whole lot of attention.

What an absolute surprise.

And Frank wanted to make sure that this surprise continued. So he wanted Newt to like him. He felt a bit like a potential stepfather bringing a child a gift. He wondered, when he had Audrey meet his birds, if she would bring them anything. Was it important to Audrey that his family like her too?

Audrey. Every thought of her caused a shimmer of pleasure to stream over his body. The pleasure dodged around some new aches and pains too, like a metal marble in a pinball machine. He hadn't felt aches like these in a long while if he ever felt them at all. Maybe, he thought, when you reached a certain age, sex switched from fluid movement and romantic endeavor to challenging movement and athletic endeavor, even when the mood wasn't the Olympics, but a romantic candlelit dinner. In bed.

He laughed. And he wondered when the last time was that he laughed all by himself in the car.

What an absolute surprise.

Inside the store, he greeted Bob. "Hey, how's it going?"

"Not bad," Bob said, hefting dog food bags from a dolly onto a shelf. "Here to get something for the family?"

Frank smiled. "Yep. The birds had kind of a tough weekend. I thought I'd get them something new to play with." Bob had an extraordinary display of bird toys, and Frank stood in front of it, mildly reminding himself to not get one of everything. He knew he spoiled his birds. But it made him happy to do so.

"A tough weekend?" Bob asked. "Are they all okay? You didn't lose anybody, did you?" He came to stand beside Frank, resting a hand on his shoulder.

"Oh, no," Frank said. "They're all fine. I just wasn't around much, and they seemed angry with me this morning. No one would even look at me. A whole perch of bird backs! I guess they might have felt neglected."

They both looked at the display. "You shouldn't feel guilty," Bob said. "It's fun to get a weekend away sometimes, and I bet they understand that. You're really a very good pet-owner." He patted Frank's shoulder. "I'm sure they're fine, but they'll appreciate something new too. You already know it's best to not let them get bored." He pointed out a strange-looking castle. It looked like it was made of adobe. "This is new. It would fit inside your big ol' cage. Birds can climb it and sit on one of the many levels, or they can pop inside. There's little nooks and crannies for roosting in there too. You can take it apart and make it into many shapes and sizes so it will keep being new to them, and it won't get in the way of your perches."

Frank considered. Aristotle might like a hidden-away roost. "I didn't really go away for the weekend," he said. "I was just next door. Audrey and I...well, we've become sort of an item, and we spent a lot of time together this weekend." He stopped and tried to think of a delicate way to explain how being right next door meant not being around much. Finally, he said, "The birds aren't used to being home alone all night."

Bob, who had started pulling toys from hangers, stopped for a moment, his hand resting on a toy with bright-colored, very un-birdlike feathers.

"An...item?" he said slowly.

Frank remembered the way Bob looked at Audrey that time they were all in the store together. That same evening that Newt nearly took his finger off. He realized he really wanted Bob to know what he meant when he said the birds were left alone all night. He needed Bob to know that Audrey was no longer available. And that the iguana who tried to bite Frank now welcomed him into the house and rode on his shoulder as easily as he rode on Audrey's. Frank never saw Newt on Bob's shoulder.

Frank felt himself smiling. Grinning, really. "It happened fast, but it feels pretty damn solid."

"Huh." Bob handed Frank the armful of toys, and then he returned to unloading his dog food bags. Frank wondered if the sudden withdrawal and end of discussion meant that Bob understood Frank's insinuations. And maybe he was just a little bit envious.

Frank sorted through the toys and kept a few, one of which was the strange adobe castle. Then he moved over toward the reptiles. "I'd like to get something for Newt too," he called to Bob. "Do you have any suggestions?"

At first, Frank only heard the sound of kibble shifting and Bob's exhalations as he heaved each bag. Then Bob said, "Audrey likes to dress Newt."

Frank remembered the bomber jacket. And he saw Newt in t-shirts and such too. Near the tanks of lizards, there was a spinning rack of reptile clothes, and Frank went over to look. Apparently, lizards were not one-size-fits-all. "Do you know what size Newt is?" He'd never considered having to fit clothes to an iguana before.

"Best bet's a medium," Bob said. "The last things she bought were small, but he's growing pretty steadily."

Some of the clothing looked like they would fit adults and Frank wondered just how big Newt was going to get. He thought he remembered an early conversation with Audrey where she mentioned the possibility of Newt's growing to six feet. For a second, he wondered what it would be like to live with an iguana who, if upright, would be just as tall as Frank was. He wondered if Newt would fit in his house, or if his birds would fit in Audrey's. Who would get to use the picture window in Audrey's home or the bay window in his? His birds needed the light and the view, but Newt needed time in the sun too. Maybe they could install a second bay window. Or buy a new house, together...

Frank shook his head out of the future. He'd had one weekend with

Audrey, a surprise weekend, a wonderful weekend, but it didn't mean a future together. Yet. He was making a quilt of bird feathers and lizard leather and laying it over a bed that wasn't made yet. He laughed at himself, then found a bright yellow t-shirt with the Geiko Gecko on it. "This is the Geiko Gecko," the print said. "But I am a green iguana. I don't sell insurance."

Frank laughed again, this time out loud. Then he thought of the kids Audrey met when she walked with Newt around the block. This shirt might help her to answer questions when she had Newt out and about. So he selected the yellow shirt and then he took his things to the counter.

Bob met him there. He saw the shirt and grinned. "I remember ordering this. I thought Audrey would like it. Newt too." He began beeping the prices with his wand. "Audrey is a real nice woman, Frank."

"She is." For a moment, Frank found himself profoundly wishing he was back in high school and had a bunch of guys to talk to in the locker room. It was great talking with Theresa about Audrey, once Theresa decided she was okay with a friend role. But he never really went into explicit detail. Not like he would with guys in a locker room when he was in high school and even in college. It was going to be great having Theresa as a friend, but there were some topics that were limited between them because she was a woman. He wanted to share his great luck, his accomplishment, his, well, triumph. He wondered if he should be ashamed for thinking this, but he wasn't. He wanted to crow. He did well with Audrey. He thought he knocked it out of the park. And more than once! At least, she seemed to have a wonderful time. Several times. He wanted to hear what other guys were doing, what other guys were finding out. Sex was always an adventure, always a fact-finding mission, and he'd learned early on that the more comparisons there were, the better. He wondered if he should join a gym if old guys in the locker rooms there would share like boys in high school. Maybe they moved on to sharing secrets in the steam room. Maybe there were tricks and tips he didn't know about. Sexual moves for the aging.

His knee twinged. Like about that. How to keep a woman happy without killing your knees. Without straining your hips. Without making your belly folds flap painfully, hers too, when things got a little vigorous. He actually had a few bruises on the underside of his belly, and he was certain that Audrey might have a few too. Though he had to admit, when he was making this woman happy this past weekend, when she was making him happy, he didn't care if his knees took him straight to hell. He was in heaven.

He looked at Bob, who glanced up at him in between beeps. "You know," Bob said, "I was thinking about asking Audrey out myself. Guess you beat me to it."

"Guess so." Frank shifted uneasily. "Glad I did. I mean, you own a pet shop. I'm sure Audrey loves that."

Bob nodded. "Audrey's special. It's hard to find a woman who actually cares for an iguana. She's not a kitten sort of woman, you know? Or a puppy. She didn't go for anything cute and fuzzy. Not even a rabbit or a guinea pig. She went for an iguana." Bob shook his head. "I shoulda made my move," he said, and he sounded wistful. "She's quite a woman."

Frank wasn't expecting to feel sorry for another man on a day when he was feeling so happy for himself. Back when he was in high school, when there was a real locker room and real locker room talk, no one ever felt sorry for the sad guy. The one that got left behind. Everyone laughed at him. Frank was that sad guy, more than once. Now, Bob was the sad guy, but Frank didn't want to laugh at him. Though at the same time, he wanted Bob to know that he and Audrey performed beautifully together.

Well, that was sort of Neanderthal, wasn't it? Frank felt like he wanted to rip his shirt open and beat his chest, declaring his sexual prowess in front of Bob. But he redeemed himself a little bit, didn't he, by feeling bad about it? Frank thought life was confusing when he was a kid. Now it was confusing all over again. Each age and phase seemed different, but each one also brought about the sense of adolescence, of angst and uncertainty and always having to find the way, whatever the way was, and if there even was only one way to be.

"There's other women," he offered to Bob. "You have other customers, right? You must get lots of women in here."

Bob shrugged and bagged the purchases. "Customers who are our age are mostly married."

After saying goodbye, Frank went out to his car. He thought again about going to the mall but decided to resist. Instead, he'd go home, give the birds their new toys, have some lunch in the living room so he could watch them have fun, and then he'd take a nap. Maybe Audrey would want to see him tonight.

With that thought, he texted her. Romance, he figured, was likely done digitally these days. "Thinking about you," he wrote. He hoped she didn't write in text-speak. Somehow, "Thnkng abt u" didn't have the same impact.

In a second, his phone pinged. And it was Audrey! There was that pinball pleasure zing again. "Thinking about you too! Hope your day is going well. How about dinner tonight?"

No text-speak. And she was thinking of him, and she seemed eager! He glanced toward the pet store and, through the haze of the sunlight, he could see Bob moving around. He wondered if Bob noticed he hadn't left yet. Maybe Bob thought he was talking to Audrey right now. He straightened in his seat, allowed his Neanderthal smile to grow unabashed. He raised his phone a little, so his carefully typing fingers could be seen through his windshield. "How about I cook for you?" he texted back. "I'd like you to meet the birds."

"Okay!" she answered. "I'll come over after I feed Newt and turn the television on for him." A second later, she texted again. "I hope they like me."

A woman who chose an iguana. A woman who left her television on for her lizard, just like Frank left it on for his birds. And a woman who wanted his birds to like her. Delighted, Frank turned the car on, then texted a smiley face. He liked smiley faces. He understood that one, but he didn't understand all the other emoji things that came on his phone. Who needed that many faces? And what was with the pile of poop? He thought about including a heart, but that felt like maybe he was moving too fast. Instead, he would pick up some flowers to have on the table at dinner. When she returned to her house, he would make a show of wrapping them and sending them with her.

If she went home.

What an absolute surprise.

Now he had to stop at the florist again, as well as the grocery store before going home. Idling at a stop sign, he thought over his morning. The visit to Susan's resting spot. The coffee with Theresa and the accepted offer of friendship. His discussion with Bob, the desire for a locker room. The sweet texting with Audrey, the happy face.

He still felt badly that Bob was sad.

Frank sighed and pulled into the parking lot of the grocery store. He thought of the doughnuts he shared with Theresa the other day and decided to get some. They would make an interesting dessert, served with good strong coffee to keep them energized. Just in case. And he'd make something nice for dinner. Chicken? Steak? Pasta? With wine.

And then he had his thought.

Theresa wasn't a cute and fuzzy type woman either. Though she wouldn't like an iguana, clearly. He remembered her reaction when she saw

Newt in Audrey's picture window. But she could use the company. While she was a bit scattered in her personal habits, she still liked tidiness and beauty. She liked colorful jewelry on top as much as she liked plain white underclothes beneath. She also liked class. She was a classy woman.

She wasn't impressed with his birds, and she didn't like the iguana. What type of animal would Theresa like?

Bob, despite working around animals all day, always dressed so neatly. He wore button-down shirts tucked into his khakis. He kept his hair combed. He was clean-shaven. There was an earring in his left ear, which Frank always thought gave him a nod to the wild side.

Theresa had her wild side. Frank remembered that wild side very, very well.

Colors and jewels. Tidiness. Something pretty. Maybe a fish? Maybe a lot of fish?

Frank texted Theresa. "Theresa," he said, "I was just thinking about me and my birds and Audrey and her iguana. You need something too, for some company around the house. How do you feel about aquariums? I know a great place to buy one. The store is run by a really nice guy. Always has his hair combed. And he has an earring."

He didn't use text-speak, and he knew she didn't either. He wondered if Bob did. He hoped not.

As he got out of the car, he stood for a moment, facing the big reflective windows of the grocery store. In his car, there were bags with offerings for the six birds and for Newt. Now, it was time to find an offering for Audrey.

Audrey. What an absolute surprise.

Frank decided. In the middle of this wild winter, he would pull out his summertime grill and cook steaks. He would stand in the cold and breathe out steam which would mix with the steam from the heat of the grill. He would serve doughnuts for dessert.

It was on to something new. Everything was new. Frank was beyond delighted.

Chapter Nineteen

Can birds of a feather flock with a lizard?

At work on Monday, Audrey found that she couldn't stop smiling. Usually, she hated Mondays. Her department was trashed from weekend treasure shoppers, and the racks all had to be redone. Audrey waved across the aisle to Gilbert, then spoke to her associate on duty in the Women's Department and sent her to work on the accessories, which were always worse off than the clothes. Shoppers would pick something out, then find something else on the other side of the floor and grab that instead, leaving the first item in the wrong place. Being the manager, Audrey could pick and choose the jobs she wanted for herself, and today, shuffling and restoring the stacks and racks of fabric, bright, pastel, patterned, plain, seemed like a wonderful thing to do.

She found herself looking forward to lunch as well. That didn't used to happen either. But then, she didn't used to look forward to going home to say hello to her iguana. And she didn't used to pat her iguana goodbye as she headed off to work or kiss a man out the doorway of her home late at night either, especially after waking up with him that morning. And really wanting to wake up with him again. To Audrey, it felt like Newt ushered in amazing changes in her life. She didn't know how, but Newt seemed to open her to new opportunities. Rabbits were supposed to have lucky feet. Maybe Newt had lucky spikes.

Audrey was glad she was alone on the floor at that moment because she giggled. She giggled when no one else was there to make her giggle or to giggle with. She felt goofy. She felt wonderful.

Annabel's and Vicki's shifts began later than Audrey's, so their lunches would typically be later too. Audrey decided she would leave in time to give her ten minutes before they showed up in the food court. She'd be able to get her meal and collect herself. She wondered if they would giggle with her. Annabel was more the snicker and leer type. Vicki was so serious. But a few days ago, Audrey wouldn't have suspected herself to be the giggle-type either. Maybe Annabel and Vicki had it in them too.

Tonight, after dinner with Frank, she would call Clara. Unless she ended up staying over at Frank's. But then what about Newt? He'd never been home alone all night before. So maybe Frank would stay with her again. But then what about the birds? That wouldn't be fair to them.

Audrey paused, thinking she would feel the urge to sigh now, instead of giggle. Even when things were wonderful, there was still stuff to work out. But then she giggled anyway. She even snorted.

As Audrey giggled and pondered giggling, an older woman came onto her floor and began to browse through the racks. Audrey recreated a double-decker table of tidy piles of V-neck t-shirts, sorted by color and size, and kept an eye on her, this woman shopping alone on a Monday morning. The woman went from rack to rack and picked out a few things, draping them over her arm. A navy blue jacket. An olive green dress. Black form-fitting yoga pants, just like Audrey wore, black A-line skirt. A couple sweaters in turquoise and lavender. All winter clearance. Audrey noticed she kept going back to a rack near the fitting rooms and pulling out a white blouse with large bright red flowers on it. It was silky and a button-down, with the first button starting right at between-breasts level, guaranteeing a deep V cut. It wasn't winter clearance, but it was on sale for thirty percent off. The woman looked at it, put it back, looked at it, put it back, shopped around, looked at it, put it back.

Finally, Audrey approached her. "You seem to be having some luck!" she greeted the woman. "Would you like me to start a fitting room for you, so you don't have to keep carrying those?"

"Oh, yes, thank you!" The woman handed over her pile and then shook out her arm. Close up, Audrey could see that the woman was a little older than she thought. She was possibly in her early seventies.

Audrey took the clothes back and unlocked the room closest to the three-panel mirror set up on the main floor of the fitting area. Inside the little room, she carefully arranged the woman's selections on the bar. She was so happy when the store replaced the hooks with the bar...it allowed you to spread your selected pieces out and see them all as you tried each one on, rather than piling one in front of the other. When she was shopping for herself, Audrey always liked to set the piece she was most excited about at the far right, and then work her way from the left, so that the anticipation built.

Going back out to the floor, she found the woman in front of that same spring sales rack again. She was holding the red-flowered blouse. "I think that's so pretty," Audrey said. "And it's on sale too."

The woman looked at the blouse, fingered the material, started to put it back, then looked at it again. "Tell me honestly," she said. "Do you think it's too young for me?"

Audrey took the blouse and then held it tucked under the woman's chin. The red of the flowers pinked up her cheeks. But the deciding factor was when the woman erupted into a smile. The blouse was bright. So was she.

"I think it would look lovely on you," Audrey said. "I don't believe in 'too young'. You should wear what you like. If you like it, it looks good on you."

The woman wrapped her arms around the blouse, and Audrey let go of the hanger. "Thank you," the woman said. "I'm ready to go in the try-on room now."

Audrey led her back, then returned to her work. She glanced over at Gilbert as he straightened out a shelf of knick-knacks and home decor. He was wearing a bright blue and pink checked shirt with tan Dockers, and the shirt was set off by a tan tie. He looked good. She wondered how he chose that; if he stood in front of a fitting room mirror for a long time, if he wondered if the clothing was too young for him. Or in his case, too old. Gilbert was young. She remembered he called her a cougar. Audrey, apparently, wasn't young. Though when she kissed Frank goodnight last night, she certainly felt young. She felt young, well, since Friday night, when she was a girl out on a first date.

Did men ever wonder if a certain type of clothing was too young?

Audrey stepped back from her rack and let her gaze sweep the floor. There was the Juniors department. The Misses. The Women's. There was Activewear and Career. Not to mention Lingerie. On the men's side, there was Men's. Unless you counted Boys, but Audrey didn't count Girls.

Why was it set up this way? Audrey couldn't remember a time it was ever any different.

Yesterday morning, when she and Frank finally got dressed, she chose her kaleidoscopic Victoria's Secret bra and panties. She had her back to Frank as she pulled on the panties, then the bra. As she turned to face him, before reaching for her jeans and sweater, she remembered questioning herself when she bought the set and the others. She wondered if she was too old. But Sunday morning, watching Frank's eyes widen, she didn't feel like she was too old for her undies. He wasn't too old either, to have such a reaction. The undies didn't last long – and when she attempted to dress again later, she laughed as she smacked his hands away, though she reached out and goosed him when he finally moved off. He looked damn good in his boxer briefs. And she didn't once consider if he was too old to be wearing them.

Why did women even have to think about these things? Why was clothing assigned an age?

The woman came out of the fitting room. "I'm ready!" she called. She put some things back on the reject rack. She kept the black skirt, the black pants, the turquoise sweater, and the red-flowered blouse. She set that with particular reverence onto the check-out counter.

"Oh, good!" Audrey said, going to the cash register. "You're keeping the blouse!"

"I am. It looks great with the skirt and the pants." She leaned forward. "I thought about picking up a black cami to wear under it, you know, to cover up just a bit. That V-neck is pretty deep. But then I thought no. Why should I?" The smile on her face dimmed the fluorescents. "I wouldn't have worn it with a cami ten years ago. Why should I now?"

And why should she? Audrey remembered reading an article about how you shouldn't show any cleavage after a certain age. About how turtlenecks were a nice substitution. The word substitution was actually used, as well as the word camouflage. As if women past a certain age were supposed to completely cover up and even disappear.

"You know what would be great under it?" Audrey said and then glanced around like she was about to commit a sin. Which, in department store land, she was. She was about to send a customer to a different store. "Go to Victoria's Secret. They have great bras." For emphasis, she stood straight and thrust out her chest.

The woman looked momentarily shocked, but then delighted, and even admiring. "Thank you! I never went in there. I thought it was for the young folks."

"It's for women," Audrey said firmly. "It's just for women. If you have breasts, you belong. If you go, ask for Annabel. She's terrific and will help you find just what you need. Tell her Audrey sent you."

The woman laughed, took her bag, and left. Audrey was sure she knew where she was going. Quickly, Audrey pulled out her phone and texted Annabel. "I've just sent a woman your way," she typed. "Lovely woman. Thinks she's too old to show a little cleavage. She just bought a terrific blouse with bright red flowers on it. Find her a knock-out set in red."

Annabel sent back a smiley face.

At lunch, Audrey threw caution to the wind. She got a Whopper and not a Junior. And fries. And a shake. When Annabel arrived, she noticed. "Wow, Audrey," she said when she sat down. "What's gotten into you? I think this is the first time I've seen you without a salad."

"I decided to eat what I wanted to eat. Isn't that amazing?" Audrey held up the Whopper as if it was a prize she'd just won.

Vicki sat down with her lettuce-wrapped something-or-other. Probably tofu. Blech. Vicki eyed Audrey's burger. "If that's what you want to eat, sure."

"It is. And that," she said, pointing to Vicki's tray, "is what you want to eat. It's all about choice, isn't it? Like Clara said." Audrey bit into what she thought was the best burger of her life. "So guess what?"

The other women were chewing, so they raised their eyebrows.

"I slept with Frank. And I slept with him again. And again! So many agains!" So much for giggling. Audrey was off, unabashedly howling. "Oh my god, oh my god, it was incredible."

Annabel and Vicki each struggled to swallow fast. "You did!" Annabel said.

"You didn't!" Vicki said.

"I did! And it was just like this burger! I did what I wanted, asked for what I wanted, and I didn't feel guilty about it! And neither did he!" Audrey turned to Vicki, who looked horrified. To Vicki, sex meant one thing, and Audrey rushed to assure her that wasn't it. "Vicki...it was wonderful. It was amazing. There was nothing 50 Shades about it." She dropped her burger, took Vicki's hand in her two greasy ones, and said, "Vicki, I said yes. That's what makes the difference. I said yes. And if I would have said no, he would have respected that. That's what makes the difference too."

Vicki sat back and wiped her hands with a napkin, but she had a small bemused smile.

"That sounds sort of...mushy," Annabel said. "I thought you meant you had a great leap in the sack."

"No!" Audrey said. "It wasn't a leap in the sack, Annabel. I've had leaps in the sack. And I've had times that I thought I was moving toward mushy and then it turned out he wasn't. But this was, without my thinking it was going to be! I didn't know what it was going to be. I just knew it was what I wanted. With him. And it was wonderful!" Audrey decided she needed to look on thesaurus.com for other words for wonderful. She was going to need them. She wiped drippings off her face and was mindful of her fingers, then grabbed both women's hands. "I figured out what was different. You know what it was?"

They shook their heads. Annabel looked skeptical; Vicki continued to look bemused.

"When I've been with other men, I would watch them watching me, and I could see them thinking, Does she like me? Do I look okay? Does she like what I'm doing? It was like being with a checklist. A worried checklist. A worried checklist who looked at me like I was a checklist. Someone who wanted to make sure he was checking off all the things on my checklist. But with Frank, he was looking at me and seeing *me.* He was thinking, Look at her. Oh, look at her. And I was looking at him and thinking, Oh, look at him. And it was amazing."

Annabel sat back. "When I'm with a guy, I'm usually picturing what we look like together. Like I'm up above the bed or something."

"You're also probably trying to remember his name," Vicki said and earned herself a swat.

Audrey laughed. "That's what I mean! I wasn't! I wasn't watching it like I was on a television screen. I was right there. All I saw was him."

Annabel and Vicki looked at her for a few moments. Audrey saw blankness in their expressions, but curiosity too. In both, she saw, "Could that happen to me?"

It could. Audrey hoped it would. Before they were fifty-five.

Vicki finally said, "He sounds really nice, Audrey."

Audrey knew what it took for Vicki to say that a man could be nice. And she hoped that if Vicki believed that a man could be nice to Audrey, then maybe there was a man that could be nice to Vicki too.

"I'm seeing Frank again tonight. He's making me dinner and introducing me to his parakeets."

Both Annabel and Vicki burst out laughing. "Ohmygod, it's serious," Annabel said.

"Well, Newt likes him. I hope his birds like me." Audrey wondered if birds could differentiate between people. They had such tiny heads with such tiny brains. But she knew she wanted Frank to believe that his birds liked her. And if they really, really could, then she hoped they would.

They ate for a while, all of them mindful of the ticking minutes of a lunch hour. Audrey discovered it was really hard to chew neatly when your mouth kept forming a smile.

"So what does this mean, exactly," Vicki said slowly. "I mean, for your favorite topic: feminism. You've been all caught up on that, having us do the postcards and talking to Annabel about her "not the F-word" shirt. And now you're all gaga, Audrey. You're goopy. You're, like, a puddle."

Audrey laughed; Vicki was right. She felt like a puddle.

"But what does that mean for you as a feminist? Can you be all…okay, I'm going to use this term carefully…girly and still be a feminist? I mean, Annabel is like a man-eater. She could be like those bugs that mate and then rip the head off the male. She uses and casts aside. She's not all goopy and girly. But you…all of a sudden, you're like one step away from buying a bridal magazine and picking out a pattern for your china."

Annabel, Audrey noticed, didn't object to the man-eater statement. She frowned, but then she just sat back. They all did. They considered.

"I'm thinking…" Audrey said, "I'm thinking that this doesn't have anything to do with if I'm a feminist or not. I'm thinking that whether or not a woman likes or loves a man has nothing to do with it. It's about supporting what's right for women. Being submissive isn't right. Being abused isn't right." She looked directly at Annabel. "A 50 Shades relationship isn't right. It's letting a man be the master. But being in love, wanting to spend your life with a man, or with a woman, I don't see that as being a feminist issue. It's just being human. Wanting to be partners with someone. Wanting to be respected and loved and enjoyed. I guess I don't see a problem with that."

"But what if a woman wants a man to be her master?" Vicki asked. "What if that *is* her choice?"

They stared at each other. They were back to it being about choices.

Audrey sighed. Then she chose the saltiest of her fries and popped it into her mouth. "I think I'm about to say something that is going to be unpopular," she said around her mouthful. "But I think if a woman chooses to have a man be her master – in a serious way, I mean. Not just sex play, but in everything, like he gets to choose everything for her, from her clothes to her friends to what she does. If a woman chooses to give up her choice, then I don't think she can be a feminist. And I think feminists, male and female, have the right to say that that's a line that can't be crossed. How can giving someone else all control in all things be good for you or good for women? For anyone?"

"But what about abused women?" Annabel asked. "That happens in abusive relationships, doesn't it? Where the man starts to take control of everything?"

Audrey nodded. "It does happen. And that's exactly what I mean. A woman doesn't choose to be in an abusive relationship. It happens over time, the man eroding her sense of self-esteem and self-worth. He takes her choice away; she doesn't give it. But here, I'm talking about when a woman chooses to give away control. Like in that stupid movie. Those stupid books. That main character...what was her name?"

"Anastasia," Annabel supplied.

"Right. Anastasia isn't a feminist. And neither is the woman who wrote those books." Audrey chewed thoughtfully for a moment. "I might even go so far as to say the women who read them...and enjoyed them...aren't feminists either."

"I don't give anyone control," Annabel said. "I don't let anyone use me. I mean, I'm just not ready to settle down yet. But I still like to be with men. I just want to have a good time. They understand that going in. So do I."

"So that means the man-eater label isn't really you. It's just where you are right now." Audrey looked at Vicki, who took a few seconds, but then nodded.

"And I *don't* want to be with anyone right now," Vicki said. "Not in any way. Annabel doesn't want to settle down, but she still wants to have sex. I don't want to be with a man at all. That's okay too."

"It's all choice," Audrey said. "It's what we choose. And as long as we're not being hurt, it's okay. No one has the right to hurt us, to make us submissive, to use us. And no one has the right to take our choice away."

They all nodded.

"Wait a minute," Vicki said. "You said male and female for feminists. You think men can be feminists?"

Audrey backtracked in her head to what she'd just said. And yes, she did say that. She remembered her discussion with Gilbert. "I guess I do," she said. "If being a feminist means supporting women, believing that women are equals, then yes, of course, a man can be a feminist." Audrey didn't know if she would have said this, years ago when she wore her original fish bicycle t-shirt. But now...it made sense. Women believing women could be equal to men was important. But men believing it was even more so.

"Is Frank a feminist?" Annabel asked.

"I guess I'll have to ask him." Audrey hoped so. It hadn't really come up yet. They'd been too involved in what was coming up...and coming up, and coming up. And what she was wearing or not wearing. She giggled again, and Annabel and Vicki looked startled. Audrey quickly changed the subject. "Did you help that woman I sent to you this morning?" she asked Annabel.

Annabel grinned. "Bright red deep-cleavage bra and matching boy-cut panties. She left in the whole outfit – the bra, panties, great black pants, and that blouse. She looked incredible."

They explained their morning to Vicki. Vicki played with her lettuce droppings. "If I came over to your store, Annabel," she said quietly, "would you fit me? With something not too bizarre or slutty?"

Annabel looked at her and considered. "I can see you in this gorgeous champagne lace set we have. Yes, Vicki, I would fit you. And you'd feel great."

Audrey picked up her shake cup. "To us," she said.

They toasted.

As they each deposited their trash and went off to their stores, Audrey decided she would stop on the way home and pick up a bottle of wine to bring to dinner. And maybe she'd stop at the pet store too. She could pick up little I-hope-you-like-me gifts for the birds. And maybe something new for Newt too, so he wouldn't feel left out while she was gone this evening, leaving him home alone while she spent company with a man and six parakeets.

. . . . .

"Hey, Bob!" Audrey called out as she entered the store. Bob's silhouette was back by the aquariums, the lights in the tanks morphing him into a shadow puppet. There was someone else there too, and Audrey hoped she hadn't interrupted a sale.

She walked over to the bird display and studied it. She only saw Frank's birdcage from outside, and it seemed to be quite large. It filled his entire bay window. She didn't know what the birds already had, and she didn't want to get any duplicates. Though with six birds, maybe a duplicate wasn't such a bad idea. If the birds were at all like humans, they wouldn't always like to share.

"Hey, Audrey." Bob was suddenly at her elbow. "Are you thinking of getting a bird?"

Audrey laughed. "No, Newt is all I can handle. I wanted to pick up a present for my neighbor's birds. You know him. Frank, remember? He was in here the night Newt tried to bite him."

"Sure, I know Frank." Bob considered the toys. "I know all his birds too.

238

How is Newt with Frank now?"

"Oh, he's great!" Bob looked startled, so Audrey figured she should dial down the enthusiasm. "Frank watched him for me one day when I was gone until late. And he's been over a few times. And, well, we're dating now." She blushed and found herself delighted that blushing and giggling were still in her repertoire. She glanced at Bob, who didn't seem surprised at her news and she wondered why. "Do you know what toys Frank's birds have?"

Bob nodded. "He's bought most of them from me. Here's something he doesn't have." Bob handed her a perch with a plunger on one end. "Frank likes to let his birds loose from time to time. This perch will attach to windows or walls so they could have a place to sit while they look outside or around the interior of the room."

Audrey thought of Newt and his tree. She knew Frank ordered one too. Birds and perches did seem to go easily together. "This is perfect, thank you, Bob. I'll get three of them, so they don't always have to take turns. Wait, make that six. He has six birds, right?"

Bob looked over his shoulder, and Audrey wondered again if she was interrupting a sale. "Yes, six. Lucky, Plucky, Ducky, Aristotle, BlueBoy, and Butch. Aristotle is shy, Butch isn't, and the others are all scattered in between. If you don't need me right now, I'm going back to the aquariums. I have a lady here who wants to buy a 20-gallon. That's going to take a while, so just let me know when you're ready to check out." He handed her six perches, each with a different color plunger.

Audrey wondered if they coordinated with the birds' feathers. She glanced at the bird cages in the shop and admired the rainbow birds could be. "Thanks, Bob." She watched him go, then turned to the iguana supplies, looking for something new to keep Newt busy over dinnertime tonight. There were so many hammocks, and Newt already had several. She considered shirts, but shirts weren't entertaining, at least not for the wearer. Newt didn't really play too much with toys. There were treats, of course, but she was going to have to fix his dinner and give it to him before she left for Frank's, and the treat would have to wait until she came home. She was about to give up when she saw a selection of DVDs. These were new.

One was nothing but iguanas. There was no narration, the description said. Just film of iguanas in the wild and in zoos and in people's houses. Whatever sound was going on during the filming was on the DVD so Newt would hear the natural sounds of the jungle, the zoo enclosure, and the houses of others. Newt liked television, though Audrey was never quite sure what he could really see. But this was like television, especially for iguanas. This would do.

She carried her things to the counter and then called for Bob. When he came up, the fish woman came with him, keeping one hand on his arm until he walked around the counter. Then she stood at the counter's side, not the front, like most customers, and she leaned against it.

"Audrey, this is Theresa," Bob said. "She's buying an aquarium."

"Oh, how great!" Audrey said. "I've always loved looking at fish. I think they're relaxing. I always see aquariums in doctor and dentist offices. Maybe that's why. The relaxing, I mean.'"

Theresa laughed. "They are fun to watch. I just want something in my house that's beautiful to look at and will keep me company." She looked away. "I lost my husband last summer."

"Oh, I'm so sorry," Audrey said and noticed that Bob paused in his ringing up. "I'm sure the fish will help. My iguana keeps me company all the time."

"Your...iguana?" Theresa tilted her head. "Did Bob say your name is Audrey?"

"Yes, that's right." Audrey was puzzled. Did she know Theresa from somewhere? Maybe Audrey helped her with choosing clothes at the store?

Theresa watched as Bob did the bagging. "Iguanas don't sit on perches, do they?"

"Oh, no," Audrey said as Bob laughed outright. "He's too big for a perch. That's a gift for a man I'm dating. Well, for his birds. He has six."

"Six!" Theresa said. "Wow. That would be quite the household if you end up together. The two of you, six birds and an iguana!"

It would be, Audrey thought. She wondered if birds and iguanas could get along and thought about asking, but that seemed like she'd be jumping too far ahead. She didn't mind blushing out of pleasure, but she didn't want to turn red with embarrassment. She paid and accepted the bag from Bob. "Well, you both have a good time setting up the aquarium. Bob is great," she told Theresa. "When I walked out of here with Newt that first night, I had everything I needed. And he hasn't let me down since."

"That's good to know." Theresa smiled at Bob. He smiled back.

Audrey noticed Theresa took Bob's arm again as they made their way to the dark alcove lit only with aquarium lights. Then Audrey tucked the bag under her arm and hurried to the car. She still had to stop for wine. What kind of wine do you get for a man with six birds and who is cooking something for dinner and you haven't the faintest idea what?

Audrey remembered Frank's arms around her, and she smiled. She'd figure it out. Frank would likely enjoy anything she picked out. And she would enjoy anything he cooked.

•　　　•　　　•

Audrey stood with Frank in front of the birdcage. Frank pointed out and introduced each bird, but the only two Audrey was sure about were BlueBoy since that was pretty obvious, and Ducky, who she assumed was the yellow one. She remembered Bob saying that Aristotle was the shy one, and sure enough, there was a bird that took one look at her and then popped inside this castle thing set up in the bottom of the cage. Altogether, the birds were a little intimidating. They moved so fast! And made startling sounds! The only time Newt moved fast was when he greeted her whenever she came home. Otherwise, he was very deliberate. And he really didn't make any noise. But the birds! They fluffed and fluttered, squawked and chittered, feathers flew, seed flew, poop fell everywhere.

Newt was litterbox-trained.

But Frank. Frank was delightful, as she watched him interact with his birds. Audrey decided you could tell a lot about how a man would treat a woman by how he treated his pets. If that was the case, Audrey was going to be treated very, very well.

Despite there still being snow on the ground, Frank insisted on grilling steaks outside. Inside, he turned on the fireplace in the living room and then set a very nice table in the small dining nook, something Audrey's house didn't have. There were fresh flowers placed in the center of the table. He put her wine in a bucket of ice, though it was a plastic ice cream bucket that he dug out from the cabinet under his kitchen sink. Audrey laughed.

"I'm not exactly fancy," Frank said.

"Neither am I," she said. "For my party on Saturday, I used my sink as an ice bucket."

Frank didn't sit across from her at dinner, but beside her. He ate with his left hand so he could hold hers with his right. And every few bites or so, he kissed her. Audrey's blushing was back, but thankfully, she didn't giggle. Until she did. And then she was mortified. She wanted to laugh deep and low, seductively. But she giggled. Frank responded by kissing her again. She gave up on being seductive and focused on being seduced.

She waited until after dinner to bring out the perches. "I brought the birds a little something, Frank. I know it seems silly, but I wanted them to like me."

He sat back and smiled. "Well, that's a coincidence. I bought Newt something too. And talk about silly; I already know he likes me." He grabbed a bag that was tucked under the table on one of the empty chairs.

Audrey laughed over the yellow shirt while Frank exclaimed over the perches.

"I'll clean off the table and then, would you mind if I let the birds out to try these?"

Audrey hadn't thought about that. But she supposed there was no better way to get used to the six of them. Maybe five, if shy Aristotle stayed inside. "Sure, if you'd like to." She wondered if she could ask for a bathrobe or something to wear over her clothes. She didn't want to be pooped on.

Frank busied himself sticking up perches. One went on the bay window and one on the dining room window. He placed the perch just a bit higher than the tree. Another perch went on the wall behind the couch, and one went, for fun, Frank said, on the television. He stuck one in the entryway to the kitchen, and then he brought one to the window above the sink. "Only Butch usually ventures this far," he said. "He usually sits on the kitchen table. I've tried to get him to the windowsill, but he's scared of the sink. If he likes the perch, he'll be able to see out into the back yard, where the birdfeeders are."

Audrey sat carefully on the couch as Frank reached for the birdcage door. She wondered if this would go down in the history books as the weirdest date ever until she realized that that honor could also go to spending the night with a woman and her iguana. Five of the six birds eagerly came out and first flew to the dining table to see if there were any crumbs. Aristotle came out, but just hopped to the top of the birdcage. Audrey studied him, the way he sat, puffed up a bit, head sunk into his shoulders. His eyes moved everywhere.

"Frank," she said softly. "Could you lower the perch on the bay window, so it's near Aristotle? Maybe he'd go on it if it was close."

Frank did so, but said, "It's not all that different from where he's sitting already."

"No, but it's a little different. Maybe he'd do it if it was just a little different." Audrey startled when one bird flew over and landed on her knee. Frank reminded her that this was Butch, the ringleader.

"He's likely checking you out," he said.

"Um...hi, Butch." The claws on his toes dug through her pants into her skin. It felt like she was being stepped on by thumbtacks. Not deep enough to be really painful, but she knew he was there. She couldn't help but notice his legs and toes looked like twigs. She wondered if that was nature's intention – to have the legs of birds blend into the branches they stood on.

Frank sat on the couch next to her. BlueBoy immediately landed on his shoulder. "You don't have to hold so still, Audrey," Frank said. "He'll move with you. I'm glad he's being friendly. If Butch likes you, they all will."

Audrey wondered how you could tell if beady bird eyes were being friendly. Overall, she much preferred Aristotle's distant approach to Butch's. She looked up to see that Aristotle had indeed moved up to the lowered perch. "Look, Frank," she whispered. "Aristotle is on the perch!"

Frank looked over and beamed. "You were right! See, you're not just an iguana expert. You're a birder!"

"I don't know about that." But Audrey smiled at Butch, and he preened a little. "Can I touch him?"

"Sure. He likes to have his head rubbed."

Just like Newt. Carefully, Audrey took her index finger and rubbed Butch's head in the direction of his feathers. She read once that animals, especially cats, didn't like their fur brushed backward. She figured the same could be true for birds. Butch was surprisingly soft. He pressed his little head against her finger.

"I think you passed the test, Audrey," Frank said and leaned in to kiss her. As he leaned in further, both Butch and BlueBoy squawked and took off. It didn't take long for Frank's kisses to grow deeper and more intense. Audrey kept one eye open, watching the birds' reactions. She swore their eyes got bigger.

When Frank took her hand and pulled her to her feet, Audrey guessed where he was going to lead her. Dessert wasn't going to be the doughnuts she spotted sitting out on the kitchen counter. She asked, "Do you need to put the birds back in their cage?"

He hesitated. "Well...let me just put Aristotle back. The others should be okay for a little while." He walked over to the bay window and offered his finger to Aristotle. He promptly jumped on, and when Frank lowered him into the cage, he hopped immediately onto a perch near the back. Audrey swore she saw him sigh with relief. Frank said, "Aristotle really only comes out to please me, I think. He's perfectly happy in the cage. He feels safe there."

"Will the others follow us into the bedroom?"

Frank laughed. "Well, my dear, what made you think I was going to take you there?" He winked. "But I was. I'll shut the door. Just like you did at first with Newt."

Audrey followed him down the hallway, but then stopped. She thought about what she'd said to Annabel and Vicki just that afternoon. That a man listening when you said yes was the important thing. And so was listening when you said no. "Frank, I'm not comfortable with this."

They were right by the bedroom door, and Frank turned around, looking surprised. "What's wrong? Did I do something?"

"No, not at all." She kissed him, quickly, to reassure him. "I'm just not comfortable with the birds loose. What if one of them gets hurt while we're...well, back here? I'd never forgive myself. What if one of them flies into the closed door, trying to get to you? I just can't, Frank."

Frank closed in for a huge hug. "Oh my gosh, Audrey. You're wonderful. You care about the birds! You just...you just put them first!"

Audrey shrugged. "Well, they're your family, Frank. Like Newt is mine."

He kissed her, and the kiss went so deep and so long, Audrey began to regret putting the birds first. Then he said, "So let's go neck on the couch for about fifteen minutes. Like kids, remember? We can pretend our parents are right upstairs."

Audrey laughed; she remembered dates like that in the family rec room in the basement.

"The birds can have their free time, and then we'll put them back in the cage, and we'll have ours. With the bedroom door open."

Audrey agreed, particularly to the necking and the free time. They waved at Butch as they went through the kitchen. He was strutting on the perch on the window above the sink and talking nonstop to the birds at the outdoor feeder.

Audrey remembered to look on the couch cushion before sitting, just in case, there was a bird there. And then, oh, the necking. She wondered if it was still called that. She wondered if petting was still called petting. She thought that was a stupid word for it when she was at an age where petting wasn't quite foreplay yet. And then...the only thing she was wondering was how long fifteen minutes could last. She wasn't so sure it was actually fifteen minutes when Frank declared it so, but she was glad he did. She was amazed when he stood by the cage and whistled, and all the birds filed back inside, greeting Aristotle. Butch was last. He stopped for a minute on the open cage door, chattered at Frank and spread his wings, but then went inside. Audrey rose to kiss Frank as he closed the cage's door.

"I bet," she said, after planting a kiss on the spot on his neck she already knew he liked, "if you stood by the door of the bedroom and gave me a whistle, I'd come flying in too."

Frank smiled and pulled her down the hallway. He dropped her hand when they reached the bedroom door. He stepped inside, turned and whistled.

Audrey didn't give his lips a chance to unpucker.

• • • • •

Audrey didn't stay at Frank's all night as she wasn't happy about leaving Newt home alone. Frank thought it was best that he stay with his birds too since he was gone most of the weekend. But both of them made the walk from Frank's bedroom to Audrey's front door last as long as possible. He kissed her soundly before walking away. He didn't go into his house until she went into hers. As soon as she closed her door, Audrey wanted to open it again, call to him, tell him to bring his birds over and stay the night.

But they really needed to talk to Bob first. Bob would know if iguanas and birds could get along. Audrey hoped so. She really, really hoped so.

Newt was on the couch, watching the iguana DVD. Audrey was so grateful for the wraparound feature. She sat next to him, and he swung his head toward her. Then he climbed from the cushion to her lap and then onto her shoulder and pressed his face against hers. She was glad he wasn't angry.

"Let's go get our snack, Newt," she said. "I'm sorry it's late."

Newt ate his treat – more banana slices and just a bit of strawberry - and Audrey made do with a slice of her own banana bread and a mug of coffee. Fully tanked. She didn't believe in decaffeinated. If you were going to drink coffee, she figured, drink coffee. So she did, at all times of the day. She was sleepy, but she knew sleep wouldn't be coming any time soon, even without the help of the caffeine.

"I had a really great time with Frank tonight, Newt," she said. "And I know you like him." But now that she was away from Frank, in the quiet of her own house, sitting next to her own iguana, she began to perseverate, to niggle at her happiness, peck at it, wondering if there was anything to it. Just over 72 hours ago, Frank was the guy next door who waved at her, had a birdcage in his window, and fed the wild birds in several feeders in his backyard. Then he became the nice man who watched Newt for her once. After that, he became a date. And suddenly...well, suddenly, they were familiar with each other's beds. She had known of Frank for a long time, almost a year, since he first moved in. Known of not knew. But now, overnight, it seemed, she really knew him, really really knew him. In that biblical way, as they used to say when she was in junior high. But she didn't really know him-know him. Really really know him, yes. Know him-know him, no. But she wanted to. She wondered what his middle name was. She wondered why she kept coming up with that as the way to know a man. She knew Frank had this endearing mole on his left shoulder blade that in the middle of the night on Sunday, she kissed. And he woke up. She knew how he smelled. She relished his arms. She loved his kisses. His breath on her ear or her neck made her shiver, but with warmth, not cold. And then with heat.

Audrey felt like she was the one who'd awakened.

When Audrey and Newt were done with their snack, Audrey cleaned up the kitchen, then closed down the house for the night. She looked out her kitchen window and didn't see a patch of light shining on Frank's yard, so she assumed he was going to sleep too. She bridged Newt to her shoulder, and they went down the hall to the bedroom. On a whim, she texted Frank. "Going to sleep now. Just wanted to say goodnight one more time."

Frank's reply was immediate. "I'm glad you did. I was just thinking about you. Goodnight, sweetheart."

Sweetheart. How long had it been since she was called sweetheart?

She sent him an emoji of a pink heart. She hoped it wasn't too soon.

After she changed into a nightshirt, she and Newt went on the computer. Going to Facebook, Audrey looked down her list of contacts, seeking out Clara. The green dot next to Clara's name meant she was probably still up and online. She sent her a message. "Hey, Clara. Are you up? Or did you forget to sign off of Facebook?"

"I'm up," Clara answered, almost as fast as Frank texted. "Hot flashes keeping me awake. What's got you up?"

Audrey asked to Skype, and in a moment, Clara's face lit up her computer screen. "Hey, Audrey! Hi, Newt! Why are you two up so late? Don't you have to work tomorrow? Or are hot flashes getting to you too."

Audrey laughed. "Well, yeah, but not the same kind you're having." Audrey quickly filled Clara in on everything that happened since Clara signed off on the postcard party on Saturday.

"Wow," Clara said. "You don't fool around, do you? But then again, yes, you do." She wiped her face with a towel. She was lit only by the shine from her own computer screen, and Audrey could see the vague outline of cabinets and a refrigerator behind her. Clara was alone in the dark in her kitchen. The rest of the family must be asleep. "So why aren't you sleeping the sleep of the sexually satisfied?"

Audrey shrugged. "Well, it's just...do you think I'm moving too fast? I mean, we went out on our first date on Friday. And I slept with him on Saturday. And I've slept with him more times now than I would have a few years ago in the first month of a new relationship and it's barely been 72 hours. I broke my own rules. I didn't even ask to see proof of his good health and lack of STD's." She rested her chin on her palm. "Come to think of it, he didn't ask for mine either. That's sort of stupid, isn't it? In this day and age." And it was. Audrey knew it. Frank just felt safe, and she went with her gut. But she was sure there were women out there that regretted the lies their guts told them.

"Too fast...sort of stupid..." Clara seemed to consider this as she took a sip of what looked like wine.

"Doesn't wine make you hotter?"

"Who the hell cares?" Clara toasted her and took another sip. "I'm going to be hot, no matter what. So I might as well enjoy it."

"Hang on, I'll enjoy it with you. Talk to Newt for a minute. Newt, you stay here. Don't you budge from this desk." Just in case, Audrey tossed pillows on the floor as a safety net. Then she went to the kitchen, listening to Clara chatter away to Newt. Wine poured, she made her way back. It felt decadent to be drinking wine after she brushed her teeth, though that diminished when she discovered what wine tasted like on top of toothpaste. She took a slug and swished it, trying to rid herself of the fresh mint and just get to the alcohol. "Okay," she said when she sat back down.

"Look, Audrey," Clara said. "I don't want to get all grim reaper on you here, but you know, we're not getting any younger. We get told as we grow older that we should slow down, but doesn't it seem like time is moving faster? It's moving faster because we're running out."

"Jesus," Audrey said and took another slug.

"I know. Grim Reaper. But it's true. Now is not the time to move slowly. Audrey, did he make you feel good? And I don't just mean physically."

Audrey thought of all the hours since Friday night. Of the giggles and blushes. The sighs and the moans. The touch of Frank's hand on her shoulder, his laugh as she joined in, the way he listened to her. The way he looked at her. The way he bought her iguana a t-shirt. And texted her, just to say hello, just to say goodnight. The way he found a way to make his birds happy and to make Audrey happy, all at the same time, without leaving anyone out. She thought of how he cheered for her when she put the birds first. She hadn't left anyone out either.

The way he called her sweetheart.

Audrey was going to use the W-word again. "It was wonderful," she said. Newt bobbed his head.

Clara smiled. "Then don't worry about it. You always were a worrier. But I remember your wild side too." She waggled her eyebrows. "Maybe you need to tap into that now. Your wild side, within the safety of Frank. Put salve on that worry wart by asking him about his health record tomorrow. But also let yourself feel your own safety, the safety of knowing who you are now, and what you're about."

"I know that?"

"Of course you do. More than you ever have."

And maybe Audrey did. She knew that she loved going to work every day, even if it was what some would call "just" a job in a department store. She loved her house. She loved her iguana, and she loved her friends, all of whom were fairly new to her, even Clara, who was a return. And she loved being with Frank. She could say she loved making love to him if she wanted to be romantic. But she could also just be flat-out honest and say she really, really enjoyed the sex. But she also enjoyed what came before and after, no pun intended. And for them, in between.

"It took me a while to figure out who I was and what I was about," Clara said. "You remember me back then. You remember the militant feminist. I'm still a feminist, just not so militant. I'm more methodical now, logistical, logical. And I'm fine with that; I actually think I accomplish more this way. I'm also a bisexual who has chosen to settle on this side of life. I chose to have a husband, and I chose to have children with him. Some people, especially those who are still militant lesbians, think that bisexuals aren't real, that we're just heterosexuals who play at being gay from time to time. I actually heard the term 'suburban bored white lesbian' the other day, in reference to being bisexual." She laughed, but then shook her head. "I reacted to that pretty strongly when I heard it. But then I settled back down. I know who I am. I know what I am. And I'm real. I'm also pretty damn happy with how things have turned out."

And even though Clara was sitting alone, sweating in front of a computer in her kitchen, Audrey believed her. Clara proved you could be happy even when you were alone and uncomfortable. She had family all around her, asleep, but still all around her. Audrey, the woman who used to be Clara's very best friend, was right in front of her on the computer screen. Of course, Clara was happy.

Audrey was happy too. Frank was just a house away. Her friends were close by. Her iguana was right here. Clara was in front of her. She could go to sleep alone, but she wasn't really alone. Things could be moving fast, but fast might be just on time.

"Thanks, Clara," Audrey said. "I'm going to try to sleep now."

"Me too." They tapped their wine glasses on their computer screens and chugged the dregs. "Audrey, 1 am so, so happy you looked me up on Facebook. You're like the piece that's been missing from my life. 1 am just amazed and grateful, to have you back."

"Oh," Audrey said. It wasn't a hot flash that made her want to melt. "Oh, me too."

Then they signed off for the night.

Newt rode on Audrey's shoulder as she brought her wine glass to the dishwasher and then responsibly brushed her teeth again. Years ago, fully immersed in her wild side, she wouldn't have. Now, she did. After childhood, she didn't think much about losing teeth. Now, she knew it was possible again, and without the promise of another tooth to fill the gap. That wild unbrushed-teeth part of her life was over. But the wild part of drinking wine late at night while discussing boys with a good friend...still there.

Audrey lifted Ooshi the cow off her bed as she prepared to unmake it. She hugged the cow to her chest and thought of the man who gave him to her, the last man she considered as a potentially serious relationship. She thought she was heartbroken when he was gone.

She enjoyed being with him, being part of a steady couple. She dressed up for their dates, and for the better part of their three years together, all of her new clothing purchases were with him in mind. Did he like this color? Had he commented on that style? He admired her legs, so she wore more skirts and dresses, where she ordinarily would have worn leggings and jeans. He said he loved to see her curves, so she wore form-fitting tops, though she really preferred loose, flowy blouses. He commented on how good she looked when she wore make-up, so she did, every time she saw him. When they began to sleep together and he stayed overnight in her apartment and then this house, or she stayed with him, she would wash off her make-up after love-making, but then put on some light eye shadow and lip-gloss so she would wake up as his version of looking good.

He won Ooshi for her soon after she bought this house. She'd talked about buying a house for about six months before she did so, wondering if he would offer to buy one with her, or offer to move in, or offer to marry her. She thought she was ready for that. She knew she was ready for a house and when she found and fell in love with this one, she went ahead and bought it and hoped the man she thought she loved would join her there, once he saw how perfect it could be. Instead, as she prodded him more toward meals at home and movies on DVD and microwave popcorn, wine in glasses she chose from Gilbert's side of the store and bought with her discount, beer that she kept chilled for him in the fridge, he pulled away. He began to work late. Weekends, when he invited her out to a bar or a party, and she said no, he still came over, just later. And later. Very late. Then he stopped inviting her. And then he stopped coming over. No more phone calls. No more texts or emails. There wasn't even a goodbye. Audrey texted him a couple times to no avail, and finally, after six months of silence, she checked the obituaries to make sure he hadn't died. She googled his name to make sure he hadn't gotten married or arrested. He hadn't. Then she gathered the few things he kept at her house, and she threw them away. But she kept Ooshi.

Audrey remembered thinking it was weird that she didn't miss him, even though she told herself she did, even though she thought she felt heartbroken. Now, she realized she wasn't looking at him, she was looking at them, at what they could be as a couple. At what she thought a couple should be. She was form-fitting him, and herself, into a mold. The heartbreak was because the opportunity was gone, not because he was gone.

In the closet in the guest bedroom, Audrey knew, there were rows of dresses and skirts and form-fitting tops that she never wore anymore. She never would. They weren't who she was. They weren't what she was about. This weekend, she thought, she would bag them up for Goodwill.

But not Ooshi. She kissed the stuffed cow on the nose. She loved Ooshi. She remembered that man's smile when he handed the prize to her, and she remembered how she squealed and kissed him. She wore jeans that night, and a t-shirt, it was a county fair after all, but she still had on make-up. This was a memory she could keep. And she would keep the cow. She didn't love

Ooshi because that man wanted her to. She loved Ooshi because she loved Ooshi.

She patted the stuffed cow on the head and set him on her desk chair. After unmaking her bed and turning on the electric blanket, she fashioned Newt's nest and settled him into it. Then she climbed into bed beside her iguana. This no longer seemed like such an unusual thing.

Audrey closed her eyes and remembered Frank's weight next to her. She remembered his weight on her. She thought of her wild side, and she thought of how she asked for what she wanted, and Frank said yes. She thought of how Frank didn't ask for anything she would have said no to. And she thought of how nice it was to wake up in the morning with his hand resting on her waist, his body curled into hers.

Nice. There was that word again, that word she said she didn't want.

But maybe, she did. Maybe nice was wonderful. Maybe the N-word and the W-word were synonymous. And maybe, like climbing into bed with an iguana, she didn't want nice to be an unusual thing.

•   •   •   •   •

After work the next day, Audrey and Frank went to Bob's pet store. They decided to go out for dinner afterward, leaving birds and lizard home alone that night and just have time with each other. Audrey complained she was going to get fat, as she was eating way more than she was used to. Frank promised that the next time he made her dinner, it would be a chef salad if that's what she wanted. Audrey laughed but remembered how good those steaks were.

Bob was alone in the store when they walked in. He had a pile of cat toys in front of him which he was attacking with a gun that shot red sticker labels. "I'm putting these on clearance," he said when he saw them. "Too bad neither of you have a cat. You could buy five of these for what one would have cost you at Christmastime."

Audrey remembered the feather-on-a-pole toy that Bob tried to tempt Newt with. She sifted through the pile. "Only cat toys?"

Bob shrugged. "I have more of these left over than dog toys, or any other kind of toys. Not sure why. Want to buy a cat? You could get toys cheap."

"I think we have enough of a zoo, thank you," Frank said. Audrey agreed.

Bob shot another toy. "So what brings you two in here? You were each here just yesterday. I hope Newt and the birds liked their presents."

Audrey blushed. She realized that was why Bob didn't seem surprised when she said she and Frank were dating. He already knew.

Frank said, "We need to ask for your expert opinion. Do you think it's okay to have Newt and the birds under the same roof?"

Bob startled. "Are you guys moving in together already?"

They looked at each other and Audrey decided to let Frank answer that. She'd definitely pictured it. She thought of her conversation with Clara last night, saying that now wasn't the time to move slowly. She wondered if Frank pictured it already too.

"No," he said, after searching Audrey's eyes. "At least, not yet. But we do live right next door to each other. And we both feel guilty when we leave either Newt or the birds home alone. So we thought they could sort of...come along for the visit."

Audrey couldn't help it. She snorted. Visit?

Bob, however, nodded seriously. "Oh, I see. And you're right, it is something to consider. Iguanas aren't carnivores, but they are omnivores. They eat primarily veggies and some fruits, as you know, Audrey, but they have been known to munch on small animals too, out in the wild. Tiny birds, like finches or canaries, tend to freak out around an iguana. Especially one that is past babyhood."

Oh, no. Audrey thought of the night before, the flurry as the birds tried out their new perches, sat on the couch, sat on her. Would Newt eat Butch? Would he go after shy and submissive Aristotle? Animals on the hunt always seemed to know where the weak link was in the herd. Or in this case, flock. Though it was difficult to think of Newt as a hunter.

Frank seemed worried too. "Okay, but how about parakeets? Are my guys okay around Newt? They're not tiny like those." He nodded toward the cages where yellow and white canaries flitted.

Bob nodded. "Typically, medium-sized birds, like parakeets, are okay around domesticated iguanas. I've even seen photos of parakeets perching on an iguana's back, much like you see photos in the wild of birds settling on crocodile's or alligator's backs. I'd move slowly with this, keep the birds in their cage at first, then maybe let them out a few at a time, to see what Newt does."

Audrey thought of the night Newt snapped at Frank's finger, how fast he moved, how fast things changed. There'd been no warning to Newt's sudden aggression. Would they be able to stop him if he went after one of Frank's birds? What bird would Frank use as a guinea pig? Likely, Butch, she figured. But how awful it would be if something happened… "Can we use something to test him out?" she asked. "A toy bird? A stuffed one?" She picked up a bird-shaped cat toy, complete with bright pink and purple tail feathers.

Bob shook his head. "You don't want to do that. You don't want to make him think that birds are toys. Just keep the birds in their cage for a while. Let Newt get used to them. And notice how much interest he takes in them. Watch for the signs, Audrey. Upraised spikes. Shaking his dewlap. Anything that looks like danger is brewing."

Newt wasn't dangerous. There'd only been Frank. Nothing before, nothing after. And now, he liked Frank. It just took a little time…and Frank's feeding him. Audrey pictured Butch, the ringleader, carrying a strawberry in his beak and dropping it at Newt's feet. Could Frank train him, the way he trained them to go into the cage at his whistle?

Bob kept on talking. "Iguanas actually like to lay on top of bird cages. Cages are usually in windows, and you already know that Newt likes windows, Audrey. Parakeets are usually tolerant of this, and if one of Newt's toes dangle through the slats, they'll likely leave him alone."

Audrey realized she'd only thought of Newt biting the birds, not the other way around. She looked at Frank in alarm.

He must have noticed. "If they did peck at him, it wouldn't really hurt him, though, would it, Bob?"

Bob shook his head. "Nah. Parakeets have little beaks. Hard to get through the leather of an iguana hide." Then, as if to continue a lesson, he said, "Now you'd have to worry if you had a bigger bird. A parrot, a cockatiel, something like that. They would likely attack the iguana."

"No upgrades," Audrey chided Frank and waggled her finger at him. He laughed. "So basically," she said to Bob, "go slow." She thought that this action was in direct contrast to Clara's advice: now was not the time to go slow. But apparently, Newt and the birds would make sure they did. Maybe, Audrey thought, it was a compromise. Not a bad thing. They lived next door to each other and were able to explore their relationship pretty easily and quickly. Their families would make sure they kept it real. "If I bring Newt over to Frank's, should I bring some of his stuff? His litterbox? A hammock?"

"That's a good idea. It will make him feel more at home. And all Frank has to do is pick up the cage and carry it over. The birds will be surrounded with familiarity, even in a new environment." Bob glanced over their heads at a clock. "Well, not to hurry you two, but I have to close up and get going."

He looked at Frank. "I have a date tonight. I helped a woman pick out an aquarium yesterday, and she was worried about setting it up properly. So I'm bringing everything over tonight. She promised me a nice home-cooked dinner. She even let me pick the menu." He licked his lips. "Fried chicken. Coleslaw. Apple pie. I've been hungry for summer, I guess."

"I think we all have," Frank said. "I grilled out steaks last night. It was cold but worth it."

"So you asked the fish lady out? Theresa, right?" Audrey asked Bob and then wondered why Frank looked startled. "That's great. She seemed really nice."

Bob blushed.

When they walked out of the pet store, Frank took Audrey's mitten into his gloved hand, and Audrey felt ridiculously safe. It was one thing to have palms fitted together, skin to skin. But Frank's warm fingers wrapped around her fat mitten just felt right. Even though it was only a few steps to the car, she leaned her head against his shoulder. And in the car, she kissed him.

"Well," he said, "it looks like iguanas and birds are doable."

Audrey wondered if he felt as delighted, and as cautious, as she did. "That's a good thing, right?"

He laughed. "Of course it is! But not tonight. Tonight, we'll have a nice, feather-free, spike-free dinner. Maybe this weekend, we'll introduce them all. I think the temps are supposed to go up at week's end so Newt won't get chilled coming over to my house. If you'd like, before we do this, I'll get a litterbox set up and a hammock and maybe some of those patio bricks he likes, so that you don't have to keep hauling them back and forth."

"Really?" Somehow, Frank making an investment in her iguana felt more serious than the proverbial buying of jewelry. "That would be great. I can get some bird stuff for my house too. Some of those perches. And I already have Newt's tree."

They chose a quiet family-style restaurant. Audrey had her salad, loaded with ham and turkey and cheese, and Frank decided on breakfast with scrambled eggs and sausage and a stack of pancakes. Their talk was quiet and intimate and important with its lack of importance; a couple filling each other in on their days, paying attention, making eye contact, laughing, blushing (for Audrey), and much hand-holding. Even without the mitten, Audrey felt safe. She decided it wasn't ridiculous at all.

• •• • •• • ••

That night, instead of heading into Audrey's bedroom, they curled into each other on the couch as they watched television. Newt sat stretched from Audrey's knee to the top of her thigh, his tail curled against her stomach, but he put one foot on Frank's knee. Audrey and Frank both complained softly of aching muscles and joints and bruised nether regions and decided that tonight was just for quiet and recovery and recalibrating.

When Frank left, Audrey watched out the picture window as he walked down the sidewalk to his house, raising the gloved hand that held her mitten so snugly earlier that evening. She saw his breath puffing out in a silver cloud in the dark night, and she thought how his breath had just become hers as they kissed goodnight. Audrey remained there for a while, after Frank went inside, and admired the dark night. She thought about how much brighter dark looked, now that she was thinking about someone, and she knew someone was thinking about her too.

Then she stood in the middle of her living room, a couple months after her fifty-fifth birthday, in the middle of her life, if she lived to be one-hundred and ten. On her birthday, this room and this house felt empty to her, despite its being filled with her possessions and memories. Now, Newt sat on his tree beside her, and a few months ago, there'd been no tree and no Newt. There'd been no Clara and no Annabel and no Vicki. Audrey had been wearing an old tired bra and old tired panties. She thought she was old and tired.

And now? Well, now.

If Audrey was in her twenties or her thirties, maybe even in her early forties, she would have whooped and danced around the room with wild, stamping, head-banging, hair-flying abandon. For that matter, if Audrey was in her twenties or her thirties, maybe in her early forties, she wouldn't have sent Frank on his way with just a warm kiss. There wouldn't have been the careful, but grateful nursing of aches and pains in a body that added something new, yet familiar, recently to the routine of every day and night. A reminder of time passing. And a reminder to appreciate.

Audrey found her postcard and looked at it again. She would mail it tomorrow, along with everyone else mailing theirs. Among all the hundreds of thousands of postcards That Man In The White House would receive, she wondered if he would look at hers. If he would care that he wasn't her answer. If he would care that he raised a whole bunch of uncomfortable questions in her life.

Just a short time ago, she would never have made a postcard, never participated in a protest not necessarily geared toward changing the world, but expressing what she felt. She might not have ever found value in expressing what she felt.

After putting her postcard back in its spot on her kitchen table, she returned to Newt's tree and bridged her arm. "Time for bed, Newt," she said.

In Frank's house, she knew he was likely saying the same thing to his birds. To Lucky, Plucky, Ducky, Aristotle, BlueBoy, and Butch. And she knew that Frank was likely still thinking of her.

As she was still thinking of him.

In her bedroom, Audrey unmade the bed and patted Gloria where she sat on the bedside table. Gloria called herself a "hope-aholic". Just a short time ago, on her fifty-fifth birthday, Audrey would have called herself anything but. But now?

Oh, now.

Everything was different. Everything was nice.

Everything was wonderful.

Audrey decided she didn't need a thesaurus at all. She just needed a dictionary, to house the new H-word she was using to describe herself, an H-word that she always wanted. She was happy.

Epilogue

January 20th, 2018

Goodnight, Audrey. Goodnight, Frank. Goodnight, Newt. Goodnight, Lucky. Goodnight, Plucky. Goodnight, Ducky. Goodnight, BlueBoy. Goodnight, Aristotle. Goodnight, Butch.

    Goodnight...

Audrey slipped her mittened hand into Frank's gloved fingers as they started the procession up the mall and then toward the White House. In their free hands, she and Frank carried picket signs. Hers proclaimed "Power to the Polls!" and Frank's said, "Power to the People!" and boasted both the male and female gender signs. They walked with Vicki and Annabel and Clara, and Clara held hands with her daughter, Sylvie, on one side, and on the other side of Sylvie was Clara's son. With Clara's other hand, she held her husband's. Audrey just met the male members of Clara's family a couple days ago, as they climbed into Clara's big van to make this trek to the nation's capital. Audrey felt exhilarated.

At home, Newt and the birds were being carefully tended to by Bob and Theresa, who agreed to stay in the house and pet-sit. They wanted to see the new house anyway, as Audrey and Frank decided not to choose either of their homes when they finally moved in together, but to make a new life in a new house. The new house had a big picture window in the front, for Newt and his tree, and a bay window in the breakfast nook in the kitchen, perfect for the birdcage. Though as predicted, Newt liked to lay on top of the bird cage. And the birds, when let out, made a beeline, or a birdline, for Newt's tree. Their tree was in the new dining room, but they seemed to like to take what was Newt's. He liked to sit in their tree too.

There were only five birds now. Aristotle, gentle, shy Aristotle, passed on shortly after the move. Audrey knew that Frank wondered if the stress of new surroundings killed him, and she knew that Frank felt guilty. Bob reassured him that wasn't the case, but it was a hurt that Frank carried close to his chest. They buried Aristotle in the new back yard, under a red maple tree, and Frank bought a stunning bird bath as a memorial, with an angel sitting on the edge, her little feet in the water and her palm upraised with an Aristotle lookalike resting there. It would serve, they knew, for all the birds and for Newt, in their time. Audrey vowed she would pass that time with Frank, and he vowed his life to hers.

Audrey found herself using the H-word often, and the W-word too. It was wonderful. And nice too. She was surprised to find out that nice was exactly what she always wanted, and wonderful was a wonderful addition, and happy was the cumulative result. She gave her wild side a nod every now and then too, especially on nights when she knew she didn't have to work the next day.

Under Audrey's winter coat, she wore her fish bicycle t-shirt, and she knew Clara did too. Frank, as always, laughed when he saw it. Audrey always knew that fishes didn't need bicycles. And she knew now that a woman didn't need a man. But it wasn't a sin or even a strike against feminism to want one. To love one. And she could relish the joy that such a partnership could bring. Especially with a man who saw her, heard her, respected her, and loved her. A man who saw her as his equal, without question.

Audrey was fifty-six now. Time, as Clara predicted, was flying faster and faster. And Audrey was running right along with it, rather than standing still as it rushed around her. But with Frank, there were also plenty of moments that just seemed to come to a stop for a languid, lovely, delicious bubble of time and privacy meant only for them.

With her fat mitten, she squeezed Frank's fingers. He squeezed back, then awkwardly leaned over and planted a warm kiss on her cold cheek.

In the middle of the crowd, Audrey blushed, her cheeks red with the wind's chill, with life's warmth, with joy, with contentment, with love. And then she giggled. Unabashedly.

The End

Kathie Giorgio is the critically acclaimed author of five novels, two short story collections, an essay collection and two poetry chapbooks. Her work has appeared in hundreds of literary magazines and anthologies. Giorgio is the director/founder of *AllWriters' Workplace & Workshop*. She lives in Waukesha, Wisconsin, with her husband, writer Michael Giorgio, her daughter Olivia, a dog named after Ursula LeGuin, a large cat named Edgar Allen Paw, and a teeny cat named Muse.

Thank you so much for reading one of our **Women's Fiction** novels.

If you enjoyed the experience, please check out our recommended title for your next great read!

The Apple of My Eye by Mary Ellen Bramwell

"A mature love story with an intense plot. This book has something important to say." –William O. Shakespeare, Professor of English, Brigham Young University

View other Black Rose Writing titles at www.blackrosewriting.com/books and use promo code **PRINT** to receive a **20% discount** when purchasing.

9781684333479